Gerald's Party

Robert Coover is the author of some twenty books of fiction and plays, his most recent being *Noir* and *A Child Again*. He has been nominated for the National Book Award and awarded numerous prizes and fellowships, including the William Faulkner Award, the Rea Lifetime Achievement Award for the Short Story, and a Lannan Foundation Literary Fellowship. His plays have been produced in New York, Los Angeles, Paris, London, and elsewhere. At Brown University, he teaches 'Cave Writing' (a writing workshop in immersive virtual reality), and other experimental electronic writing and mixed-media workshops, and directs the International Writers Project, a freedom-to-write programme. Coover currently splits his time between the United States of America and London. *Pricksongs & Descants*, *Gerald's Party* and *Briar Rose* and *Spanking the Maid* are all published in Penguin Modern Classics.

ROBERT COOVER

Gerald's Party

PENGUIN BOOKS

PENGUIN CLASSICS

Published by the Penguin Group
Penguin Books Ltd, 80 Strand, London WC2R ORL, England
Penguin Group (USA) Inc., 375 Hudson Street, New York, New York 10014, USA
Penguin Group (Canada), 90 Eglinton Avenue East, Suite 700, Toronto, Ontario, Canada M4P 2Y3
(a division of Pearson Penguin Canada Inc.)
Penguin Ireland, 25 St Stephen's Green, Dublin 2, Ireland (a division of Penguin Books Ltd)
Penguin Group (Australia), 250 Camberwell Road, Camberwell, Victoria 3124, Australia
(a division of Pearson Australia Group Pty Ltd)
Penguin Books India Pvt Ltd, 11 Community Centre, Panchsheel Park, New Delhi – 110 017, India
Penguin Group (NZ), 67 Apollo Drive, Rosedale, Auckland 0632, New Zealand
(a division of Pearson New Zealand Ltd)
Penguin Books (South Africa) (Pty) Ltd, 24 Sturdee Avenue, Rosebank, Johannesburg 2196, South Africa

Penguin Books Ltd, Registered Offices: 80 Strand, London WC2R ORL, England

www.penguin.com

First published in Great Britain by William Heinemann Ltd 1986
Published in Penguin Classics 2011
1

Copyright © Robert Coover, 1986
A portion of this novel appeared previously in *Anteus* under the title *The Interrogation*

Set in 10/12.5 pt Monotype Dante
Typeset by Ellipsis Digital Limited, Glasgow
Printed in England by Clays Ltd, St Ives plc

978-0-141-19298-7

www.greenpenguin.co.uk

For John Hawkes, who, standing beside me in a dream one night long ago, long before we'd become friends, and remarking upon another author's romanticization of autumn (there seemed to be hundreds of them actually, stooped over, on the endless tree-lined streets before us), observed wistfully: 'It's so true, people still do that, you know, count the dead leaves. Ten, nine, eight, seven, six, five, three, four . . .'

None of us noticed the body at first. Not until Roger came through asking if we'd seen Ros. Most of us were still on our feet – except for Knud who'd gone in to catch the late sports results on the TV and had passed out on the sofa – but we were no longer that attentive. I was in the living room refilling drinks, a bottle of dry white vermouth for Alison in one hand (Vic had relieved me of the bourbon), a pitcher of old-fashioneds in the other, recalling for some reason a girl I'd known long ago in some seaside town in Italy. The vermouth maybe, or the soft radiance of the light in here, my own mellowness. The babble. Or just the freshening of possibility. My wife was circulating in the next room with a tray of canapés, getting people together, introducing newcomers, snatching up used napkins and toothpicks, occasionally signaling to me across the distance when she spotted an empty glass in someone's hand. Strange, I thought. The only thing on my mind that night in Italy had been how to maneuver that girl into bed, my entire attention devoted to the eventual achievement of a perfectly shared climax (I was still deep into my experimental how-to-do-it phase then), and yet, though no doubt I had succeeded, bed and unforgettable climax had been utterly forgotten – I couldn't even remember her face! – and all I'd retained from that night was a vision of the dense glow of candlelight through a yellow tulip on our restaurant table (a tulip? was it possible?), the high pitch of a complicated family squabble in some alleyway billowing with laundry hung out like bunting, the girl's taste for anchovies and ouzo, and my own exhilarating sense of the world's infinite novelty. Not much perhaps, yet had it not been for love, I knew, even that would have been lost. I passed among my guests now with the bottle and pitcher, sharing in the familiar revelations, appraisals, pressing searches, colliding passions, letting my mind float back to those younger lighter times when a technically well-executed orgasm seemed more than enough, feeling pleasurably possessed – not by memory so much as by the harmonics of memory – and working my way through the congestion meanwhile ('She was great in *The House of the Last Hymen*,' someone remarked, and another, laughing, said: 'Oh yeah! Is that the one about the widow and the pick?' No, I thought, that was *Vanished Days* . . .) toward a young woman named Alison: not only, uniquely, a vermouth drinker – thus the bottle in my hand – but virtually the sole cause and inspiration for the party itself. Alison. Her name, still fresh to me, played teasingly at the tip of my tongue as I poured old-fashioneds for the others (and not a pick but—): 'A little more?'

'Thanks, Gerry! You know, you're the only man I know who still remembers how to make these things!'

'Ah well, the ancient arts are the true arts, my love.'

'Like poison, he means. Take my advice and stick with the beer.'

'More in the fridge, Dolph, help yourself. Naomi—?'

'What? Oh yes, thank you – what is it?'

I poured, glancing across the busy room at Alison, now profiled in a wash of light cast by the hanging globes behind her – like a halo, an aura – and I knew that, crafted by love, that glow of light would be with me always, even if I should lose all the rest, this party, these friends, even Alison herself, her delicate profile, soft auburn hair ('Ouch, Dolph! Stop that!'), the fine gold loops in her small ears –

'Hey, golly! That's enough!'

'Oops, sorry, Naomi . . . !'

'Steady!' shouted Charley Trainer, charging up to lick at her dripping hand. 'Yum!'

'What is this, some new party game?'

'Ha ha! Me next, Ger!'

I heard the doorbell ring, my wife's greeting in the hall. Sounded like Fats and Brenda, but my view was blocked by the people pushing in and out of the doorway: Knud's wife Kitty gave Dickie a hug and he ran his hands between her legs playfully, Yvonne looking wistful, her husband Woody shaking the hand of an old man who said: 'In Babylonia, y'know, they used to drown folks for sellin' beer too cheap – we visited the holes they dipped 'em in!'

'Love the ascot, Gerry! Très chic! Cyril and Peg here yet?'

'Yes, I think so. In the dining room maybe. Old-fashioned?'

'Mine's a stinger.'

'Ha ha! don't kid me!' someone butted in, crowding up behind me.

'I can show you pictures.'

'Try it and see!'

Laughter rose lightly above the drone of music and chatter, then ebbed again, throbbing steadily as a heartbeat, as people pressed close, parted, came together again, their movements fluid, almost hypnotic, as though (I thought in my own inebriate and spellbound state) under some dreamy atavistic compulsion. I squeezed, myself compelled, past a group of serious whiskey drinkers hustling a painted-up redhead with pickaninny pigtails (Ginger: one of Dickie's girls), ignoring their disappointed glances at the vermouth bottle in my hand, and made my way toward Alison (Kitty, flushed and happy, crossed left of me, just as Patrick in immaculate green passed right, someone singing 'It's No Wonder' on the hi-fi), feeling the excitement of her as I drew near.

The glow, profile, it was different now, yet overlaid as though stereo-scopically by the way I'd seen her just before. And by that earlier time across the dimming auditorium. We'd met a few weeks earlier in a theater lobby during intermission. Friends of friends. We'd exchanged passing reflections on the play, and Alison and I had found ourselves so intimately attuned to each other that we'd stopped short, blinked, then quickly, as though embarrassed, changed the subject. Her husband had given me his card, my wife had said something about getting up a party, I'd said I'd call. On the way back to our seats, passing down parallel aisles, Alison and I had exchanged furtive glances, and I'd been so disturbed by them that the play was over before I'd realized that I'd not seen or heard any of the rest of it: only by asking my wife her opinion of the last act did I learn how it came out. Now Alison's glance, as I pressed up beside her at last and refilled her glass with vermouth, was not furtive at all, even though there were several other people standing around, watching us, waiting for refills of their own: she was smiling steadily up at me, her eyes (so they seemed to me just then) deep brown puddles of pure desire . . .

'Somehow,' I said pensively, holding her gaze, seeking the thought that might connect us to that heightened moment at the theater, 'I feel as though all this has happened before . . .'

'It's an illusion, Gerald,' she replied, her voice smooth, round, almost an embrace, my name in her mouth like a cherry. She reached into the old-fashioneds pitcher for an ice cube without taking her brown eyes off me. There was a peculiar studied balance in her stance that made me think of those girls in advertisements out on the decks of rushing yachts, topless, their bronzed breasts sparkling with sea spray, hair unfurling, legs spread wide and rigid in their tight white denims like cocked springs – though tonight in fact she was wearing a green-and-gold silk charmeuse dress of almost unbelievable softness. The peculiar thing about love, I thought, gazing deeply into those beckoning pools of hers which yet reflected my own gaze, the reflected gaze itself a reflection of that first numbingly beautiful exchange (that night at the theater she'd been wearing a Renaissance-styled suit of cinnamon panne velvet with a white ruffled blouse, the ruffles at the cuffs like foliage for the expressive flowering of her hands, her auburn hair, now loose, drawn then to her nape by an amber clasp), is that one is overwhelmed by a general sense of wanting before he knows what it is he wants – that's why the act, though like all others, seems always strange and new, a discovery, an exploration, why one must move toward it silently, without reason, without words, feeling one's way . . . 'You know, I'll bet you're the sort of man,' she said, as though having come to some sort of decision, her voice gloved in intimacy and, yes, a kind of awe (I felt this and drew closer), 'who used to believe, once upon a time, that every cunt in the world was somehow miraculously different.'

'Yes – ah, yes, I did!' I glanced up from her gaze: we were alone. Our thighs were touching. 'Hot *what*— ?' someone hooted behind me, and I thought, this may not turn out quite as I'd imagined after all. My wife, in the next room, pointed, her hands high above her head, at Tania's empty glass. Tania, smiling broadly over the faces between us, held it up like a signpost. 'Each one a . . . a unique adventure.' Alison was licking the ice cube before dropping it into her glass of vermouth, and, watching her, I seemed to remember the ice wagons that used to call at my grandmother's house, the heavy crystallized blocks that had to be chopped up (this memory was soothing), the ice chips in the truck beds, the little girl next door . . . 'But I was young then . . .'

'Ah, but it's true, Gerald!' She smiled, sucking coyly on the cube. It sparkled like a fat gem between her lips. She let it ooze out like a slow birth and drop – *plunk!* – into her vermouth. 'Each one *is* . . .'

And just then Roger came through, interrupting everybody, asking if we'd seen Ros.

I understood Roger's anxiety, I'd witnessed it many times before. Roger loved Ros hopelessly – loved her more no doubt than the rest of us loved anything in the world, if love was the word – and he was, to his despair, insanely jealous of her. He'd found her, as though in a fairy tale, in a chorus line, a pretty blonde with nice legs and breasts, a carefree artless manner, and an easy smile (yet more than that, we'd all been drawn to her, her almost succulent innocence probably, and a kind of unassuming majesty that kept you in crazy awe of her, even in intimacy – during my own moments with her, I'd found myself calling her Princess), and he'd been overwhelmed at his good fortune when she took him to bed with her the same night he met her. That there might be others who shared in his fortune, he could hardly believe; in fact, to the best of his ability, he chose *not* to believe it, which was the beginning of his grief. Instead, he pursued her with the relentless passion of a man with a mission, striving to fill up her nights so there'd be no room for others, begging her to marry him, and because in the end you could persuade her to do just about anything, she did. And went right on living as she always had, barely noticing she'd even changed her address. Poor Roger. She loved him of course: she loved all men. He was still in law school at the time and had difficulty finding the money for them to live on. Eager to help, she took a job as a nude model for a life-drawing class in a men's prison, and nearly drove him mad. She'd plan a big surprise for him, take him out to dinner, joined by another man who'd pick up the bill and offer to drive Roger back to the library after. She returned to the theater, to acting, unable to stay away, and so then neither could he, doing his studying in the back rows during rehearsals, almost unable to see the texts through his tears. Backstage, of course, her thighs were pillowing cast, crew, and passing friends alike, but Roger wasn't even aware of that – just the scripted on-stage intimacies were enough to plunge him into all the desolation he could bear.

So when he came through now with that look of rage and terror and imminent collapse on his face, breaking up conversations, shouting over the music, demanding to know if we'd seen Ros, I smiled patiently and – though in fact I couldn't remember having seen her since the moment they'd arrived – said, 'I think she's in the kitchen with my wife, Roger.'

5

'No, she's not!' he cried, turning on me. The light gleamed on his damp face almost as if he were drawing it to him. 'I've just come from there!'

Some people were still dancing out in the sunroom, or conversing in remote corners, slipping off to the toilet or wherever, but most of us in here were by now watching Roger. Our relative silence made the music – oddly romantic, nostalgic (a woman was singing about mirrors and memory) – seem to grow louder. I remember Roger's law partner Woody stepping forward as though to offer consultation, then shrugging, turning away, as a woman sighed. Parties are clocked by such moments: we all knew where we were in the night's passing when Roger's anguish was announced. He glanced fearfully from face to face (Dickie, leaning against a doorframe near Vic's daughter Sally Ann, winked and cast an appraising eye on Alison beside me), then down at the floor. Roger turned pale, his eyes widening. We all looked down: there she was, sprawled face-down in the middle of the room. She must have been there all the time. 'Ros – !!' he gasped and fell to his knees.

Alison touched my arm, pressed closer. I could almost feel the warmth of her breath through my shirt. 'Is she all right?' she whispered.

I opened my mouth to speak, perhaps (as though obliged) to reassure her, but just then Roger turned Ros over. Ros's front was bathed with blood – indeed it was still fountaining from a hole between her breasts, soaking her silvery frock, puddling the carpet. I could hardly believe my eyes. I had forgotten that blood was that red, a primary red like the red in children's paintboxes, brilliant and alive, yet stagy, cosmetic. Her eyes were open, staring vacantly, and blood was trickling from the corners of her mouth. Roger screeched horribly, making us all jump (some cried out, perhaps I did), and threw himself down upon her, covering her bubbling wound with his own heaving breast.

Alison's hip had slid into the hollow above my thigh, as though, having pushed past me for a moment to see, she was trying now to pull back and hide inside me. It felt good there, her hip, but I was wondering: How has it got so hot in here? Who turned up the lights? Is this one of Ros's theatrical performances? I glanced inquiringly up at Jim.

Jim was staring down in surprise at Ros like everyone else, his thick square hand on the back of his head, his professional instincts moment-arily enthralled. Roger screamed again— 'Ros! Ros, what have you *done?!'* – releasing Jim from his stupor: he knelt, felt her wrists, her throat, peered under Roger at the wound, closed the girl's eyes, concern clouding his face, actually darkening it as though (I thought) in closing Ros's eyes, some light in the room had been put out. Alison trembled slightly and reached behind her to touch my hand: the thought had not been wholly mine (a responsive tremor made my head twitch), but hers as well. Jim looked up at me, his coarse gray hair falling down over one eyebrow. 'She's dead, Gerry,' he said. 'She seems to have been stabbed to death.'

I looked around at the shocked faces pressing in, but I couldn't see her: she must have gone to the kitchen. Even in this crowd of friends, squeezed up against Alison, I felt alone. The house was silent except for the upbeat wail, oddly funereal, of the show tune playing on the hi-fi. Roger shrieked – *'No! No! No!'* – and someone turned the music down. 'What's happening?' Tania cried, and pushed through the jam-up in the doorway. Jim, standing now, was wiping his bloody hands with a white handkerchief. I saw that his sleeves were rolled up, yet seemed to remember him kneeling beside Ros in his suit jacket still. Memories, I realized (recalling now the sudden gasps, the muttered expletives of disbelief, the cries rushing outward from the body through the door like a wind: *'It's Ros! She's been killed!'*), always come before the experiences we attach them to. Comforted somehow by this insight, I brushed past Alison's hips, bumped gently by each firm buttock, and went to the kitchen, looking for my wife.

She was at the counter, decorating a tray of cold cuts with little sprigs of fresh parsley. She wore a brown apron with purple-and-white flowers on it and held a butcher knife in her left hand. There was no blood on it, but it startled me to see it in her hand just the same. Perhaps she'd been slicing the roast beef with it. 'Ros has been murdered,' I said.

My wife looked up in alarm – or maybe the alarm had been there on her face before she turned it toward me. 'Oh no! Where— ?'

'In the living room,' I said, though I wasn't sure that was what she'd meant by the question. I was having trouble breathing. She stared past my shoulder toward the door, her mouth open, little worry lines crossing her forehead. There were plates and glasses in the sink behind her, but the counter was wiped clean. I wondered if she wanted me to hug her reassuringly or something. But I had these things in my hands. 'What . . . what do you think we ought to do?' I asked.

With difficulty, she pulled her gaze back to me. 'I don't know, Gerald,' she said softly, touching her cheek with the back of the hand holding the knife. 'Probably we should call the police.'

'Yes. Yes, of course,' I said, and went back out front, thinking of my wife with a butcher knife in one hand and a bouquet of parsley in the other, and trying to remember the special telephone number for emergencies.

But Alison's husband was using the phone. He was murmuring secretively into the mouthpiece, his head ducked, a sly grin on his thin bearded face. I tried to interrupt him, but he waved me away without even looking up, puckering his mouth as though blowing a kiss into the phone and chuckling softly. 'Listen,' I cried, 'there's been a murder!'

'Yes, I know,' he said coldly, putting the receiver down. 'I've just called the police.' I was troubled by the way he stared at me. It occurred to me that I knew almost nothing about him: only his name and address on a white card.

I followed him back into the living room where Roger was still carrying on pathetically over Ros's corpse. Tania had knelt beside him and was trying to console him, draw him away from the body, but he was beyond her reach. Beyond anybody's. He was wild with grief, looked a terror, his front now as bloody as Ros's. His face seemed twisted, as if a putty mask were being torn away from it, and people watching him were twisting up, too. Vic's girlfriend Eileen had apparently fainted and was lying on the gold couch. Jim was sitting by her, holding one wrist, slapping her face and her palms gently, while Dickie at the end of the couch, keeping her shoes away from his bright white pants and vest, held her legs up so the blood would flow to her head. Vic flung what was left of his drink up her nose and that brought her to with a snort, but she went on lying there, whimpering softly to herself. Vic said something about a 'stupid cunt,' and Jim said: 'Take it easy, Vic. She's had a severe shock.'

The contrast was there for everyone to see: Roger and Ros, Vic and Eileen. It seemed to bring a kind of ripeness to the room. Alison gripped her husband's hand tightly and stared over at me as though in supplication, but what was it she wanted? I felt lost and confused, a stranger inside my own house. I did, however, remember now the special phone number for emergencies. Her husband, watching me, withdrew his hand from hers to smooth down the fine black hairs of his beard. 'There's nothing we can do until the police come,' I said at last. Alison seemed helped by this: she sighed, her slender shoulders relaxing slightly, and turned to gaze compassionately across the room at Eileen on the couch. Her dark hair fluttered wispily, as though filmed in slow motion, as she turned her head, and I thought: I understand myself better because of this woman. This was true of my wife, too, of course.

Tania, still trying to comfort Roger, was now completely bespattered with blood herself. 'Oh my god, Gerry!' she cried, showing me her bloody dress, her dark expressive eyes full of dismay and sorrow (I felt my own eyes water: I bit down on my lip), her nostrils flaring. '*This is terrible!*'

Roger, as though in response, suddenly tilted far back, clutching his face with bloody hands, and let forth an awful howl, scaring us all, then pitched back down upon Ros's ruptured breast, still amazingly spouting fresh blood.

Eileen at that same moment cried out. We looked up. Vic was standing over her at the couch, his legs spread, elbows out, the back of his thick neck flushed, and the way she was curled up with one arm flung over her drawn face, I had the impression Vic had just struck her. Dickie had backed away, clearly wanting no part of it. When our eyes met for a moment, I frowned in inquiry, and Dickie, tugging at the ivory-buttoned cuffs of his plaid jacket, shrugged wearily in reply. 'No . . . !' Eileen sniveled.

'We've got to be patient!' I said sharply, but no one appeared to be listening. Even Alison was distracted. Her husband was studying a Byzantine icon depicting the torture of a saint, a curious piece my wife had bought at an auction. Mr and Mrs Draper came in and began to discuss it with him. He turned away. I felt there was something I should be doing, something absolutely essential, but I couldn't think what it might be. It didn't matter: I'd had the same sensation many times before – just a little while ago in the kitchen, for example – and knew it for what it was: the restless paralysis that always attends any affront to habit.

Not always had I read this feeling rightly, I should say. There was the terrible night, for example, of our first son's stillbirth. Little Gerald. I'd been by my wife's side throughout the daylong ordeal that preceded it, holding her hand through the ferocious pain that was tearing her apart: a small fineboned woman exploding with this inner force growing increasingly alien to her as it struggled, though we did not yet suspect this, against its own strangulation, having tried, its cord twisted, to breathe too soon – oh, how I'd loved her then, loved her delicacy, her courage, her suffering, her hopes, even the fine cracks disfiguring her belly, the veins thickening in her legs, her swollen teats, fierce grimace, cries of pain. It had been Jim who had suddenly guessed the truth and rushed her into the delivery room. But too late, the child was dead. Afterward, drugged, she'd slept. 'It's all so unreal,' I'd said, contemplating the wreckage of so much natural violence, 'so unbelievable . . .' Jim had given me a sedative to take and, wrapping one arm around me, said I should go home, get some rest, come back early in the morning. Leaving the hospital, then, I'd had this same feeling: that there was something important I should be doing, but I couldn't think what. Halfway home, dreading the emptiness there, still a bit awed and frightened, I'd thought of a woman I'd been seeing occasionally during the final months of my wife's pregnancy, and it had occurred to me that she too must be needing solace, understanding, and needing too the opportunity to be needed in this calamity, needed by me, even if only this last time (yes, it was probably the last time), and I'd supposed that this must be the important thing I had to do, that thing I couldn't put my finger on. And so, full of sorrow and distress and compassion, I'd gone by. But I'd been wrong. She'd been shocked, disgusted even. 'My god, have you no feelings at all?' she'd cried, still only half-awake, her face puffy from sleep and her hair loose in front of her eyes. 'That's – that's just it,' I'd explained, tried to, love (I'd supposed it was love, for someone) thickening my tongue. 'I need someone to talk to and I thought—' 'Christ, Gerry, go find a goddamn shrink!' she'd shot back, and slammed the door. I'd gone on home, feeling sick with myself (what kind of filth are we made of, I'd wondered miserably, nauseated by my own flesh, its dumb brutalizing appetites and arrogant confusions), and had found my mother-in-law waiting for me there: she'd come to help with the new baby and she was all smiles. It was like a strange nightmare memory: my mother-in-law smiling . . .

I looked up from Ros's corpse and saw Jim's wife, Mavis, standing there like something hung from a hanger, locked in a helpless stupor, her soft red mouth agape, her eyes puffy and staring. I knew how she felt: Ros was like her own daughter, or so she often said. Jim was clearly shaken, too, but had the defenses of his profession: right now, playing the family doctor, he was counseling Vic's daughter Sally Ann. Sally Ann wore, as usual, a white shirt open down the front and knotted at the waist, and tight faded blue jeans with a heart-shaped patch sewn over her anus that said, 'KISS ME.' She'd painted her eyes and lashes to appear grown-up, but had only made herself look more a child. Earlier, Dickie had been moving in on her, but now she was alone with Jim. Maybe they were talking about her father: Vic was sitting heavily on the couch, his large shaggy head in his hands, Eileen stretched out limply behind him, looking less alive than Ros. Jim smiled gently and Sally Ann sighed petulantly and looked away. Tania's nephew Anatole was hovering furtively at the outer edge of their conversation, a look on his tense angular face that seemed to say: I *told* you this would happen! But then, he always had that kind of look on his face.

His aunt, still on the floor beside Roger and the body, had sunk back on her heels, her half-lens spectacles dangling on a chain around her neck, her celebrated vitality utterly drained away. The crowd of people around her watched as she rubbed her eyes with the tips of her long bloodstained fingers, pressed her lips together, and looked up at Mavis beside her. Mavis seemed to be trying to speak. She slumped there over Tania, staring bleakly, working her soft mouth fitfully around some difficult word, her squat pillowy body otherwise lifeless. Anatole, noticing this, tugged at Jim's arm, but Jim was still reasoning patiently with Sally Ann and appeared not to notice. Patrick, taking a seeming interest in Jim's counsel, had joined them, sidling close to Anatole, a tumbler of vodka and grapefruit juice – Patrick's famous 'salty bitch' – in one hand, French cigarette in the other. Sally Ann glanced over at me suddenly, her eyes flashing, then stamped her foot and left the room. Beyond them, I could see Alison, alone, her head down: was she crying? 'Who . . . ?' Mavis finally managed to blurt out, and the other conversations in the room died away. Jim looked toward his wife at last, then away again, focusing on the doorway leading in from the hall. Someone in red moved past it. 'Wh-who . . . ?' It was the question, I knew, that had been quietly worming through us all. Patrick took a nervous puff on the cigarette held like a dart between the tips of his fingers, watching Mavis now over Anatole's shoulder. Dolph came in with a can of beer in his hand and popped it open. Jim was talking with Mr and Mrs Draper, nodding his head in agreement as Mr Draper gesticulated broadly. I had the feeling he was describing some kind of pyramid or temple. Mavis's plump white arms hung limply at her sides, palms out. She lifted her head slowly and we waited for her question. I felt people crowding up behind me like mustered troops. Or a theatrical chorus. Somebody was chewing potato chips in my ear. Vic stood up. 'Who— ?'

The front doorbell rang.

'Ah! they're here!' I exclaimed, and went to answer it, greatly relieved. The thick clusters of guests parted, murmuring, as I passed through. I could hear Roger moaning behind me, Tania speaking gently with Mavis. Old Mr Draper stepped forward and clutched my forearm with his gnarled white hand, surprisingly powerful. He tipped his head back to peer down his lumpy nose at me and said: 'There's someone at the door, son!'

'I know . . .'

There were people filling up the hallway, too, watching expectantly. I'd forgotten we'd asked so many. I could see my wife trying to squeeze in from the dining room, wiping her hands on the bib of her flowered apron. 'Can you get it, Gerald?' she pleaded from the back of the hall.

'Yes,' I called over the heads between us as the bell rang again. 'Don't worry, it's all right!'

Dickie, stepping out of the downstairs toilet, still zipping up, seemed incongruously amused by this exchange. The tank refilled noisily behind him. He glanced up at Vic's daughter Sally Ann, staring down at me from the staircase landing over his head, her tanned belly pressed against the balustrade. 'Hey,' he grinned, fingering the buttons on his white vest, 'it's free now.'

'Never mind,' she snapped and continued up the stairs, switching her fanny huffily.

My wife backed away toward the dining room, looking momentarily defeated, lost in the crowd. Mrs Draper, standing near me, touched my sleeve and said: 'She's so pale, the poor dear. She needs a little sunshine.' The Drapers, complete strangers to me, had been belaboring everyone all night with tales of their retirement-age tourist travels, such a tonic, they'd said, and I'd found myself wondering earlier if my party might be part of some package tour they'd bought. But it was true, we hadn't had a holiday in years . . .

The bell rang a third time and I reached hastily for the doorknob, only to discover I was still carrying the bottle of vermouth and pitcher of old-fashioneds. I looked around for some place to set them down, but the door opened and a tall moustachioed man in a checked overcoat and gray fedora entered, followed by two uniformed policemen. 'May we come in?' he asked politely, but more as a statement of fact than a question: he was already in.

'Of course. I'm sorry, I was just—'

'Inspector Pardew,' he explained with a slight nod of his head. 'Homicide.' He removed his gloves carefully, finger by finger, tucked them in his pockets, unbuttoned his overcoat. The two officers watched us impassively, but not impolitely. They were armed but their weapons were holstered and the holsters fastened. The taller one carried photographic equipment and what looked like a paintbox, cables and cords looped over his narrow shoulders; the short one had a toolkit and a tripod. 'Now, I understand there has been a murder . . .'

'Yes, a girl—'

'Ah.' He slipped out of his overcoat, reached for his fedora, gazing thoughtfully at Dickie's girl Ginger, who had just, as though prodded from behind, stepped up beside me. 'Of course . . .'

Ginger, under his steady gaze, kept shifting her weight nervously from foot to foot, fumbling at my elbow to keep her balance. Her long lashes seemed almost to click metallically when she blinked them and her pickaninny-style pigtails quivered like little red Martian antennae.

Inspector Pardew handed his coat and hat to me, but, glancing away from Ginger, saw that my hands were full. This caused him to frown briefly and study my face. There was something incisive and probing about every move he made, and his gaze chilled and reassured me at the same time. I tried to explain: 'I was serving drinks. I – I'm the host and I—' But he stopped me with an impatient flick of his hand, a disinterested smile. He folded his coat on the seat of a hall chair, placed his fedora on top of it, smoothed down the few hairs he had left on the top of his head, and, still wearing his white silk scarf, strode on into the living room, his thumbs hooked in his vest pockets.

The hallway emptied out as the others, rapt, curious, followed him in, some circling through the dining room to get there ahead of the rest. Ginger, made awkward by her own self-consciousness, picked out her steps behind the others as though negotiating a minefield. Or maybe it was just the exaggerated height of her glittering red stiletto heels that made her walk that way. The two police officers paused in the doorway to watch her go. It was hard not to watch. She wore an alarmingly eccentric costume which seemed to be hand-sewn from printed kerchiefs of Oriental design, intricately multicolored but primarily in tones of mauve, crimson, emerald, and gold. They were stretched tight in some places, hung loose and gaping in others. Sort of like Ginger herself. Dickie called her a walking paradox: 'More cunt inside than body out, Ger. Fucking her's like pulling a prick on over your condom.' I watched, too ('What's within's without,' as Tania would say, 'without within . . .'), but when I looked back at the policemen, a faint smile on my face, it was me they were staring at. Nothing malevolent about their stare, but something was clearly bothering them. They bulked large and alien in the living room doorway, their brass buttons and leather straps stranger to me than Ginger's kerchiefs, their noses twitching, and, though nothing was said, it felt like an interrogation. I found myself running over the night's events in my mind as though hunting for dangerous gaps in the story (but it was the gaps I seemed to remember, the events having faded), my smile stiffening on my face. It was like crossing a border: what might they look for? what might they find?

But then Roger started bellowing wildly again and, touching their hands to their holsters, they whirled around and, in a crouch, the tall one bobbing on a leg that seemed shorter than the other, left me.

I released a long wheezing sigh, aware that I'd been holding my breath for some time. My arms ached with the weight of the bottle and pitcher, and I could feel sweat in my armpits and on my upper lip. Tania's husband Howard came down the stairs behind me. 'What's going on, Gerald?' he asked softly, looking a little flushed, his hand at the knot of his red silk tie.

'Ros has been murdered,' I said. I felt like I'd just been the victim of something. Or might have been.

'Is that so . . . !'

*

I went into the dining room to leave the vermouth and old-fashioneds on the sideboard with the rest of the drinks. I noticed that all the ice in the pitcher of old-fashioneds had melted and, recalling Alison licking the ice cube, shuddered at the world's ephemerality. I looked at my hands as if to see time falling through them like water. My wife came in with the cold cuts. 'Can you move that empty tray, Gerald?' she said.

'It was the police,' I told her, my voice catching in my throat. 'They're in looking at Ros now.'

She nodded. She seemed paler than usual and her hands were taut, the blue veins showing. I thought of her stubborn taciturn mother upstairs and wondered whether my wife, drifting prematurely into sullen stoicism, was a victim of her genes, her mother, or of me. I took the empty tray away and she set the cold cuts down, cautiously, as though afraid they might leap from her hands. There were four different kinds of cold cuts, laid out in perfect rows, lapped like roof tiles and spaced with parsley and sliced tomatoes. Perhaps I should find someone to be with her. 'Don't bother Mother just yet,' she said, as though reading my mind. 'There's no need to upset her, and there's nothing she can do.'

'No,' I agreed. It felt like a recitation, and I remembered something my grandmother, a religious woman, had once said about freedom. 'Besides, Mark's just getting settled down and . . .'

She nodded again, leaning over the cold cuts as though studying a dummy hand in bridge, her slender nape under the tightly rolled hair (free to do what we must, my child, she'd said with her sweet clenched smile, free to do what we must) sliced by the thin pallor of the fluorescent light from the kitchen behind her. 'You'd better go back in there, Gerald,' she said without looking up. 'You might be needed.'

Once, somewhere, long ago, I recalled, her nape had shone that way from the light of the moon: was it on the Riviera? during a transatlantic cruise? The memory, what was left of it, saddened me. It's not enough, I thought, as I left her there – it's beautiful, but it's just not enough.

On the way back in, I passed Vic coming out. He looked terrible, his large-boned face ashen and collapsed, thick hair snarled, eyes damp, movements clumsy, his blue workshirt sweaty. 'You already out?' he asked sourly, poking an empty whiskey bottle at me. I pointed toward the sideboard, clustered round now with other guests (through the door into the TV room I could see Dickie arguing with Charley Trainer's wife Janny:

'Me? You're crazy!' he shouted – she was biting her little pink lip and there were tears starting in the corners of her mascaraed eyes, but she continued to stare straight at him), and again found myself with something in my hand, this time the empty tray. I seem to be having trouble letting go of things tonight, I said to myself (to Vic I said, 'Down below, on the left . . .'), and set the tray down behind the antique prie-dieu. 'What a fucking mess,' Vic grumbled, and gave the doorjamb a glancing blow as he bulled through. I didn't think he was drunk: it was still early and Vic could hold his liquor. It was more like some final exasperation.

In the living room, Inspector Pardew, ringed round by a crowd of gaping faces, was crouching beside Ros's body, examining the wound, while the two officers, their criminalistic gear beside them, held Roger up a few feet away. Roger was apparently in a state of shock, eyes crossed, head lolling idiotically on his bloodstained chest, legs sagging outward at the knees like an unstrung puppet's. One side of him hung lower than the other, due to the mismatched sizes of the two policemen supporting him, adding to the poignancy of his grief. Tania, who was now kneeling by Mavis, watched Roger with concern. Mavis was sitting lotuslike in the spot where before she'd been standing, her legs apparently having ceased to hold her up. She stared dull-eyed at Ros's corpse, but seemed to be gazing far beyond it. It was as though, in her quiet matronly way, she had guessed something that none of the rest of us had become aware of yet, and the knowledge, as visions have been known to do, had struck her dumb. Ros's wound had at last stopped flowing, but the blood seemed almost to be spreading on its own: through the carpet under Mavis's bottom to Roger's feet, up the shoes and uniforms of the two policemen, down Tania's front and Kitty's knees, even turning up on Jim's white shirt, Michelle's cheek, the Inspector's drooping moustache.

'Ah!' the Inspector exclaimed now. 'What's this— ?!'

He asked for a pair of tweezers and the women scrambled about, looking for their handbags. Naomi, another of Dickie's entourage, a bigboned girl over six feet tall with naturally flushed cheeks and long blond hair clasped at the nape, lurched forward impulsively and emptied out her shoulderbag all over the floor: compacts, cigarettes, lipstick, earrings and bracelets and spare hairclasps, postcards, safety pins, a handkerchief, combs and coins, birth-control pills, antacids, ticket stubs, zippers and buttons, a driver's license, body and hair sprays, maps, matches, tampons and timetables, thread, newspaper clippings, breath sweeteners, photographs, chewing gum, a ladies' switchblade, addresses, tranquillizers, credit cards, hormone cream, shopping lists, a toothbrush, candy bars, a dog-eared valentine, flashlight, vial of petroleum jelly, sunglasses, paper panties, and little balls of hair and dust all tumbled out – even a tube of athlete's foot ointment, a half-completed pecker-sweater, one knitting needle, and one of my Mexican ashtrays – but no tweezers. 'I'm just *sure* I had some,' she insisted, scratching around at the bottom of her bag, turning it upside down and shaking it. My wife, I knew, kept a pair in the upstairs bathroom, and I wondered if I should go get them. 'I have a fingernail file,' offered Mrs Draper. Tania stood with a grunt, putting her spectacles on and fishing through her pockets, but then Patrick produced a silver pair from his keyholder.

The Inspector studied Patrick skeptically a moment, squinted down his nose at the tweezers, then with a shrug bent over the body once more, his white scarf falling over Ros's breasts like theater curtains. Jim knelt beside him, observing critically. Working with meticulous care, the Inspector extracted what looked like a bloody hair, or a thread maybe, from Ros's wound. He held it up to the light a moment, then sandwiched it carefully between two glass slides he'd been carrying in his pocket. Watching him, I had a sudden recollection of my biology teacher in high school, fastidiously tugging on a pair of transparent gloves, finger by finger, before dissecting for us the fetus of a pig. The gloves, I remembered, had made his hands look as wet and translucent as the pickled fetus, and when he'd had them on, what he'd said was, 'All right, boys and girls, ready for our little party?'

Dickie came in, but without Janice, and stepped up beside me, tooth-pick in his teeth, hands stuffed in the pockets of his crisp white pants. He looked harassed, chewing fiercely on his pick. It was ironic to see him so unsettled by a person as simple as Janice Trainer – even Chooch, her husband, liked to say that under all that makeup there was nothing but a doublejointed flytrap on a broomstick, and most people supposed he was being generous. 'Hey, Ger, what the hell's going on?' he whispered around the toothpick.

'Pardew is examining the body.'

'No, I mean, what's Naomi doing down there on her hands and knees with her shit all over the floor?'

'*Sshh!*' Howard admonished. Others were glaring.

Indeed it had become very quiet. The Inspector, bending closely, was probing the wound again with Patrick's tweezers (Patrick, flushing, winced, his teeth showing), and there was an attentive stillness, almost breathless, in the room. Jim stood with a frown on his square face, troubled about something. Is the hole the empty part in the middle, Daddy, Mark once asked me, or the hard part all around? I didn't know the answer then and I didn't know it now. Distantly, I could hear the thuck of darts hitting the dart board down in the rec room. Almost like the ticking of a slow clock. The chopping of ice. The bib of Ros's blood-stained frock was in the Inspector's way: he pulled part of it aside and one white breast slid free.

Whereupon Roger started screaming wildly again, shattering the silence and making us all jump. Patrick squeaked and dropped his drink, Mavis groaned, and Tania cried, '*Oh my god!*' sinking to her knees again.

Roger, eyes starting as though to fly from their sockets, struggled desperately to reach Ros's body, the two police officers hanging on, grappling for balance and handholds, their veins popping. 'Kee-rist!' hissed Dickie between his teeth, and Naomi, picking up her things, dropped them again. One of the officers lost his hat and the other stumbled once to his knees, but they managed to subdue Roger and pin him back against a wall. 'Easy now, fella, easy!' gasped the shorter one, pressing his knee into Roger's bloodsoaked groin, then, glancing at me over his shoulder, he shook his head as though sharing something privately with me and blew his cheeks out.

Inspector Pardew, absorbed in his examination, noticed little of it. Using the glass slides as a makeshift magnifying glass, he peered closely at the wound, poking and probing, muttering enigmatically from time to time. He picked Ros's breast up once by the nipple to peer under and around it, but he seemed disinterested in the breast itself – if anything, it was an obstacle to him. I couldn't get my eyes off it. Ros was famous for her breasts, and seeing the exposed one there now, so soft and vulnerable, its shrunken nipple looking like a soft pierced bruise, pecked fruit, I felt the sorrow I'd been holding back rise like hard rubber in my throat. I glanced up and found Alison watching me, tears running down her cheeks. She smiled faintly, and it was a smile so full of love and understanding that for a moment I could see nothing else in the room, not even Roger in his despair or poor, drained Ros, such that when I heard the Inspector ask, shouting over Roger, '*How long ago did this happen?*' I realized that it was at least the second time he had asked it and that he was looking straight at me.

'I – I can't remember,' I stammered hoarsely. I looked at my watch but I couldn't see the dial.

'Here, use mine,' said Dickie.

'Wait a minute— !' barked Pardew, rising.

Dickie smiled, shrugged, took his watch back. I rubbed at my eyes: there were tears in them.

'Hey! Where's Sally Ann?' shouted Vic, blundering in. He seemed to be asking Eileen, who was sitting up now, face buried in her hands, looking distraught, and I was invaded by the same feeling I'd had earlier with Alison: that all this had happened before. But then it went away as Sally Ann appeared in the doorway and said: 'What do you want, Dad?' I glanced across the room at Alison, still watching me, damp-eyed and gently smiling, looking almost fragile now in her soft satiny dress with its slashed sleeves, its frail silken folds. She touched the glass of vermouth to her lips. No, I thought, as Vic grunted ambiguously and shoved his way out of the room again, I hadn't really had that feeling with Alison before. I'd only wished to.

'The *time*,' the Inspector was insisting. 'This is *important*— !'

'How long,' I asked, turning to him, not really thinking about what I was saying, my mind on an earlier Alison, playful and mischievous, now nearly as remote to me as that girl from Italy (and I recalled now from that night, as though my memory were being palpated, the splatter of a pot on a cobbled street, a wail, something about gypsies in another country, and the way the girl's pubic hair branched apart like brown bunny ears: discoveries like that were important then), 'does it take ice to melt in a pitcher?'

'Ice?' exclaimed the Inspector, genuinely astonished.

'I'm sorry. What I mean is—'

'*Ice*— ?!'

'When you came in,' I tried to explain, 'I was—'

'Ah yes,' interrupted the Inspector, 'so you were.' He drew a large Dutch billiard pipe and tobacco pouch from his pockets. Roger's ravings had subsided to a soft whimper, and he'd sagged lopsidedly into the arms of the policemen once more. The tall one stared at me coldly, leaning on his short leg, a dark line of sweat staining the collar of his shirt. The short one had unbuttoned his blue coat, and his shirtfront, stretched over his bulging low-slung belly, was soaked with blood. He nodded me back to the Inspector, who asked: 'I wonder . . . has the murder weapon been found?'

'No,' I replied. He peered at me closely, one finger in the bowl of his pipe like an accusation. Inexplicably, I felt my face reddening. 'We left her exactly—'

'Yes, yes, I'm sure.' He lifted his gaze to the ceiling as though studying something there, and involuntarily, the rest of us looked up as well. Nothing to see: a plain white ceiling, overlapping circles of light cast on it by the various lamps in the room. In some odd way, in its blankness, it seemed to be looking down on us, dwarfing us. I wondered, staring at it, if Alison might not be thinking the same thing – or, knowing I'd be having such thoughts, refuting me: there *is* no audience, Gerald, that's what makes it so sad. Hadn't I said much the same thing the night we met: that the principal invention of playwrights was not plays or actors but audiences? 'Curious . . . ,' mused the Inspector. He was gazing down at Ros again. As though directed, so then did we. Her breast was covered by the frock once more, but now her legs seemed farther apart, the silvery skirt riding halfway up her stockinged thighs, and she had some kind of apparatus stuck in her mouth. An X-ray unit maybe. 'You'd think a girl like her . . .' He paused thoughtfully, zipping up the tobacco pouch. What had he meant? There was a heavy stillness in the room, broken only by Roger's muffled sob, a low hum (the hi-fi? or that thing in Ros's mouth?), and the labored breathing of the two police officers. Inspector Pardew sighed as though in regret, then looked up at me: 'But excuse me, you were speaking of an ice pick, I believe . . .'

I started. 'No . . . ice!' It was a cheap trick. Not to say a complete absurdity. And yet (I was finding it hard to catch my breath), hadn't I just been . . . ? 'There – there was ice in the pitcher I was carrying when you—'

'Of course.' He smiled, making an arch pretense of believing me. He tamped the tobacco into the bowl of his pipe, returned the pouch to his pocket, withdrew a lighter. 'So you've said . . .'

'You think she might have been killed with an ice pick, do you?' I shot back, though I felt I was blustering, inventing somehow my own predicament. Where did all this come from?

'I don't know,' he replied, tucking the pipe in his mouth, watching me closely. Behind him, Jim was shaking his head at me. Most of the others simply looked amazed. Or distracted. 'Do you?'

'We – we don't even *have* an ice pick, Inspector,' I replied. This seemed more sensible, but I still felt like I had lost my place somehow. 'Our refrigerator has an automatic unit which—'

'One moment!' cried Pardew, his attention drawn suddenly to something at the other side of the room. 'Unless I am very much mistaken, we shall find what we are looking for in that white chair over there!' Pocketing his unlit pipe, he strode over to it, guests parting to form a corridor. We all saw it now: something glinting just behind the cushion at the back, red stains on the creamy velvet. 'Aha!' he exclaimed as he lifted the cushion. I half-expected him to produce an ice pick from under it, absurd as that seemed, but there was only a knife. I recognized it: it was my wife's butcher knife. Just as I'd seen it in the kitchen. 'It's been wiped clean, I see,' he observed, picking it up with a handkerchief from his trousers pocket. 'But there are streaks on it still of something like blood . . . !'

Distantly, in another room, half-lost in shadows, I saw my wife, slipping back toward the kitchen again. She was gazing tenderly at me over the heads of our guests, through the bluish haze of cigarette smoke and what seemed almost like steam (I wiped my brow with a shirtsleeve), looking more serene than I'd seen her for months. Yet pained, too, and a bit forlorn. Love is *not* an art, Gerald, she had once shouted at me in rare anger but common misunderstanding: *It is a desperate compulsion! Like death throes!* 'What? What did you say?' I asked.

The Inspector was holding the knife up in front of my face. The handkerchief in which he cradled it was wrinkled and discolored, clotted with dried and drying mucus. 'I said, do you recognize it?'

'Yes, it's ours.' I looked up into his penetrating gaze. 'It's from our kitchen.'

'I see . . . and who would have access— ?'

'Anybody. It hangs on a wall by the oven.'

'Hmmm.' He stared down at the knife, lips pursed, twisting one end of his moustache meditatively – then he arched his brows and, handing the knife to Anatole, blew his nose in the handkerchief. Anatole studied the knife skeptically, weighed it in his palm, tightened his fingers around the handle, tested the cutting edge with his thumb, and then, while the Inspector stared absently into his filthy handkerchief, passed it on to Patrick, crowding in at his elbow. Patrick jumped. Someone said: 'Is that it?' Patrick, panicking, held it at arm's length between thumb and forefinger as though it might contaminate him. He pushed it toward the distracted Inspector, back at Anatole who shrugged it off, then thrust it at Dickie. Laughing, Dickie tossed it up in the air, caught it by the handle, wiped the blade on the seat of Patrick's green trousers ('Naughty boy!' squeaked Patrick, twisting about, trying to see over his hip where Dickie had wiped), and handed it on to Charley Trainer, who had just come in with his wife, Janice, she still looking a bit weepy. Charley said: 'What is it, huh, some kinda joke?'

And so it went around the room, passing from hand to hand as though seeking recognition, approval, community, and, as I watched, it suddenly and finally came home to me: Ros, our own inimitable Ros, was dead. All those breathless hugs: gone forever. And now everything was different. Fundamentally different. I felt as though I were witnessing the hardening of time. And the world, ruptured by it, turning to jelly.

'Tell me,' said Inspector Pardew, looking up from his handkerchief, 'is your wife here?'

'Yes, of course, in the kitchen – but she had nothing to do with this!'

'Who said she did?' asked the Inspector, eyeing me narrowly. He stuffed the wad of yellowed handkerchief back in his pocket. The knife was still moving like a message around the room. It reached Tania on the floor, who explored it dreamily with both hands, her eyes closed. 'All the same, we'd better interview her,' said the Inspector to his assistants, nodding toward the back of the house.

'Yessir,' said the shorter one, as the Inspector set up a tripod, un-wrapped some film. 'Can you handle him, Bob?'

The tall one, Bob, nodded grimly and gave an extra twist on Roger's arm, but just then Tania opened her eyes, lifted her spectacles onto her nose, and, frowning curiously at the knife in her hands, leaned over and touched its tip to Ros's wound. '*WrraAARGHH!*' screamed Roger and broke free.

'Oh no— !'

'*Stop him!*' somebody shouted.

The two policemen managed to cut him off from the body, but they were unable to lay hold of him. He lurched violently about the room in a wild whinnying flight, blind to all obstacles, slapping up against walls and furniture, tangling himself in curtains, leaving not mere fingerprints behind but whole body blotches, and howling insanely as he went. People tried to duck out of his way, but he slammed into them just the same, knocking them off their feet, sloshing them with Ros's blood, making them yell and shriek and lash out in terror. I saw Mavis tip backward on her round bottom, her thick white legs looping gracefully over her head like surfacing porpoises. Some guy behind her crashed into the fireplace in a cloud of dust and ashes, still holding his drink aloft, big Louise slipped on Ros's blood, Howard hit the wall like a beanbag, spectacles flying. Roger was a man possessed. The police chased him, stumbling through the wreckage, knocking down what Roger missed, but there was no catching him. Glasses were spilling and smashing, tables tipping, potted plants splattering like little bombs, lamps whirling, camera gear flying like shrapnel; someone screamed: *'Get down! Get down!'* I was glad my wife was well out of it, but I was afraid for Alison. She was standing in the middle of the uproar as though chained there, her eyes locked on mine, the tears drying on her cheeks, her smile fading. And then I couldn't see her anymore as Roger pitched suddenly toward Ros again, tripped over Tania ducking the wrong way, and fell upon Naomi, who was trying desperately in the confusion to get everything back in her bag again. Naomi squealed as she sprawled under his weight and all her stuff went flying again. Before the police could reach him, Roger was back on his feet, half-galloping, half-flying through a flurry of paper and toilet gear, plowing into Patrick, caroming off big Chooch Trainer, whose eyes popped and crossed at the force of the blow, and sending Woody and Yvonne, who'd just come in with fresh drinks in their hands, scrambling back through the door again on their hands and knees.

'Hey, listen, Ger, do me a favor,' whispered Dickie in my ear as we watched all this (Anatole and Janice were just being knocked over like toy soldiers, Anatole's black jacket and Janny's pink skirt billowing behind their fall like lowering flags), 'tell that silly slit to get off my case, will you?'

I looked up at him (the short officer was clomping about furiously, his foot caught in the toolbox), standing tall and trim in his white vest and trousers, dark plaid sports jacket, blue tie, his blond hair swept back with care, a cool half-smile on his lips, yet a kind of loose panic in his eyes. 'Who, you mean— ?' And just then Roger hit me. I felt the blood spray up my nose like wet rust and I crumpled to the floor under a creature moist and cold as a slug, but with roaring breath and flailing crablike limbs, and massive with its own furious but mindless energy. It was some kind of monster I was grappling with, not Roger, and the sheer bloody reality of it terrified me. Maybe I was even screaming. I saw the police grab at him, but he leaped away, kneeing me in the stomach, and they fell on me instead. The short cop's hat had slipped down over his eyes, and in his blindness he seized my wrist, threw me over onto my face, and twisted my arm up to my neck, nearly breaking it. 'Hey!' I cried, and something cold and hard knocked up behind my ear.

'Hold it, Fred!' gasped the other one. 'It's the host!'

'Wha— ?' The officer on top of me, snorting and blowing, leaned toward my face, pushing his hat up with the barrel of his pistol. 'Whoof – sorry, fe – fah! – fellah!' he wheezed, letting go my arm. His face was smeared with blood and sweat like warpaint and his shirtfront had popped its buttons, his blood-red belly pushing out in front of him like a grisly shield. He holstered the gun he had pressed to my head. 'I thought it was the— poo!— bereaved!'

Roger had got as far as Inspector Pardew, who was holding him calmly away from Ros's body with one hand, while brushing irritably at the specks of blood on his white scarf and three-piece suit with the other, muttering something about 'a stupid waste of energy.' He frowned impatiently at the two policemen and, abashed, they got off me and (the short cop kicked the toolkit off his foot, there was a clatter of wrenches, glass cutters, and hammers, Kitty exclaiming: 'Knud will never believe this!') took hold of Roger, dragging him away, still screaming, into the next room. I sat up, massaged my twisted arm. My head was ringing, and there was a sullen pain deep in my stomach where Roger had kneed me. The others were picking themselves up, mumbling, coughing (Janny, snuffling, said: 'Where's my shoe?'), surveying the damage.

'Jesus! Remind me not to ask you any more favors!' groaned Dickie in my ear. 'That one fucking near killed me!'

He sat beside me, wiping his face with his shirttail, his bright white vest and trousers peppered with blood as though riddled with punctures.

His redheaded girlfriend Ginger, who had somehow kept her feet through it all, now fell down. I saw Alison in a corner, straightening her tights under the softly drawn folds of her skirt. Her husband seemed not to be around, had apparently missed it all. Had I seen him stroll disdainfully out when Roger launched forth? Or perhaps he'd gone before. Alison looked so vulnerable. I wanted to touch her, be touched, and just thinking about that eased the pain some. 'She sure has a sweet ass on her,' acknowledged Dickie, following my gaze. 'Tight and soft at the same time, like bandaged fists.' As though to model it for us, Alison turned her back and smoothed her silk skirt down. I sighed. Between us, in debris and rubble, Ros lay like a somber interdict. 'Reminds me of a dancer I used to know who could pull corks with hers. Who is she anyhow, Ger?'

'People we met,' I said noncommittally. Dickie had energy, but no subtlety. He was like an artisan who had the craft, but no serious ideas, and what he didn't finish, he often spoiled. 'What do you think's the matter with Naomi?' I asked.

We watched her, looking utterly stricken, go hobbling out of the room taking little baby steps, clutching her skirts tight around her knees, her shoulderbag spilled out behind her. 'Christ,' Dickie muttered, struggling to his feet, 'she must've shit her pants!' And he followed her out.

Across the room, near the fireplace, Tania's husband, Howard, held his spectacles up for me to see: both lenses cracked. Like everyone else, he was splattered all over with blood, making him look like his red tie had sprung a leak. The indignant expression on his flushed face seemed to suggest that he blamed me for the broken lenses.

'Now then, one thing I don't understand,' insisted Inspector Pardew calmly, one hand at the knot of his tie as though to draw himself erect: 'Why did you speak of an ice pick?'

'Not an ice pick,' I replied wearily, looking up at him from the floor. 'Ice.' Even as I spoke, my words seemed, like the punchline to one of Charley Trainer's shaggy dog stories, stupid, yet compulsory. Something Tania had once said about art as the concretizing of memory lurked like a kind of nuisance (we'd been talking about her 'Ice Maiden' and the paradoxes of the 'real') at the back of my mind, back where it was still throbbing from the revolver's knock on the skull. I hoped both would go away at the same time. The knife was nowhere to be seen, though it could have been anywhere amid all that wreckage. 'I was trying to get at the time, working backward . . .'

'Gerald was serving drinks,' Alison said, coming over through the clutter to stand above me. Her voice was clear and musical, and it mellowed somewhat the Inspector's expression. She let her hand fall softly into my hair, her silk dress caressing my ear like a blown kiss. Legs passed my head, moving toward the dining room. 'Did you ever notice how blood *smells?*' someone whispered. 'It was about an hour ago.'

'Ah, that's better!' The Inspector reached into his vest pocket and pulled out a fob watch. Beyond him, Mavis lay on her belly still, staring vacantly, Tania kneeling beside her, speaking softly into her ear. Smashed film gear lay scattered around them, the tripod's legs bent double at the joints like broken ski poles. I rose achingly to my feet, helped by Alison. The touch of her hands on me was wonderfully comforting. My wife's fat friend Louise passed us on her way toward the back of the house, disapproval darkening her face like a bruise. The Inspector, his chin doubling, stared down at the body (I was thinking about Ros again, those gentle body massages she loved to give and receive between orgasms, the way she held your face in both her hands when she kissed you, even in greeting, and the soft silky almost phantasmal touch of her finger as she slipped it dreamily up your anus), idly winding his fob watch; then, pocketing it, he looked up and said: 'I'm afraid I'm going to have to ask everyone to turn their watches in to me, if you don't mind.' I sighed when Alison took her hands away, and in response she smiled. Her nose and cheeks were freckled with blood, and there were larger spots between her breasts, but she wore them gracefully, like beauty marks. 'Come along, hurry it up, please!'

My own watch was on an expansion band and simply slipped off, but Alison's band was a complicated green leather affair with three different buckles. 'Here, let me help,' I said, taking her hand in mine. A warm flush of nostalgia swept over me as, like a boy again with bra hooks, I fumbled with the buckles, her fingers teasing my wrists, her free hand falling between our thighs.

I wanted to hold on to this moment, but Pardew interrupted it. 'I'll need someone to collect them,' he said. I knew he was looking at me, and I smiled apologetically at Alison. Her eyes seemed to be penetrating mine, reading feverishly behind them, while her free hand stroked the inside of my thigh as though scribbling an oath there. Or an invocation. 'And I'll want those of all the people outside this room as well.'

'Allow me,' offered Mr Draper, stepping in behind us from the dining room with a roast-beef sandwich in his bony fist, and Alison took her hand away. 'I may not be good for much, old as I am, heh heh, but takin' up collections is one thing I can still execute, as you might say.' To my embarrassment, he turned to Alison and presented her with his sandwich, softly mangled at one end. 'Here, hold this for me, will you, dear?' he said. 'Can't seem to get these new choppers through the durned thing.' He saw me staring and clacked his teeth once for me as a demonstration. 'Store teeth, y'know,' he explained wistfully, removing his suit jacket and rolling up his sleeves. 'Perils of a long life, son, nothin' works like it used to.' And he winked meaninglessly, snapping his braces.

'Thanks, Mr Draper,' I said, handing him our watches.

'My pleasure, sir!' He strapped mine on his arm, dropped Alison's into a pocket of his baggy trousers, then went off on his rounds, gathering watches onto his arms and into his pockets, greeting everyone boisterously: 'I'll take your watches, please! At my age, I need all the time I can get!' Followed by a mechanical chuckle like some kind of solemn ratification. Ame-heh-heh-heh-hen.

'I'm sorry,' I said to Alison, trying to disassociate myself from him, 'I've never seen him before tonight.' Certainly he was out of place here, he and his wife both. I supposed my wife had invited them. 'The old fellow's been badgering me all night to look at some snapshots from his tourist travels. I think he's a bit—'

'I know, I've seen them all.' She smiled, but when I reached for her hand, she pulled it away. Absently, she began eating the old man's sandwich. Dolph came by with a can of beer in one hand, gazing at something across the room, and Alison winced, bumping me with her hip. She reached into her teeth and pulled out a little piece of string. 'Tell me about her, Gerald. The girl . . .'

'Ros?' I looked down at the body. Inspector Pardew was chalking out an outline of her. It occurred to me that she'd been jostled somewhat during Roger's recent rampage. One arm and leg had shifted and her head was tilted a different way. Did that matter? Exposed film plates lay beside her like last words and the apparatus had fallen out of her gaping mouth. 'She was an actress. Not a very good one. Her problem was, she could never be anyone on stage but herself. Mostly she was in chorus lines or shows where they needed naked girls with good bodies.' Roger seemed to have quieted down. 'Did you see *Lot's Wife*, by any chance?'

'No, I don't think so.' She chewed, watching me closely, eager, it seemed, merely to hear me speak, no matter what about. The Inspector, having completed his chalk outline of the corpse and some of the stuff around it – including, I noticed, some of the junk that had fallen out of Naomi's bag and out of the toolbox – was now moving Ros's limbs about as though looking for something under them. Mr Draper's croaky old voice could be heard out in the hallway, saying: 'Watches, please! Take time off! Thank you, thank you! Your time is my time! Yeh heh heh . . .'

'She had the title role, probably her best part, one of them anyway. She'd been getting little but walk-ons before then, back row of the chorus, even nonparts like one of Bluebeard's dead wives or the messenger at the door who never enters, and mainly because Roger blew up such a storm whenever something a little more adventurous came along. So when the chance came to do *Lot's Wife*, she could hardly turn it down.' I felt as though I were shaping the words for her, rounding them, smoothing them, curling them in over the little gold loops: and that she felt them there, sliding in, caressing her inner ear, and that it made her breathe more deeply. 'The play was a kind of dionysian version of the Bible story in which, after being turned to salt and abandoned by Lot, she was supposed to get set upon by ecstatic Sodomites, stripped, stroked, licked from top to bottom, and quite literally reimpregnated with life. At the end, Lot returns, sees his mistake, repents, and joins the Sodomites, now no longer as her husband of course, but just one of her many worshipers, which is supposedly an improvement for him.'

'And Roger, I take it, was not so wise.'

'I'm afraid not – of course, Lot probably had some help from the director.'

'Roger had not seen the script.'

'Oh, he'd seen it all right.' I smiled. 'That was exactly the problem.'

Pardew was down on his hands and knees now, fishing about under Ros's skirt with the tweezers. He had filter papers in one hand, empty pillboxes, tape, and a pick glass on the floor beside him. Alison watched him a moment, distracted, the last bite of her sandwich held out absently like a coin about to be dropped in a meter. The two policemen had returned and the short one was holding Ros's limbs in various positions at the Inspector's instructions, while he nosed around. The other was making sketches of the scene. They seemed a bit subdued.

Alison turned back to me, her face softened by a momentary sorrow. 'The problem— ?'

'He turned up at the first rehearsal with a gun at his head, saying he'd pull the trigger if she didn't leave the play and come home with him, and since Ros couldn't say no, that's what she did.'

'Turned back. Like Lot's wife, after all.' She popped the last bite in. I saw a neat row of gleaming white teeth sunk into red flesh, crisp green lettuce, dark rye painted with yellow mustard. If even that arouses me, I thought, I'm pretty far gone . . . 'Yet you said— ?'

'Well, the author refused to let the play go on without her. He insisted she'd inspired him to write it, a dream he'd had or something, and she had to play the lead. So they talked Ros into having Roger temporarily committed. Because of the suicide attempt. For his own good, they said, and it probably was.'

'Until the show closed.'

'That's right. Ros visited him every day in the ward to cheer him up, never told him she was in the play, and he never asked.'

'An old trouper, after all. And so,' she added, not wryly, just sadly, staring down at her hands, 'everybody lived happily ever after.' She brushed the crumbs away, tongued a bit of sandwich from her teeth. For some reason I thought: Am I forgetting something? What I remembered was an old beggar in Cadiz who did tricks with coins. His last trick always was to stack as many coins on his tongue as people would put there, then swallow them. Or seem to. I made some remark at the time about 'pure theater' and the woman I was with said: 'I know a better trick but it is not so practical.' The old fellow climaxed his act by belching loudly and producing a paper note in 'change,' and the truth about the woman was that she was mistaken. 'And was the play a success?'

'It had a good run.'

In fact, she packed them in. But mainly because they invited the audience to join in, and the same crowd kept coming back night after night to lick the salt. True believers. Her breast, I saw, had fallen out of the dress again. It seemed less important now. The Inspector, peeling down one stocking, had found a run, which he peered at now through his pick glass. 'There's another one here at the back, Chief.' Alison touched my hand. 'You loved her very much.'

'Yes. Along with a thousand other guys.' I watched Pardew and his two assistants tugging her dead weight this way and that, watched her breast and head flop back and forth together as though in protest at the mockery of it, thinking: How quiet it has grown! I lowered my voice: 'She had something . . . very special . . .'

'I might have guessed,' Alison said. She was grinning. 'Unique, I think you said before. . .'

I smiled, leaning toward her touch. 'Mm, but hers *really* was, you see,' I said, brushing at the specks of blood on Alison's nose, letting the truth slip away now, or at least that kind of truth, letting myself be led, 'and not just in the eye, so to speak, of the beholder . . .'

'Ah, poor Gerald!' she laughed. 'When will you ever learn?'

She stifled her laughter: people were staring at us. Even the police had glanced up from the body. She covered her mouth, forced a solemn expression onto her face, peeked up at me guiltily. She waited until the others had looked away again ('Calipers, please,' the Inspector muttered), then whispered: 'But it was her breast that made you want to cry.'

I nodded, conscious of Alison's own breasts, tender and provocative under the soft silken folds of her dress, the nipples rising hard now like excited little fingers, seeming to reach through the bloodstains in the delicate jacquard pattern as though to point hopefully beyond. 'Her sex was a secret, known only to millions, her dark side, you might say . . . her buried treasure . . .' No longer: the police had their noses down there now, arguing about something. Her thighs had been pulled apart and the curled tip-ends of little straw-colored pubic hairs could be seen fringing the legbands of her panties. For some reason, it was making me dizzy. The glossiness of her panties or something. 'But her . . . her breasts,' I continued, taking a deep breath, forcing my gaze away (somewhere a toilet flushed; down in the rec room, the darts players were still at it), managing to draw myself back to Alison's eyes once more, 'her breasts were her public standard, what we knew her by . . .' The placid depths of Alison's eyes calmed me. I felt certain that everything was going to be all right. Somehow. 'Her innocence and her light, you might say. The good white flag she flew.' I smiled as our legs met: she touched her throat. 'Flags . . .'

'In the dark and dangerous land of make-believe,' whispered Alison, not so much completing my thought for me as marrying her thought to mine in a kind of voluptuous melodrama.

'Yes . . . yes, that's it . . .'

There was something truly extraordinary about Alison's eyes. Sometimes they seemed to penetrate my head as though copulating with it like a man, and then as quickly they'd go soft, almost opaque, inviting me in. Or they'd suddenly seem to pick up light from somewhere and cast it twinkling back at me, suggestively, mischievously – then just as suddenly withdraw it again, hide it, daring me to come and look for it. 'Bewitching . . .'

'Pardon?'

'Your eyes, Alison . . .'

'Ah, that must be the wormwood.' She grinned. There was a simple gaiety in them again, and I could feel her releasing me.

'Wormwood?'

'The vermouth. That's where the name comes from.'

'I always thought it was just some kind of wine, I didn't know I was giving you wormwood—'

'Oh yes. The flowers anyway. And sweetflag root and cinchona bark and coriander seeds and sandalwood – shall I go on?'

'I take it you're trying to tell me something.'

'Mmm, after that sandwich—'

'I'll be right back,' I said and lightly touched her hip. 'Don't move.'

'*Nobody* moves!' barked the Inspector, glancing sharply up at me from under Ros's skirt. 'Nobody leaves this house without my permission!'

'I'm not – it's only – just an errand,' I stammered. 'The dining room . . .'

Pardew studied me closely a moment, hooded by Ros's silver skirt like a monk. He stroked his thick moustache, glanced thoughtfully at Alison, then nodded and returned to his work, snipping through the legband of Ros's panties now with a tiny pair of manicure scissors. He made two crosswise cuts, an inch or two deep, then peeled away the little flap of silk as though easing a stamp from an envelope. Jim came in with his black bag and handed the Inspector a probe with a light on the end of it, and the others in the room pressed closer. The Inspector looked up at me and frowned: 'Off you go, then!'

Something, as I turned away, was worrying me, something just at the edge of my vision. The way Ros's stockings had been rolled down to her ankles like doughnuts maybe, making her seem pinioned, the stark face-powder whiteness of her bare thighs under their silvery canopy, the shadows beyond, Jim shaking down a thermometer . . . Or was it that tube of lipstick I'd noticed, its greasy red tip extended as though in sudden excitement, lying not far from Mavis in the chalked outline of one of my wife's fallen plants like a child's crayon on a colouring book drawing? Or Tania, scrambling out of Roger's way a moment ago, still clutching the— ?

'Boy, they sure tore up jack in here,' remarked Daffie in the doorway: one of Dickie's girls, regal tonight in her sleek indigo sheath. Her drink looked like pink lemonade, but I knew it to be straight gin tinted with juice from the maraschino cherries jar. 'Your whole house looks like it's suffering from a violent nosebleed, Ger.'

'Well, it just goes to show,' I said vaguely.

'You mean never hire a lip as an interior decorator?' She smiled, drawing deeply on a small black cigarillo. Over her shoulder, just inside the dining room, I could see Dolph's burry head with its bass clef ears, and beyond him a crowd of people jammed up around the food and drink. At the sideboard, under one of his wife Tania's paintings (a conventional subject, 'Susanna and the Elders,' yet uniquely Tania's: a gawky self-conscious girl stepping over a floating hand mirror into a bottomless pit, gazing anxiously over her shoulder at a dark forest crowding up on her – no elders to be seen, yet *something* is watching her), Howard was stirring up a fresh pitcher of martinis. I was afraid he might use up all the dry vermouth, but Daffie had taken a gentle grip on my forearm, holding me back. 'You know, Ger,' she said softly, smoke curling off her lower lip as she spoke, 'there's something funny about those cops.'

'What's that, Daffie?'

'Scratching around in Ros's drawers like that,' she said. Daffie was a model, one of the best, but in the soft-focus photos you never saw the worry lines, the dark hollows under her eyes, the nervous twitching of her nostrils. 'I don't know, but it's, well – it's like they've been there before.'

'They're professional. They've seen a lot of murders.'

'No, I mean . . .' She hesitated, withdrew her hand, took a stiff jolt of iced gin. 'I want you to do me two favors, Ger.'

'Sure, Daffie. If I can . . .'

'One, tell that pint-sized ham-fisted ape behind me to stop messing around behind the scenes,' she said loudly, Dolph's ears reddening like dipped litmus paper as he disappeared around the corner, 'and two . . .' She leaned close, touched my arm again, lowered her husky voice: 'Be careful, Ger . . .' Then, bracing herself, her elbows tucked in, she drifted on into the living room (both the Inspector and the short cop, Fred, had their heads under Ros's skirt now, Bob standing by with a test tube), moving with exaggerated elegance as though to demonstrate for me her sobriety. What she showed me, though, was a backside splattered head to foot with blood, a split skirt, and tights laddered from cheek to heel like torn curtains.

Most of the people in the dining room were crowded around the chafing dish on the table, spearing miniature sausages out of a barbecue sauce that bubbled lazily over a low blue flame. Squeezing through them on my way to the sideboard, Daffie's warning still echoing in my ear, I was reminded (I felt flushed through by fear as though it were a sudden passion) of a night at the theater when we went backstage to see Ros after a play. On that occasion, too, I'd been cautioned, but by my wife, who, seeing Roger standing guard at Ros's door and looking utterly demented, had clutched my arm, whispered her warning ('Be careful . . .'), shouted at Roger to give Ros our love and blown him a kiss, and then had dragged me away through the frothy bustle of actors and their friends and hangers-on and on out the backstage exit. I'd thought she'd seen something more specific than Roger's monstrous but by then familiar affliction – and indeed perhaps she had, for what she'd said when we got outside was: 'I sometimes get the feeling, Gerald, that the world is growing colder and colder.' Having just watched a corny but loving play about a houseful of prostitutes with an innocent virgin and old-fashioned boy-meets-girl romance on their hands, I'd wanted to say that, yes, and Ros was the flame at which all chilled men might well warm themselves; but instead, sensing my wife's deep disquiet, what I'd come out with was: 'You think Roger's going crazy?' 'No,' she'd replied, drawing me closer to her as we came out onto the street, pressing her cheek against my shoulder, 'what scares me is I think he's going sane.'

I greeted Howard at the sideboard and, noticing that the pitcher of martinis he was stirring was only about half-full, asked him (the flush had passed; I thought: a passion, yes, but passion's passion) how the vermouth was holding out, but before he could answer, his wife's nephew Anatole, hovering crowlike beside him, shot me a dark long-lashed glance and asked bluntly, his voice breaking: 'How much longer are you going to put up with this horseshit?' Then he glared at his tumbler of bourbon and ginger ale as though discovering something trenchant there and, flinging back his long black hair with a toss of his head, promptly drank down most of it.

'The vermouth's not the *problem*, Gerald!' his uncle Howard snapped. 'But there's no *ice* and the *gin* is all gone!' He seemed unusually peevish. His cracked specs maybe. Behind them, when he looked up at me, his eyes appeared broken up and scattered like little cubist exercises, and probably the world seen through them looked a bit that way as well.

I laid a consoling hand on his shoulder. 'Don't worry, Howard, there's ice in the kitchen and more gin down here below. Excuse me, Anatole.' I knelt for the gin, and the boy jerked backward, thumping up against Vic, just coming for a refill of his own. Vic swore, Anatole stammered an apology, and Howard said: 'And *someone's* stolen the fruit knife for the *lemons!*' Looking up, I saw then that he'd been using his scout knife. His hands, stained and soiled, were trembling.

'Those three dicks probably borrowed it,' said Vic sourly, his speech beginning to slur. 'I think they're in there now, trying to peel Ros's cunt with it.'

Anatole laughed, took a nervous puff on his French cigarette, and said: 'That's just it, those stupid turds can't see what they're looking straight at!'

'I'm afraid the whole fucking species has much the same problem, son,' Vic growled, cocking one shaggy eyebrow at Anatole. 'Like bats in daylight, we can't even see when we're pissing on ourselves.' Vic was a hardnosed guy with a spare intellect, but he had a weakness for grand pronouncements, especially with a few shots under his belt. I handed Howard a new bottle of gin, pushed the cabinet door shut with my knee, poured a wineglass full of vermouth for Alison, and then, on reflection, one for myself as well.

'Here's a good one,' said Anatole. He was reading the cocktail napkins Kitty and Knud had given us, which were decorated with the usual party gags based on lines like 'Please don't grind your butts into the carpet,' or 'Thou shalt not omit adultery.' The one he showed us was of a policeman frisking a girl bankrobber. He had her face up against the wall, her skirt lifted and her pants pulled down (as though on cue, the cop with the test tube limped in, pushing people aside, and snatched the salt away from Mrs Draper, went bobbing out again), from which heaps of banknotes were tumbling out, and what he was saying was: 'Now, let's get to the bottom of this!'

'Tell me,' said Vic, plunging his fist into Howard's martini pitcher for a couple of ice cubes, Howard sputtering in protest, 'where do you think the cop got that line? Did it come natural to him as a simple horny human, or did it get thrust on him somehow?'

Anatole flushed, a nervous grin twitching on his thin lips. 'You mean about free will or— ?'

'I mean, has he emptied his own incorrigibly shitty nature into the vacuum of an occupation here, or has the job and society made him, innocent at birth, into the crude bullying asshole that he's become?'

'I – I don't know . . . I guess a little of both—'

'Just as I thought,' grunted Vic, 'another goddamn liberal.' And he turned away as though in contempt, sucking the ice cubes, squinting down at some of the other cocktail napkins, held at arm's length.

Anatole, badly stung, looked to Howard for support, but his uncle, absently stirring the martinis, was distracted, his head bent toward the TV room where several couples were necking. Ah. Probably the true cause of his bad temper: I'd interrupted his little spectacle. Howard the art critic. At the far wall, Charley Trainer's wife, Janice, was in a stand-up clinch with some guy whose back was to us, her arms wrapped round his neck schoolgirl-style, her pink skirt rucked up over her raised thigh. Our eyes met for a moment and what I saw there, or thought I saw, was terror. 'I guess I'll get something to eat,' Anatole muttered clumsily and slouched off toward the dining table, looking gangly and exposed. 'I'm feeling drunk or something . . .'

Ginger was over there, jabbing clumsily at the sausages in the chafing dish with a toothpick. She caught the tip end of one, lifted it shakily toward her little comic-book 'O' of a mouth. It fell off. As she bent over, stiff-legged above her heels, to pick it up, Dolph stepped up behind her and, as though by accident, his eyes elsewhere, let his cupped palm fall against her jutting behind. Anatole saw this, spun away, found himself moving on through the doorway into the living room, puffing shallowly on his cigarette stub.

'You were pretty hard on him, Vic.'

'He's all right. But he's all style and no substance. He needs to grow up.' Ginger rose, holding painfully with her fingertips the hot sausage, furry now with dust and lint. She looked around desperately for some place to put it, finally gave up and popped it in her mouth, then brushed at her rear end as though flicking away flies. 'Isn't she the one that cunt-hungry fashion plate brought here tonight?'

'One of them.' Dolph took his hand away and (Vic, moving like an aging lion, now stalked off into the TV room, flinging open doors, peering behind furniture) rubbed his nose with it. Poor Dolph. Bachelor-hood, since his break-up with Louise, had not sat well on him. Ginger blew out her cheeks around the hot sausage and bobbed up and down on her high heels, her halo of carroty little pigtails quivering around her heart-shaped face like nerve ends.

'Hey,' I said when Vic returned (Howard had left us, taking up a position over near the dining table where he still had a view into the TV room, his fractured lenses aglitter with myriad reflections of the candles on the table), 'fatherhood doesn't last forever, you know.'

'She's a fucking innocent, Gerry, and I'm telling you, if that cocksucker gets his filthy hands on her, so help me' – he ripped a wadded-up cocktail napkin apart in demonstration – 'I'll tear his balls off!'

I believed him. It was what made Vic more than just an armchair radical: he could kill. 'I'll get some more ice,' I said, taking the bucket along with me, dumping the empty bottles in it, and Vic called after me: 'If you see Sally Ann, damn it, tell her I want to talk to her. Right now!' Alison's husband came through just then with Roger's law partner Woody and his wife, Yvonne, and as I passed them I heard them laugh together behind me. All three were carrying croquet mallets: had they been playing out there in the dark?

Louise stood up suddenly when I entered the kitchen, almost as though I'd caught her at something. She'd been squeezed in at the breakfast bench, watching my wife whip up what looked like an avocado dip – or perhaps helping with some of the chopping: there was a little cheese board and knife in front of her – and she nearly took the buttons off the front of her dress trying to jump out of there.

Patrick, halving a grapefruit at the counter with a small steak knife, exclaimed: 'My goodness, Louise! I felt that all the way over here!'

'You don't have to leave, Louise,' I said, raising my voice as the dishwasher thumped suddenly into its wash cycle. 'I've only come for some ice and mix.'

'Let her go, Gerald,' my wife called out, getting to her feet. 'She's just eating up all my potato chips anyway.'

'Are you still making more food?' There was a huge platter of freshly prepared canapés on the counter, empty tuna cans and cracker boxes scattered about, dip mix packets, bread from the freezer, the wrappers still frosty, home-canned pickles and relishes up from the cellar, smoked oysters on toast squares. And something was cooking in the oven. 'I thought you had everything ready *before* the party.'

'So did I. But it's all going so fast.' Louise glanced suspiciously past the bucket of empty bottles I was carrying to the two full wineglasses in my other hand, as without a word but accompanied by the splashy grind of the dishwasher, she shifted heavily toward the dining room. 'Did you notice how many sausages were left in the chafing dish?'

'Not many. Should I turn the flame off?'

'No, I've got more.' She went to the refrigerator and brought out a ceramic bowlful, bumping the door closed with her hips. 'Louise, would you mind?' she called, stopping her at the door.

'My, what cute little weenies,' Patrick remarked as Louise, flushing, took the bowl from my wife's hands.

'Can I fix you a drink before you go, Louise?' I called, but, averting her face darkly, she backed out through the dining room door without replying. 'What's the matter with *her?*'

'She was badly bruised in there,' my wife said, speaking up over the dishwasher. She brought the avocado dip over and set it on the butcherblock worktable in the middle of the room, under the big fluorescent lamp, and I thought of Alison again, that play we'd seen. 'Don't you notice? Everything that happens,' she'd said that night, 'happens where the light is.' 'Didn't you see her face?'

'Ah, was that a bruise . . . ?' I poked my nose in the fridge: about a dozen cans of beer left – Dolph must be drinking them six at a time.

They were squeezed in there among dishes and dishes of prepared foods, tins of sardines, anchovies, pimentos, bags of sliced and chopped vegetables, pâtés, and dozens of sausages and wrapped cheeses.

'She said Roger bumped her cheek with his elbow,' my wife explained over her shoulder, pulling hot bread out of the oven, hurrying it gingerly to the butcherblock.

'I'm afraid her *face* isn't *all* that's bruised,' Patrick announced archly. 'It's a good thing for you this house has firm foundations!'

'Now, Patrick,' my wife scolded playfully (her busy hands, slender, a bit raw, stirred dips, arranged biscuits and crackers, sliced bread), winking at me as I dragged a case of beer up to the fridge, 'she's not *that* heavy!'

'My dear,' declared Patrick, one hand on his hip, the other holding his glass up as though in a toast, 'I had already fallen when Louise went down, and when she hit the floor *I skidded three feet in her direction!*'

My wife laughed and waggled an admonishing finger. 'Patrick, you're a scandal!' Patrick, looking smug, lit up one of his French cigarettes, and she put a saucepan of water on to boil.

'By the way,' I said, realizing that this had been bothering me for some time now – in fact since I'd talked to Daffie – 'where did they take Roger?' This last was shouted out in relative silence, as the dishwasher timer suddenly clicked over, and it made my wife and Patrick start. Frightened me, too, in a way. They turned away. I lowered my voice. 'I, uh, didn't see him in the dining room.'

'They took him into your study,' my wife explained. She put a lid on the saucepan, staring at it as though estimating its contents. 'They said the TV bothered them.'

'Really?' I pulled the cold beers forward, packing the warm cans in at the back. 'I don't even think it's on.'

'Knud was watching something.'

'He fell asleep.'

'You know, he told me a really *weird* story tonight,' said Patrick, sucking up some of the crushed ice from his salty bitch.

'Knud?'

'No, Roger, of course. Before the – before . . .'

Shoving things around to make room for the beer, I discovered at the back an old bottle of tequila, still about a third full. Must have been in there for years.

'He said he came home one night and Ros was gone.'

'Nothing weird about that. The weird thing was to find her at home. Say, how long's it been since we were last in Mexico?'

'Eight and a half years, Gerald – but don't interrupt. Tell us about the story, Patrick. What happened . . . ?'

'Well, it's very peculiar,' said Patrick, stubbing out his cigarette, his bright eyes squinting from the smoke, his voice losing some of its mincing distance, mellowing toward intimacy. 'He said he arrived home from the office late one night and Ros was gone, but there in her place, sitting in a chair by the window, was a strange old lady. Roger said the only word for her was "hag." An old hag. She had long scraggly white hair, wild piercing eyes, a hunched back, and she was dressed in pitiful old rags. He said he felt a strange presentiment about her as though he were in the presence of some dreadful mystery. He asked her why she'd come, and she replied that she'd been told he was a great lawyer and could help her in her misfortune. She claimed to possess a fabulous wealth which she wished to share with all the world, but which had been taken away from her by a wicked and spiteful son and locked in a secret vault. Moreover, her son was seeking to have her declared mentally insane and put away, and she wanted Roger to force the son to release the fortune for the benefit of all and to prevent her unjust incarceration. Well! Roger said he understood immediately that it was a parable she'd been speaking, one meant for him alone, *he* was the selfish son, and his treasure – well, he told the strange old woman that though he sympathized with her plight he was unable to do as she asked. "For shame!" hissed the old woman. "You'll burn in hell for your lack of charity!" Mortified by his own weakness, he buried his head in his hands, and when he looked up again the hag was gone. He ran to the door and found Ros, lying in a swoon in the corridor outside, her hair loose and wild, her clothes torn.'

'In a swoon— ?'

'That's what he said. You should have seen his eyes when he told us! He said he carried her into the bedroom, fearing for her very life. He sat up with her all night, weeping buckets, kissing her feverishly, pleading for her forgiveness, until at last she came around. He begged her to tell him all that had happened, but she said she couldn't remember a thing since she'd left the bank that afternoon.'

We were both staring at Patrick in silence when the dishwasher popped suddenly into its rinse cycle, making us all jump. I laughed. My wife said: 'It must have been a dream, don't you think, Gerald?'

Even over the noisy churning of the dishwasher, we could hear Mr Draper's booming voice on the other side of the door: '*Yes, heh heh, you might say I've got a lot of time on my hands!*' Patrick started up uneasily. 'Probably,' I said. 'Or maybe a play Ros was in . . .'

'*Time, heels! Yeh heh heh!*'

'Do you think they'll *keep* my tweezers?' Patrick asked anxiously, tugging his cuffs down over his wrists, his eye on the door. 'They're real silver!'

'Speaking of silver, I forgot to tell you, we're invited to Cyril and Peg's big anniversary party,' my wife said, peeking into the kettle of water. The way she held the lid made me think of the Inspector hooded by Ros's skirt.

'Are they here yet?'

'A – a gift from my mother— !'

'Cyril and Peg? I think so.' She poked around in the refrigerator and found a carton of eggs. 'Didn't they come with Fats and Brenda?'

'*It's Old Man Time here, soaks! I mean, folks!*' Mr Draper sang out jovially, bumping in through the door, and Patrick slipped stealthily out behind him. Mr Draper wore wristwatches chockablock up both arms like sleeves of armor and his pants bagged low, their thin suspenders stretched tight, weighted down by his deep bulging pockets. 'Come along now, heh heh, no present like the time!'

My wife, using a ladle, dropped the last of the eggs into the boiling water, checked her watch, then peeled it off and handed it to him. 'Mine was your first, Mr Draper,' I said, showing him my empty wrist.

'Call me Lloyd, son! You – oops, nearly forgot!' The old man reached into his hip pocket and pulled out the butcher knife the Inspector had found. 'Iris said to return this to you.'

'Why, thank you, Lloyd. Looks like it needs a good washing.' As she turned to put it in the sink, our eyes met. 'Are you all right, Gerald?' she asked, smiling at me as she might at our young son.

'Yes, only I – I keep forgetting things . . .'

'Wasn't there someone else here when I came in?' asked Mr Draper, peering over his spectacles, just as Dolph came thumping in for another beer.

'He left,' said my wife, turning her bottom away from Dolph as he passed. She winked at me.

'Christ, have I got a thirst!' Dolph exclaimed, swinging open the refrigerator door.

'Gerald just put some in, Dolph.'

'Cold ones to the front,' I said. It was coming back to me, the knife, loose in the room like a taunt, then someone reaching for it, picking it up . . .

Dolph pulled a beer out and popped it open, took a long guzzle, all the while holding the door agape.

'Excuse me, sir,' smiled Mr Draper, coming forward (yes, Naomi, Naomi picking it up and putting it in her bag, Mrs Draper making her take it out again – it must have been just before Roger hit me). 'It's time—'

'You already got mine, Dropper,' grumped Dolph, wiping his mouth with his sleeve (and some big woman, fallen among my wife's potted plants, greenery in her hair like laurel, a silly look on her face as though she'd just remembered something she wished she'd forgot). 'That one with the gold band halfway up your arm – don't lose it!' He belched and the dishwasher shut down. 'That's better!'

'Time is never lost,' Mr Draper declared, lifting his chin so as to peer grandly down over his long warty nose, 'only mislaid!'

'Jesus, what a night,' wheezed Dolph, ignoring the old man. He shook his burry head as though in amazement, hauled out another beer. 'It's starting to look like a goddamn packing house in there, Gerry!'

My wife blushed, wiped her hands on her checkered apron. 'I'll go tidy up in a minute, Dolph.'

'Is this guacamole?' Mr Draper asked at the butcherblock.

The two glasses of vermouth sat there, pools of pale green light on the maple top beside the dark pudding of mashed avocado. Like two halves of an hourglass. I hurried over to the fridge, filled the bucket with ice. 'You're right, Gerry,' Dolph said, watching me ('Well, it has avocados in it,' my wife was explaining, 'but it's not as spicy – would you like to try some?'), 'you sure as hell couldn't stab anybody with *that* thing.'

'Yes indeedy, ma'am – if you have a spoon. I don't think I can chance those crispy things. New store teeth, you know.' He grinned sheepishly and pushed them halfway out of his mouth at her.

Dolph squeezed his empty can double and tossed it in the bin, then, belching voluminously, popped the other one open. 'I'll take that bucket in for you, Gerry.'

'Thanks, Dolph. Oh, hey – this bottle of tonic, too.'

Mr Draper smacked his lips generously. 'A real treat, senyoretta!' he beamed. She smiled again, but less buoyantly. Her courage was slipping, and I could see the anxiety and weariness crowding back. 'But I must fyoo-git!' He lifted his manacled arms: 'Time, like they say, hangs heavy – yeh heh heh!' And he left us, Dolph having preceded him without farewell.

'Are you fyoo-gitting, too?' my wife asked, her apron twisted up in her hands.

'Well, duty,' I said, picking up the two glasses.

'Someone . . .' She hesitated, staring at her hands. 'Someone said there was a valentine.'

'What? A valentine?'

'In Naomi's bag.'

'Ah, well, what *didn't* she have in there! Even our—'

'They said it was from you.'

'From *me*! What, a valentine to Naomi?' I didn't know whether to laugh or be offended. But she seemed to be trembling, so I set the glasses down and took her in my arms. 'Hey, has Louise been working on you again?'

She turned her head into my chest, wrapped her arms around my neck. At least, I was thinking, she didn't ask about the cock sock. 'Gerald, I'm afraid . . .'

'Come on, *you're* my only valentine. You *know* that,' I said, and lifted her chin to kiss her.

But there was a sudden rush of chattery laughter as the door whumped open and in came Charley Trainer with Woody's wife, Yvonne, and a tall skinny man he introduced as Earl Elstob. We pulled apart. I recognized Earl by the mismatched pants and sports jacket, green socks and two-toned penny loafers, as the guy who'd been in a clinch with Charley's wife in the TV room a little while ago. What I hadn't seen before was the awesome overbite that nearly hid his chin from view. One of Charley's insurance projects no doubt; he often brought them to parties to soften them up.

'Hey!' boomed Charley affably, wrapping his free arm around my wife's waist; the other carried glasses and a half-bottle of scotch. '*Hey!*'

My wife, getting out a fresh handtowel, said, 'Goodness! I've got so much to do!' and Earl Elstob, grinning toothily, asked us if we knew what a constipated jitterbug was. Charley Trainer har-harred and lumbered over to the fridge for some ice cubes. He grabbed ahold of two, and a half-dozen fell out. 'You're lookin' beautiful!' he said to the room in general, and Yvonne, a huge splotch of blood over the left side of her face, thrust her empty glass out and cried: 'You goddamn *right!*'

My wife picked up the avocado dip and offered it around, Charley slopping half of it out on the floor with his first dip. He stooped with a grunt to wipe it up with his fingers, hit his face on the edge of the bowl in my wife's hands, came up with a green blob over his right eye like some kind of vegetable tumor. 'What izziss stuff anyhow?' he asked, licking his fingers. Big Chooch they called him back in his college football days: Choo-Choo Trainer, last of the steamroller fullbacks. In those days he could sometimes be stopped but rarely brought down; now, any time after happy hour, you could tip him over with your little finger.

'One who can't *jit!*' Earl Elstob hollered out, just as my mother-in-law came in, looking down her nose at so much noise, to get cookies and milk for Mark. Charley backed out of her way, crunching ice cubes underfoot, and bumped into the cabinets, sending things clattering around inside.

'There's some vanilla pudding for him in there, Mother,' my wife said, exchanging a cautionary glance with me. 'Behind the bean salad.'

'Mark's still not asleep?' I asked. Yvonne seemed to be crying.

'Not *yet!*' my mother-in-law snapped, giving me a fierce penetrating look which had more in it than mere reproach. She slammed the refrigerator shut, snatched down a box of candies from the cupboard, and, jaws clenched, planted a button of chocolate in the middle of the little bowl of pudding – *fplop!* – like some kind of immutable judgment.

Charley Trainer, staring down at it, suddenly went limp and morose, his thick jowls sagging. 'That poor damn kid . . .,' he muttered tearfully, the avocado dip now slipping down over his eyebrow as though he were melting, and my wife shook her head at him, her finger at her lips.

Charley stared at her foggily, failing to understand, opened his mouth to speak, and my wife, in desperation, grabbed up the dip again: 'Charley! A little more . . . ?' Yvonne stifled a sob.

'But . . . but I *loved* her— !'

'We all did, Charley. Here . . .'

I had a catch in my own chest and felt suddenly I had to get out of here (Mavis over the body, working her jaws: it was like trying to turn a key in a stiff lock, my chest felt like a stiff lock) – but as I grabbed up the glasses and turned to go, Tania came bursting in, her bangles jangling, holding her bloodsoaked dress out away from her body as though it were hot soup spilled there, crying: 'My god, look at this! What am I going to *do*?'

My mother-in-law took one glance and replied matter-of-factly: 'It should be soaked in a chloride-of-lime solution. If that doesn't work, try salts of sorrel.'

'Protein soap will do just as well,' my wife said, turning the fire off under the boiling eggs. 'Just a minute and I'll get you some, Tania.'

Her mother sniffed scornfully and paraded out with the milk and pudding, her chin high, old dark nylons whistling in deprecation, Earl Elstob holding the door for her, while slurping at his drink. 'One who – huh! *shlup*! – can't jit?' he repeated hopefully. Yvonne had buried her face in her hands, her short straight hair, rapidly going gray, curtaining her face. It was the first time I'd seen her break down since the day she first learned about her breast cancer.

Tania picked up the steak knife Patrick had used to cut his grapefruit, touched the point with her fingertip. 'Janny was crying, too,' she said, peering up at Charley over her half-lens spectacles.

'Janny's not very flexible,' Charley rumbled apologetically, wiping away the green dip in his eye.

Yvonne lifted her head, flicked her hair back from her face (I saw now that the eyelash on the side splashed with blood was thickly clotted and her penciled eyebrow was erased: it looked like that side of her face was disappearing), blew her nose and wailed: 'God gave me a blue Louie, Charley!'

'Well, give'm one *back*, Yvonne! God-*damn* it!'

Tania had discovered and examined the cheese knife on the breakfast table, and was now poking through the silverware and utensils drawers. My wife glanced up anxiously from the sink where she was draining the water off the eggs. 'Is there something you need, Tania?'

'Yes,' said Tania, closing a drawer, while Charley staggered around the room dropping cubes in drinks and on the floor and pouring scotch, 'maybe I *will* rinse this dress out.'

'The soap's up in the bathroom,' my wife said, running cold water over the eggs. 'In the cabinet under the sink, or else the linen cupboard – Gerald, could you look for it? It's in a blue box . . .'

'Sure . . .' A whiff of herbs rose to my nose from the cool sweating glasses in my hands, and that now-familiar sense of urgency washed over me again. 'As soon as I—'

'Is that my wife's drink?' It was Alison's husband, standing behind me in the doorway, one hand in his jacket pocket, the thumb pointed at me like a warrant, the other holding a meerschaum pipe at his mouth. 'She's been *waiting* . . .'

'Ah! Yes, I was just—'

'Two of them? Well . . .' He clamped the pipe in his teeth, took both glasses as though, reluctantly, claiming booty. 'I'll see that she gets them.'

'Now, *there* goes a pretty man!' exclaimed Yvonne as the door slapped to, and Earl Elstob, as though suddenly inspired, asked: 'Say, huh! yuh know the best way to find out if a girl's ticklish?' Charley was fishing about in the refrigerator and things were crashing and tinkling in there. He came out with that bottle I'd noticed earlier, dragging dishes and beer cans with it, and, holding it at arm's length, stared quizzically at the label, then shrugged and poured some in his glass of scotch. 'He looks like Don the Wand!'

'Juan?'

'Yeah, or the Scarlet Pippin – Pimple – what the hell— ?'

'Hey!' Charley laughed, waggling the bottle. 'Y'know why the— ?'

'Pimpernel,' my wife said.

Tania took my arm. 'C'mon, Gerry. Let's go get cleaned up.'

'No, wait!' Charley rumbled. 'Jussa – ha ha! – jussa goddamn minute! Why'da Mexican push his wife till she – hruff! haw! – fell offa cliff?'

'Uh, that's sorta – *shlup!* – like a shotgun weddin',' Earl yucked, sucking.

'Check on the toilet paper while you're up there, Gerald!' my wife called as Tania, her arm wrapped in mine, pulled me through the door, whispering: 'There's something I have to show you, Gerry – something strange!'

'You know, huh, a case of wife or—'
'What *cli-iii-iif-fff*?' howled Yvonne.
'*And handtowels!*'
'No – haw haw! – *wait . . . !*'

As we pushed through the people around the dining table, making
our way toward the hall, Tania said, 'Just a sec,' and reached in to inspect
some knives and skewers, her dress rustling as it brushed others. Over
by the sideboard, Alison, discussing Tania's painting with Mrs Draper,
pointed up at something, then adopted 'Susanna's' pose, one hand down
in front, the other, holding the vermouth, at her breast, and looked back
over her shoulder. Our eyes met and she smiled brightly, dropping the
pose as though, still Susanna, exposing herself. She raised her fresh glass
of vermouth at me, invited me over with a jerk of her head '(*In a moment!*)
I mouthed silently, pointing at Tania's broad back (she was slipping
something into the pockets of her dress), then blew her a kiss just as her
husband, who'd been standing in the TV room doorway, turned around,
fitting his pipe into his mouth. He froze for a second, teeth bared around
the tooth-white pipe, staring at me, and I wiped my lips with the hand
with the kiss in it as though I had something hot in my mouth. Alison
looked puzzled. Her husband lit up thoughtfully in the shadows behind
her.

'Hey, these horseradish meatballs are terrific, Ger! Is there any more
of the dip?'

'Uh . . . probably. In the kitchen, Talbot. Ask my wife.' Earlier, Iris
Draper had remarked on the dimness of the light in here, the relative
brightness of the rooms around, comparing it to some mantic ceremony
or other she'd come across in her tourist travels, and though at the time
I'd found her chatter about 'secret chambers' and 'illumination mysteries'
naively pedantic, now as I gazed at the candlelit faces of my friends
gathered around the table (Alison had been drawn back to the painting
by Iris and her husband, and now seemed glowingly mirrored there) –
bruised, crumpled, bloodied – it all seemed strangely resonant. 'What's
the matter with your ear, Talbot?'

'Hit the goddamn fireplace with it.'

'Whew! Did you show that mess to Jim?'

'Yeah, he had to put three stitches in. Hurt like hell. Good excuse to soak up more anaesthetic, though – oh, oh, the old ball-and-chain's calling. I was supposed to bring her one of those fancy whatchamacallits in the seashells. See ya in a minute.' I noticed one of Ginger's kerchiefs on the floor where he'd been standing and stooped to pick it up, also some toothpicks, spoons, a mustard knife, parsley sprigs, and a ripped-up cocktail napkin. The joke on the napkin, when I pieced it together, was of a frightened young suitor, his knees knocking together, asking a towering irate father with fumes rising from his head: 'May I have your d-d-daughter's hole in h-handy matrimony, s-sir?'

Someone's breast was touching my elbow. 'Hi, Gerry.'

'Hey, Michelle.' Her breast burrowed into the crook of my arm as if seeking shelter. 'You all right?'

'I think so. Awful, isn't it?'

'What happened to the fucking scotch, Ger?'

'Charley's got it in the kitchen.'

'Is he sober enough to be trusted with it?'

'I don't know, Noble – but there's more down there in the cabinet.'

'Listen.' He leaned close, dead eye toward us, good one keeping watch. There was something not quite clean about Noble's breath. 'Chooch's wife knows something,' he whispered, and Michelle backed off a step.

'Janny? She doesn't know the time of day.'

Noble shrugged, his lids heavy. 'Maybe. But she's been talking to the cops. I think she's naming names. I'd check it out if I were you.' He took Ginger's fallen kerchief from my hand, casually popped his false eyeball into it, and knotted it up.

'Come on,' said Tania, taking my hand. Across the room (Michelle 'oh'ed' as Noble, squinting, unknotted the kerchief and showed it to be empty), Alison and her husband were moving parallel with us toward the living room, and again we found ourselves exchanging furtive glances. What had she said that night we met? I'd been speaking of the invention of audiences, theater as a ruse, a game against time. 'Yes,' she'd said, smiling up at me over the ruffles at her throat (I gave Tania's hand a little squeeze, as I'd no doubt squeezed my wife's hand that night at the theater), 'and that's why the lives of actors, thought frivolous, are essentially tragic, those of the audience, comic.'

The short policeman, the one called Fred, pushed in from the front room, blocking my view of her. At the table, he picked out three or four forks, held them up (Noble was prying his eyelid open, revealing the false eye back in place, gold backside out: Michelle gasped), chose one and turned to go, but got stopped by Woody, Roger's law partner. They huddled for a moment, watched closely by Tania's husband, Howard, standing stockstill against the wall, his broken lenses twinkling, and it looked to me, before I lost sight of them, like Woody gave the cop some money.

'Who's that playing darts downstairs?' Tania asked in the hallway.

'I don't know.' I was still thinking about Noble, his pocked face dark with apprehension: Ros had told me he'd been brutal to her once. Down below, the darts could still be heard striking the board, but the conversation, if any, wasn't carrying up the stairs. 'Cyril and Peg maybe.'

Tania considered this, twining the laces of her peasant dress around one finger. Noble had tried to shove the handle of a hairbrush up her bottom, she'd said, apparently as part of yet another amateur magic trick, and when it wouldn't go, he'd beat her with the other end of it. In the doorway of the living room ('I'm not a prude, Gerry,' Ros had declared, 'but it didn't even have round edges – what was he so mad about?'), Jim was swabbing Daffie's elbow with a ball of soaked cotton, Anatole and Patrick watching. Daffie made some remark to Anatole that made him blush, then looked up and winked at me.

'Curiously,' Tania said, fluttering her arm in a kind of salute at her nephew as she passed, 'Peg was just talking about Ros. She said she'd always been a little jealous of her because, in spite of the crazy life Ros led, she was never unhappy, as far as anyone could tell, while Peg, talented, well-educated, orderly, comfortably married to Cyril for over twenty-four years now and never a serious quarrel or a single infidelity, could not truly claim to have been happy a single day of her life. It seemed so unfair, she said, like all the things you get born with and can't help.' Tania paused at the foot of the stairs to look back at me, one hand, knobby with heavy jeweled rings, resting on the banister, and I thought of Ros, bouncing goofily down a broad ornate staircase in a play in which she was supposed to be a stately middle-aged matron, descending to receive the news of the death of her husband, whom she herself had poisoned. 'But then one day Peg saw Ros in a terrible state, all in a frazzle and close to tears, and the cause of it was simply that Ros was trying to learn her lines for a new play, something she always found almost impossible. She said it was a revelation, not about Ros, but about herself: she said she'd never see her own marriage in quite the same way again!' Tania's dark eyes crinkled with amusement as she thought about this, her lower lip caught in her bright white teeth, then she said: 'The wound – it wasn't made by that knife, you know. It was more like a puncture than a gash . . .'

'Yes, that's how it looked to me, too.'

From the stairs as we climbed them, I could see over Jim and Daffie and their audience into the living room, where Inspector Pardew seemed to be demonstrating something to his two assistants. Ros was out of sight, but her chalked outline, blood-drenched at the heart, was clearly visible, ringed about by the legs of watchers-on. Things still looked pretty smashed up and scattered in there, but from this angle the peculiar thing was the complex arrangement of chalked outlines, which reminded me of the old star charts with their dot-to-dot drawings of the constellations.

On the landing, in front of another of her paintings, Tania paused and raised her spectacles to her nose. 'Look,' she said. It was a painting of 'The Ice Maiden,' an extraordinary self-portrait in glacial greens and crystalline blues, viewed as though from the surface of an icy mountain lake. The Ice Maiden – Tania – was swimming up toward the viewer, her dramatic highboned face distorted with something between lust and terror, a gold ring deep in the throat of her gaping mouth, her right arm stretched out, sapphire-ringed finger reaching toward the hand of an unseen swimmer, like Adam's toward God's in all those European paintings. Behind her – below her – swirling up from the buried city streets of her childhood through a fantastic tapestry of crystal ice: blind frozen images from her other paintings up to then – 'The Thief of Time,' 'The Dead Boy,' our 'Susanna,' the tortured 'Saint Valentine' with his bloody erection, the orgiastic couples of 'Orthodoxy' and the dancing 'Unclean Persons,' 'The Executioner's Daughter' in her pratfall, the pettifogging privy councilors holding a meeting on 'Gulliver's Peter,' plus a number I didn't know – and one of these, a woman poised in astonishment, had had her face scratched out.

'My god!' I cried. 'Who's done this— ?'

'It's what I wanted to show you.'

'It's – it's *terrible!*' I touched the scarred area.

'Gives you a funny feeling, doesn't it? Like somebody's made a hole in the world . . .'

'But then that girl, I was never sure – it was *Ros*, wasn't it?'

Tania nodded. 'It wasn't a very good likeness. I did it from memory and from other sketches.'

'Do I know the painting it's from?'

'No, I never finished it.' She seemed to think about this for a moment, staring at the obliterated face, as though, like the Ice Maiden, being sucked down into it. 'Did you ever see that play, *Bluebeard's Secret*, the one—'

'Yes, Ros had a bit part. Or nonpart. It was the only reason we went to see it. I . . . well, I guess I didn't—'

Tania smiled. 'I know. All that self-indulgent melodrama, phony symbolism, pompous huffing and puffing about free will and necessity – just a lot of sophomoric mystification for the most part and a few bare bosoms. But I came away from it with an idea for a painting, Gerry – more than an idea: it was like some kind of compulsion, a desperate, almost violent feeling. A painting is like that sometimes. It can start from the most trivial image or idea and suddenly, like those monsters in the movies, transform itself and overwhelm you. That's what happened to me with "Bluebeard's Chambers." I came home with nothing more than the idea of doors, the color blue from the lights they used, and Ros. And yet—'

'But she hardly—'

'I know, that was the point. Part of it. I meant to have a lot of doors in my painting, doors of all sizes, some closed, some partly open, some just empty doorframes, no walls, but the various angles of the doors implying a complicated cross-hatching of different planes, and opening onto a great profusion of inconsistent scenes, inconsistent not only in content but also in perspective, dimension, style – in some cases even opening onto other doors, mazes of doors like funhouse mirrors – and the one consistent image was to be Ros. As you see her there.' As she spoke I could feel the surge of excitement she must have felt as the idea grew in her, filling her out, as though her brain, sixth sense organ, were being erotically massaged. I loved this power she had: to be excited. It was a kind of innocence. 'Only from all angles, including above and below, sometimes in proportion with the scene around her, sometimes not, sometimes only a portion of her or perhaps strangely distorted in particulars, yet essentially the same basic pose, a being dispossessed of its function. And as she disappeared into her own multiplicity, Bluebeard himself, though not present in the painting except in the color, would hopefully have emerged as the unifying force of the whole.' She sighed tremulously. 'But I couldn't handle it. Too many doors at once, you might say.' It was like a tide ebbing. Her voice softened. 'And Ros was not just fidgety – she was almost fluid. Never the exact pose twice – even twice in the same minute. But the colors were good, and eventually they led me to this one, a painting I'd been wanting to try for years.' She stared now at her own image, beautiful, yet frightening in its intensity. 'I think now if I tried again . . . the "Bluebeard," I mean . . .'

She didn't finish, but I felt I knew: she'd try scratching the faces of all the Ros figures, just as it was here. 'Why not, Tania? Maybe you're ready for it now.'

She smiled wanly, curling a few strands of her deep black hair around one long pointed fingernail, painted a deep magenta. 'It's so late, Gerry . . .' In reflex, I glanced at my empty wrist. Below us, people were arguing noisily about what they'd seen or heard before the discovery of Ros's body, and I heard my own name mentioned. Tania touched my arm. 'Come on. We've come this far, we might as well wash these stains out.'

As we started up, I found myself thinking of that town in Italy again, a staircase, the hotel probably where I took that girl with the bunny-ear pubes – no, wait: some city to the north. Paris. Yes, a walk-up ('I think of him, you know,' Tania was saying, she was apparently talking about Bluebeard still, 'as a man who wished to share all he had with the world . . . but could not . . .'), bare bulb on the landing. Over an Algerian restaurant on the Left Bank. Then who was I with? Oddly it seemed like Alison. But later, on the bidet—

'Sometimes I think art's so cowardly, Gerry. Shielding us from the truth . . .'

'Well . . . assuming the truth's worth having . . .' We'd had this conversation before. Vic's daughter Sally Ann slouched against the banister at the top of the stairs, watching us.

'In other words, scratching that face out was the same thing in the end as painting it in . . .'

'No, Tania, the one takes talent, genius, the other—'

'Ah! But you don't say which!'

There was a new patch on Sally Ann's blue jeans, just over the crotch – the first thing I saw, in fact, as we climbed past her – that said 'SWEET

MEAT' in bright fleshy colors. She was slumped against the rails, body arched, rolling a cigarette. Or maybe a joint. 'Hey, your father's looking for you,' I said, and then, because she was staring so intently at me, I poked my finger in her bare navel and added: 'Deli Belly.'

She jumped back, dropping her handiwork down the stairs. 'Oh, Gerry, that's stupid!' She slapped at my hand, then pranced on down to the landing.

'Someone's got a crush on you, Gerry,' Tania observed.

'I always did have more luck with poets than painters,' I sighed, and stooped to pick up another of Ginger's kerchiefs on the top stair. In Paris, climbing, I was carrying some books with plain green jackets, a print bought from a stall along the Seine, and I stooped for . . . for . . . a coin? a ring? a button maybe, a brass or silver button . . .

The bathroom door was closed. I started to knock, but Tania with her customary lack of ceremony walked in. 'Well, *that's* pretty,' she declared, and turned on the ventilator fan. Dickie was in there, cleaning Naomi's bottom over the toilet. She was straddling the thing, bent over and facing the wall, skirt hiked, elbows resting on the water tank. Dickie looked very unhappy, smoking self-defensively with one hand, dabbing clumsily at her big hindend with the other. His shirtsleeves were rolled up, his plaid jacket hanging on the doorhook. 'Hey, Ger! Just in time!' he cried, flinging his butt into the paper-clogged stool. I saw he'd used up all the toilet paper on the roller and a box of tissues besides. '*You're* the host, *you* can wipe her goddamn ass!'

'No, thanks, you're doing fine,' I protested, but he was already washing up. Yes, the restaurant smells below, the creaky climb, the bare bulb, the bidet – but cold water. And a smaller fanny, plump but like a little pink pear, softly creased by the bidet lips, not two big melons like this – ah! my wife's!

'I'm so *embarrassed*,' Naomi said. I was directly behind her, down on my haunches by the linen cupboard, reaching for more toilet paper (these genuflections, these child's-eye views!), and her voice seemed to be coming out of her high looming behind. 'I've never done anything like this before – you know, poohed at a party. But I was so scared— !'

'It was what you'd call a moving experience, Nay,' said Dickie, reaching for a towel. I found Tania's protein soap down there as well. Only it was in a white box with blue lettering, not a blue box. I noticed a worn wooden handle behind the soap and grabbed it up – an old ice pick! *Where had this come from—?!* 'Christ! Even the goddamn towels are covered with shit!'

Dickie came over to get a clean one from the cupboard and I shoved the thing out of sight, covering it up hastily with the nearest cloth to hand. It was uncanny, I hadn't seen one in years – as best I could remember, the last time was at my grandmother's house when I was still a boy – it was almost as though . . .

'What you need is a bidet in here,' Tania said, sprinkling soap into the tub and churning the water up with her hands.

'*What*—?!' I gasped. Naomi's bottom reared above me, seeming to watch me with a suspicious one-eyed stare, pink mouth agape below as though in astonished disbelief.

'A bidet. It's what they're for, you know, washing bottoms.'

'Yes, sure, but oddly I – I was just thinking about—'

'Can you beat that,' said Dickie, tossing the towel over Naomi's bent back. 'I always thought they were for cooling the beer in.' He leaned close to the mirror, scraped at a fleck of blood in front of his golden sideburns. 'Oh, by the way, Ger, I don't know if you saw what's left of the poor bastard on the way up, but Roger's no longer with us, you know.'

'*Roger*—?!' It was like a series of heavy gates crashing shut, locks closing like meshing gears. I stumbled to my feet.

'*I knew it!*' gasped Tania, clutching her arms with wet hands.

Dickie unzipped his white trousers and tucked his shirttails in, frowning at the bloodstains on his vest. I braced myself on the cupboard shelves. 'But . . . but who—?'

He raised his eyebrows at me in the mirror as though to say I already knew. And I did. 'They used croquet mallets,' he said with a grimace, zipping up. 'The grand fucking round, Ger – it was awful.'

'But did you see it? Couldn't you do anything about it?'

Dickie, framed in lights, smiled enigmatically. I recalled now the thud of the policemen's blows, the shrieks, the thrashing about, the sudden stillness: we all knew what they were going to do when they took Roger out of the room. Maybe I'd even been told . . .

'Dickie asked them to stop it,' Naomi said from behind her bottom. 'But they didn't pay any attention to him, it was like they couldn't even hear him, maybe because of the screaming, they were like standing on his head all the time. And we couldn't stay, I was starting to . . . to poop again . . .'

Dickie turned his cuffs down, buttoned them, adjusted his tie. 'Woody said the cops were claiming self-defense,' he said, pulling a hair off the fly of his pants. He touched the top of his head, took out a comb.

Tania turned off the taps, got slowly to her feet, using the tub for support. 'Self-defense. Yes . . . maybe it was . . .' Tears filmed her big dark eyes. She'd been with me in the hallway when the two of them arrived tonight, Ros radiant, all smiles, Roger jittery as usual, trying to swallow down his panic as Ros went bouncing off into the living room, hugging everybody – it seemed so long ago! Like some kind of ancient prehistory, utterly remote, lost, an impossible past . . . 'He was the most dangerous thing in the world, after all. A child . . .'

'Hullo, folks! It's your ole ticker taker!' shouted Mr Draper, pushing heavily in, his glittering arms held out like a robot's. 'Just pass the time, please, any old time! Yeh heh heh!'

Dickie, carefully combing his fine blond hair back over the thin spot on top, grunted, slipped off his all-gold wristwatch, and, still checking himself in the mirror, held it out to Mr Draper: just then, one of the light bulbs surrounding the mirror sputtered and went out.

'Hey!' Dickie exclaimed, his arm outstretched, watch waggling at the end of it as though on the same circuit as the bulb.

'Everything I've painted so far,' Tania sighed, staring down at her dress, hands clutching her laces, 'is shit . . .'

'Could you slide it on there for me, son? Can't bend my doggone arms anymore!'

Once, during a thunderstorm, when the lights had gone out suddenly, my son had asked: 'Which is real, Daddy? The light or the dark?' 'The light,' I'd replied, just as my wife, entering behind me, had said: 'The dark.' Then, as now, I'd felt inexplicably guilty of something I couldn't define. I found a new bulb on the second shelf, then pushed the linen cupboard door shut behind me, leaned against it.

'Which . . . if I am what I've painted . . .'

'My watch was in my shoulderbag,' said Naomi, sniffling. 'I'm sorry . . .'

'Now, now, child, don't cry over lost time! When you get as old as me, you'll – say! looks like you folks need a plumber there!'

'I'm going to fix it in a minute, Mr Draper.' He peered at me over his spectacles as though discovering me for the first time. I was thinking about my wife still. What had she said about the TV? I couldn't remember. But I felt somehow I shouldn't leave her alone too long. I held up my arm shakily, as Tania, beside me, began undoing the laces of her dress. 'You've already—'

'Yep, I've got yours, son, I know. I may have lost most everything else, but I still got my marbles. And Lloyd's the name, lad, or is your memory lettin' *you* down in your old age?' He chortled drily and winked, then gazed pensively at Naomi's backside. 'Y'know, a curious thing happened to my wife and me in the catacombs of Calcutta—'

'You can't have love *or* art without the imagination, but it's dangerous,' Tania murmured, removing her half-lens reading glasses and setting them on the edge of the tub. 'Roger said that . . .' He had also explained to me once that, in the theater, when business was bad it was *brutal*, and when it was good it was: *murder*.

Talbot's wife Wilma came in just then, asking if we had any aspirin. 'For Talbot,' she explained, peering at herself in the mirror over Dickie's shoulder. 'His ear's hurting him so much, I'm afraid the dope's going to drink himself silly, and you all know how, when Talbot's looped, it's goodbye – why, hello there, Lloyd! My, you've got quite a collection!'

'Oh, it's not *my* collection! No, I'm – heh heh! – I'm not *keepin'* time, I'm just, as you might say, hangin' on to it for the *time bein'*!'

Dickie, still primping, stepped aside to let me at the medicine cabinet. I caught a glimpse of myself in the mirrored door before I swung it open, and I was shocked at how rumpled and bloody I looked – and how natural it seemed . . .

'Oh, Lloyd,' Wilma was saying, 'you do pop out with the wittiest things! You ought to be on television! I was just talking to your wife, and she said how you had everybody on the bus out to the pyramids just in stitches about mummies and mommies and—'

'In *stitches*, did you say— ?'

'Oh my goodness! It must be catching!' She fussed at her perm, which had come undone in places, loose curls poking out like released springs.

'Don't you mean *all wound up*? Yeh heh heh!'

In the cabinet, my wife's manicure set lay scattered on the bottom shelf. The tiny curved scissors were gone. The tweezers, too, for that matter. And was that a bloody hair – ? No . . . no, a piece of red thread. I was overwrought. Dickie puffed his chest and smoothed down his vest, then reached for his plaid jacket.

'I've lost touch,' Tania muttered. She gazed sorrowfully down at Naomi straddling the toilet and pursed her lips. 'I've got to get back to landscapes again . . .'

'You know, by coincidence Talbot and I were just discussing yesterday, Lloyd, the idea of touring the – just give me the whole bottle, Gerry. If I can tranquillize the jerk maybe I'll have a little fun myself for a change – we were just saying we maybe ought to visit Africa and the Middle East next year, so we must get together! You and Iris can tell us what to take, the good places to eat, nightclubs – Dickie, where are you going? I didn't mean to chase you out!'

'Don't leave me, Dickie!' Naomi begged.

'The most important thing about Africa and the Middle East,' Lloyd Draper was saying, 'is that they're two different places . . .'

'Dickie, *please!* What am I going to *wear?*'

'Go as you are, Nay, you'll have them rolling at your feet!'

'And of course it depends on what you're keen on. Some folks like the cities, some the countryside, some the resorts.'

'But what if it all starts *up* again— !'

'Didn't I see some disposable underthings in your shoulderbag, dear?' Wilma asked.

'I'm a temples-and-tombs man myself, though Iris goes more for the arts and crafts.'

'*Were* there?'

'Paper panties, Dickie, a package of them,' I called, unscrewing the dead bulb. 'You can't miss them, they're all chalked out—'

'You can send Howard up with them, Dickie,' Tania shouted. In the mirror, I saw her, her laces loosened, emptying her pockets onto the bathtub ledge. 'I have to talk to him anyway!'

'All wound up! Lloyd, however do you do it? Say, wasn't that absolutely horrid about poor Roger! I just heard about it on the way up!' I unwrapped the new bulb and screwed it in, feeling it pop alight under my fingertips. That hole in Tania's painting. All along I'd been supposing Roger might have done it. Now I didn't think so. 'They say he was very brave, but as I told Talbot, such bravery, Talbot, we can do without! If they want to ask you anything, you just – but then there's nothing to worry about really, Talbot always makes a good impression in interviews, heaven knows he's had enough practice! Are you leaving us, Lloyd?'

'Yes, eh, I'm afraid I mustn't take any more time – or rather, I *must!*' He chuckled, but his heart wasn't in it. His arms and pants as he lumbered out seemed suddenly to be hanging a couple of inches lower.

'Dear me, it seems I'm chasing everybody away tonight!' I took the towel off Naomi's back, hung it on the rod by the basin, tossed all the other towels into the clothes hamper. 'Close the door, please,' she begged, 'it's bad enough without everybody—' 'Oh, I'm sorry, dear. My, you're the very model of patience!'

'With Dickie, you have to be.'

Wilma checked herself quickly in the mirror, turned away in disappointment, fumbling in her handbag for makeup. 'Do you think those policemen down there know what they're doing?' she asked idly, uncapping a tube of lipstick. 'Well, I suppose they do.' One night I was backstage talking with Ros in front of her mirror (she liked it best when she could do her lips in a cherry red), when an actor came rushing in, leaned over her shoulder, popped her breasts out of her costume, and kissed them with loud sucking smacks, crying: 'Yum! I just *love* them!' – then dashed out again, shouting: 'Two minutes, sweetheart!' She reached over, flushed with excitement, took my face in both her hands, and whispered: 'Wait for me, Gerry!' – then gave me her breasts to kiss, tucked them in, and rustled out. But she never came back. Not that night. It was a long way from the stage to her dressing room and, as often happened, she just didn't get that far.

'Before you start that, Gerry,' Tania grunted, 'could you help me off with this damned dirndl? It's a bit tight through the middle.'

Of course, if I'd been more patient . . .

'Still, poor Roger! Wasn't it frightful, I still can't get over it!'

. . . But in those days I believed in energy and ingenuity: that there was nothing beautiful in the world but what you worked for.

'Do you think the visit of that old witch had anything to do with it?'

'What witch?'

Which was a long time ago . . .

'I think it's snagged on my bra!' Tania called from inside her skirts, as I tugged on them. I could almost hear Ros giggling under there, trying to guess who was behind her by feeling between his legs. Ah, Ros . . . I was beginning to choke up again. 'At the back!' I pushed my hand up under the heavy material and unhooked the bra clasp: her full black-nippled breasts tumbled out of their straitjacket like a landslide and Tania was free. 'Thanks, Gerry!' she gasped, and shook the dress out. 'This damn thing's worse than a corset!'

'It's beautiful, though,' sighed Wilma. 'Wherever did you get it, Tania? No, don't tell me! I'd look as plain in something like that as I do in this. Why is it that no matter how much I spend I always come out looking like a hostess for a ladies' club?'

Tania fastened her bra back on, hiking her heavy breasts into the cups, then knelt to spread her dress into the soapy water. I was struck by all the color on her face and down into her neck, against the sudden vulnerable milkiness of her naked back, its soft flesh (I was thinking of age, time, loss – Ros's giggle like a hollow terrifying echo now – and the fruitless efforts to rise above them) deeply imprinted by the checks and crosses of the waistband and bra straps. I unrolled some toilet paper, took a preliminary swipe at Naomi's behind as though to fight back. 'I feel so ashamed,' she said. 'Dickie shouldn't have left you to do this—'

'No, it's all right.'

'It's a crime,' complained Wilma, patting at her hairdo. 'Even this movie star mirror doesn't help!'

There was a sharp knock at the door and I opened it, the pad of soiled toilet paper in my hand. It was my wife's mother. 'Mark needs to use the bathroom,' she said testily.

'Sure. Tell him to come on in.'

'Not while *you're* in there!' She glared angrily past my shoulder at the three women.

'Then why don't you take him downstairs?'

'Can't do that. There's a dead person down there.'

'Ah, you . . . you know, then. I'm sorry . . .' She stood there, rigid in her implacable distrust and isolation. I knew it was hard for her here, I wanted to reach out to her, make her feel at home, but she shrank from all such gestures as though to avoid defilement. 'All right then. Just a minute.'

'Hurry, Daddy! *I can't wait!*' my son called from behind her.

'I'm just going anyway,' said Wilma, squeezing past us. She rattled the aspirin bottle: 'Gotta give Talbot his fix. Hello there, Mark – say, that's a handsome sweatshirt! You look like Little Boy Blue! Remember me? Auntie Wilma? No?'

'What am I going to *do*?' Naomi whimpered. 'I can't go out there like this! And if I let my skirt down it'll get all dirty— !'

Tania dried her hands on a large bathtowel, then wrapped it around herself like an Indian blanket. I retrieved the used handtowel from the clothes hamper. 'Here, put this between your legs, Naomi – I'll hold it for you, just let your skirt fall over it . . .' She straightened up, towering over me as I crouched to hold the towel in place: a big girl.

'Can I come in now?'

'Not yet!' said my mother-in-law as the skirt fell.

'That's it – now hold on to it, both sides . . . !' She clapped her hands front and back and I came out from under the skirt. Even standing, I had to look up to her.

'Please tell him not to take too long,' Naomi pleaded softly as we stepped out, Tania wrapped in her towel, Naomi strutting stiff-legged, feet wide apart like a mechanical soldier, holding her tummy and behind. 'I feel so stupid . . . !'

My son rushed past us, one hand inside his pajama pants, followed by my mother-in-law, straight-backed and icily silent. 'Don't flush it! It's all stopped up— !' The door slammed shut on my warning, and I could hear her snapping the lock into place. At the same moment, across the hall, the door to her room snapped open, and Woody's cousin Noble came out, tie loose around his neck, buttoning his shirtcuffs, heading for the bathroom. 'It's busy,' I said, and Noble, looking somewhat distant, his good eye as dull as his bad one, nodded and moved on downstairs.

Tania had meanwhile started telling me about Roger and the bad time she'd had when he found out about Ros posing for her – 'There were just the two of us women in a closed studio, but he couldn't bear the thought of other men even seeing Ros's naked image – when he came storming over, he didn't even knock, Gerry, he just smashed the door down!' – but I was only able to follow part of it, my eye caught now by Alison. She was with a group of people down on the landing – her husband, Wilma, Lloyd Draper weighted with watches, Woody, Noble still doing himself up, and a handsome dark-suited woman I didn't know but remembered from Roger's rampage (the dignity of her fall, even as her pendant rose to strike her on the nose) – and maybe they'd all been looking at Tania's painting before, or simply had run into each other there on the landing by chance (her husband shook hands now with Noble), but just as I spied her there, she turned, smiled suddenly at discovering me, and then, watching her husband (he was being introduced to the woman beside her, as Lloyd Draper clumped heavily on down the stairs), tossed me a kiss by kissing her hand, putting it behind her back and flipping it up at me from her rear. 'As it happened, the day he came to wreck my studio, Ros wasn't even there. Howard was up on a little pedestal, posing for me in a pink leotard as a privy councilor, and he nearly died of shock and mortification when Roger came crashing in.'

'I should imagine . . .'

Woody had something he was showing to everybody, and as they all leaned closer to see it, or perhaps to sniff at it ('I haven't been able to get him to pose for me since . . .'), Alison slipped away and came hurrying up the stairs, her hair flowing, her breasts bouncing gently in their silken pockets. 'I've been looking all over for you!' she whispered. She took my hand, pulled me urgently into the darkened sewing room doorway (or what we called the sewing room), out of sight from those below, and kissed me. There was an incredible taste of something like herbs and mountain air, and a strange feeling, almost of a lost memory, swept over me – but just for a moment: laughter rattling up from below broke in on us. She glanced back over her shoulder, as I licked my lips. 'He has a piece of that girl's underwear.'

'What?'

'That man down there. The lawyer? He has a piece from her panties.'

'Woody?'

'I saw them cutting them up. I thought the policeman – the main one with the moustache – had something in mind. But apparently he forgot and the pieces started getting passed around. Like souvenirs or something . . .'

'Ah, that explains . . .'

'I've heard a thousand stories about her tonight.' What I was thinking about was the money. And what Ros once said about time and love. 'You're right, you certainly weren't the only one . . .' She turned back and gazed up at me as though pained by something, then, unfastening a middle button, ran her hand inside my shirt. 'When it's like a river,' Ros had said, 'it scares me. What I want it to do is just *ooze*.' There was a faint rustling in the sewing room darkness beyond us, a couple, perhaps more than one. I saw something red, a dress probably, and a glimmer of flesh. Alison's mouth opened under mine and I closed my eyes, let my free hand slide down to grip one supple buttock. She kissed me, tonguing my lips apart, murmured into my mouth: 'They killed her husband, Gerald. It was terrible.'

'I know. I heard. I'm still not completely over it.' Behind me, Naomi was telling Tania about her childhood, her mother's cruelty and the cruelty of all her mother's lovers.

'Didn't you expect it?' Alison whispered, licking my lips.

'I guess I did. That's not what upset me. It was—'

'Learning something you already knew – you said that during the intermission that night we met.'

I recognized now the source of that feeling I'd had since she came up the stairs. She stroked my chest gently, and I (I peeked past the doorframe – Noble was into another act down there now, making his cigarette vanish, then, with a bulge of his false eye, reappear from inside his mouth, now lit at both ends) pulled her closer to me, curled my hand around both firm cheeks, amazed at the familiarity of them. I disbelieved in fate, hated plays and novels whose plots were governed by it, but now, with Alison's silky bottom filling my hand like an idea the mind . . . Naomi was telling Tania about being tied up and locked all day in a closet without a potty, then getting whipped with a belt for wetting on her mother's pink suede pumps. Alison nibbled at my throat.

'But it was more than that even,' I whispered into her ear, a gold loop glinting there like a wish. Or a promise. I heard somebody grunt hoarsely in the sewing room shadows, then a soft stifled whimpering sound. Alison found a nipple, drew a gentle circle around it as though inscribing a target. 'I think what struck me was not so much learning something I already knew, as the sudden recognition that in fact it *had* to be *learned*.'

Alison gasped softly, her bottom flexing in my grip as though to squeeze my hand, and looked up at me, her brown eyes swimmingly wide in a kind of awe, excitement, wonder. Her fingers tugged at my nipple. 'That's funny! I was just thinking the— !'

The bathroom door banged open behind us and my son came bounding out, calling my name – I let go of Alison and turned, squatting (my shirt jerked against her hand, a button ripped), just in time to catch him up. 'Good night!' he shouted, giving me a big kiss. There was a large white 'SUPERLOVER' emblazoned on his sweatshirt.

'Good night is right, chum! You know what time it is?'

'Daddy, do I look like Little Boy Blue?'

'Well, you don't look much like Red Ridinghood, do you?'

'But Little Boy Blue's a *little* boy!'

'Not really. They just put that in the poem to make it sound better. He doesn't like it either.' Naomi, still holding on to the two ends of the towel through the skirt, rocked stiffly back and forth on her way back into the bathroom. 'And you know, it wouldn't hurt you to imitate Boy Blue and go crawl under—'

'That's a funny lady! Does she always walk that way?'

'I don't think so. She must have got wound up too tight.'

'Daddy . . . ?'

'Yes?'

'Daddy, somebody's broke all my soldiers!'

'What— ?' Why did that startle me so? 'Hey, don't cry!'

'They took all the *heads* off! All my *best ones!* From the *Waterloo!*'

'Easy, pal! We'll get new ones! Here, wipe your eyes with this . . .' My mother-in-law was glaring impatiently down on us, her arms folded.

Alison ran her fingers into the hair above my nape. 'I'll see you in a few minutes,' she murmured, and Mark smiled up at her through his tears.

'Not you, mister!' I said, getting to my feet and handing him over to his grandmother. 'You're off to bed!'

He blinked, surprised. 'You look scary, Daddy!' he exclaimed, backing away.

'We've been playing monsters,' I laughed, and made a face.

'Can I play?'

'Not yet. When you grow up.' I winked at my mother-in-law, but she turned her head away, her lips pinched shut.

'Oh gosh, help!' Naomi called from the bathroom. 'I've dropped part of it!'

I turned to touch Alison's fingertips in farewell, but she was already at the head of the stairs. She waggled her hand behind her back and waved at someone down on the landing, and I heard my son's door slam. The heads?

In the bathroom, Tania was sliding open the shower curtain which my mother-in-law had apparently drawn shut. 'Like variations on a theme or something,' she said, and Naomi, in some distress, replied: 'Well, that's exactly the problem! It seemed so unfair!'

'Here, let me help.' I knelt and reached up under her skirt to hold the towel against her buttocks, but it had dropped down in front and I accidentally stuck my finger in her vagina. 'Oop, sorry, Naomi . . .' I found the loose end. 'Okay, now pull your skirt up, I've got it . . .'

She hiked her skirt and, gripping it with her elbows, straddled the toilet stiffly once more. 'Ouch,' she complained as she leaned low onto the watertank, keeping her rear high so the skirt wouldn't fall back over it. 'I think it's getting hard!'

'Heavens!' exclaimed Tania, casting a professional eye upon the sight. 'Red, green, brown, yellow – what have you been eating tonight, Naomi?'

'Just what was out on the table.'

'Look, there's even a little piece of string!'

'It's a shame to wash it away,' I said, dipping the dirty towel under the hot water faucet in the sink. 'Maybe we ought to frame it and hang it on the wall.' A monster: yes, I was: there was blood at the edge of my mouth.

Tania, smiling, knelt to her task, wrapped still in the bathtowel, which slowly loosened as she squeezed and kneaded the dress. My grandmother, rolling out pie dough, would tell me stories about the wilderness, about the desperate, almost compulsive struggle against it as though it were some kind of devil: 'We had to domesticate it, now look what we got for it.' I could still see her old hands, dusted with flour, gnarled around the handgrips of the wooden rolling pin, her thin wrinkled elbows pumping in and out as she talked. Once she'd told me the story of a man in love with his own reflection who went out ice-fishing one day and drowned himself. She'd said it was her cousin. Tania held the sudsy dress up to study it. 'By the way, Naomi, where did you get this switchblade?'

'Switchblade?' I touched my throat: a tiny red toothmark.

'It was in your shoulderbag.'

'Golly, I don't know – I don't know *half* the things in that bag!'

'My favorite Mexican ashtray, too!' I scolded, turning away from the sink and clapping the hot towel against her backside. Naomi oohed gratefully. 'And, say, what's this about a valentine?'

'Did I have a valentine in there, too?'

'Somebody said it was from me.'

'Did you give me a valentine?'

'No, dummy, that's just the point.' I took the compress away: it seemed to be softening up. I rinsed the towel out and applied it again, molding it to the curves of her moony cheeks. 'What I want to know is who *was* it from?'

'Honest, I don't understand a thing you're saying. I don't think I ever got a valentine in my whole life.' She sighed tragically. 'Except once, a long time ago. And then it was more like giving it than getting it.' She shuddered at the recollection. Or maybe at the chill when I took the towel away for another rinse. 'My mother let one of her men friends spank me. It wasn't the only time, but this time she didn't even pretend I'd done anything wrong. Mother said it was a valentine, for him or for me, I don't know which she meant, but he could slap it until it was bright red, a little bright red heart. They laughed and laughed all the time they smacked it.'

'That's what I like,' said Tania, 'a happy ending.' She had a painting by that name, the darkest, most depressing piece she'd ever done, her vision of the lust for survival. 'A cartoon,' she called it.

'Well, it was so . . . so humiliating!' Naomi's bottom did seem to be blushing at the memory, but mainly it was the warmth that was turning it rosy. 'And there were others – an old man, I remember, who used a thing he called his "stinger," and another one—'

Tania laughed, pushing the dress under. 'All these family stories! They remind me of my own father the day he gave me my first box of paints.' She lifted her dress out of the water to examine it, her arms bubbly with pink suds up to the elbows. '"Tatiana," he said, "there are no lies in the world, so everything you paint will be true. But not everything will be beautiful."' She glanced at me over her pale fleshy shoulder, then plunged her dress back into the ruddled suds once more.

'Ow,' said Naomi, trying to peer past her bunched-up skirt at her behind, 'it feels all prickly now like when you skin your knees!'

'It's a little raw. I wonder if we still have any baby oil around . . . ?'

There was none in the medicine cabinet or on the shelves below the sink, but I found half a bottle at the back of the linen cupboard: thus life provides these little markers, I thought – then closed the door quickly. I'd nearly forgotten. How was I going to get that thing out of here? Should I even try? And what would I do with it? In my palm, the oil felt like sweat. I spread oil on one buttock, my mind racing through the house like a scanner (the clothes basket at the bottom of the chute? the loose floorboard in my mother-in-law's room? the deep freeze?), then puddled out another palmful for the other one.

'Actually, spankings and valentines go together,' Tania remarked. 'Saint Valentine was himself whipped before they beheaded him, and the Church has got a special kick out of beating lovers ever since.'

'Beheaded—?' gasped Naomi. Her buttocks clenched, and I thought of Alison, the way her hips had flexed in my grip, and a wave of anxiety swept over me. It was as though something were rushing down upon me which I wasn't ready for, and I remembered my own mother, hurtling down a ski slope toward a broad bulge of mud – we'd hit an unusual dry spell that winter, and the snow had got worn off in places; the rest of us could ski round the muddy patches, but my mother still hadn't progressed beyond the snow plow. We could see her streaking down a ridge toward the big glistening mud patch, a sickly smile on her face, and there was nothing we could do. 'Sit down! Sit down!' my father had cried, but she just kept coming, her eyes getting bigger and bigger. And then suddenly she'd stopped. I didn't remember the fall, I must have looked away, but it was terrible, and she was in the hospital for a long time afterward. It was not only our last ski trip. It was the last time we ever went anywhere as a family.

'Well,' said Tania with a sigh (of course, I could simply turn it over to the police – why did that seem so impossible?), 'they had to chop *something* off . . .'

I rubbed the baby oil into those big cheeks, bigger than my own, thinking back on my son when he was tiny, his little bottom like two fat knuckles, narrow and pointed, his life still simple then, his memories wholly utilitarian and unfocused. Now . . . One of his drawings was stuck up on the wall over the clothes hamper. It was a picture of a castle with a war going on, blood and flags flying, bodies scattered like jacks. There was a big figure up on top that was presumably Daddy. He had a long thing hanging down between his legs which Mark said was for killing the bad guys, and he was throwing somebody off the ramparts. Mark said sometimes the picture made him laugh and sometimes it made him afraid, but he wouldn't tell me who it was that was getting thrown off. 'The only Saint Valentine story I remember,' I said, dribbling a little more oil into my hand and spreading it into the creases of the thighs and the furrow between her cheeks (I could feel her muscles relax as I worked the oil in – her tummy sagged and her thighs gaped a little as though her pelvis had distended), 'was how he restored the sight of a blind girl.'

'That's nice . . .' she whispered. I oiled the surface of her anus in little circles as though polishing a button (perhaps, I was thinking, recalling my son's question, it's neither the hard part nor the empty part, but something in between), then pushed my fingertip in, twisting it gently; she groaned and squeezed her cheeks together in pleasure and gratitude as I pulled it out: 'I – *oh!* – like stories like that . . .'

'Yes, well, naturally both she and her father got converted, and so consequently got *their* heads chopped off, too, bright eyes and all.'

'Yuck! Why'd you have to go and *spoil* it?'

'Ah, well, who's to judge him?' Tania sighed. She was wearing pink suds now all the way to her armpits. 'Probably, like all of us, he only wanted company . . .'

I capped the oil, set it aside, then gave Naomi's buttocks one final vigorous rub, making them gleam rosily, buffing away their playing-card pallor. If I could get that thing out of the house, I thought, I could bury it in the garden. 'You like that girl, don't you, the one with the pretty hair . . . ?' she asked softly, her voice jiggly from the massage.

'How's that?'

'You were-her thi-hi-hinking about her ju-hust now, I-hi-hi could tell-ll-ll . . .'

'Actually I was thinking about all those pee-hee-heople downstairs, and what they're going to do-hoo-hoo to me if I don't get back down there.' This was a lie. I *was* thinking about Alison. She was all I'd been thinking about all night. Except for Ros of course. I spread the excess oil around the sides of Naomi's hips and down her thighs, gave her cheeks a final slap, straightened up. And my wife. 'There! that should—'

'You want to make love to her, don't you, Geoffrey?'

'Gerry.' I wrung out the towel, tossed it in the hamper, washed up.

'Gerry . . .' Naomi seemed to have grown fond of her position, or maybe she was falling asleep. Her voice was just a drowsy murmur. 'How would your wife feel about it?'

I glanced at Tania in the mirror, her broad back to me like a stone tablet. A soft sympathetic stone tablet. 'She wouldn't like it.' I wiped my hands, combed my fingers through my hair. 'I'll go get something for you to wear, Naomi.'

But when I opened the door, there was Howard kneeling down behind it, his eye where the keyhole had been – the package of paper panties hit the floor. He snatched at them. 'I – I'm sorry, I, eh, just dropped – they slipped . . .'

'Is that you, Howard?' Tania called, and he popped erect as though on wires. She wrapped herself in the bathtowel, pulled the door open. 'Well! *look* at you!'

He stood there in the doorway holding the package of panties in his chubby fist, weaving slightly, knees bent, a silly smile on his flushed blood-flecked face, one shirttail out, red silk tie dangling loose. 'I just – hic! – brought these – this, you see. Dickie, eh . . .' He thrust the package at me, but it had been opened and what reached me was only the cellophane wrapping: the panties lay in a soft heap at his feet. Tania picked them up, glanced at them curiously, then handed them to me with a wink. 'Howard, Howard!' she clucked, tucking in his shirttail. He giggled idiotically. 'You've popped all your buttons!'

'Here, Naomi, Howard's – Naomi? *Hey!*'

She started up with a snort, blinking her eyes, her skirt slipping down her shiny bottom. 'Oh . . .' I could hear Tania asking her husband for his scout knife: 'Which one's the leather punch, Howard?' Naomi smiled sleepily, leaned her head on my shoulder, looping her arms softly around my neck. 'Can you help me,' she yawned, 'just one more time.'

'You're a big girl, Naomi, you can—'

'Please, Geoffrey? I always split these things . . .'

I knelt with a sigh and, clumsily, one hand braced on my back, the other on the sink, she pushed her feet through the legholes. I could see it was going to be a tight fit. 'Are these your size, Naomi?'

'How should I know?'

Tania opened the linen cupboard. Maybe she was looking for some place to hide Howard's knife. There was nothing I could do about it – the panties were caught halfway up Naomi's thighs and had to be inched the rest of the way. 'You'd think the oil would help,' I complained, one eye on Tania.

'Your wife, ahem, asked me to tell you, Gerald, she needs some things from the top shelf of the pantry and – burp! – can't find the ladder.' The ladder was *in* the pantry, but never mind, I understood. Naomi lifted her skirt out of the way, as I tugged at her flesh, pushed at the band. 'I think we're almost there, Naomi . . . easy now!'

'Mmf! Whoo – thanks!' she gasped, helping me at the crotch. Howard's head was twitching from trying to look at Naomi and not look at her at the same time, making his thick fractured spectacles flutter with reflected light and his pink jowls wobble. 'Now, just so I don't have to bend over . . . !'

'Also, eh, something about food stuck in the freezer, and the garbage was filling up and, well, she seemed . . .'

'Yes, all right, Howard, tell her—'

'You know, it's funny,' Naomi interrupted, 'but these pants feel like they've already been worn by someone.'

Tania smiled; Howard was gone.

Naomi wriggled her hips to let the skirt drop. 'Maybe I *could* do something to help, Geoffrey – I mean, if you want to see that girl. Like, you know, I could go talk to your wife for a while maybe, or get her to go to the basement with me and play darts or something . . .'

'It's too dangerous, Naomi,' I said, wiping my hands. 'She throws a wild dart. Anyway, I don't see why you—'

'Love!' she said with a kind of sweet breathless tremor in her voice. 'It should have a chance, wherever and whenever it appears. It's so rare . . . and wonderful!'

Tania snorted. 'Roger once told me he thought love was the most evil thing in the world – and seeing what he got out of it, you can hardly argue with him.'

'Oh golly— !'

'Don't bring up Roger, Tania, I've just got her all cleaned up.'

Tania smiled wanly, leaning back against the linen cupboard, wrapped in her towel like a desert mystic, the tip of my ascot peeking out between her feet. I glanced up at her face, but it told me nothing. 'It was that day he came breaking into my studio. Once he'd calmed down, we had a long talk together. He knew what was happening to him . . .'

'But that wasn't love, that was something . . . something *crazy!*'

'He told me he used to believe, before he met Ros, that love was a kind of literary invention, that people wouldn't fall in love at all if they didn't read about it first. He said he always thought that we learned our lines about love, as it were, from fairy tales, then went out in the world and acted them out, not even knowing why it was we had to do it. But he said he forgot all that when he met Ros, forgot everything. He said she left him completely stupid, an illiterate, a wolf-child, a man utterly without a past, she invented him where he stood – it was as if he'd been concussed, suffered some kind of spectacular fusing of his entire nervous system, reducing it to the simple synchronous activity and random explosions of a newborn child.'

'I can understand that,' said Naomi softly, staring at me. 'It's great . . .'

'He was terrified, He said it wasn't that he needed to possess her, it wasn't even selfishness, not in the way one would think. And he didn't feel protective, didn't feel kind or generous toward her, didn't especially want her to be happy or successful or feel fulfilled – it was something much more immediate than that, something much more frightening, it was something almost *monstrous . . . !*'

'Oh my . . . !' Naomi fled, holding her tummy, brushing past Vic's girlfriend Eileen, who had just come in behind us, looking dazed still, one whole side of her face now swollen and turning blue.

'You'd think, after such a colorful childhood,' I said, wiping the sink, then tossing the towel in with the others (yet I, too, was thinking about love), 'she'd be a bit more callused.'

Tania laughed drily. 'My god, Gerry, I knew the girl's parents. Her father was a teacher and poet, her mother a musician, played the viola, gentlest people in the world. I'm sure Naomi's never had a real spanking in her life. Not that she couldn't use one . . .' Eileen set her empty glass down on the rim of the basin, stared at us bleakly for a moment as though trying to place us, then dropped the seat of the toilet, lifted her limp skirt, pushed her pants down to her knees, and sat to pee. 'Or maybe she's at the wrong party . . .'

'It's blocked, Eileen,' I said. I noticed that my electric razor was missing. Not (Tania was staring down at her dirndl in the tub of suds, lost in thought, it was as good a moment as any) in the linen cupboard either. 'You should use the one downstairs.'

'Somebody's in there,' she replied dully. 'I think it's Janice Trainer and some guy.' I hung fresh towels on the racks, got out a washcloth and soaked it in cold water. Eileen looked down at her shoes and, peeing disconsolately, said to them: 'I'm sorry . . .'

'Here, Eileen, hold this against your face.'

'It's so sad,' she said, 'and there's nothing we can do about it.' She blew her nose in the washcloth. 'And the worst thing is, I don't feel a thing. That's what's horrible. They're both killed and I don't feel a thing.'

'You feel sad.'

'I felt sad when I came here.' She'd left the door open: Alison didn't seem to be around, but the sewing room light was on. I felt vaguely frightened and wanted her close to me again. Eileen twisted her finger in her cotton drawers, looked up at me. 'Your wife was asking for you, Gerry.'

'I know. I'm going.'

'Gerry, do me a favor,' Tania said, stopping me just as I stepped out the door.

'It's . . . it's not over, you know,' Eileen murmured softly behind her, posted there as above some deep abyss. Her urine had dwindled, but now it started up again, rattling against the clog of paper like a disturbing thought.

'I'm worried about Mavis. Something about that look on her face. I can't get it out of my mind. Check on her for me, will you?'

'Sure, Tania. Should I— ?'

But something she'd seen past my shoulder had made her frown suddenly and close the door. I turned to look: the two uniformed officers were coming up the stairs. Nobody in the sewing room now except Sally Ann and Dickie. My mother-in-law's room was locked. The policemen had paused on the landing, hats tipped back, arguing about something around mouthfuls of food: it seemed to be about which sandwich was whose, but the party noises from below drowned them out. In the sewing room (little Gerald's room actually – left more or less as it was ever since the stillbirth, the walls still a bright green, decals on all the furniture and closet doors, only a couch and a sewing machine added), Sally Ann was trying to thread a needle, and Dickie, cuddling behind her, had reached around and pushed his hand down inside her jeans. She glanced up, saw me watching, pulled his hand out as though to kiss it, and stabbed it with the needle. As the policemen started up the stairs again, alerted by Dickie's yell, I decided it might be a good moment to get changed. Also I needed time to think. Too much was happening too fast and I was beginning to feel like my mother on that ski slope, sit down, sit down.

'Can't you tell them to be a little more quiet?' my mother-in-law scolded, standing sentinel at the doorway of my son's room.

I smiled at her, then edged past a stack of dirty plates and crumpled cocktail napkins into our bedroom and closed the door.

The room was quiet, hushed almost, lit only by the dense yellow glow cast by the bedside lamp, and I felt the jitteriness ebb away. I crossed the room to draw the curtains shut, catching a glimpse of myself in the wall mirror as I passed it. Hmm. Once I'd cleaned up, I should go say good night to Mark again so he wouldn't carry that face into his sleep with him. Unless, of course (recalling Naomi's valentine), he needed it.

Tania's 'Susanna and the Elders' had hung where the mirror was until something she said one night made us move it to the dining room. Her husband, Howard, writing on a painter he disliked, had called his work 'bedroom art,' meaning too private and self-indulgent. I'd argued that all good art, being a revelation of the innermost self, and thus a kind of transcended dream, was 'bedroom art,' but Howard would have none of it. 'This widespread confusion of art and dreams is a romantic fallacy,' he'd said, 'derived from their common exercise of the brain's associative powers – but where dreams protect one's sleep, art disturbs it.' Tania had agreed: 'I don't paint in bedrooms, I don't even *think* about painting in bedrooms, and I certainly wouldn't hang one of my paintings in one, any more than I'd go to a party in haircurlers and pajamas.' So we'd put the mirror there and moved 'Susanna' down to the dining room (admittedly, we'd hung it in the bedroom in the first place for no better reason than that the forest colors went well with the curtains and russet-canopied four-poster), and truth to tell, it did seem to take on more power down there.

Tania and Howard had arrived with Anatole tonight just minutes before Roger and Ros – in fact, I was still taking their coats when I heard

Ros laughing on the porch – so we were all there in the hallway together for a moment, a moment that now in retrospect seemed almost magical. Ros had given each of us a big hug (I remembered Anatole blushing and staring at the ceiling as she smashed her breasts against him, Howard adjusting his spectacles knocked askew) and announced she'd just got a new part in a play – I'd had the impression at the time that it was news to Roger as well, and dismaying news at that – and then off she'd gone, the last time I'd seen her alive, best I could remember, to pass her hugs around. Ros was a great hugger. She always made you feel, for about five seconds, like you were her last friend on earth and she'd found you in the nick of time, and now, as I searched through the clothes hanging in the closet for something to wear, I found myself remembering all her hugs like one composite one: not a girl hugging, but hugging, girl-shaped. I picked out some soft linen slacks and a rust-colored open-collared wrap-tie shirt, tossed them over the back of a chair. Have to change shoes too. And socks: I was wearing blue.

Ros sometimes asked us, if we were visiting her backstage, to help her change costumes. I say 'us': I was seldom lucky enough to have her all alone. And anyway, somehow you were never really quite alone with Ros even when there wasn't anyone else around. But it didn't matter. One of the best times I ever had with her, in fact, was the day I arrived to find a photographer there shooting stills. I was married by then and so was she, so we'd seen each other only rarely, but her greeting was the same as if we'd been actively lovers. That is to say, exactly as it always was. What the photographer was after were simple straightforward publicity stills of Ros in rapture, but whenever she tried to *act* ecstatic, she always looked like she had a fly up her nose. The photographer said he'd be glad to help her work up the real thing himself, but he wasn't loose enough, as he put it, to shoot pix and jism at the same time, so he asked me if I'd do him the favor of pulling Ros's trigger for her. For the sake of art, he added with a professional grin. I protested – weakly, as Ros had just thrown her soft arms around me and given me another breathless hug: oh yes! let's! – that my wife had slightly less magnanimous notions about art and duty, and I couldn't take the risk of an uncropped photo turning up somewhere. Ros, of course, didn't understand this at all, but the photographer, a married man thrice over, thought about it for a moment, then suggested: why not wear a mask? So we got the keys to the costume trunks, locked ourselves in a rehearsal room where they had some colored lights, mirrored walls, and a few loose props, and enjoyed an enchanted hour of what I came to think of as an erotic exploration of my own childhood. I was severally a clown, a devil, a scarecrow, skeleton, the back half of a horse, Napoleon, a mummy, blackamoor, and a Martian. I played Comedy to Ros's Tragedy, Inquisitor to her Witch, Sleeping Beauty to her Prince Charming, Jesus Christ to her Pope. Sometimes the mirrored images actually scared or excited me, altered my behavior and my perception of what it was I was doing, but Ros was just the same, whether as a nymph, a dragon, an old man or the Virgin Mary: in short, endlessly delicious. The photographer occasionally joined in – just to keep his hand steady, as he put it – and once we balled her together without masks, dressed only in red light and jesters' bells. I probably learned more about theater in that hour or so – theater as *play*, and the power of play to provoke unexpected insights, unearth buried memories, dissolve paradox, excite the heart – than in all the years before or since. After the third orgasm, it all became very dreamlike, and if I didn't have a set of prints locked away down in my study to prove that it actually happened, I probably wouldn't believe it myself. I enjoyed no particular costume so much as the strange sequence of them – a kind of odd stuttering tale that refused to unfold, but rather became ever more mysterious and self-enclosed, drawing us sweetly toward its inner profundities – but from the photographer's viewpoint, the best was probably one of the simplest, a variation on Beauty and the Beast in which Ros wore only a little strip of diaphanous white cheesecloth and I dressed up in a gorilla suit. He said her astonished expression as she gazed up at the monstrous black hairy belly with a little white pecker poking out was exactly what he'd been looking for.

I smiled, feeling grateful. My bruises hurt less. I felt I could stay here forever, wrapped round by memory and the soft light and fabrics of my bedroom; but then I heard my mother-in-law scolding someone out in the corridor. I sighed, kicked my shoes off, peeled off the socks, removed my belt and laid it over the chairback with the clean clothes, lowered my trousers (all that blood in the crotch, hers: I shuddered, pained by this sad final gift), and had one leg out when Vic's daughter came in. 'Hey, I'm changing, Sally Ann!'

'That's all right, don't mind me – I just want to sew this patch on.'

She peeked back out into the hallway (I heard someone protesting, something like a scuffle on the stairs – what I read on Sally Ann's hindend was 'SEAT OF BLISS'), then eased the door shut. 'Everywhere else, there's always somebody *bothering* me.'

She padded barefoot across the room to my wife's dressing table, pausing there to admire her navel in the mirror. I'd pulled my trousers back up, partly to hide the erection I had from thinking about Ros, and stood holding them. 'Come on, I've got a houseful of guests! I've got to get dressed and—'

'Well, go ahead, for goodness' sake,' she said with an ingenuous smile, studying my open fly, 'don't let *me* stop you!' She turned her back to me, pushed her blue jeans down, her little bikini pants getting dragged along with them. She stepped out of her jeans, very slowly pulled her panties back up, then sat down on the dressing-table stool, her little bum stuck out like she was trying to get rid of it. 'I mean, we *do* know what men and women *look* like, *don't* we, Gerry?' She laid her blue jeans across her lap, took up her needle and thread as though conducting me with a baton. I noticed now the two whiskey glasses on the dressing table, the half-eaten sandwich, open jar of petroleum jelly, smelled the alien perfumes, the sweat and smoke. Even here then . . . 'Look, I won't even *watch* if that's what's bothering you,' she added, gazing at me mischievously in the dressing-table mirror.

'Have it your own way,' I said, turning my back on her. I saw now that the bed had been rumpled, the covers tossed back over loosely. I lifted them: there was a bloodstain on the sheet, a small brown hole burned by a cigarette, coins, crumbs, a wet spot, and someone's false eyelashes. Well . . . and the lamp's yellow glow: it came from one of my wife's nighties, draped over it.

I removed my trousers and tossed them on the bed, feeling fundamentally deceived somehow, just as Sally Ann said 'Ow!' and came prancing over to show me her thumb, which she said she'd pricked with the needle. 'Kiss it for me, Gerry,' she groaned, squeezing up behind me, her voice schoolgirl-sultry.

'Now, see here, damn it— !' I snapped, whirling around, and the ice pick, wrapped in my ascot, fell out of my shirt on the floor at our feet.

'Gerry— ! My gosh!' she squeaked, stepping back, still holding her pricked thumb up with its tiny bead of blood.

'It's not mine,' I said lamely. 'It just . . . turned up . . .'

She squatted to pick it up. 'It's so – so *sexy!*' she gasped, stroking it gently. She wound it up carefully in the ascot once more and handed it back to me. 'I'll never tell, Gerry!' she whispered gravely and, standing on her tiptoes, threw her arms around my neck and kissed me. 'Cross my heart!' I tried to twist away, but she held on to my nape with one small warm hand, pointing down at the hard bulge in my shorts with the other: 'See, you *do* like me, Gerry! I felt it pushing on my tummy – you can't hide it!'

'Don't be silly, it gets that way by its—'

'Can I see it?'

'What? No, of course not!' I pried her hand away from my neck.

'Please, Gerry!' She blushed, her worldly pretensions evaporating. 'I've never really, you know, seen one . . .' She touched the tip of it gingerly through the cotton. 'Not . . . not sticking up like that . . .'

'Don't kid me, Sweet Meat, I've read your ads.'

'Don't make fun of me, Gerry. I was . . . all that was just for you. You're so experienced, I thought you'd . . .' She ducked her head, sucking at her pricked thumb. 'I was just showing off . . .' Her knotted shirt gaped, showing the firm little bubbles inside with their pink points like new pimples. I could hide it inside one of my wife's hatboxes, I thought. Or her boot maybe, a sewing basket . . . 'I feel so dumb . . .' She leaned against me, putting one arm around my waist, pulling my shorts down with the other.

'Hey— !'

She started back in amazement, holding on to the shorts. 'Wow! Is that supposed to go in . . . in me?' she gasped, cradling it in both hands. 'Doesn't it, you know . . . hurt?'

'Only when you swallow,' I said drily, tugging at my shorts with my free hand, trying to back away.

'Wait, Gerry!' She held the shorts down firmly with one hand, clutching my rigid member with the other. 'I'm not as dumb as you think, honest – but in all the pictures they showed us at school, it was always hanging down like a lump of taffy, I never saw one all stiff like this!'

Maybe it was so; but her curiosity both angered and saddened me and I thought again of my walk that night through the laundry-laden streets of that seaside town of Italy: what a fool I was! 'Sally Ann, please . . .'

'But look – there's the penis and there's the scrotum, right? And the scrotum contains the epididymis, the seminiferous, uh, somethings, and the vas deferens, which I can just feel, I think, at the back . . .' The illusion of novelty, that old shield against time: her fingers stepped tentatively between my thighs like a traveler in a strange city, excited by the possibility of the next turning, poor child . . . 'At school, we girls called it the "vast difference" . . .'

'Very funny.' She pushed the shorts down further, thrusting her hand deeper, maneuvering my penis with the other like a lever – and in truth I felt like some kind of antiquated machine, a museum piece, once an amazing invention, the first of its kind, or thought to be, now seen as just another of time's ceaseless copies, obsolete, worthless except as a child's toy, disposable. I regretted my sarcasm.

'And then the perannum—'

'Perineum.'

'The perineum, the anus, the – may I try to feel the prostate, Gerry?' She held my organ gently now, the tip of it resting in her bared navel, as her finger probed speculatively up my rectum, and I thought: yes, the vast difference: a schoolgirl's titter was what it was worth. Yet: maybe that was enough . . . 'It's all so soft and squishy and—'

'*SALLY ANN!*' roared Vic as he came crashing in, the door slamming back against the wall with a bang, his face pale with rage and anxiety.

Startled, she jerked her finger out – *ffpop!: 'Yow—!'*

'Oh, Dad!' she groaned. 'For crying out loud . . . !'

'*If that goddamn sonuvabitch—!*'

'Daddy, stop it! You're making a scene!'

'Holy smoke . . . !' I wheezed, touching my anus gingerly: yes, it was still there.

Vic blinked, looked around blearily. 'Oh, hullo, Gerry. Sorry. I thought – well, I didn't see that bastard around anywhere, and . . .'

'Really! You'd think it was the Middle Ages!' She sighed petulantly, then, sniffing her finger, tipped my penis up for one last glimpse of it from the underside: 'It's all goosebumpy,' she murmured, sliding the foreskin up and down, 'just like the neck of an old turkey!'

'Sally Ann, your father—'

'I can take care of myself!'

'Goddam it, you don't *know* that guy, baby!' Vic insisted, stumbling heavily about the room. He looked like a runner who'd just finished a mile and was trying to keep from falling over.

Sally Ann groaned, gave me a sympathetic grimace and a final squeeze, let go at last, as Vic fell heavily on the stool. I pulled my shorts up, caressing away the twinge in my anus. *'Now*, you've just sat down on my *jeans!'*

'Sorry,' he muttered, standing again, his eyes averted.

'You're drunk, Daddy, and you don't know what you're doing,' Sally Ann scolded, tugging her jeans on. Vic had turned his back momentarily, drinking deeply, so I stuffed the ascot and ice pick under the mattress. There was something else under there already – a meat skewer? More picks? 'I'm not a child, you know!'

'You coulda fooled me,' Vic grumbled, and wiped his mouth with his sleeve. His blue workshirt, half-unbuttoned and bloodstained, was sweaty at the back.

'Oh, Daddy, you're such a pain,' Sally Ann said, checking herself in the dressing-table mirror, pressing one hand against her flat tanned belly, untying and loosely reknotting her shirt when she saw me watching; but it was her mortality, not her childish flirtations, that I saw there. Something Tania had once said about mirrors as the symbol of consciousness or imagination. Maybe we'd been talking about her painting of 'Saint Lucy's Lover,' the one with all the eyes. It had started, I remembered, with one of her little parables on wisdom, her painterly belief in immersion, flow, inner vision, as opposed to technique, structure, reason. Just as mirrors, she'd said, were parodies of the seas, themselves symbols of the unconscious, the unfathomable, the formless and mysterious, so were reason and invention mere parodies of intuition. What one might expect from Tania. What impressed me at the time, however, was her definition of parody: the intrusion of form, or death (she equated them), into life. Thus the mirror, as parodist, did not lie – on the contrary – but neither did it merely reflect: rather, like a camera, it *created* the truth we saw in it, thereby murdering potentiality. Sally Ann, watching me curiously through it, had clutched the collars of her shirt and tugged them closed as though chilled. 'What . . . what's the matter . . . ?'

I gazed at her mirrored image, unable to see her shadowed back between us. A great pity welled up in me. 'You are too willful . . .'

'You can goddamn well say that again!' growled Vic, looking up. 'Now the rest of the night I want you downstairs where I can—'

'Oh, pee!' she pouted, clenching her little fists to her sides. 'Both of you can kiss my elbow!'

Vic lunged at her: 'Why, you little— !' But she was out the door. He stood there glaring furiously for a moment, his broad sweat-darkened shoulders hunched; then the strength seemed to go out of him and he sank down again on the dressing-table stool. I sat on the edge of the bed to pull the clean socks on, tie my shoes, and relieve the tingling between my cheeks. I was thinking still about death and parody and mirrors and the essential formlessness of love (my mother-in-law appeared in the doorway, glared at us, and snapped the door shut), and about how I might explain it all to Alison. And then: how she'd gaze up at me . . . 'You keep a bottle up here somewhere? Under the mattress or something?'

'You might find some hair tonic in one of those drawers . . .' And so what about marriage then, Gerald? Just another parody? I seemed to hear Alison ask me that.

Vic grunted. His face was in shadows, but his shaggy white hair was rimmed with light right down into his sideburns. He spied the two glasses on the dressing table, sniffed them, chose one, dumped the cubes from his own glass into it. I transferred the things from the pockets of the old pants to the new, shocked again at the obscenity of the bloodstains (and how had I come to pocket a can-opener, this medicine dropper, these shriveled oysters and bumpy little marbles?), then threaded my belt through the linen loops. 'Jesus, what am I going to do, Gerry?'

'I don't know, do you ever talk to her?'

'Talk to her! What the fuck about? My father was a happy-go-lucky tough-ass illiterate coal miner, hers is a sour bourgeois overeducated drunk – what could we possibly have in common? Hell, she understands my old man better than I can understand either of them!'

'That figures.'

'Come on, don't get supercilious with me, pal— !'

'I only meant—'

'You meant what we all know: love blinds. I ruined myself as a thinker the day I knocked up my wife. I haven't been worth stale piss ever since.' I couldn't argue with him. He hadn't written a thing since Sally Ann was about six years old, and had slacked off long before that. But I didn't believe it was that simple. It's one thing to reduce the world to a mindless mechanism, another to live in it. Flow had surprised him, offended him, dragged his feet out from under him. Even now, as he reared up and paced the room restlessly, he seemed to slip and weave. 'Let me tell you something about my old man. Just because he could belt the shit out of you, he thought he was tough. And smart. The sonuvabitch was full of cocky aphorisms, proverbs – he had the secret. And you know what it was? Power. This cringing yoyo, who spent his whole life slaving away down in the nation's asshole when he wasn't in the breadlines, believed in power like kids believe in fairy godmothers. He still does. Still talks tough and acts smart and lies there in his goddamned hospital bed in the old folks' home waiting to be blessed with it. With Sally Ann, on the other hand, it's experience. Spoiled, naive, unable to grasp anything more complicated than a goddamned confession magazine, a girl who wouldn't recognize the real world if it rolled over her, and what she believes in – guides her whole life by – is experience!'

'What are you trying to tell me, Vic?'

'That I *know* what my fucking problem is, goddamn you – but what burns my ass is that I can't seem to do anything about it!'

'Well, you're coming around in your old age . . .'

'What, to paradox? Hell, no, I've always accepted that – I just don't make a religion out of it like you do, that's all.'

I took a sip at the drink Vic had turned down: something between a Manhattan and a gin rickey. Awful. Against the light: lipstick smears on the far rim. Full lips. Cherry red. 'And what do you suppose Eileen believes in, Vic?'

He sighed, finished off his drink, chewed an ice cube. 'I can't imagine. Ecstasy maybe? Belly laughs?'

'You're awfully hard on her – why do you even go out with her?'

'She's got a comfortable hole I can use. And when I'm done I can go away and she doesn't complain.'

'Is that fair?'

'I don't know. I don't think about it.'

I shook my head. 'I don't think I could enjoy it that way.'

'Well, you're more considerate than I am. You give parties, I don't.'

'Maybe the trouble, Vic, is that you've never been in love.'

His sour laughter boomed out. 'No, you silly shit, you're right – I've loved, god-*damn* I've loved, but *in* love is one fucking place I've never been! Except . . .' He paused, sobering some, ran his broad hand through his hair. 'Except once maybe . . .' He leaned against a bedpost, his craggy face softening.

'Anyone I know?'

He sighed, rubbed his jaw, lurched away from the bedpost. 'Yeah.'

I drank in silence while he paced. He was clearly in pain. Not Eileen's kind of pain, sullen and stoic: it was more disturbing than that. He seemed riven by it, his stride broken, his vision blocked, and I thought: Yes, I've known all along – Eileen on the couch, Vic standing over her, his back to the rest of us, his neck flushed, fists doubled . . . 'Ros,' I said.

He nodded. 'It was right after my wife and I broke up.' His voice was husky, and as though to cover, he cleared his throat and sucked up another cube to chew. 'I needed somebody quick and easy,' he said, the words crunched with ice. 'No complications.'

'Like Eileen.'

'Like Eileen. Only it didn't turn out that way.' He sighed: more like a groan – then dropped onto the stool as though undermined. He sat there, his back bent, elbows on his knees, staring mournfully into his empty glass. 'We ran into each other at a political rally. Roger was defending some prisoners who'd rioted down at the jail—'

'I know. I read about it.'

He grunted. 'For some reason, he'd dragged Ros along. Probably afraid to leave her on her own anywhere. The rally was held on the steps of the courthouse, and those of us who were organizing the thing were up on the porch, under the colonnade, facing the crowd. I was pressed up against Ros when we first arrived, and pretty soon we found ourselves holding hands and asses and finally all but jerking each other off – Jesus, I was horny! We must've excited everybody within thirty yards of us!'

'Where was Roger?'

'Up front with all the main characters. He was pretty nervous about her as usual, but though he kept craning his head around, he couldn't really see anything – except for the flush on Ros's face and the way she twitched around.' He paused, licking idly at the melting ice, his thick brows knitted. 'You sure you want to listen to this?'

'Yes . . .'

'It's not just a cheap cocksman's brag – I mean . . .'

'I know.'

He leaned forward again, staring off through the far wall. 'She was wearing a soft woolen skirt, lambswool maybe. I never notice women's clothes, but I know every goddamn thing she had on that day. By feel anyway. I don't remember for sure what color the skirt was – a greenish plaid, I think – but I'll never forget what it felt like to grip her cunt through it.' The fingers of his right hand closed around his knee. 'A fat furry purse, a little soft bristly stuffed animal that you stroked between the ears – Christ, I'm getting a hard-on just thinking about it!' He scratched his crotch, sucked up a cube, spat it back again. Tears glinted in the corners of his eyes. I screwed the lid on the petroleum jelly. 'Anyway, it came my turn to speak, and I whispered to Ros before I left her how fucking unhappy I was, and how much I needed something human to happen to me. She was waiting for me when I'd finished – I don't know what I said out there, but it must have been good, taut and hard and nothing wasted, my whole body working on the message, as it were – and when I got back she pulled me gradually behind the others and finally on into the building, smiling toward Roger all the while. She knew the courthouse pretty well, I guess because of having to go there with Roger at lot. She hurried me up some stairs, down a corridor, through an empty courtroom and into a little cloakroom where the judges' robes were hung. We could hear the speeches and chanting and applause from in there, so we were able to time it pretty close. Or I could anyway. I don't think it mattered to her. Probably we weren't up there more than ten or fifteen minutes, but thinking back on it I feel I spent the best half of my life in that cloakroom, and I left enough seed in Ros and all over those fucking robes to turn a desert green! Jesus! I knew it was crazy, adolescent, unreal, but I didn't care. I came down out of the goddamn building about three feet off the ground! It's too bad we weren't storming the fucking barricades that day, I could've died a happy man!' He smiled broadly, thinking about this, and for a moment, a glow of warmth and innocence lighting up his craggy face, he looked like a different man. Then the skepticism returned, the sour shrewdness, the weariness: he glanced up at me to see how I was taking it, shrugged at my sobriety (oh, I knew it, knew what she could do, knew what I'd lost, what we'd all lost), set his glass down. 'It was so goddamn beautiful, Gerry . . .'

'Yes . . .'

'Fucked me up politically though. My head was useless, she blew a hole right through it. No will. Everything was body.' He seemed, guiltily, to savor the thought. I was thinking about that old joke of Charley's: making it stand up in court . . . 'A weird kind of connection. For me anyhow. The illusion of . . . owning time . . .'

'I know. We have the past, we have the future, but what we never seem to be able to get ahold of is the present.'

'Yeah, well, the present is in the hands of a very few.' I could see his jaws grinding under the heavy sideburns.

'Have you seen a lot of her?'

He peered up at me under his shaggy gray brows, his eyes damp, then back down at his empty glass. 'We met a few times afterward, but as you know, with Roger it's not easy. And it was against my principles, in ruins as they were by then, to fuck another man's wife, so finally I got enough self-control back to bring an end to it. The fucking anyway. I still wanted to be around her whenever I could, even if I had to exercise my imagination a little and get my rocks off in a substitute. I mean, no offense, but Ros was pretty much the reason I came here tonight. Just to be . . . well . . . and now . . .' He bit his lip, reared up, and began stalking around the room again, rubbing his face with one thick hand, breathing heavily. *They're using a goddamn fork on her down there, Gerry!* he cried.

'A fork— ?'

Those fucking cops! He smashed his fist into the wall. I recalled now that view I'd had into the living room over the heads of Daffie and Jim and the others, Inspector Pardew on the floor on his knees, reaching back over his shoulder toward his two assistants like a surgeon asking for a scalpel. Vic whirled around suddenly and bulled out, fists clenched, slamming past some people just outside the door: Dolph and Talbot spun back against the wall, Charley Trainer fell on his arse, his scotch flying, a woman giggled nervously. *Beautiful!* exclaimed Charley from the floor, his face dripping whiskey, and the woman, a rolypoly lady I didn't know but judged from her rouged cheeks, colorful print dress, bloodied broadly at the belly, short socks and loafers (why did I think of her in a garden?) to be Mrs Earl Elstob, tittered again. There was a crash down on the landing and somebody cried out. 'Jesus, what was that?' Dolph asked thickly, bumping up against the back of the fat lady, who looked surprised and moved away.

'Maybe he forgot about the stairs,' Talbot said, and licked his palm. His bandaged ear made him look like he was growing a second head.

I gave Charley a hand getting to his feet, hauling him up out of the dirty dishes. He'd sat square in a plateful of Swedish meatballs, but he didn't seem to care. 'Physical contact – I *love* it!' he declared, weaving, and flung his arm around me, the bottle of scotch at the end of it thumping heavily against my shoulder. 'You're a wunnerful guy, Big G!' He belched sentimentally, his eyes crossed, and Dolph echoed him more prosaically.

'I heard that one before,' said Talbot stupidly. They looked like bloated parodies of horny teenagers, papier-mâché caricatures from some carnival parade, and for a moment they seemed to be wearing their mortality on their noses like blobs of red paint: yes, we're growing old, I thought, and felt a flush of warmth for them.

I started to pull away, but Charley hugged me tight, the neck of the whiskey bottle pressing up cold and wet under my ear. 'Hey, I *love* this fella!' he exclaimed to the fat lady, and she commenced to giggle. 'Honess t'god, Gladys, he's my oldess 'n bess friend! He's a – he's a *prince!*'

'Oh you!' she tee-heed, her face flushed and blood-flecked.

'No, *s'true*, Gladys! He's a real goddamn *prince!* And I wanna tell ya something— !'

Oh oh. 'Listen, Charley, no kidding, I—'

'Charming,' said Dolph drily, a bit slow in his beery distance. 'Prince Charming.'

'Pleased, I'm sure,' giggled Gladys, holding out a reddish hand, and Talbot, taking it, said: 'And this is our fairy godmother, Prince. Make a wish – *any* wish!'

'I wish I had another beer,' said Dolph quietly, his face flattening out, and Charley, laughing loosely and dragging me lower as his knees sagged, said: 'No, wait a minute! Ha ha! This'll kill ya! We were out inna country, see—'

'Keep it clean,' admonished Talbot, holding a small patch of silk to his nose. He sniffed and, winking, offered me the scrap: I turned away, clamped still in Charley's grip. Distantly, I could hear Woody's wife, Yvonne, complaining loudly and drunkenly.

'I *awways* keep it clean, Tall-Butt, you *know* that!' Charley was rumbling, drooling a bit at the corners of his mouth. 'I soak it three times a day in hot borax, beat it on Saturdays, n' hang it out to air on Sundays – how clean can ya *get*? No, cross my heart – ask Gladys here, she's *seen* it!'

'Oh my!' she gasped as the others yukked it up. 'I've . . . I've never been to a party like this before!'

'Firss time fr'evrything, my love!' Charley declared, the dark pouches of his left eye flexing in a drunken wink. 'I'll drink to that!' said Talbot confusedly, and Charley, staring at us quizzically, mouth adroop and eyes rheumy, asked: 'Whawere we talkin' about? Hunh? God-*damn* it, men!'

'The . . . the prince . . . ?' whispered Gladys.

''*Ass* it! You got it! By God, Gladys, you *got* it!' He slumped toward her, pulling me with him (once in a film when the heroine said her lover took her breath away, Charley's wife Janny had sighed wearily and said she knew just how the lady felt, and I thought of her now, blanched with the terror of some knowledge, as though – could this be it? – as though hugged once too often . . .), resting his empty glass on her big round shoulder. Down below, Yvonne was hollering something about the sky falling in. 'You got it,' he growled, '*an' I want it!*'

She squealed again, clapping a pudgy hand to her mouth, and the big soft mounds of her bosom bobbled with giggling, watched glassily by Dolph and Talbot. Charley winked at me, hugging me close, but behind all the clowning I saw a soggy sadness well up in his blue eyes, a plea: help me! it's terrible, old buddy, but this is all I can do . . . !

'I think your wife's about to bust a vessel down there,' Dolph put in, crumpling his beer can and dropping it in the hallway clothes hamper. 'She asked me to tell you—'

'Yes, I know.'

'You got a goddamn mess downstairs, you wanna know the truth,' Charley declared, frowning drunkenly down his nose at me. 'We come up here t'get away from it all, Earl's sister here'n Doll-Face'n ole Tall-Butt'n me – all us birds of a feather, we gotta, you know, go *flock* together!' Talbot grinned sheepishly, glancing toward the head of the stairs, Dolph's ears turned red (he pulled a spare can of beer out of his back pocket as though in self-defense), Gladys looked blank. ' 'N hey! we'd be honored t'have yer company, you ole scutlicker, if you careta join us— ?'

'Thanks, but I have to go see what my wife—'

'Woops, I feel rain, boys!' Charley hollered, ducking, as Dolph popped the beer open, and I was able to squeeze out from under his arm at last. 'We better get under *cover!* There was a slap, a nervous titter, something about age and beauty, while ahead of me, Yvonne: 'Just break the goddamn thing off, Jim, and throw it away – what the hell do I need it for anyway?'

'C'mon back, Ger, when you get a chance! Awways room for one more!'

The mess in the hall seemed to be worsening – not just the dirty plates and glasses (picking my way through it, I was reminded of a similiar occasion, stepping gingerly by moonlight through the wreckage of an ancient ruin somewhere in Europe, I was there with some woman, she was Czech, I think, though she said she was French), but pits and crusts, ashes, butts, napkins, toothpicks: I stuffed ten glasses full of debris and picked them up with my fingers in their mouths (I'd been experimenting around a lot and felt the need for tradition, something stable – but the ruin was a terrifying cul-de-sac, capriciously dangerous in the moonlight, and the woman's sudden wheezing appetite for oral sex scared the blazes out of me; afterward, so I was told, she threw herself down a well), paused a moment to listen at my son's door. My mother-in-law was reading to him: '. . . endeavoring to appear cheerful, sat down to table, and helped him. Afterward, thought she to herself, Beast surely has a mind to fatten me before he eats me, since he provides such plentiful entertainment . . .' The way she read it, it sounded like a Scripture lesson – no wonder Mark had been telling us lately he didn't like fairy tales. As I listened to her recount the trials of beauty in a world of malice and illusion, I was reminded of my own grandmother's bedtime stories, variations mostly on a single melancholy theme: that people are generally better off not getting what they think they want most in this world. For her, the Beast's miserable enchantment would have been paradise compared to the Prince's eventual regret.

Yvonne howled with pain and swore fiercely. 'Take a grip on something,' I could hear Jim grunting, and Yvonne bellowed again: '*Waaah! Woody—? Where's Woody?!*'

I rushed toward the stairs, worried suddenly about my wife – how long had I been gone? what were the police thinking about that? – and crashed into Alison's husband, just stepping out of the bathroom: two glasses slipped from my fingers and exploded on the floor. 'Oops, sorry!' I exclaimed, shaken.

'It's occupied,' he replied flatly, touching his beard. I caught just a glimpse of the drawn shower curtains and what looked like my wife's apron on a hook as he pulled the door firmly shut behind him (probably I should call a plumber, you could smell it all the way out here) and waited for me to precede him down the stairs. If in fact he meant to follow.

'It's okay, Yvonne,' some woman urged (I'd already turned toward the stairs, as though compelled, as though following some dancestep pattern laid out in footprints on the floor), and Yvonne cried: '*Okay— ?!* What the hell do you *mean* it's okay?!'

My knees flexed involuntarily on the top step: it was (like a sudden wash of color, the fall of a memory scrim) the ski slope again – not now the one on which my mother fell (Yvonne lay sprawled on the landing, one foot sticking out at an angle under Jim's seat as he bent over her, worried onlookers pressed around), but the recurrent ski slope of my dreams, impossibly sheer, breathtaking, ambiguously crosshatched, disasters at the base: my tip (watched always by rows of dark spectators and now as though pushed from behind) into oblivion . . . 'Yvonne— !'

'Gerry!' Yvonne cried, looking up at me (they all looked up, Iris Draper, Howard, that woman I'd seen with Noble, Anatole, Daffie, Ginger, as though I were something painted on the ceiling – all but Jim, now gripping Yvonne's foot by its heel and instep). 'They're *after* me, Gerry!' The dark side of her face, bruised and bloodied, glistened with tears (the skis were off, I was walking down stairs again), but the eye looked dead: it was the near side alone that seemed to be speaking to me: 'They're taking me away by *pieces!*' As she said this, Jim pulled steadily against Daffie on the leg, twisting it inward (the toes had been sticking out at ninety degrees), actually stretching the leg as though indeed trying to screw it off, and there was a harsh grating sound – '*Yowee! Lord love a duck, Jim!*' she yelped and her free leg kicked out, catching Ginger in the back of the knees and making her sit abruptly, her narrow rump thumping the stair with a crisp little knock. '*Use a little grease!*'

'That's got it, I think,' Jim grunted, holding her foot with one hand and wiping his brow with the other. The grating sound echoed in my head like the faint harmonic of some lost memory. Jim pushed her skirt back to study the symmetry of the two legs, and I thought of Ros again, a game we used to play which we called 'Here's the church, here's the steeple . . .' I was breathing heavily. 'All right, let me have those splints, son . . .'

Anatole, down a few steps behind him, handed him a pair of croquet stakes, the spikes still muddy. I knelt next to them, bracing myself on the glasses I was carrying. 'It was Vic,' Daffie panted, squatting alongside ('Oh, Gerry,' Ros would say, 'did we? I just don't remember!'), and Anatole said: 'He was after the cops.' I could hear his stomach gurgling; he didn't look all that well. 'He ran straight into the living room and grabbed the fork away from them— !'

'The *fork*— ! What was he, *starving* or something?' Yvonne squawked, her head resting now in the lap of Noble's friend. Ginger unpinned a kerchief from one shoulder and handed it to Jim, searched her body for another. Over our heads, Howard and Mrs Draper seemed to be arguing about Tania's painting of 'The Ice Maiden,' Iris finding it too unskillful and farfetched. 'If that's all he wanted, why the hell didn't he ask? Do I look like the resisting type?'

Daffie, leaning over the railing ('But of *course* there's distortion,' Howard was insisting, 'there's *always* distortion!'), called out: 'Hey, Nay, is that a fresh drink? Bring it up here like a good old dog! We got an avalanche victim who needs it bad!'

'I wouldn't,' said Jim. He was tying Yvonne's two legs together with Ginger's kerchiefs. 'She's probably got some fever, a drink could make her sick.'

'Make me *sick!* Oh boy! That's a good one!' Yvonne hooted. 'Just *look* at me! *Sick* would be a goddamn *improvement!*'

I looked through the railings and saw Alison in the hallway gazing up at me. She glanced past my shoulder, pursed her lips, then beckoned me with a faint little nod and disappeared from view, replaced by Kitty, rushing past, clutching her shirt front together, a flushed grin on her face. Ginger, perched awkwardly on two steps, her ankles wobbling above the stiletto heels, had meanwhile bent over and run her hand between her knees and up the back of her skirt: she smiled suddenly, her little red pigtails bobbing, and whipped another kerchief out, then grabbed her rear as though it were all falling apart back there, crossed her eyes, and tottered bowlegged down the stairs, past Naomi coming up. 'It's just too ambitious,' Iris Draper said flatly (I glanced into the cluster of glasses under my hands, disconcerted suddenly by the sense of being anchored outside time: I jerked my fingers out of them), and Howard sighed with disgust.

'Gosh, what *happened?!*' asked Naomi, staring wide-eyed at Yvonne's bandages. She leaned down to offer Yvonne her drink, provoking a disapproving sigh from Jim, and there was a sound like a paper sack being popped, then a slow soft tear. Naomi smiled sheepishly at me and shrugged, and Yvonne said: 'Thanks, honey, you just saved an old lady from a fate worse than life!' She tossed the drink back as Jim, nose twitching, asked: 'What's in that thing?'

'I don't know,' Naomi said. 'I just found it.'

'Yum!' wheezed Yvonne. 'Pure bourbon!'

'Smells like a salad.'

Below us, Dickie laughed, and Daffie, saddened by her glance over the railing ('But please,' Howard was arguing, 'there's not arts *and* crafts, there's only art *or* crafts!'), said: 'Roger once told me a funny thing. He said all words lie. Language is the square hole we keep trying to jam the round peg of life into. It's the most insane thing we do. He called it a crime. A fucking crime.'

'You mean he . . . he thought it was a crime to be insane?' Naomi gasped, looking distressed, and Yvonne, smacking her lips, declared hoarsely: 'My oh my! That oughta put some chest on my hair!'

The woman cradling Yvonne's head winced and exchanged a sorrowful glance with Jim, who said: 'The thing now is to get you more comfortable. Here, son, you're young and strong, you take that side and I'll – can you manage the legs, Gerry?'

'Sure,' I said as the doorbell rang. 'Ah . . .'

Jim glanced up from under Yvonne's right arm, a shock of gray hair in his eyes. 'That may be the ambulance . . .'

'Ambulance?'

'The police wanted an autopsy on Ros.' Anatole, under the other arm, looked startled and annoyed. Jim pivoted toward the foot of the stairs just as Woody appeared there, coming in from the back. The doorbell rang again. 'They said here and now, but I told them this was not the place for it . . .'

'*Woody!*' Yvonne wailed, breaking into the tears she'd been holding back.

I nodded and set her feet down gently. 'Thanks, Jim. Just a minute, I'll let them in.'

'Where've you *been*, for chrissake?!'

'I'm sorry, I was in conference,' her husband said, hurrying up the steps with his cousin Noble. As they brushed past me, Noble took a last impatient drag, then flicked his cigarette butt over the railing (Patrick, below, ducked, glaring – behind him: a line of people at the toilet door). 'I just heard – are you all right?'

'All *right*?! Are you *crazy*?' She was bawling now, all bravura swept away in the sudden flood. Wilma had started for the door, but hesitated when she saw me coming, turned to check herself in the hallway mirror instead. 'It's gonna take three goddamn *trips* just to get all of me *home*, Woody! *Baw haw haw!* How can I be *all right*?!'

'She's had a rough time,' the woman who'd been holding her said, her voice sharp, and Woody, behind and above me, muttered something apologetic about an interrogation: 'I'm sorry, the police needed help opening some drawers – I think they're on to something . . .'

'It's the ambulance,' I explained to Wilma's reflection, but when I opened the door it wasn't. It was Fats and Brenda.

'*Ta-daa-aa-ah!*' Fats sang out, his arms outspread like a cheerleader's, a big grin on his face, and Brenda, squeezed into a bright red pants suit, did a little pirouette there on the porch, one hand over her head, and, snapping her gum, asked: 'Hey, am I beautiful? Am I beautiful?'

'But . . . what are you guys doing out there?' I asked in confusion.

'I give up, man,' Fats replied, rolling his eyes and thrusting a bottle in a paper bag at me. 'What are *you* guys doin' in *there*?'

'But I thought – I thought you'd already—'

'Sorry we're late, lover,' Brenda said breathlessly, pushing in and pecking my cheek ('She's too *heavy* for him,' Patrick was complaining through the banister rails), 'but it took – hi, Wilma! – it took me an hour to get into this goddamn pants suit!'

'It's gorgeous!' Wilma exclaimed, holding her breasts. 'Where'd you ever— ?'

'And I got so turned on *watchin'* her,' Fats rumbled with a grin, unzipping his down jacket, 'that I made her get *out* of it again!'

'Which was damn near as hard as getting *in* – God help me if I— *pop!*— have to pee!'

'Never mind, I can't wear pants anyway,' Wilma sighed ruefully, turning back to the mirror and giving her hair a pat. 'The last time I tried it, Talbot said I reminded him of an airbag.'

'Gettin' *in*,' Fats admitted, jabbing a stiff thick finger at us ('Or maybe it was Archie who told me that . . .,' Wilma mused), 'it was pretty hard, okay.' The finger drooped: 'But gettin' out . . .'

'Or Miles . . .'

'Listen,' I broke in, 'you have to know, something terrible has—'

'What? Do I hear somebody at the dartboard?' boomed Fats, tossing his jacket on the chair over the Inspector's overcoat: the fedora (now dented as well as spotted, I noticed) fell brim-up to the floor. Above us, glasses kicked, clattered and tumbled. 'Lemme at 'em!'

'Talbot likes to do it with mirrors,' Wilma added, turning away from her reflection. Fats, over her shoulder, was slicking down his pate, someone was hammering on the toilet door: 'The police are here, Brenda. Ros has been—'

'*Hey*, baby!' Fats boomed out over our heads. 'Whatta they *done* to you?!'

'It's been a helluva ballgame, Fats!' Yvonne declared from halfway down the stairs, her arms around Jim and Anatole, Woody carrying her bound legs, Noble cradling the middle: 'Don't let it sag, Noble!' Jim gasped. Patrick's face was screwed up, his body tense, as though sharing the burden.

'He says it makes him feel like a movie star,' Wilma explained to no one in particular. 'It only makes me feel depressed.'

'Well, old Fats is here now, honey – you just point out the bad asses who *done* this to you!'

'Easy!' puffed Jim as they reached the bottom, crunching glass underfoot, and Michelle came over to see what was going on. Up on the landing, Alison's husband was expounding on something to Howard and Mrs Draper, pointing into the depths of the Ice Maiden's mouth.

'Say, Gerry, your wife—'

'Yes, yes, I know, Michelle—'

'Wait a minute, what's all that *red* stuff all over everybody?' Brenda cried.

'It's just what it looks like,' said Wilma. 'Wait'll you see the living room . . .'

'All I can say,' said Noble darkly (Daffie, stepping down, turned her back to the hallway mirror, presenting us with a mocking before-and-after contrast that seemed almost illusory: a time trick that Tania might have used), 'is it had better come out!'

The downstairs toilet door opened just then: and it wasn't Janice Trainer who emerged, but the short cop, shirttails dangling, still struggling with his buttons: 'Awright, *awright!* Christ!' he muttered, his face flushed, and ducked into the living room.

'Blood always does . . .'

'They still won't give them back to me,' Patrick was whispering to Woody. Woody nodded, grunting sympathetically: 'See me about it later, Patrick. We'll see what we can do.'

'Roger went crazy,' Michelle explained to Fats, but he wasn't listening: 'Here, man, you ain't lookin' so good,' he said, taking over from Anatole. 'How 'bout lettin' ole Fats have a cuddle now?'

Anatole, starkly pale, gave up his burden gladly, and as they carted Yvonne off to the living room ('I'm okay! Send me in again, coach! I'm not finished yet!' she was declaiming), he turned to Brenda and said, his breath catching: 'That woman was there when they killed him. He gave her something.'

'Who, sweetie?' Brenda asked, smiling up at him (Patrick, behind the boy's shoulder, bristled). 'Killed who?' She blew a teasing bubble, popped it, sucked it in.

'It was nothing,' Daffie shrugged. She held her elbow cradled in her palm, cheroot dangling before her face. 'I saw it. He gave her a small gold earring, that's all.'

I started. 'What kind of— ?'

But the phone rang and Daffie went to answer it. 'Who?'

'*Bren!*' Fats bellowed from the living room. '*It's Ros! Our little Ros! She's DEAD!*'

'*What? Ros— ?!*' she cried and went running in there in her tight red pants (there was a thump, a curse): '*Oh NO— !!*'

The tall officer appeared, scowling, in the doorway, leaning on his short leg, and Daffie with the phone said: 'It's for your boss, kiddo.'

'Fucking bastard,' muttered Anatole under his breath, and Michelle whispered: 'I once had a dream about something like this.'

Howard came down, his hips swiveling with drunkenness, and announced petulantly: 'The upstairs toilet is blocked, Gerald!'

'I know, don't flush it. I'm going to call a plumber. As soon as the phone's free.'

'Only it was at the art school, a boy who'd been painting me – he was dead but he kept on painting and I couldn't get away . . .'

'Have you seen Talbot, Howard? I can't find him anywhere.'

Inspector Pardew now stood in the living room doorway, thumbs hooked in his vest pockets under the drapery of his white silk scarf, his impeccability marred only by the dark stains and chalk dust on the knees of his trousers. He gazed thoughtfully at Wilma, then at each of us in turn. Anatole brushed past him, thumping his shoulder (the Inspector seemed not to notice, his eyes falling just then on his overturned fedora), and Patrick followed nervously, making little whimpering noises probably meant as apologies. 'It was so strange,' Michelle was saying softly, 'but then it suddenly became a movie we were all watching. Only I still didn't have any clothes on. I wanted to get out of the movie theater before the lights came up, I was so afraid . . .'

Pardew picked up the fedora, smoothed out the dent, brushed it on his sleeve, and, glancing casually at the label of Fats' jacket, placed his hat on top of it. He seemed all the while covertly interested in Michelle's description of her attempt to push, naked, past all the people in the movie house of her dream ('I kept hearing them all laugh, but every time I turned around, they'd be like gaping statues, fixed in some kind of awful terror – and the scary thing about it was I couldn't find any aisles . . . !'), ignoring Daffie behind him, holding the phone at her crotch like a dildo and blowing smoke at the back of his head. 'Is that for me?' Iris Draper asked, leaning over the banister, her spectacles dangling on a golden chain, and Wilma said: 'That reminds me of the time Talbot took me to a professional wrestling match, and Wolfman threw Tiny Tim, who weighed about five hundred pounds, right in our laps.' Yes, the trouble with ritual, I thought, is that it commits you to identifying the center (Pardew, staring at the front door, seemed momentarily nonplussed), which is – virtually by its own definition – never quite where or what you think it is . . .

'But then I was in the film again that I'd been watching and I was crying over the dead boy, yet all the time I felt like I had to go to the bathroom . . .'

'I know what you mean, dear! When Tiny Tim came crashing down—'

'Yes, yes,' Inspector Pardew was saying (he had the phone now and Daffie had vanished), 'I'm doing everything I can.' Howard, hands outspread for balance, wobbled past us into the dining room, muttering something about 'that stupid boy,' and Michelle, taking my arm, her hand like gossamer, whispered: 'It's so eery down here without any music. It makes everybody feel lost or something . . .'

'Put something on if you like,' I said.

'Well, because it's very complicated,' Pardew barked. Ginger crossed behind him, tiptoeing springily toward the toilet, her red pigtails trembling, kerchief tails lifting and dipping. She tried the door but it was locked. 'Yes, yes . . . in her chambers. Just an agonal phenomenon probably. We'll get prints later. No, that's smashed up.'

'Do you think it – it would be all right?'

'Sure, Michelle, why not?' I touched her hand gently: so frail, yet the knuckles were sharp and hard. I was thinking of Susanna in Tania's painting, that fixed artificial way she stood, and then Alison, miming it, the puzzled look on her face – and now Michelle, who'd posed for the painting in the first place, soft beside me, so light, almost wraithlike, yet brittle: a sequence, as it were, of interlocking figures, 'Susanna' a kind of primal outline, like Pardew's pale chalk drawings on my living room floor (he glanced up at me, phone at his ear, and I heard the cries from in there: such an emptiness under them, yes, music might help), for the subsequent incarnations . . . 'Something quiet.'

'It's a problem of dynamics, you see. She was a blonde and – what? How should I know?' Pardew turned and, picking his nose, watched absently as Ginger pressed an ear against the toilet door, both hands pinched between her thighs, mouth puckered, kerchiefs dangling loosely like bits of laundry. 'No, she was married. Probably. Yes, of course I did, but we got nothing from him we could use.'

A kerchief fluttered to the floor, and Ginger, her thin legs tensed above her high stiletto heels, bent stiffly to pick it up just as Earl Elstob banged out of the toilet, wiping his shoes on his pantlegs: 'Woops!' he exclaimed as the door batted her behind and sent her flying. He watched her bellyflop and, eyes agoggle, pink mouth pertly agape, skid across the hall, then he looked up, blinked, and grinned toothily. 'Hey, uh, didja hear about the ole lady who – *shlup!* – backed into the airplane propeller?'

'Well, I *know* it's too bad,' the Inspector snapped, scowling at his fingertip as he turned away, 'but it can't be helped!'

Michelle pulled me on toward the living room, saying something about my being forgiven (I was worried about this: where had the time gone?), or someone wishing to be forgiven. 'What's that?'

'Fiona. She told me all about it.'

'She did?'

'Well, a dipping refractometer maybe, if you have one – we can see what's going down here . . .'

'She said she knows how upset you were that night and she should have been more understanding, but her own guilt feelings made her fly off the handle like that.' Elstob's got the word for it all right, I thought, as we stepped into the front room (he was yuk-yukking dopily behind us, helping Ginger back up on her spiky stilts, the Inspector meanwhile describing someone as a 'spoiled weak-willed ladies' man with a propensity for dare-deviltry and an inflated ego' and outlining his equipment needs): all these violent displacements, this strange light, these shocked and bloodied faces – it was as though we'd all been dislodged somehow, pushed out of the frame, dropped into some kind of empty dimensionless gap like that between film cuts, between acts . . .

'Waah! I'm getting reamed by those goddamn posts, Jim!'

'It's your big ass, Yvonne, it's too heavy!' Noble grunted.

'It's *terrible*, Bren! I can't *believe* it!'

'Hang on, we'll get you braced up.'

People stood in hushed awkward clusters, gripping drinks, cigarettes, crushed napkins, watching Yvonne get settled noisily onto the couch, or Fats and Brenda keening unabashedly over Ros's body in the far corner, or just staring at the people drifting uneasily in and out of the room. The blood, drying, seemed to have sunk back slightly from the surface of things, giving them another dimension. Like visual echoes, hints of hidden selves. It was almost as if (footprints had trampled Ros's outlines, disturbing the contours, laying down around them tracks of checks and arrows, a patina of graying chalkdust) the room had *aged* somehow . . . 'She knows it was never meant as unkind – if anyone was being cruel that night, she said, she was – but under the circumstances, you know, after what had just happened, where you were coming from and all, and then with your penis moving inside her and her face, wet, on your cheek, almost like something had been skipped over, well, suddenly she—'

'What in the world are you talking about, Michelle?'

'You know, Fiona. She was telling me about the night you—'

'*Yipes!*' Yvonne yelled, jerking upward against her bindings and swatting reflexively at Jim, who, with help from Noble and the woman he was with, was trying to push an extension leaf from our dining table under her: 'There's *slivers* in that goddamn thing, Jim!'

'Don't be silly, I'm sliding it *under* the cushions.'

Alison and her husband appeared in the dining room doorway: they seemed to be arguing about something, but he was smiling. The two policemen went out past them, then came in again through another door.

'Well, then, something's *biting* me, I – *OWW!*'

'Aha,' said Jim, reaching under her and pulling out a shard of broken glass, stained with blood, part of a microscope slide maybe ('How could this be *happenin'*?!' Fats was weeping, Brenda hugging him, Woody squatting beside them offering counsel, or perhaps just telling them what he knew: 'It's *crazy!*' 'Oh my *god*, Fats!'), and Yvonne shrieked: 'Yah – is that blood *mine*— ?!'

'I don't think so . . .'

'Fiona said it was sort of like going from one room to the other without using the door,' Michelle whispered, leaning on my arm (Alison was gone again), 'but she didn't mean to—'

'Well, you've got it all wrong!' I snapped angrily, turning on her (poor girl – I hadn't even been listening), as Yvonne cried out: 'Honest to god, Jim, I think you guys pulled a fast one on me! This isn't my *body!*'

Startled, Michelle took her hand away, and I saw my wife in the sunroom watching us, a broom in her hands like a flagpole, Louise squatting fatly in front of her with a dustpan (and yes, I was aware now that much had been done: tables and chairs had been righted, debris cleared away, plants repotted – there were even fresh bowls of peanuts and rice crackers here and there, clean cloths on some of the tables). 'Well, I don't know, Gerry, it's what she *said*. Anyway, she's here somewhere, you can ask her yourself.'

'Fiona— ? But I'm sure we didn't—'

'I never had this gray hair! And where did this fat *ass* come from?'

'I think she came with Gottfried.'

'Gottfried— ?' But, with a cautioning glance past my shoulder, she'd slipped away. I turned ('Fats! Look! Somebody's stolen her rings!' Brenda cried, as Woody, suddenly interested in a bowl of black olives on a lamp table, left them, whereupon the tall cop, Bob, appeared in the doorway, one hand on his holster, his eyes asquint, lips tensed; then he relaxed and dipped out again) and kissed my wife on the cheek. She was wearing a blue-and-white apron now with red hearts for pockets, a mauve-and-crimson kerchief around her hair. 'I was just looking for you,' I said ('How come all the hard parts are flopping around now and the nice soft parts have gone hard? Eh, Jim?'), and brushed at a streak of dirt near her eye. 'Someone said you needed me . . .'

'Oh no,' she smiled, stooping to pick up a mashed tamale. She seemed amused, surprised even, but her voice betrayed her. She cleared her throat. 'Louise is helping.' As though on cue, Louise came lumbering up behind, but as I turned to thank her, she veered away, rolling off toward the back of the house ('Hell of a surgeon you are! You left me the rotten tit and took all the rest! I'm not *me* anymore!') with her dustpan and bag of garbage. My wife dropped the tamale bits in a pocket, stared at the brown smudges on her fingertips, then wiped them on her apron. 'The upstairs toilet is stopped up.'

'I know. I'm sorry.' I watched her as she untied the kerchief from around her hair and stuffed it in one of the red hearts in the apron, the brilliant kerchief making the heart seem dull. There was a thick smell of chili and warm chocolate. 'I'm going to call a plumber, but right now the police are using the phone.'

'Have you been into your study . . . since they . . . ?'

'I had to get something *off* my *chest*, he told me! Make a *clean breast* of it, he says!'

'No, but I heard. Poor Roger. It's terrible.'

'Now, hell, it's the only *dirty* thing I got *left!*'

'Woody said that they made people come in and confess to things in front of him. Awful things.' Over in the glow of our carmine-shaded table lamp, Woody now offered a black olive to Patrick, Anatole slumping, hand to stomach, into the white easy chair beside them like a frail shadow. 'The only thing harmless in this world,' Roger had once said – we'd been speaking enviously about Dickie's success with women, Roger had remarked gloomily that for him it would not be success but a catastrophe, and I'd said: 'We're not talking about affairs, Roger, emotional engagements, just harmless anonymous sex,' and he'd burst out in dry laughter, tears in the corners of his eyes, repeating my phrase – 'is death.' 'And they . . . they showed him the photos . . .' Alison had just reappeared. She and her husband had joined Fats and Brenda at the body and were exchanging introductions, Brenda smiling and weeping at the same time, Fats rubbing his big nose, shaking his head sadly. 'They want to . . . to talk to me now, Gerald. An interview, they said . . .'

'Yes, I'm sure . . .'

They all gazed down at Ros, their faces crinkling with pain at the sight. I felt my own cheeks pinching up around my nose. I was with Fats and Brenda the night they went to see *Lot's Wife:* they'd both stepped forward when the audience was invited up, and Ros had welcomed them to her body like old friends, their faces smoothed out then by a kind of glazed rapture. But theater, I thought, as the four of them raised their heads almost in unison, is *not* a communion service. No, a communion service may be theatrical, but to perceive theater as anything *other than* theater (I was talking to Alison now, she was smiling eagerly up at me, her auburn hair falling back from her slender throat) is to debase it. 'So what did Michelle have to say?'

'What—?'

My wife sighed. 'You were talking together when I—'

'Ah, yes, nothing – a dream she had . . .'

'I might have guessed.' She touched her brow lightly with the back of her hand and, leaning slightly on her broom as though to steer herself by it, gazed off across the room. 'Why is it that people always tell you their dreams, Gerald?'

'I don't know. Maybe they think I don't have any of my own.' I tried to recapture the thought I'd just had about the debasement of theater, but to my annoyance I'd lost the thread. I didn't remember much of Michelle's dream either. 'It was about being trapped in a movie house without exits.'

'Did she have any clothes on?'

Alison's husband had left the room, but Dickie, Wilma, and others had joined the little group around Ros. Brenda, her jaws snapping vigorously at the gum, admired Dickie's white vest, showed off her pants suit. Alison looked around – for me, I felt sure – but her view was blocked (there was something I wanted to tell her about this, something I'd been thinking about all night) by Jim, who was talking quietly in the middle of the room with Howard and Noble's girlfriend. Jim rolled his sleeves down and buttoned them, lit a cigarette, glanced up at me. 'Listen, I really am sorry – but, well, I needed a moment to myself. You understand. Alone.' My wife hooked her free arm in mine. I wanted to tell her about Tania, about the damaged 'Ice Maiden' and Eileen's premonitions, Mark's headless soldiers, the blood on our bedsheets, what I'd found in the linen cupboard – but she seemed unusually fragile just at that moment, twisting her wedding ring on her finger as though to screw up her flagging courage, so what I said was: 'Mark's fine . . .'

'Yes . . . He said you were playing monsters with Uncle Dolph and some silly lady who said he was little.'

'Wilma, he meant.'

'Was Dolph with Wilma?'

'No, but . . .'

'Peg said it wouldn't last. I guess she was right.' She sighed. 'I wish they were still together.'

'You mean Wilma— ?'

'Louise and Dolph.'

'Ah.' I had the peculiar sensation, briefly, that this conversation was both unlikely (Jim showed the tall cop the shard of glass he'd found: the officer shook his head and handed it back) and, word for word, one we'd just been having a few moments before. Of course, all conversations were encased in others, spoken and unspoken, I knew that. It was what gave them their true dimension, even as it made their referents recede. It was like something Alison had said to me about the play we were seeing that night we met – or rather, not about the play itself, but the play-within-the-play, in which the author's characters had taken on the names of the actors playing them ('self-consciousness reified,' Alison had called it – or perhaps she'd been reading from the program notes: I watched her now as she scratched at something on the bare flesh of her chest between the silken halters of her dress, overseen approvingly by Dickie, Jim and the cop having parted between us like curtains) and then had improvised a sketch based on what had supposedly happened to them that day out in the so-called real world: 'If that's what life is, Gerald, just a hall of mirrors,' she'd mused, blowing lightly on her cup of intermission coffee, the tender V of her chin framed in ruffles and brown velvet like an Elizabethan courtier's, 'then what are we doing out here in the lobby?' 'I don't know,' I said (Alison was laughing now at some remark of Dickie's – he was pointing at his own behind – and her husband, rejoining them with drinks for Fats and Brenda, licked his fingers and smiled with them), 'they never seemed very happy.'

'Who, Yvonne and Woody?'

'No . . .' I realized that she had changed the subject and had just been telling me about Yvonne's crying jag, brought on by Earl Elstob's joke about the retired brassiere salesman who liked to keep a hand in the business (my wife said: the brassiere salesman who wanted to keep working but had already retired): 'She couldn't stop, it just kept pouring out, so she'd gone running upstairs to be by herself, and she'd just reached the top when Vic hit her and knocked her right back down again.'

'She seems almost to be seeking out her own catastrophes,' I said, although I wasn't sure the line was my own. 'Vic was upset about Sally Ann. I'm sure he meant no harm.'

'That's what you always say.' She tipped her head against my shoulder, the broom handle cradled in the crook of her far elbow, index fingers linked. She yawned. 'But why did he want the fork?'

'Well, and Ros, too, of course.'

'I feel I should know what you mean, Gerald,' my wife said after a moment, lifting her head and unlatching her fingers to tug briefly at her bra strap, 'but I don't.'

The doorbell rang and the tall officer, unsnapping his holster, bobbed out into the hall. 'I'll get it,' I said, starting to disengage myself, but before I could move, a tall woman in a frilly black gown came swooping in like a huge bird, trailing feathery chiffon wisps, her hands clasped at her breast: one of Ros's actress friends, the one who'd played the Madame in the bordello play and Nancy Cock in *The Mother Goose Murders*, though she'd once been an opera singer. 'I came over just as soon as I heard!' she cried breathlessly. 'Where *is* she?'

'You mean Ros? She's—'

'Good God! I'd never have recognized her!' she gasped, staring in amazement at Yvonne on the couch. Yvonne, speechless for once and equally amazed, stared rigidly back as though into a mirror. '*Ros!* What have they *done* to you—?!' She threw herself on Yvonne, who now found her voice and used it for screaming blue murder, Jim dragging the woman off and redirecting her.

'*NOW she's broke the OTHER one!*'

'Easy, Yvonne, You're all right . . .'

'*Waahhh!*'

'*Ros, love! It's me, Regina!*' the woman wailed, pitching herself, arms outflung, through the people around the body (Fats' face was screwing up again as though to cry, and Brenda, gum in her teeth, was grimacing) and – though she seemed frantically to be trying to arrest herself in mid-air – on down on Ros: there was a windy rattling sound and Ros's head bounced up off the floor briefly, then hit it again, jaw sagging slackly at an angle. '*Oh Christ, no!!*' Regina rasped, stepping on her dress and tearing it in her haste to scramble to her feet. She looked around desperately and found herself staring at Anatole, slowly going green in the white chair, lips pulling back, his eyes agog with a horror reflecting her own. Then she clutched her mouth and ran teary-eyed out of the room: 'Nobody *told* me she was *dead* – !' she gurgled as she passed.

'My goodness! Poor Regina!' my wife whispered, drawing closer. 'I hope she makes it to the bathroom!' Ros lay wide-eyed and gaping as though frozen in perpetual astonishment, truer than any she could ever have play-acted, her limbs now disjointedly akimbo, her wound thick and dark between her breasts. 'I just like to be looked at,' she used to say. I could hear the sweet childish lilt in her voice. 'Do you think they're . . . they're simply going to leave her there . . . ?'

'No, Jim has called an ambulance,' I said, a catch in my throat. Alison, following Regina's flight, had – as though cued by the folk music starting up softly around us – discovered me at last: the pained shock on her face gave way to a gentle sadness, and she turned to her husband and took his hand. I felt my own shoulders relax as, not unlike mockery, the stringed instruments behind me tensed and slackened. I gave my wife a little reassuring hug and said: 'Don't worry, it'll be here soon.'

'Sometimes I feel I hardly knew her. Ros, I mean. She seemed so obvious, there was always something so direct, so *immediate* about her – and yet . . .'

'Well, maybe that's all there was.'

'How can you say that, Gerald? Even bare skin is a kind of mask . . .' Dickie, never one to patronize melodrama, had, even while Regina was still clawing the air helplessly in her grim descent, left the group around the body, but they were joined now by Noble and his girlfriend. Noble, fresh drink in his hand and cigarette dangling in his thick lips, seemed almost intentionally to scuff through the chalked outlines as he wandered over, to kick at objects on the floor. 'Don't you remember? *You* told me that the night we went to see that awful incest play about Jesus and his family.'

'*The Beatitudes*, you mean . . .' She was right, of course, and it was true. Noble turned his glass upside down, making Brenda gasp, but nothing poured out; then he took a long slow drink.

'It's that kind of openness, *directness*, that's the hardest to understand, to really *know*.' Alison glanced up at me and seemed about to make some gesture or other (Noble had just turned his empty glass over, pouring what seemed like pitchers of whiskey out on Ros and the floor), but just then the tall officer returned, blocking my view of her, and told Anatole to get out of the easy chair. He was threatening him, or so it seemed, with a pair of scissors. Anatole grumbled but dragged himself weakly to his feet, and Brenda, watching him, said something that made Fats laugh and turn his head to watch. 'It was what you said about amateurs and professionals, how it was easy to see how people *learned* their parts, but the mystery was the part that *wasn't* learned, the *innerness*, the – what did you call it?' Lloyd Draper clumped through in all his golden armor: 'Time passes!' he called out with a kind of leaden cheerfulness. Reflexively I glanced again at my naked wrist, reminded of Alison's slender hand when I stripped her watch from it, that mischievous grin under her freckled nose (I was recalling my thoughts about blocked views now, the special chanciness of live theater, the uniqueness of each spectator's three-dimensional experience, the creative effort, as in life, to see past sight's limits, all those things I'd wanted to talk to her about), the taut excitement of her body as her finger circled my nipple, its pad brushing it lingeringly across the top, the nail in turn underscoring it as though to italicize it with some gently ambivalent threat . . .

'Gerald . . . ?'

'Ah, the . . . the innateness?'

'Yes. What's in the sack?'

'I don't know, a bottle of something. Fats brought it.' I handed it to her, and she peered inside, saying: 'Fats? But I thought they'd already . . . ?' I had apparently missed seeing the short cop, Fred, leave the room, but he entered from the dining room now with a freshly made sandwich, just as his gimpy partner, tugging his cap brim down over his brow, went lurching out: they collided in the doorway, the sandwich popping out of Fred's hand onto the floor, and Bob, backing up with his scissors uplifted like a sword, stepped in it with his short leg (there was distant applause: the folk album was a recording from a live theatrical performance), squirting catsup and mustard out over the carpet. I felt my wife wince as his foot came down. 'I hope we have enough food,' she murmured. Alison was distracted by Brenda and Anatole. 'Everyone seems to have starved himself before coming tonight, and those two are the worst of all.' Bob scraped the mess off his boot on the rung of a chair, as, out in the hall, the doorbell rang again.

'Oh no, not more . . . !'

'Maybe that's the ambulance.'

'I've got everything for moussaka, I think. And I could fix some eggrolls and chicken wings . . .'

'Can I help clean up?' asked Naomi, rushing up with an ashtray full of cigarette butts and olive pits. She cast me a meaningful glance (I could hear new voices out in the hallway, loud and insistent, and there were quick bursts of light) and dropped the ashtray. 'Woops!'

'Oh, Naomi! I just *cleaned* in here!'

'Honest, I'm all thumbs!' She squatted to gather up the litter, smiling at me and nodding toward Alison.

My wife knelt in front of her, reaching toward a little constellation of spilled pits ('You know, I think I'm beginning to like other people's parties better than my own,' she sighed), then paused, her hand outstretched, sniffing curiously.

'I'll see who it is,' I said, pulling away (someone was shouting: 'As if it weren't bad enough— !'), just as Soapie, an old acquaintance of ours from the city newspaper, painstakingly seedy in his sweaty press hat, black horn-rimmed spectacles, tweed sports jacket and frayed tennis shoes, came striding in with his photographer Leonard: 'There she is, Leonard! Beautiful! Looks like she's screaming or something! Don't miss that bottle of pills! Or – wow! – the pinking shears!' He greeted Woody and Patrick – 'No, hold it! Just like that! Got it, Leonard?' – then waved at Noble, slapped Fats on his paunch ('Howzit goin' champ?' 'Not so dusty, Soap . . .'), lit a smoke, watching Alison slip around behind Woody and Patrick, aimed Leonard at Brenda. 'Holy moley, Yvonne!' he cried. 'What kinda party games you been playing? Leonard, get a picture of that mess!'

'Get my good side, Leonard! The *back* one!'

Leonard, dipping and twisting, fired away, Soapie instructing. Some ducked, some smiled painfully, others turned away as though to ignore the newsmen. Behind me, over the simple throbbing chords on the hi-fi, I could hear my wife laugh and say: 'Darts! Goodness, Naomi, I don't know which end you throw at the target!'

'Whoo-*eee*,' exclaimed Soapie, rubbing his finger along a blotch on the wall and tasting it, as Leonard crouched for a shot, through legs, of the soles of Ros's feet, 'this is the real stuff! Did she get it with her socks down like that?'

'No, she—'

'She just got a part in some new play, didn't she? I heard that some-where – something about a rapist who turns out to be the President or God or the Pope maybe, I forget which—'

'She said it was about a private eye who—'

'Yeah, you think there's any connection, Ger?'

'You mean with the murder?'

'Not likely, hunh? *Nothing* private about our gal Ros, right? I'll never forget that toyland musical where she was a limp puppet with strings tied to her bazongas, but nothing else! What was it— ?'

'*The Naughty Dollies' Night*—'

'Right! Sensational! Just so long as she didn't have to act, eh? Why was she carting around all this junk, by the way?'

'Well, actually that's not—'

'I mean, like *pipe* cleaners? Wacko!' He scratched out a note, his cigarette between his teeth like a blowgun. 'Best ever, though, was that pillar-of-salt thing – remember that, Leonard?'

Leonard licked the thick brush under his nose and rolled his eyes, then focused again on Yvonne, who, pulling some strands of stiff gray hair under her nose, said: 'What would you say to a pillar of blood blisters, Leonard?'

'Yummy,' Soapie remarked absently, watching Brenda put her arm around a wobbly Anatole, Howard trying to hide himself in the shadows of the drapes. Soapie picked up a fallen ashtray, stubbed his butt out in it, then tossed the ashtray over in a pile of swept-up debris, fished his pack out for another smoke. I saw we didn't have to worry about how to get the stains out in the white easy chair: they'd been cut out. 'This is where you found her?'

'No, more like . . .' Suddenly we were all looking around on the floor. 'Here!' I said, pointing down to her chalk outline. It was almost completely trampled away, a ghost drawing.

'Are you kidding?' argued Noble. 'That's where I was standing.'

'She was over – here!' said Wilma, pointing down at another outline, this one of Ros spread-eagled. 'Here's the place!' Yvonne stretched round in her bindings, trying to see, winced, sat back hurt and frustrated. I was afraid she might start crying again. 'Then what about this one?' Fats asked, standing over a third, and Lloyd Draper, disencumbered now of his timepieces, came in and, thumbs hooked in his red suspenders, pointed down at yet another, this one of Ros curled up, near the foot of Yvonne's couch. 'Here's where she was, young fella, the poor thing.'

Soon everyone was arguing about this, moving around the room from outline to outline as though on a guided tour, plumping for one chalk outline or another, even Dickie, winking at me and grinning around a toothpick, pointing at the place where Roger had knocked me down. 'You can see the bloodstains here at the heart.'

Yvonne reached out and took my hand, slipping something into it. 'Listen, do me a favor, Gerry,' she whispered ('So what, they've all got bloodstains!'): a small gold loop, an earring . . .

'Sure, Yvonne—'

'Whatever happens, just don't let them take me away!'

'But no one's—'

'Please?' She squeezed my hand, held it tight, her own hand trembling. 'Promise?'

'Of course I promise. But nobody's going to—'

'I love you, Gerry,' she whispered, while around us the argument raged on: 'Her legs were together! Like this one!' 'No, apart! Here!' 'You *care* . . .'

'Do you like this one better, Leonard? Okay? Then, let's get started!' By a kind of vote, they'd chosen the one chalk drawing I knew to be impossible, for, until Roger had knocked it over running wild, our brass coffee table had stood there. Now, Soapie instructing, Fats, Woody, his cousin Noble, and Alison's husband began shifting the body. '*Easy—!*'

'Jesus, she's so fucking *cold!*' Noble complained, letting go and wiping his hands on his trousers, and Lloyd, patting him on the shoulder, took over for him. 'That's right, old man,' grumped Noble, 'it's more in your line.'

'Really? In a *swoon?*' his girlfriend asked, fingering her medallion, and Patrick, commanding a small group with his tale of Roger and the old hag, nodded gravely: 'That's what he said.'

'You've got it all wrong,' Brenda butted in (she was clinging to Anatole, or maybe holding him up), and Patrick went red, his eyes narrowing. 'You always overdramatize, Patrick.'

'By the way, Yvonne,' I whispered, rubbing the little golden earring gently between my fingers (I'd just, averting my gaze from the resettling of poor Ros, caught a glimpse of Alison past the bent back of her husband: she'd also turned away and was now watching the tall police officer, Bob, scrape dried blood off the walls into little pillboxes, and I thought, captured once more by the illusion of pattern: What love shares with theater is the poetry of space . . .), 'who's that woman who came with Noble? I missed her name when—'

'Who, Cynthia?' Yvonne hollered out, and the whole room seemed to stiffen. 'With that one-eyed pig? Come *on*, Gerry, give the lady credit – that's my husband's new mistress!'

'Oh, I'm sorry— !'

'Sorry? What's to be sorry?' What had Tania said earlier about Yvonne? I should have been listening. The earring seemed to be dissolving between my fingers like a melting coin. 'I mean, what the hell, you can't blame him – who wants to poke his little whangdoodle in me and catch a goddamn cancer?' Her voice was breaking. 'Right, Soapie?'

'Right,' replied Soapie absently, tipping his hat back and lighting up. 'Okay, that looks terrific – don't worry about the stockings, just leave them down like that, it's a nice touch. So what do you think, Leonard?'

Yvonne burst into tears again, and Cynthia, holding her hand, cradled her head against her stomach. 'I'm so goddamn miserable, Cynthia!'

'I know. It's okay . . .'

'Reminds me of a sailor I once saw clapped in bilboo-boots,' Lloyd Draper drawled, staring down his long lumpy nose from the foot of the couch.

'Hey, Ger!' Soapie called, arm outstretched. 'Come over here a minute!'

'Iris and me were in Singapore at the time, thought bilboos had gone out of fashion, but nothing does really. Let an idea come into the world and you're stuck with it till the cows come home, seems like.'

'You weren't here! You didn't see him! How do *you* know what he said?' Patrick cried, becoming a bit hysterical as Brenda linked her plump fingers with Anatole's and smiled icily back at him, grinding her jaws.

Soapie guided me around behind Ros's body, then stepped back (something cracked under his sneakered foot, he kicked it aside: glass, it glittered) to peer at me through a frame made by his thumbs and index fingers: 'That's it, Ger, just – no, turn a little to the right, *your* right!' While Soapie focused on me through his fingers (I tightened the ties on my rust-colored shirt which had fallen loose, the earring pressed to the hollow of my palm with two oily fingers), Leonard knelt behind my ankles shooting Ros's profile against the lights. 'Okay, good – now where's your wife?'

Michelle, hands crossed at her shoulders and elbows tucked in, danced alone in the sunroom now, swaying trancelike to the whining nervous music. 'I guess she's gone back to the—'

'That's okay, never mind.' Soapie pulled Alison away from her husband to stand beside me. 'Just need a warm body.' Her husband went over to watch Leonard, who was setting up a tripod about fifteen feet away, the tall cop complaining: 'Somebody has stepped on my X-ray unit . . . !' 'I'm telling you, Patrick, I *know.* I was the one who sent that old lady *to* him! She's a welfare client of mine.' Brenda popped her gum, Patrick bit his lip; Anatole, looking confused, gazed through both of them, letting himself be fondled. 'No, not like tin soldiers – relax, you two! More like you're talking or joking about something!'

Woody started to slip away, but Soapie clutched his sleeve and guided him behind Alison, jostling her slightly, so that, having tried not to, we touched.

'Excuse me,' I said, clearing my throat, but Alison was looking the other way: yes, the left one was missing.

'I feel so exposed,' she muttered between her teeth, tugging at the green silk sash at her waist.

'Hey, Doc— ?'

'I can see now why the old lady came away convinced that Roger had a goddamn screw loose!' Brenda laughed behind us, and Patrick hissed: 'That's stupid!'

'Well, he wasn't stupid,' Wilma said, 'he certainly wasn't.'

'Somebody's going to *pay* for this,' the cop swore as he limped past us, and Anatole said: 'Can I sit down again?'

Jim had come over and, directed by Soapie, had removed his jacket once more and rolled up his shirtsleeves. He plugged the stethoscope into his ears, knelt down in front of Ros: 'Like this?'

'You got it, Doc – but sit back so's you don't block the view! And here – let's open her up in front like you're listening to her heart or something.'

'Jesus, Soapie! Do we need that?'

'Leonard needs it. Flesh keeps him awake. Besides, how else will all her fans recognize her?' Leonard pretended to doze off until the breasts appeared, then perked up and started fiddling with his camera with jerky speeded-up motions. 'Barfo! What did they ram in there, a steam drill?'

'It wasn't that large before,' said Jim, glaring up at Bob, who was back with a miniature vacuum cleaner, sucking dust samples up through little filter papers from cuffs, hems, pockets, shoes: I closed my fist around the golden earring. '*Someone's* made it *worse*.' His gray hair lifted and fell as Bob's vacuum sweeper passed over it.

I heard the thin rattle of applause again, as Soapie plumped up the shrunken breast by pulling the cloth tight under it: Michelle, alone in the sunroom, no longer danced but stood impaled as it were by her own trance, eyes closed, clutching her shoulders as though trying to hold herself in. 'Okay, the rest of you people back there: step in closer, come on, crowd around— !'

'What? Are we having our picture taken?'

'Hey, leave a little room for ole Fats!'

'You know, it's curious,' I murmured, 'we've had that painting in the dining room hanging there for years, and only tonight did I notice for the first time that Susanna was wearing gold loops in her ears . . .'

Alison caught her breath, glanced up. 'I've got to see you,' she whispered, letting the hand between us curl around my thigh for a moment, as the others pushed up around us. I wanted to show her what I had in my hand (I was sure it was in there, though in fact I'd lost the feel of it), but we were ringed round with spectators. 'As soon as this is over . . .'

'I look such a fright,' Wilma was protesting, primping nervously at my shoulder. 'But then I guess that's nothing new.'

Photos, Tania believed (Soapie had pulled the shades off some lamps, bent others up to aim the light at us, using Cynthia and Alison's husband to hold the shades in position), did not preserve the past, they only distorted it. Memory, left alone, even as it purged and invented, was always right. Photography could only be defended, she felt (I understood this, recalling the collection of old postcards my grandmother used to let me play with as a child), as a fantastic art form.

'Okay, we're getting there!' Soapie dropped his butt on the carpet, ground it out with his heel. 'Why's it getting so cold in here?' Yvonne, left to herself, wanted to know. 'Howard? Come out from behind those drapes! Don't be shy, press up in there – say, what's wrong with that kid?'

'He's not feeling so great, Soapie.'

'Well, hold him up!'

'This reminds me of the time Archie took me to one of his high school reunions,' Wilma said.

'I've told you, Patrick, they're yours,' Woody was murmuring just behind my ear. 'If you want them, take them. You're perfectly within your rights.'

'Only I ended up in their group photo somehow and Archie didn't.'

Bob came over, pulled a thermometer out of a hole in Ros's side I hadn't noticed before, and left the room, scowling at it. Alison had felt me flinch and now gave a little squeeze. 'They couldn't get it into her behind,' she whispered, 'there was something in there. They had to punch a hole through to her liver.'

'Ah . . .' Was this what I'd wanted to know?

Jim, sighing, put an adhesive strip on the hole and covered it with a loose tatter of her dress. 'We oughta get Cyril and his goatee into this picture,' somebody remarked, and Wilma said: 'Did you know Peg had a tattoo?'

'Come *on* now, frenzied neighbors,' Soapie called out, 'let's show a little *life* there! We don't wanna make our readers have to guess which one's the victim!'

'A little red heart – right where you usually get your flu shots . . .'

'What's that about Cyril?'

'My old corpus delicious isn't good for much anymore, but – heh heh
– if you need another bystander—'

'Not that badly, old-timer. But I tell you what, if you can find one of
those cops for me –' Anatole burped ominously. 'Woops! Hang on, kid!
Are we ready, Leonard?'

'Who, Fiona— ?'

Jim stood, unlocked his knees, and paced around in a little circle. 'Foot
went to sleep,' he explained apologetically.

'Hold it, Leonard! Fats, stop crossing your eyes like that! You got no
respect!'

'You mean the one with the big nose?'

'*Sshh!* She's around here somewhere!'

'Are you ready, Doc?'

'That's really hard to believe!'

'Whoa, look what's just blowed in! Get in here, gorgeous, and show
these amateurs how it's done!' It was Regina, leaning in the doorway
behind Leonard, gripping the doorjamb, looking drained as though she
might have coldcreamed her face and just wiped it off. Her black hair
and costume were limp, her lips still drooling. Slowly she lifted her head
and found herself staring directly at Anatole, staring helplessly back.
Briefly they reflected each other, gasping, eyes watering, hands sliding
upward to clutch at their gaping mouths – then Anatole, swallowing hard
against the bubbling sounds in his throat, lurched forward, falling over
Ros's body ('*Unf!*' Jim grunted), picked himself up and staggered out of
the room, hand to mouth, Regina having just, with a muffled gargle,
preceded him. 'Hey, you clowns, come *back* here!' exclaimed Soapie, his
press hat flying, as Leonard struggled with his tipped camera, and Brenda
asked: 'Who *is* that boy anyhow?'

'Tania's nephew.'

'Oh yeah?' She cracked her gum. '*Cute!*'

'Awright, just straighten the knees out where he hit her, Doc,' Soapie
shouted (I heard a hissed whisper: '*Bitch!*'), 'we haven't got all night.'
I glanced into my hand: yes, it was still there. I held it between my
fingertips, letting my palm air out, recalling the little magic shows I used
to do for my grandmother with coins and cards and little balls. The trick,
always, depended on distraction, a lesson, as it were, in the way the world
worked. Lloyd Draper had returned meanwhile with the short cop in

tow, Fred now carrying a big steaming slice of pizza in both hands, and Soapie, flicking away the cigarette he'd just lit up, pulled Fred over to join us around the body. 'Here by the head maybe . . . yeah, that's – listen, gimme that garbage! Now, one step back . . . right, hold it! That's terrific!'

'Should I have my gun out maybe?'

'What do you think, Leonard?' Soapie asked around a mouthful of pizza, his head cocked (behind the lights, the doorbell rang again), and Fats said: 'Say, is there eats?'

'Yeah, all right, why not?' Soapie mused, handing the rest of Fred's drippy pizza to Leonard. Leonard folded it up and stuffed it all in his mouth, then wiped his hands on Yvonne's bindings ('Psst! Do me a favor, Leonard,' she whispered, 'go get me a drink!') and, oozing oily juices from under his scruffy clump of moustache, bent down (he bugged his eyes at her and winked: 'Ah, you're a nut case, Leonard,' she grumped) behind his viewfinder again. 'Come on, let's get a hump on, Soap, while there's still some groceries left!' Fats whined, and Soapie said: 'No, don't point that wart remover at the body, sarge! What kinda sense does *that* make? Aim it more toward Ger there!'

'Hey— !'

'I got the safety on,' Fred assured me with a wink.

'Talbot! Come on in here! You can take the kid's place – make room for him there, Bren!'

'How 'bout if we move this tab in round the table and do a little *in*-terior *dec*-oratin' at the same time?' Fats suggested hopefully.

'At least you might tuck your shirt in,' sniffed Wilma as Talbot wobbled over, a dippy smile on his face. He had his own jacket on, but the pants he was wearing now – agape at the waist and baggy at the ankles – were mine.

I glanced down at Alison, feeling vaguely apologetic, and caught her looking up at me. She blushed. 'I was thinking about that play we saw,' she whispered, 'what you said that night about happy endings . . .'

Talbot, weaving blowzily in front of us and accompanied by a nimbus of sweat and bathpowder, belched. He seemed puzzled by the sight of Ros's body at his feet, Fred's upraised revolver. He braced himself on Jim's shoulder and lifted his feet high over Ros's body, as though straddling a fence. Alison, leaning back against me to make room, scratched furtively at the back of my thigh, her hair aglow with a light that was almost magical – except that it came from the lamp her husband, lost in the shadows behind it, was beaming at her. Talbot stumbled into our midst, peered blearily up at me. 'Your can's leakin' all over the goddamn place,' he announced loudly, and Patrick whispered: '*Now?*'

'It's as good a time as any,' said Woody.

'Stinks, too.'

'I know, I'm going to call a plumber, Talbot,' I said, excited by Alison's hand, her pressing thigh, her toe on mine beneath the body: I squeezed the earring in my palm, recalling for some reason the wetness of that beggar's tongue as he stacked the coins. A kind of unappeasable hunger . . . 'As soon as we're done here—'

'Oh yeah, the plumber. Met him on the stairs when I was comin' down.'

'What?'

'Okay, lazy gents, let's watch the little birdie!'

'*Love* to! Pull it out there where we can see it, Talbot!'

'You saw a plumber— ?'

'Cockadoodle-*doo!*'

'*Talbot— !*'

'That's putting your best half-foot forward, Talbot,' Yvonne cawed, as Soapie went on, Leonard beginning to click away: 'Come on, everybody halo around there, squeeze up – you're not paying attention, Ger! I've never seen you like this! Give us a hug or a smooch or something! Talbot's got the idea – what's the matter with the rest of you lot? This *is* a goddamn party, isn't it – Pat, where are you going?'

'I – I'll be right back— !'

'That's *disgusting*, Talbot!'

'Oh, it's not so bad,' Brenda laughed, smacking her gum (Wilma, leaning toward Talbot in an effort to help him zip his spreading fly, had jostled us, and, as I gripped Alison's buttock for support, she gasped and said: 'I'll meet you by the cellar stairs!'), 'but there's one over there that beats it!'

We turned to look at Earl Elstob, his hand in Michelle's blouse, an erection pushing his pants out in front of him, like a plow – we all laughed, even Woody: a peculiar little barking noise – but I was wondering at the strange intense beauty of this charge between us, brief, sudden, even (we knew this, it lent poignancy, passion, to our furtive touches) ephemeral, yet at the same time somehow ageless: a cathectic brush, as it were, with eternity, numbing and profound . . .

'Don't laugh at him, it may be a tumor!'

'Terrific!' exclaimed Soapie as Leonard cranked and fired at us. 'You got it now! Ha ha! Hold it!'

Fred, grinning over his shoulder at Elstob, had lowered his gun, but now he raised it again. 'You'd be doing your little ball-and-chain a favor,' he said, holding the smile for Soapie, but staring ominously at me, 'if you told her to stop interfering with our investigation.'

'Interfering?' Alison was stroking my finger as though trying to peel back a foreskin.

'How can you even *see* me, Soapie, past that wad on Talbot's ear?'

'Yeah, sweeping up, moving things, covering up the evidence – it can get her in a lotta trouble.' I started to explain (Janny had appeared in the doorway, her pink skirt creased horizontally and makeup smeared, holding something up), but Woody was distracting the cop, muttering something in his ear about the protection of forensic evidence; to give him room (but I was thinking about my wife, how to get a message to her), I leaned toward Alison's breast. 'He *what* – ?!' roared Fred.

'I think Janny's got something for you,' Talbot mumbled. I saw it now: the ice pick, my ascot knotted around the tip – in reflex, I jerked away from Alison. She too pulled back in alarm: 'What – what's the matter?'

'Whoa! Hold the horses!' Soapie shouted. Janny was picking her way past the lights and camera, waggling the pick and ascot like a little flag. 'Only a couple more!'

'No— !'

But it was Fred who broke up the picture-taking, leaping past us to smash Patrick in the face with the butt of his gun just as he was leaning into the pile of scattered criminalistic gear in the corner. '*Hey!*' Lamps tipped, Soapie shouted something at Leonard, Patrick screamed ('[*Not in here, Janny!*]' I mouthed, backing off), Fats seized the cop by his collar and pulled him away.

'A-a-gift from my m-mother . . . !' Patrick bawled, his lip split, blood streaming from his nose and mouth as though a pipe had burst.

'Now, what'd you go and do that for?' Fats wanted to know, his big arm around Fred's throat (I'd managed to get several people between me and Janny, but she came on, smiling dimly, holding the pick high): then Bob came rocking in, cocked revolver in an extended two-handed grip, shouting: '*FREEZE!*' and Fats let go. 'Awright, awright, I can take a hint . . .'

The two officers pried the tweezers out of Patrick's clenched fist, then dragged him out, still blubbering bloodily, Bob covering us with his revolver. 'Stupid little nance,' Noble grumbled in the doorway, watching them go, and we all relaxed: I was on the move again.

'*Here*, Gerry!' Janny called, circling wide around Ros's abandoned body in her stocking feet as I ducked behind Leonard. 'We *found* it! It was under the *bed!*'

I scowled at her and shook my head, I was nearly at the door, but there she was, passing the pick on to me like a relay baton – what could I do? I grabbed it and tucked it inside my shirt. 'Thanks! I – I was just looking for it!'

She smiled wanly, a little breathlessly, her face a blank (had someone put her up to this? I glanced over at Talbot: Wilma was fussing with his clothes and he grinned dopily at me over her bent back), then suddenly, spying something past my shoulder, she yanked me back against the wall, threw her arms around my neck, straddled my thigh, and kissed me, her greasy mouth yawning, in undisguised panic. 'It's that horrible Earl Elstob,' she breathed. 'Stick your finger in me, Gerry – *quick!*'

'Eh, huh! Can I cut in?'

'Can't you see we're busy?' Janny panted, her thigh twitching mechanically between my legs as though pumping a treadle. 'Well, nothing works like it used to, old-timer,' Soapie was saying a few feet away, while across the room, Fats, giving Woody some money, seemed momentarily stunned: 'Who, *Roger*— ?' Janny's tongue dipped in and out of my ear like a swab. 'You can't find his lower lip, Gerry!' she gasped. 'It's like kissing only half a mouth! I felt like I was falling over the *edge* of something!'

Brenda was holding a little handkerchief of some kind to her nose, her eyes watering. She offered it to Howard ('I mean, French-kissing him is worse than painting a *ceiling*, Gerry!'), but he shrank back, Fats clutching her elbow in pained alarm: 'They *killed* him, Bren!' 'Oh *no*! Not Roger – !' And then, as they rushed out past Noble (the doorbell was ringing), someone on the stairs shouted down: 'You the guy who lives here?' He was leaning over the railing to peer in at us in the living room, a bulky man in cap and overalls, monkey wrench in his fist, the name STEVE stitched over his pocket. There were new voices in the hallway, the slap and bang of doors.

I eased Janny away. 'Yes . . . ?'

'Well, I can't do much with the stool, mister, I didn't bring the right tools – but it's easy to see what's fouling up your tub.'

'The tub? But I didn't know it was—'

'Yeah, some poor broad just took her last drink in it.'

'What?' I felt the pick slip, pinched it nervously against my ribs with my elbow. People were passing between us, greeting each other, pulling off wraps, asking about Ros ('In here!' one of them shouted, a woman in a yellow knit dress), there was a lot of confusion. 'Who . . . ?' But I knew, yes, even before Anatole came tumbling down the stairs behind the plumber, wheyfaced and woebegone, I knew – and the others knew, too, knew something, for there was a sudden awestruck silence as at the raising of a baton. Even the comings and goings had stopped, the greetings, the music, the footsteps, the whisper of clothing against clothing had stopped. There was only, in another room somewhere, the solitary clink of a fork against a dish.

'*Uncle Howard!*' Anatole cried.

We all turned to look: Howard was in the middle of the room, alone, down on his plump haunches alongside Ros, his hand under her silvery skirt; he gaped back at us, aghast, seemingly transfixed there in an intersection of beamed lamps, his cracked spectacles aglitter with a confusion of tiny lights as though his eyes were bursting. 'My god, what are you *doing*, Howard— ?!' a woman asked.

His mouth worked but all that came out was a little squeak. A flush, seeming to rise from the well of his dangling tie, flooded up through his throat and into his cheeks, crept behind his eyes and into his scalp. 'My, ah . . . tiepin!' he managed to stammer at last. 'I . . . eh . . . dropped—'

'*It's Aunt Tania, Uncle Howard! She's dead!*'

A sudden spasm jerked Howard's lips back into a terrible clenched grin, the flush draining away as though some plug had been pulled – then he fainted and, anchored by the hand still locked in Ros's thighs, fell over her body, Leonard's flashgun popping.

There was a pause, then a rush for the stairs, people shouting, crying, swearing. The plumber, catching my eye as they clambered past him, shrugged apologetically. 'Christ! When did all this happen?' somebody asked behind me, and Soapie said: 'That's it, Leonard! That's our story!'

'We're not exactly sure, there's an Inspector here from Homicide trying to work it out now.'

'Notch it!'

'Woody— ?'

I stood, rooted in turmoil, clasping the ice pick to my breast like precious treasure and staring down at my feet, invaded by a fearful sense of some kind of ultimate déjà vu. I was standing, I saw, in one of the police team's chalk drawings of Ros, the fetal one: what had Tania said about primal outlines? Life, she'd said (I seemed to see her again, kneeling at the tub, her arms scabbed with pink suds, peering at me over her pale turned shoulder as though to offer me something: love perhaps, or a vision of it), was nothing but a sequence of interlocking incarnations, an interminable effort to fill the unfillable outline. Yes, vague chalk drawings, that's what genetic codes were, the origin of life: questions with no answers, just endless inadequate guesses. Art, she believed, attempted to reproduce not the guesses, but the questions; this was how beauty differed from decoration – or indeed from truth, in her father's sense of the word – which was why Tania always claimed that, contrary to the common opinion, she was in fact a realist. But art was therefore dangerous: the heart of beauty was red-hot (she'd once tried, in that notorious self-portrait, to paint this heat directly) and it could burn your eyes out, sear your flesh away. Like she said tonight: 'Something almost monstrous . . .'

'Jesus, did they both die like that?' someone asked behind me. 'It's like a goddamn fairy tale!'

'No, you don't understand . . .'

'Gerald . . . ?'

I looked up, meeting my wife's gaze. There was, as always, a touch of worry in her eyes, a touch of uncertainty: even as she smiled it was there, though now she wasn't smiling. In her arms she carried a bundle of dirty clothes, and I saw that she had changed aprons again. This one was an icy blue with pink pears and yellow apples in it. 'Where did everybody go?' Yvonne wanted to know. 'Cynthia . . . ?' 'It's Tania,' I said, swallowing. 'She's dead.'

'I know.' She turned to look at the people on the stairs, holding the soiled laundry in her arms like a gift received but still unopened. She shuddered and the sleeve of my bloodstained shirt dropped and wagged from her bundle like a spotted tail. 'Can you get his finger out of there,

Jim?' someone asked behind me. 'I don't know, I think she's getting hard.'
She touched a hand to her brow, gazing past me: a towel uncoiled as
though to slip away, a blue sock fell to the floor, someone's underwear,
a handkerchief, all falling – I stopped to scoop it up for her. It lay scattered
in and around Ros's outline like conjectural apprehensions of form, like
Mark's drawings of Christmas trees (yes, I felt myself in a child's world
down here, disassociated, unseen: it slid out from under my shirt like a
duty shed and I folded my soiled shorts around it): even a pillowcase: had
she been changing the bedding? 'Thank you, Gerald. I thought I'd do a
load . . . before we got too far behind . . .'

'Whose handkerchief is this?' It was almost too filthy to pick up: I
pinched it by one corner, dropped it loosely on top.

'His.' She nodded back over her shoulder toward my study. Daffie had
paused to speak to Anatole, now lying on the stairs, staring blankly out
through the railings, and Noble, passing, whispered something in her
ear. She threw her glass of pink gin at him. 'Gerald, they've got Patrick
in there now. I'm afraid.'

I kissed her forehead, clasping a hand to each shoulder: 'Don't worry,
I'll go check on him,' I said, and stepped by her, freeing myself from
Ros's outline as I did so. 'I *believe* it,' someone said as I pressed through
the jostle in the doorway toward the downstairs toilet (Daffie was
rubbing her arm where Noble had struck her and she exchanged a
commiserating glance with me), 'but there's one goddamn thing I just
don't understand . . .'

'Wait, don't go in there,' Woody cautioned, touching my arm. 'They're
using it for a darkroom.' He glanced back over his shoulder, just as
Cynthia came out of my study. 'Everything okay?'

She nodded, businesslike. 'I loaned him my calculator, which should
help, but he still has a long way to go.' She handed Woody a gold watch
which he pulled on, then she took his arm, looked up at me. 'I'm sorry
if we caused you any embarrassment in there— ?'

'No, it was my—'

'How's Patrick?' Woody interrupted, placing a hand over hers, a hand
stubbier than her own.

'You'd be surprised. He has a split lip, some bruises, he's going to be
pretty sore – but I think he's fallen in love.'

'Patrick—?' I couldn't help smiling, and she returned it: I thought of teachers I'd had, bank managers, a doctor who treated me once for trenchmouth in Rouen. A man in lilac and gray passed us, muttering something about 'a good run' or 'cut one.' 'I mean, is anyone noticing?' he asked.

'They discovered a set of photos of the girl – the victim – being raped by some man in disguise. It's true, I've seen a couple of them – they're pretty offensive, and there's even a dagger or something in one of them. The only clue to the rapist's identity, it seems, is his exposed genitalia, so they're taking measurements, checking for peculiar marks, scars, circumcision, and so on, as you might expect.' My smile was gone. She watched me serenely. 'Anyway, when they took hold of your friend's member, it erected on them. This enraged one of the officers for some reason and he struck it with his nightstick. Quite firmly, I must say – you may have heard the scream.'

'Aha,' smiled Woody. The photos: had someone just been telling me . . .

'The Inspector reprimanded the officer and apologized to your friend, even patting him on the shoulder as he put his bruised organ away – then he returned the tweezers to him and with that the little fellow simply melted, started telling them everything he knows. When I left, it was something about a fabulously wealthy old woman who presumably came to Roger with what was a kind of parable about love and jealousy, if I understood it correctly.'

'Close enough. I remember the day Roger came into the office with that stupid story,' Woody said, shaking his head. 'He was very talented, Roger. Sometimes, in a courtroom, he could be downright brilliant, an artist in his way. But he was too ego-centered ever to make a really good lawyer.'

'I always had the feeling it was his *loss* of ego that got him into trouble,' I said, recalling Tania's account of Roger concussed by love.

'Maybe.' Woody pursed his lips like a skeptical prosecuting attorney confronting a dubious plea. It was almost as though he were preparing a case against his ex-partner. 'But maybe ego *is* absence, that bottomless hole in the center that egomaniacs like Roger keep throwing themselves into.'

Cynthia, on his arm, her gaze steady, seemed neutral, but there was something disquieting about her, too. Something odd. Now, fingering her medallion, she turned to Woody and said: 'If we're going up to see the body, we should do it soon, before Yvonne starts missing us.'

'I know – but first, damn it, there's something I have to . . .' He glanced toward the study, his face clouded, just as Fats and Brenda, in tears, holding each other up, came staggering out. 'God, it's *awful*, Bren!' 'I can't believe it! Did you see his *eyes* – ?' 'Gerry, listen, could you do me a small favor?'

'Sure, Woody, only first I—'

He laid a hand on my shoulder, leaned close. Through the doorway into the dining room, I caught a glimpse of Alison with Dickie, his arm around her, both of them laughing – she didn't seem to see me. 'Would you go in there with me? I'd really appreciate it . . .'

'Well . . .' I looked around. What was it my wife had wanted? Something from the freezer, a stepladder, fruit knife? I couldn't remember. There was a lot of activity on the stairs and I could feel it inside myself like a kind of abdominal turmoil. Alison, I saw, had both hands at her ear, her head tipped toward them – what? My hand was empty: *I must have dropped it!* Dickie smiled and she gave him a little kiss on his cheek. 'I've got a lot to do, Woody – my wife . . .' Woody was gazing at me intently, as though through me, more than just an appeal somehow. 'But, I suppose, if you really—'

'Thanks, Gerry. I knew I could count on you. We'll be right back, Cyn.'

'That's right, it nearly slipped my mind,' Cynthia said, as Woody pulled me away. 'The police were talking about your wife. I'm not sure – I think they found something in the laundry.'

'The laundry— ! But I just left her!'

'Well, I don't know when,' she called back over her shoulder. 'I really don't have much time, Woody,' I insisted, though by now it was too late, we were already at my study door.

I blinked, drew back, bumping into Woody in the doorway. I was almost unable to believe what I saw in there. Everything had been turned inside out. The desk drawers and filing cabinets had been broken open and emptied out on the floor, books dumped from the shelves. The walls, seen only insubstantially through the haze of pipesmoke and shadows (the lamps had been moved about, it was hard even to get my bearings), were smeared now with what was no doubt blood, most of the pictures torn away so violently there were holes in the plaster. There were sketches of the crime pinned up in their stead, procedural charts and instructions, a diagram of what looked like an amusement-park maze. They'd set up a lot of strange equipment, turning the place into a kind of crime lab with test tubes and burners, sieves, calipers, inkpads and rollers, odd measuring gadgets – even now the tall cop, Bob, sat at a microscope holding up between his fingers what looked like a piece of bloody flesh – ah no, the swatch he'd cut out of our white easy chair . . . Fred, wearing translucent rubber gloves, worked at a hot plate. He seemed to be boiling up some kind of soup. Photographs hung from strung-up lines like dance decorations, and brightly tagged objects – I saw knives, drinking glasses, an ax, swimming trunks, Mark's paintbox, knotted-up pantyhose, a tin of anchovies, pillboxes and specimen bottles, a blackstriped croquet ball, a pink shoe – lined the swept-out bookshelves like museum exhibits. I had the feeling my whole house was reinventing itself. 'What have you done— ?!' I gasped, and Woody said: 'Here he is.'

Inspector Pardew looked up from his paperwork. He sat at my desk behind a heap of watches, calculator in hand and dead pipe in mouth, Patrick hunched nearby, hands between his legs, muttering something about 'the woman in red.' The Inspector looked me over carefully, passed a folded bill to Woody. 'Very well.'

'Let me know if you need any help, Gerry,' Woody whispered in my ear. 'We'll be upstairs.'

'Hey, wait a minute, I thought you— !'

'*Here!* Just *look* at this!' Inspector Pardew commanded, holding up a little heart-shaped watch on a gold chain. In his other hand, I saw, he now held Alison's watch with its three opened buckles, the straps dangling from either side of its digital face like green plaited locks, the numbers blinking between them like a part. 'I tell you, time is *not* a toy!'

'Actually, I was only, uh, passing by, I have to get back to—'

'It is *not* a mere *decoration!*'

'It certainly is *not!*' echoed Patrick, scowling at me like a judge. His mouth where Fred had hit him was puffed up and purple, and there was a big bloody gap just under his nose that made him look like he was metamorphosing into a frog or something. Woody was gone, vanished in that moment that Alison's watch had distracted me, and the short cop, tracking through the correspondence and check stubs, travel brochures, books, photos, and old newspaper clippings that littered the floor, had moved over between me and the door. He wore his rubber gloves still, white powder down his front. I seemed to have trouble thinking clearly, my mind confused by all this . . . this confusion.

'It is the very *content* and *shape* of the world,' Pardew was saying. 'Look! This one doesn't even have a *face!* It doesn't have *hands!* It's like a theater marquee, reflecting nothing but our pathetic *vanity!*'

Turning back to him, I now saw, past Fred's abandoned hot plate, what I hadn't seen before: Roger, sprawled upside down in the far corner like a broken doll, limbs akimbo, legs listing against the walls as though he'd slid down from the ceiling, his right leg bent sideways at the knee, forming a kind of aleph of the whole. His face was smeared with blood, his hair matted with it, his eyes below the gaping mouth starting minstrel-like from their sockets. I gaped my own mouth (I was thinking suddenly about Tania, what she'd said: 'Like a newborn child . . . !') to suck in air. 'Are you just – just *leaving* him there— ?!'

'*Time,*' Pardew was insisting, wagging the heart-shaped watch at me (I'd turned just in time to see him hurl Alison's watch behind him as though it were contaminating him: 'It's a *mockery!* A *corruption!*'), 'we're talking about *time!*' With a sweep of his other hand, his white silk scarf fluttering about his neck as though in awe and wonder, he indicated the glittering mound of watches on the desk, and it was then, noticing a heavy ring he wore with a large red stone in it, that I realized what it was that had seemed odd about Cynthia just now: her rings. She had been wearing four of them, all uncharacteristically ostentatious, on one hand, none on the other. 'It's the *key* to it all, it *always* is, the key to *everything!*'

'Yes, pay attention, Gerald.'

The Inspector sighed, sat back, nodded at Fred. 'If you don't mind, please,' he said to Patrick.

'But I haven't finished telling you about— !'

'I know, we'll discuss it later. Now I have to speak with this gentleman.'

'But I'll be quiet! I won't be in the way! I *promise!*'

'Sergeant . . . ?'

'Please! Wait! My tweezers!' Patrick cried, fumbling in his pocket as Fred took his arm.

'I gave them back to you.'

'Yes, but –' He fished them forth, thrust them at Pardew. There were tears welling up in his eyes. 'There was a little silver chain – it's not *there* anymore!'

'Oh, I see. Well, you'll have to fill out a claim form,' the Inspector said, his moustaches lifting and falling with a dismissive smile as he handed the tweezers back. Bob was stapling a tag to the patch from our easy chair. 'We'll leave one with you before we go.'

Patrick hesitated, tugged at by Fred in his dusty rubber gloves, then plunged recklessly forward and planted a wet crimson kiss on Pardew's cheek. 'Thank you!' he burbled, his split lip bleeding afresh, as Fred collared him. 'You're so . . . so *kind!*'

The Inspector winced faintly, narrowing his eyes at Fred, and the policeman led Patrick away, still twittering and squeaking, holding himself as he hobbled along. 'In the old days,' Pardew muttered icily, 'we used to strip perverts like that in the middle of winter and scourge them in the marketplace.' He caught my frown and added: 'Well, a long time ago, of course. That old gent was telling me . . .' He touched his cheek, glanced at his fingertips. 'Do you perhaps have a handkerchief I could borrow?'

'Sure, here, I won't—'

'Thank you.' He folded it into a little pad, dabbed at his cheek with it as though at a wound. 'Your wife took mine. Said she'd wash it for me.' Bob looked up at us from his microscope, lip between his teeth like a thought he might be chewing on, then (the alarm went off on one of the wristwatches in Pardew's heap: he located it, depressed the button that turned it off) bowed his head again. 'Does your wife usually do the laundry during a party?'

'Sometimes. It depends. Why do you ask?'

He shrugged, staring at the stained handkerchief, then refolded it and applied it to his cheek again. 'I'm interested in patterns. And the disruption of patterns. That's my job. I solve crimes. Do you understand?'

I nodded. I was trying to be civil, but his bluntness and cold piercing gaze made civility seem like evasion. I felt unfairly singled out, he at my desk, I before it as though at a dressing down, but when I turned away from him, there was only poor battered Roger staring back, the pre-occupied cop at his microscope (he was working now with a piece of material from the heap of rumpled clothing at his feet, and as I watched him bend to his lens, I thought of my wife at the kitchen stove, lifting the pan lid to peer in at the boiling water – I realized I should have gone over right then and taken her in my arms, but the moment was gone, what had been done could not be undone – or rather, undone done – and I felt a flush of sorrow penetrate my chest, spread, pulsing, through my body, and leak away like time itself, like hope, like Being, that great necromantic illusion . . .), close-ups of Ros's corpse hanging from the line, the room upended and strewn with the debris of my dislodged past. What they'd done here reminded me of a line Ros once had to deliver in a film called *The Invasion of the Panty Snarfers:* 'When they stuck their noses in, it felt like everything just changed its shape!' Pardew waited still. Watching. 'I mean, patterns, and, uh, crime – murder – as . . . you know . . .' I was struggling. The Inspector narrowed his eyes: I supposed I was an open book. 'A . . . disturbance of things, and so—'

'Not necessarily. On another scale, this party of yours is the true disturbance. Maybe all conventions are, all efforts at social intercourse.' He sighed, and sighing, seemed more human. There was still a trace of blood on his cheek where Patrick had kissed him, but he'd ceased rubbing at it. 'Since I was a child, I have been troubled by, let's call it the irrational, and have been trying to find an order, a logic, behind what is given to us as madness and disorder. That hidden commonality, you see. Well, I have been in homicide a very long time now, and I can tell you, the more I run into all the surface codes and structures – as we say in the business – that people invent for themselves, the more it seems to me that the one common invariant behind them all is, quite frankly, *murder itself!*'

I felt he was confiding in me and I smiled politely, hoping only to get out of here. What I'd thought was a maze, I saw now, was only a diagram of the brain, showing the consequences of injury to the various parts. 'That's interesting, but I don't believe anyone here could possibly—'

'What? What— ?! You think I can't see what's going on here?' he roared, bolting up out of his chair in a sudden rage that sent me staggering back a step. 'I *live* in the *filth* of the world! I live at the *heart* of absolute *evil* and *degradation!* It's my *profession,* and certain things I am *good* at! I have an *eye* for them! Hatred, for example! No matter how deeply it is buried, I can *see* it! Lust, doubt, fear, greed: I can see these things like color painted on people's faces, washed into their movements, their words, and believe me, this place is *screaming* with it!'

'It – it's only a party— !' I protested.

'*Only!* Do you think I'm *blind?* You've got drug addicts here! You've got perverts, anarchists, pimps, and peeping toms! Adulterers! You've got dipsomaniacs! You've got whores, thugs, thieves, atheists, sodomists, and out-and-out lunatics! There isn't *anything* they wouldn't do!' He seemed almost to have grown. He was rigid, powerful – yet his hand was trembling as he picked up a piece of paper. 'In this world, nothing – *nothing*, I tell you – is ever wholly concealed! I *know* what's in their sick stinking hearts!'

'But— !'

'Look at this! It's a drawing of the murder scene! Only it was drawn *before the murder!* We can *prove* this! Somebody was planning this homicide all along! You see? Somebody here, *in this house!* Down to the *last vile detail* – except that they apparently meant to strike her in the womb instead of the breast – at least that must be the true *meaning* of the crime – you can see here the blood, the hideous weapon between her legs. There's the killer standing over her. *Gloating!* One interesting thing: he's bearded. That might be a clue or it might not, of course. It might be a disguise, for example, or some fantasy image of the self, a displacement of some kind . . .' He was calming some and, reluctant to stir him up again, I was tempted to let him have his 'bearded murderer.' But then he added: 'And beside him, this horned figure, his diabolical accomplice, you might say, *his own evil conscience!*' – and I felt obliged to interrupt.

'I'm afraid that's the, uh, Holy Family.'

'The what?' He looked pained, his eyes widening as he stared at me, as though I might have just grown horns myself and struck him.

'It's the Christmas scene. You know, the manger and all that. My son drew it for nursery school.'

He slumped back into his chair, staring at the drawing in disbelief. 'But – all this *blood*— !'

'There was a childbirth documentary on television the week before that we all watched. Not surprisingly, my son put the two things together. The "weapon" is the baby and the "killer's" the father, and that, eh, "diabolical accomplice" is a cow.'

The Inspector seemed momentarily deflated, his moustaches drooping, and I was sorry I had had to be the one to tell him. 'It's terrible,' he said. He turned the drawing over, applied a self-adhesive label to the back, and scribbled something on it. 'It might be worse than I thought. Your son's name?'

'His— ? Mark, of course, but—'

'Age?'

'He's four, almost five now, but he—'

'Did you or your wife ever have syphilis?'

'No!'

He handed the drawing to Bob, who asked: 'Should we get stats?'

'Probably a good idea.'

'Wait a minute! What are you— ?'

'Now as regards the missus and her laundry,' the Inspector continued icily, turning back to me. I watched Bob add a few notes of his own to the label on Mark's drawing, then put it on the shelf beside a crushed beer can and what looked like part of a truss. 'She's been a busy little lady.'

'Well . . .' It was a mistake, I sensed, to be too frank with this man. Yet, it was difficult to conceal anything from him either. 'She likes things clean, if that's what you mean.'

'I'm afraid it's not as simple as that. Let me show you something.' He nodded Bob over. The policeman picked up some jockey shorts lying near his feet, brought them to Pardew. 'She was just stuffing these into the washing machine when we stopped her. She pretended surprise, of course. Or perhaps she was really surprised. You can see that there is blood on them. Very close to that of the victim, I might say.'

'Yes, but everybody—'

'And feces, which we haven't yet identified' – he sniffed meditatively – 'as well as oil and alcohol stains, what might be lipstick, the usual. Or so we thought. But then, under the microscope, we discovered a fleck of old blue paint and a—'

'Blue?'

He smiled flickeringly. Bob, watching us, scratched out a note. 'Mmm, or green, gray, something like that, and a touch of rust. Curious, isn't it? Of course, blood, paint, rust – just a pair of dirty shorts, you might say. But we found something else. Look: do you see that hole? Well! You'll agree, only one instrument could make a perforation like that! If we find the weapon that did it, we'll have our . . . our perpetrator . . .'

I knew there was something I should be doing, or saying (at my feet lay a photo of Ros on her back, dressed in a pith helmet and gunbelt, and sucking off a tiger that crouched over her, lapping at her sex with a huge rough tongue – how did we do that? I couldn't remember, but I did remember the one we shot with Ros as the tiger: that one scared me to this day . . .), but before I could get my thoughts in order (some vague sense of entrapment: I was trying to play back the recent exchanges), Fred came back in behind me with a fresh sandwich and Howard: 'We caught him with his thumb in the old pudding,' Fred reported around a half-chewed mouthful, and the Inspector raised his brows at me as though to say: Haven't I just told you so?

Howard, sagging flabbily in Fred's grip – shirttails out, broken glasses hooked over one ear and the tip of his pink nose, thin gray-blond hair falling loosely over his brow like a lowered scrim – held his stained finger up in front of his nose, trying to focus his weak eyes on it. 'Something . . . spesh . . .,' he mumbled and put it in his mouth. Fred clipped him ferociously behind the ears, kicked him in the belly as he hit the floor.

'Stop!' I protested. 'You've got to understand – he just lost his *wife*—!'

Fred whirled round on me, whipping out his nightstick, sandwich clamped in his jaws, Bob unsnapped his holster, elbow crooked behind his back. 'All right, all right,' said Pardew, 'that will do!' The cops eased up, their hunched shoulders dropping, backs straightening, though they continued to watch me with narrowed eyes. Howard gurgled miserably into the carpet at my feet, his horn-rimmed spectacles crushed once and for all beneath him. Poor Howard. I understood what the others could not: that there was nothing mischievous or prurient about what he had done, that for him it was simply a matter of aesthetic need. He was an art critic. A good one. He had to *know*.

On a signal from Pardew, Bob and Fred hauled Howard to his feet and dragged him, weak-kneed and drooling, over to their work area. 'The important thing,' the Inspector was saying, his finger in his nose, 'is to keep your eyes open, to miss nothing, not just to look, but to *see* – true percipience is an art, but you must work at it, it's the first thing you learn in this game.' He fished a long string of mucus from his nose like a snail from its shell and laid it in my handkerchief. His two assistants were taking caliper measurements of Howard's head and face. 'I've solved crimes with my ears, my mouth, even my toes and the seat of my pants, but mostly I've solved them up here. In the old conk.'

'Well, he's got the thick lips and swollen eyelids, all right,' Fred was saying, putting the last of the sandwich in his mouth and mumbling around it, 'but the hair's too thin and the jaw's not right.'

'How about bumps?'

'It's a little like sorting out the grammar of a sentence,' the Inspector went on. He was studying the string of mucus in my handkerchief. 'You have the object there before you and evidence at least of the verb.' He folded the mucus into the handkerchief and handed it back to me. 'But you have to reach back in time to locate the subject. I say, *locate*—'

'Ah, you can keep it, I have—'

'*Take it!*'

'What about the left one?' Bob was asking, and Fred, chewing, said: 'Definitely different from the right.'

'It – he is what I came in here to tell you about,' I said, and wiped my hands on my shirt. Fred had grabbed a hank of Howard's hair and jerked his head forward: 'Crikey, look! He's wearing somebody's flopper-stoppers!' 'Fucking weirdo.' Fred plucked a strand of hair, scraped some dirt from Howard's ear, made him spit on a glass slide, while Bob scratched away in a notepad, muttering to himself. 'It's about his wife, you see – she's up in the bathtub, we just—'

'*One thing at a time!*' The Inspector rapped his briar pipe smartly against the ashtray. '*We're scientists here, not sightseers!*'

'Say, speaking of your old chamber of commerce,' Fred put in over his shoulder (they had pulled Howard over to the inkpad and roller and were undoing his pants), 'you got a real problem up there!'

'I know. There's a plumber—'

'Come on, apeshit, stand up straight!' Bob growled, kneeing Howard in the butt.

'Or *if* sightseers,' the Inspector added thoughtfully, fitting the empty pipe into his mouth, 'then sightseers of a very special kind.'

'Pardon?'

'Is that a hernia scar?' Bob asked.

Fred leaned closer. 'Looks like it.'

'I mean, sightseers not of place, but of time.' Pardew picked up some watches from the pile and began laying them out in single file. 'We tend to think of time as something that passes by,' he said around his pipe, 'a kind of endless flow, like a river, coming out of nowhere and going into nowhere, with space the theater in which this drama of pure process is acted out, as it were.' When he ran out of room on the desk, he added five or six watches at a forty-five degree angle to the last one, turning it into a kind of checkmark. 'But what if it's the other way around? What if it's the world that's insubstantial, time the immovable stage for its ghostly oscillations? Eh?' The checkmark had become an arrow. From my perspective it was pointed from right to left.

'I'll tell you one thing,' said Fred, 'that ain't the one in the photos.'

'And *if* it's a stage,' the Inspector continued, picking up a large gold pocketwatch and pointing to its face, '*if* it's there in its entirety, the script all written, so to speak, a kind of cyclorama which seems to move only because we, like these hands here, move *through* it, then it should be possible, if we could just overcome our perceptual limitations, to visit any *part* of it, including the *no-longer* and the *not-yet!*' He was jabbing at these places on the watch, and it brought to mind a play Ros was in called *Vanished Days*, the one in which, having poisoned her husband, she descended the stairs to receive the news of his death. 'This idea first came to me – and you can imagine the potential consequences for criminalistics! – when I was working on the case of the West Indian omphaloclast, wherein I ran into the problem of the exact – what are you smiling about?'

'I'm sorry. I was thinking of . . .'

'You wouldn't think it was funny if you'd been one of his victims!'

'No . . .' At the first rehearsal, she'd come bouncing down the stairs and crossed over to the guy who'd brought the news, reached into his pants, and given him a twist that had sent him yowling and stumbling into the wings. 'No, no, Ros!' the director had shouted. 'You're supposed to grab up the *clock* and wind it!' Or such at least was the legend. One of them . . .

'He actually cut them out and *ate* the bloody things!' As though finding it distasteful, the Inspector took the cold pipe out of his mouth. 'The point was, I couldn't pin down the exact moment when it happened. I could not even *imagine* it! One moment the knife was *outside* the flesh' – he demonstrated this, using his pipestem against his stomach – 'and then it was *inside:* but what was that moment in between when it was *neither?*' I too could not imagine this. I could not even make the effort.

Ros was wholly on my mind again, and I could only recall the poignancy of her hugs, the taut silkiness of the flesh around her own navel, the rich juicy flow that filled my mouth as her clitoris stabbed my tongue, and now (in another version, of course, it was not a clock, but –) – '*Stabbed!*' he cried. 'What does it *mean?* If we say, he, the murderer, *is stabbing* her, there are at least twenty ways of verifying it, but if we say he . . .' I had started violently with his first word, thinking I must have been talking out loud, and now he watched me intently. 'Is something— ?'

'No! Sorry, I . . . I was just thinking about your idea of time . . .' Trying to anyway. I couldn't seem to concentrate. The two policemen were putting Howard's shoes back on. His crushed spectacles stared up at me from the carpet beside a roadmap of Provence and a torn zipper. 'A stage, you said, a kind of space – like a fourth dimension—'

'Not fourth – *first!*'

'Yes, well, I mean the idea of events just being there, waiting for us, like stations we keep pulling into—'

'That's correct. Crimes, for example . . .' He peered up at me over his handlebar moustache and white silk scarf, his pate gleaming in the subdued light. He had returned his pipe to the ashtray and seemed to be shuffling watches like cards. We were alone, his two assistants having hauled Howard from the room, feet first, like an old sack. '*Murders* . . .'

'And – and their solutions.' It was very quiet. Fred's soup bubbled. Roger, fallen on his neck, stared at us vacantly. I lowered my voice. 'Or not: the failure to solve them. Also there waiting. Which would make us just passive observers, and you seem, well . . . more *willful* than that . . .'

'On the contrary. Will, free or otherwise, is just as much a hallucination as flowing time is, or change or meaning. Detectives, like criminals, are born, not made, for even the social forces that might be said to shape them are also part of their birthright. When we in the trade speak, for example, of the "perpetrator" of a crime, we are really speaking not of this or that actor like some character in a play, but rather of certain innate traits and tendencies borne by various individuals like seed, like wavelengths, like the properties of theorems – my curiosity, for instance, or your solicitude and hedonism.'

'I don't think that's—'

'Don't take offense. I'm merely trying to say that I am swept along by the seeming restlessness of matter like everyone else. My investigative labors may define me, but they do not account for my success. Indeed, my most famous solutions to crimes have come to me quite unexpectedly, like gifts. Visions. I use science as a discipline, but only to prepare myself as a vessel for intuition. This is the secret of all great detective work, I might say, and the most important clues, therefore, are not facts, but rather what you might call 'impressions of radiance' – like my rather luminous apprehension here tonight of some unspeakable crime-within-a-crime, some dalliance, as it were – or so I feel – with *oblivion itself!*' He watched me with that same close intensity as before, and I felt my mouth twitch involuntarily into a half-smile.

'But then—'

He looked away as though dismissing me, concentrating instead on his watches, enlarging upon his diagram: he was crossing his arrow now with a perpendicular row. 'I don't know what it is that perceives these things. I don't feel any personal identity – any "I" or "me" – I feel simply that I stand at a crossroads on this map of time – that I *am* a crossroads, that we *all* are – do you follow?' He glanced up, transfixing me with the vehemence of his gaze. 'I realize that it is not easy, that it takes an exceptional mind . . .' I chose not to contradict him, but as he returned to his display, sliding the watches from the arrow's leading edge into the middle, adding others to form a kind of field, fretted with straps and chains and buckles, I recalled a history teacher we once had who accused us of 'attending to the head of the arrow to the neglect of its tail' – which at the time we all took as a dirty joke. 'What I want – *all* I want, really – is to *see time!*' He hovered tensely above the field of watches, his hands outspread as though to scoop them all up, seeming almost to tremble with greed – and indeed they did give an illusion, all ticking, clicking, or pulsing away, of a plenitude. 'Yes . . .' He concentrated on them, his eyes narrowing. 'Now . . .' Beads of perspiration appeared on his brow and the top of his head. I, too, concentrated, afraid to move. 'Eeny,' he intoned gravely, his hands quivering rigidly in fiercely contested restraint, 'meeny, miny . . .' He reached, as though through some dense magnetic storm, for a watch. '*Mo!*' My wife's.

'Hey, look, Leonard! It's our old buddy Nigel!' Soapie shouted from the doorway, blowing in like a sudden gale: the Inspector stiffened momentarily as though buffeted, then sat back, folding his arms. Fred and Bob, who had dragged Howard out, now dragged him in again: 'Excuse us, Chief – they wanta restage this guy's examination so as to get some photos.' Pardew, his brow damp, nodded his permission, watching Soapie warily as the reporter kicked through the papers on the floor in his tattered sneakers, picked up a Mexican rattle – a dried gourd that looked like a tattooed testicle – and shook it, peered into Bob's microscope, and sniffed specimen bottles, the two policemen meanwhile hauling Howard, his feet trailing behind him, over to the work area and opening him up again. Soapie tested a magnet out on a row of needles and probes, then on Leonard's crotch – Leonard rolled his eyes, still firing away, his feet seeming to lift off the floor and fall back again – finally on the display of watches on the desk between Pardew and me. 'What's old shortcake trying to palm off on you here, Ger?' Soapie laughed as a watch jumped to his magnet. He pocketed the watch and magnet and, admiring the photos hanging from the line, lit up a cigarette, Leonard's flashgun popping away the while like magnesium bubbles. 'So whaddaya got, Nige? Who done it?'

'We have several leads,' replied the Inspector frostily, 'but we are still pursuing our inquiries.'

'Yeah? Well, what about fatty here with the red tie and inky dingdong?'

'What about him?'

'You know, abusing the habeas corpus like that, like maybe he was returning to what you might call the scene of the crime – and then, he's obviously banged to the bung—'

Inspector Pardew leaped to his feet. 'We are not jumping to any half-baked conclusions! We are not peddling headlines here – we are seeking the *truth!* '

'Awright, awright, calm down— !'

'Holistic criminalistics *rejects* these narrow localized cause-and-effect fictions popularized by the media! Do you think that poor child in there died because of some arbitrary indeterminate and random act? Oh no, *nothing* in the *world* happens that way! It is just by such simple atavistic thinking that we fill our morgues and prisons, missing the point, solving nothing!' Pardew stormed about the room, waving his arms. Soapie whipped out his notebook. 'Murder, like laughter, is a muscular solution of conflict, biologically substantial and inevitable, a psychologically imperative and, in the case of murder, death-dealing act that *must* be related to the *total ontological reality!*'

'Hold up, hold up!' cried Soapie, scribbling away frantically, hat tipped back and cigarette between his teeth. 'Jesus! How do you spell "interterminant"?'

'This death tonight was a violent but dynamically predetermined invasion of what we criminologists call a self-contained system of ritually proscribed behavior in which the parts are linked by implacable forces and the behavior of the whole is *precisely* defined by the laws of social etiology – and I *assure* you, we are *not* going to be pressured by any *hack scandalmongers* into abrogating our broader *responsibilities* and jumping to unwarranted and even irrelevant parochial *conclusions!*'

'Whoa-ho-ho!' laughed Soapie, his pencil waggling frantically across the pad in his hand. 'Violent total antilogical, uh, irreverent system . . . whew! I don't know what any of this malarkey's about, Nigel, by golly, but it should knock 'em out on the funny pages!' He dotted a few *i*'s, flicked his butt away, and, slapping his notebook shut, nodded at Leonard, who had been photographing the Inspector's bristly tirade through a foreground of test tubes and beakers. 'C'mon, Leonard, let's go get a coupla skin shots of these impeccable faucets, and then have us something to eat. Ger's old lady puts out a handsome spread.'

'Stick around,' Fred urged, coming back in with Bob, the two of them having just dumped Howard outside the door, 'this one's next!'

'Nah,' grinned Soapie, winking at me. 'He's old hat.'

'*Those shameless egotistical frauds!*' shrieked the Inspector when the two newsmen had left, and then, in a fit of decompressed rage, he began to beat his head against the far wall. '*Filthy bloated mythomaniacs who feed like dogs off the excrement of their own vile lies!*' I thought this might be a good moment to slip away, but before I could make my move, the Inspector whirled around and cried: '*Seize him!*'

'*No, wait—!*' But they had already grabbed me, twisted my arm behind my back, and were highstepping me over to their work area, my feet barely touching the floor. '*Don't—!*'

'Easy, pal!'

'We don't want to have to get rough!'

The Inspector, who was striking his temples with his fists and groaning something about 'dark fissures of the soul' and 'massive spiritual de-formity,' now threw a sheaf of photographs on the table in front of me and, jabbing a tremulous finger at the erected penis that Ros, dressed as a telephone operator, was holding in her ear, cried: 'Whose *is* that?!'

'I – I don't know,' I stammered, mine being the one she was speaking into.

'And *that!!*' he demanded, pointing now at Ros's pumping fist in a photo of the *Pietà*, then at one of Little Miss Muffet with what looked like a lamb under her skirt: 'And *this!*'

'Actually, uh, that one's from a show, I believe – a publicity still – *The Mother Goo—*'

'*What are you trying to hide?*' he screamed, banging his fists on the table, making the photos fly.

Bob tightened his grip on my arm, Fred whipped out his nightstick. '*Nothing!*'

'Nothing? *Nothing?* Then how do you explain *this?!*' he cried, flinging a valentine onto the table.

'Where did you find that?' I gasped. It was one I had given my wife long ago – I recognized the 'honeymoon hotel' with its heart-shaped shutters, a private joke: there'd been a heart-shaped hole in the door of the outhouse we had to use . . .

'Next to the body!'

'Ah, that must be the one Naomi—'

'We *know* what it is! Do you take us for *fools?* Do you *deny* you knew the victim?'

'Of course not! She's—'

'She's *dead!* I *know* that! But I need to know *how!* And *when!* Now for the last time: what have you *seen?* Eh? *What have you heard?*'

Bob tightened his grip again; Fred, still wearing the dusty rubber gloves, grabbed my belt with one hand, brought the nightstick crashing down on the table with the other – '*Dickie!*' I yelped. It was all I could think of. I could hardly breathe. I felt like I'd reflexed my testicles all the way into my ribcage. 'Somebody said— !'

'Dickie?'

They eyed me narrowly. I felt betrayed by my own desperation, ashamed of the outburst. I swallowed. 'Actually—'

'That the lily-dip in the white ducks?' grunted Bob behind my back.

'Yes,' I squeaked, 'but I only . . . Mrs Trainer said—'

Fred shook his head. 'Nothing there, Chief. We checked him out. Double on-tonder.'

'What – ?! More *lies*?!' I felt relief, even as Bob threw his free arm around my throat, half-strangling me. 'I tell you, I can't *stand* lies! They turn our consciousness to *rot* and *putrefy the spirit!* He waved a photo in front of my face of a round-helmeted cop being buggered by a masked superhero: 'Now, who *is* that?'

Bob squeezed, arching my back, and all I could see was the ceiling. Fred, sucking in wind, drew his arm back. 'I . . . I can *explain— ?*'

'Explain? *Explain?*' the Inspector raged. The ceiling seemed to be pulsating and a chemical pungency filled the air. '*Open him up!*

'*No, just a minute!*' I gasped. I groped for my buckle – 'In the end, Gerry,' my father used to say, 'we *reach* for the inevitable' – and Fred took his hand away. 'I'll . . . I'll do it . . .'

They seemed to accept this. Fred lowered his stick. Bob loosened his grip slightly, though he kept his arm around me. 'Awright,' he growled, '*out with it!*'

The three of them pressed round, boxing me in. We were all breathing heavily. On the wall in front of me they'd tacked up their charts for spectrochemical analysis: they looked like indictments, columnar and menacing, with something penciled in across the top. I studied it without seeing it, my hands at my buckle. I might as well get it over with, I thought. Who knows, I might not even be recognized. But I didn't believe it. I felt betrayed somehow. A kind of inconsolable dismay swept over me, and a loneliness, as I reached, my eyes misting over (I'd had dreams like this: some final crowded-up demand, my will erased), for my zipper.

Bob and Fred backed off, laughing. The Inspector, too, relaxed, laid a restraining hand on mine. 'That's all right,' he said quietly. 'We know it's not you. We showed your wife the photos and she said definitely not.'

'We were just kidding,' said Fred.

'Ah . . .' My heart was still in my throat. I wiped my eyes. The penciled-in notation on the chart read: 'Never confuse the objective with the subjective sections of the protocol.' It sounded like a line from a play.

'Naturally, we would appreciate any help you could give us,' said Pardew, filling his pipe from a small saclike pouch. I settled back. I'd been standing on my toes all this time, and somehow this had added to my sense of isolation and vague nameless guilt.

Bob had limped away to switch off the lamp on the microscope, shutting down the show there, and now gathered up some little boxes, plastic bags, and tools. 'Shall I knock the teeth out before we bag her up,' he asked, 'or save it till later?'

'Might as well do it now. What about the cast?'

'The stuff's ready,' said Fred at the hot plate, stirring (I could hear music now, conversations, people shouting on the stairs: where had they been before?). 'You want the whole chest or just— ?'

'All of it.' The Inspector tamped the tobacco into the bowl with his little finger. He seemed to be studying one of the odd inky prints the cops had taken. I was still having trouble breathing, and I wasn't sure my knees were going to hold me; at such times I resented my gentility, yet understood that often as not it had spared me worse. 'Be sure to get the angle of penetration.'

'I'll help with that, Fred,' said Bob, tucking his tools in his armpit.

'Careful, it's hot . . .'

'I want to thank you for coming in,' Pardew said as they left. He settled his pipe in under his drooping moustaches (I heard a glass break, laughter, someone said: 'Don't try to explain . . .'), fumbled in his pockets. 'It's been good to have someone to talk to, someone who understands . . .'

'Well, I only—'

He smiled. 'You've been more help than you know. Got a match?'

'No, sorry . . .' I slapped my ribs pointlessly.

He poked about the shelves, the worktable, finally lit his pipe from a Bunsen burner. I mopped my brow with the handkerchief I realized too late had been the one used by the Inspector, thinking (not for the first time at a party like this): I should make better use of my time than this. 'Like all intellectual pursuits,' he said around start-up puffs (there seemed to be a growing agitation outside, as though to set off the deep stillness here in my study), 'this is a lonely and thankless profession, a daily encounter with depravity, cruelty, and sudden—'

Fred burst in, looking sweaty, his eyes popping: *'They're trying to take the body away!'* he cried, then rushed out again.

'What – ?!' the Inspector roared, rearing up, his moustaches bristling.

'It's probably only the ambulance men,' I offered, but he pushed me aside and strode out in the wake of his assistant, his fists clenched and jaws set, white scarf fluttering.

★

People – some of whom I didn't even know – were piling down the stairs, thumping out of the kitchen, rushing for the living room where there was a great commotion. *'Stop them!'* they cried. *'Oh my god!'* 'He was using a hammer on her *mouth!'* In the middle of the room, two white-jacketed men and Jim were trying to lift Ros's body onto a stretcher, but the two police officers, grabbing a limb each, had engaged them in a kind of grisly tug-of-war. *'The Inspector* – grunt! – *says she stays!'*

'Sorry, pal! We got orders!'

'Oof!'

'Do something, Gerry! I can't *take* this!'

Talbot and Fats and some guy in a gray chalkstriped suit with a lilac shirt (he was familiar, I'd seen him somewhere before) were already trying to do something, struggling clumsily with the two policemen ('Talbot! You come out of there right this minute!' Wilma fussed from the side-lines), and Pardew now stepped into the melee on the other side, strad-dling one of Ros's arms (her hands were wrapped now in plastic bags, I saw, her feet as well, and her front was splotched with drying plaster as though someone had hit her with a custard pie), a long finger jabbed at Jim's lapel: 'I must warn you that any further interference will be viewed as *a criminal breach of the law!'*

'I'm *not* interfering, damn you, I'm *trying* to –'

But just then Vic strolled in ('Oh boy! look out!' squawked Yvonne, 'it's the Grim Raper!'), walked serenely up to Fred in time to the dance tune playing on the hi-fi, and chopped him – *kthuck!* – in the back of the neck. *'Yow!* Crikey, you didn't have to do *that!'* Fred howled, crumpling.

Bob let go of the body, whipped out his revolver, backed off in a crouch: *'Anybody move—!'*

Vic smiled, showing his teeth, then turned and walked nonchalantly away toward the dining room, his back to the cop. It was so quiet you could hear ice clinking somewhere in an empty glass. 'Jeez,' Fred whimpered, all curled up on the floor, hands behind his head (Jim, also ignoring the drawn weapon, knelt to examine his neck), 'we're only doing our job, for cripe's sake!'

'He's going to go too goddamned far if he doesn't watch out,' Noble grumbled to Eileen, standing listlessly by. 'What?' she asked absently, and picked up Vic's drink, which he'd left behind. Bob fired, shattering the glass: Noble threw himself down heavily behind the couch, and someone screamed, but Eileen seemed not to notice what had happened, staring in bruised puzzlement at her dripping hand and what was left of the glass. 'Give that boy a silver dollar!' Yvonne applauded from the couch, and Talbot in his drunken stupor (Wilma seemed to be feeding him aspirin by the spoonful) joined in, slapping his hands together loosely like a trained seal. 'I'm sorry,' Eileen said, and Fats, watching Bob warily, lit up a thick black cigar. 'Or maybe . . . maybe I'm not sorry . . .'

'Please,' I urged, but no one seemed to be listening. I felt locked into one of Pardew's space–time configurations, where the only thing moving was my perception of it. The Inspector had knelt beside Jim and the injured officer (Jim was fitting him with a kind of neckbrace, using a pillow from the couch and attaching it with a woman's garter belt – might have been my wife's), and Bob, covering us with his gun, now loped over to join them, leaving the two ambulance men free to carry on with removing Ros's corpse. But even as they heaved the body onto the stretcher (so light: she seemed almost to float, her torso rising and falling airily), Regina appeared in the doorway with her friends Zack Quagg, the playwright-director, and the actor Malcolm Mee, Quagg with his famous purple cape pulled on over a white unitard, Malcolm in faded blue jeans and a striped sailor shirt. Quagg was normal enough (not that my wife thought so: once in a performance he had stepped down into the audience and slapped her face with a dead fish), but Mee always struck me as dangerously homicidal. Just the parts he tended to play maybe, but his cold glassy stare and the scar on his cheek always sent a chill down my spine. Regina, hand to mouth and face averted, was pointing across the room at Ros, long white finger quivering, and Quagg, following it, swept into the room, his eyes ablaze. 'What kinda two-bit tank show *is* this?' he cried, shoving the ambulance men aside. 'That's my *star!*'

'Hey, wait a minute— !'

'Get these greaseballs *outa* here!' Quagg yelled, swinging wildly, but before he could hit anything, Fats locked him in a bearhug: 'Whoa! *Cool* it, Zack!'

'Whose company you *in*, Fats?' Quagg grunted, as Talbot staggered blearily away from Wilma and threw himself at everybody: Mee, his face icily deadpan, lashed out with a whistling left hook and knocked him cold. Anatole was there too now, thin and pale in his all-black get-up, Earl Elstob grinning stupidly at his elbow with his fists cocked. On the hi-fi, somebody was singing something about 'needing someone to talk to,' and I thought: maybe it would help if I just changed the record. 'The doc wants her tucked away outa the lights, Zack – it's no *good* for her here!' Fats gasped around his cigar, and the woman in yellow came up and kicked him in the shins. '*OW!*'

I stepped forward to explain, somewhat disquieted by the odd sensation of walking through a grid of intersecting vectors, just as Bob sprang up out of his half-crouch next to Fred, swinging the butt of his pistol: he'd have got me had not Ginger at that same moment crossed between us, wobbling on her high heels and holding the tattered remains of her costume together with both hands, and short-circuited the cop, who fell between her legs like trapped game. I ducked and they struck Anatole in their fall, propelling him into a scuffle between Mee and one of the ambulance men ('Stop that! Stop that!' I could hear Patrick shrieking over the uproar). Ginger, when she hit the carpet with Bob on her, squeaked airily as though getting her noise button squeezed, the officer cursing when his head knocked bonily on hers. 'Yuh huh,' said Earl Elstob, stumbling over Talbot, tangled up in Quagg's cape. Dolph wandered in sleepily, wearing one of my ski sweaters and opening a beer can: 'Christ, what's been going *on* down here?' Leonard, who'd been taking cheesecake shots of Daffie straddling the back of an easy chair as though horsed over it, turned away to get one of Ginger with her eyes crossed, lips puckered, and skinny legs straight up in the air like spiky red signposts, Bob between them seemingly humping away, but really just trying, in vain, to get his short leg under him. Daffie slid off the chair, walked over (Noble from behind the couch was telling someone to shut up), and kicked the cop in the face, and his gun went off again, shooting the cigar out of Fats' mouth.

'Wha— ?!' Fats exclaimed, feeling the bulb of his nose speculatively, and some guy in the doorway threw his hands up and whooped: 'Hey, I like the *pitch!*' I recognized him: the actor who'd played the wind-up sergeant-major in Quagg's soft-core production of *The Naughty Dollies' Nightmare*. Gudrun the makeup artist and a plump actress in a toga and a pair of oversize rubber galoshes, worn like slap-shoes, crowded up behind him. Knud's wife, Kitty, shouting something about official rape, had meanwhile leaped on the cop between Ginger's legs and was pulling on his ears, and now Earl Elstob, seemingly misreading everything, jumped on Kitty, pushing her skirt up. 'Can you use some talent, Zack?' hollered the actor, as he elbowed in.

'Yeah,' shouted Quagg, trying to wrest the stretcher grips away from the man in the lilac shirt, 'but first get the word out, Jacko: Ros has been ragged! Go call Hoo-Sin and Vachel and get them over here! And anyone else you can think of!'

'I'll do it!' said Regina, appearing in the doorway at the actor's elbow, and, released, he came bounding over, eyes aglitter and a smile on one side of his mouth – '*Ha ha! Hold up the exits!*' he howled – and flung himself at the lilac-shirted man.

Brenda, bending over to drag Elstob off Kitty (she'd let go the cop's ears and was struggling to keep her underpants on), suddenly yelped, spun around, and laid into Patrick. '*You little creep!*' she screamed, her fists flying.

'*It wasn't me!*' he blubbered, his split mouth bleeding anew, as Dolph slipped away (I felt Alison near me again and wondered if she understood, relative stranger here though she herself was, what was happening, and if that was why she'd drawn close to me again), sipping beer. Mee, standing on Anatole's face ('Can't somebody *do* something?' Wilma was wailing: Talbot was under there somewhere, too), seemed to be strangling one of the ambulance men – the other one had tackled Quagg and they had fallen over Ros, her plastic-mittened extremities flopping, her face masked in chipped plaster which bearded her throat and chest as well, and I felt (as a soft belly pressed up against my buttocks) newly sorrowed: 'It's almost sad,' she used to say after oral sex, 'that it tastes so good.'

'That's enough!' someone cried. 'You don't know what you're doing!'

'Someone should go get Cyril!'

'Hold the bimbo down, Malcolm, while I—'

'Wait a minute! I – *unff!* – I got an idea!'

The word 'crepitus' came to me just then, the word I'd been trying to recall since I'd first seen Yvonne on the landing (they were talking about her now, the punch-up was slackening and there were negotiations under way), and with it came a general sense of loss that embraced Ros, Tania, Yvonne, my mother and grandmother, life itself in its fleeting brevity, its ruthless erosions. Yes, I thought as arms encircled my waist, a hand slid under my shirt (Bob was getting to his feet at last, using Ginger's legs for crutches, exposing the fat little red purse between them:

it was expanding and contracting rhythmically like someone chewing), it's true: love is indeed, as a woman once whispered to me (from our balcony we could hear mullahs in minarets singing the sun down: the setting, coming back to me now like a fragrance in the air, was ripe for such sentiments), the tragic passion – not for her reasons of course (she had just left her husband to spend a strange, fleeting, but beautiful week with me in Istanbul, which was perhaps, though I'd forgotten it until now, the most beautiful week of my life), but because of its ultimate inadequacy: for all its magic, love was not, in this abrasive and crepitant world, enough. And was that, I wondered as one gentle hand caressed my nipple, the other burrowed below my belt (Ros had been abandoned and with her the free-for-all as well, people were picking themselves up, groaning, laughing – '*Hoo-eee!* that was a real dingdong!' – and the ambulance men, breathing heavily, had turned their attentions to Yvonne: 'Sure, why not? They told us to – *whoof!* – pick up a body, but they – *gasp!* – didn't say which!'), the source of its strangely powerful appeal: its own tragic inadequacy? The question itself was resonant with passionate implications, tragic or otherwise, but even as I turned to share them (out of the corner of my eye I glimpsed my son Mark, one of my ski caps down around his ears, eating things off the floor, my mother-in-law dragging him over toward me, something clutched in her white fist), Yvonne cursing raucously, screaming for help, Jim distracted by his efforts to bring Talbot around, I realized that it was not vermouth I'd been smelling (Alison in fact was watching me from the dining room doorway, looking somewhat startled), but bubble gum. 'Damn it, Sally Ann, this is no time for adolescent vamping!' I exclaimed, tearing her hands away. 'People are hurt here! Your own father— !'

'Oh, crumbs, Gerry! Stop treating me like a child! I mean, I only want to make love with you – is that so awful?'

'I just won't have it!' my mother-in-law snapped, glaring at Sally Ann's hands on my belt. She held up the ice pick like a denunciation: 'He was playing with *this!*'

'Ah— !'

'I'll take it,' said Sally Ann quietly, dropping it in her shirt. There was a patch now over the breast pocket that said: 'HANDS OFF UNLESS YOU MEAN BUSINESS.' I glanced over at Alison, but she was watching the ambulance men, a pained look in her eyes.

'Where did it come from, Daddy?'

'I – I'm not sure . . .' Fred was turning round and round, trying to get used to his neckbrace; at his feet, the Inspector was tying a plastic bag around Ros's head. 'Hey, man, what gig you working here?' Quagg wanted to know. 'What's that you're eating, son?'

'Hormone tablets,' my mother-in-law replied icily, speaking up to be heard over Yvonne's bawling as the ambulance men stretchered her away. 'And before that it was some kind of *foot* ointment!'

'No, hey, I *like* it, it's *got* something!'

'Ow, what happened?' Talbot moaned, then coughed and gagged. Jim was holding something to his nose. 'Who did I hit?'

'All you hit was that young man's fist with your silly face,' sniffed Wilma. 'And then the floor.'

'Hard, though – right? *Hard!* Ooohh . . . !'

'Take another whiff of this,' Jim said, and Talbot snorted and gagged again.

'*Gerry* – ? Do something! *Help me!*' I caught just a glimpse of the terror on her stricken face ('You know what I hate most, Gerald?' my mother once exclaimed – maybe the expression on Yvonne's face had made me think of it – 'What I really hate is *having a good time!*') as they squeezed her through the door into the hall, past the new arrivals pressing in. 'Man, somebody really chewed up the scenery in here!' one of them said: Scarborough, Quagg's lugubrious baggy-eyed set designer. He looked around as though measuring the space.

'If this is a party, Daddy, why aren't there any balloons?'

'Yeah, there was some guy went crazy, Scar . . .'

'*I'll be good! I won't complain!*'

'I didn't realize it would hurt so much,' Anatole whimpered, holding his mouth as though to keep his teeth from falling out.

'Here, try this, Mark,' Sally Ann suggested, picking up one of the condoms Naomi had dropped earlier in the evening. Alison had vanished, and in her place Ginger was just wobbling out of the room on her high red heels, her pigtails bent askew, the cheeks of her narrow behind peeping out through gaps in her costume, looking carpet-burned, others drifting away as well.

'Whoo! After all that excitement, I think I'm gonna hafta go out back and – *wurp!* – table a motion!'

Mark puffed futilely into the condom, then handed it back to Sally Ann. 'The hole's too big.'

'*What*— ?!' Brenda cried.

The tall cop was crawling around on his hands and knees. 'I lost her goddamn teeth,' he grumped.

'It's also fun to fill them up with water,' Sally Ann whispered conspiratorially, 'and drop them like bombs!' Mark grinned, his eyes lighting up under the woolly fringes of the ski cap, and my mother-in-law said: 'That's not clean! It was on the floor!' She looked up at me accusingly. 'Daddy, who's the lady in the bathtub?'

'No one, pal – now you get to bed.' I took his hand and led him toward the door, Brenda crying behind me: 'Oh no! My god, where's Fats? *Fats?!*' just as Yvonne in the hallway in front of us ('Last Year's Valentine' was playing on the hi-fi, a silly nostalgic song about time and loss, and it reminded me somehow of something Tania had once said to me about the way language distorts reality: 'I know we can't survive without it, Gerry, probably we even need all those fictions of tense embedded in the goddamn grammar – but art's great task is to reconcile us to the true *human* time of *the eternal present*, which the child in us *knows* to be the *real* one!' – which is why, paradoxically, she had always defended abstraction as the quintessence of realism) cried: '*Woody*— ?!'

'Fats said he was flyin' light,' someone said. 'I think he went to put on the nosebag.'

'*Fats*— ?!' Brenda cried, charging off toward the dining room. 'You won't *believe* it!'

'Don't let them take me away, Woody! *Please!*'

Woody and Cynthia were standing on the stairs a step or two below the landing, holding hands in their underwear, Woody in stolid boxer shorts and ribbed undershirt, Cynthia in a heavily cross-strapped brassiere and old-fashioned umbrella-shaped lace drawers, seemingly stunned into a kind of grave compassionate silence. '*Cyn*— ?! Christ all Jesus, *don't just stand there!*' There were tears in Cynthia's eyes now as she took Woody's stubby hand in both of hers (their heavy ornamentation made her hands now seem more overdressed than ever), sliding partway behind him and nuzzling her pale cheek against his bare dark-tufted shoulder. '*Help me! WOODY*— ?!'

'Daddy, why is the lady all tied up? Did she do something bad— ?'

'No, son, she—'

'*Gerry?!*' Yvonne wailed, spying me past the others, her eyes raw, her gray hair stringy and wild. She had grabbed onto the front doorjamb, and the ambulance men were now prying her hand loose. 'Goddamn it, Gerry, you *promised*— !'

'I – I'll get Jim,' I offered (and there was another thing about my mother: you could have anything she had, she was utterly unpossessive, thought of nothing in the world as exclusively her own – but she never, ever – this came to me now, and I felt, oddly as if for the first time, the unfairness of it – gave anyone any presents), but before I could let go of my son's hand, Charley Trainer came tumbling noisily down the stairs, my bathrobe stretched tight around his flab, shouting: '*Whuzz happenin'? Whuzz goin' on downair?*'

'*Charley! It's me! Help!*' Yvonne bawled from the front porch even as the door swung shut behind her, her voice disappearing as though into a tunnel, and Charley yelled: '*Hole on, Yvonne! God-DAMN it! Ole Chooch is comin'!*' But his knees started to cave about halfway down to the landing and there was no negotiating the right-angle turn there – Woody and Cynthia ducked, clinging to each other, as he went hurtling past behind them, smacking the banister with his soft belly and somersaulting on over the railing to the floor below: '*PpFOOOFF!*' he wheezed mightily as he landed on his back (I'd managed to jerk Mark out of the way just in time), bathrobe gaping and big soft genitals bouncing between his fat legs as though hurling them to the floor had been his whole intent. 'Ohh, shit!' he gasped (Mark was laughing and clapping, my wife's mother shushing him peevishly), lying there pale and, except for the aftershock vibrations still rippling through his flaccid abdomen, utterly prostrate: '*Now* wha've I done . . . ?!'

'Careful, just lie still a moment,' Jim cautioned, kneeling by his side and palpating gently his neck and collarbone, while above them Cynthia was saying (Woody seemed to be putting yet another ring on one of her fingers): 'Woody, you shouldn't . . .'

'Who the hell was runnin' innerference?' Charley groaned, as Jim reached under and ran his hand slowly down his broad back.

The phone rang, but as I turned to answer it, Fats and Brenda, tears streaming down their cheeks, came blundering through from the dining room, making us all fall back. 'Oh my *god*, Brenda,' Fats, stuffing the last half of a cheese-dog in his jaws, cried as he stumbled over Charley's upturned feet ('Unf! Get his goddamn nummer, coach!'), 'this is too *much!* Not *Tania*— !' And then, picking himself up, he staggered on up the stairs behind her, Woody and Cynthia pressing up against the banister to let them by. 'Yeah,' somebody was saying into the phone ('Woops! Damn!' Woody muttered as the ring slipped through the railings and hit the floor near Charley – 'Gerry, could you pass that up to me?'), 'it's Ros! A cold curtain, man – that's it, gone dark! You comin' over?'

'Hey, Ger,' Charley moaned softly as I dug under his ear for the ring: it was elaborately worked with a heavy stone, somehow familiar, 'I'm in trouble.'

'Right, Hoo-Sin's already here – just this minute walkin' on,' the guy on the phone was saying, out of sight now behind all the people gathering around, concerned about Charley, who still lay flat out, motionless, my bathrobe twisted around his thick torso like a bit of rind. 'Is it his heart?'

'Has to be – he's *all* heart, ole Chooch . . .'

'But I don't *wanna* go! I wanna see Unca Charley do it again!'

'And Gudrun, Prissy Loo, the Scar . . .'

'You'll be okay, Charley,' I said, handing the ring up to Woody ('Great – and bring Benedetto,' said the guy on the phone, 'we'll *need* a groaner!'), 'Jim's here, he—'

'Naw, I mean – didn't Tall-butt tell ya?' He was nearly crying, his eyes puffy, his nose purple. 'I juss found out . . . the reason ya can't take it with ya . . .'

'Ah,' said Jim, pausing thoughtfully in his trek down Charley's spine.

'. . . Is cuz *it* dies before *you* do!'

'He's got a slipped disc,' Jim said. 'We need to double his knees back and see if we can pop it back in place.' 'Oh my! let *me* help!' exclaimed Patrick, getting a laugh, just as Lloyd Draper stepped up and remarked down his nose: 'See here now, looks like you've had a little tumble, young fella!'

'Since Ros died, Ger, I juss can't . . . can't . . .'

'For goodness' sake, Charley!' cried his wife, Janice, padding in breathlessly, zipping up the side of her pink skirt. 'What have you been doing – trying to fly again?'

'Yeah,' he mumbled, winking at me through his tears ('Ros is the only one,' he used to say while reproaching himself, with that comical hangdog look in his eyes, for his clumsy haste and artlessness in lovemaking – 'The nicest thing about Charley,' Janice liked to say, 'is that there's none of that wham-bam-thank-you-ma'am stuff with him – it's always quicker than that!' – 'who's ever *thanked* me after . . .'), 'I awmoss had it there f'ra minute!'

'Hey, everybody!' Janny cried, bouncing up and down. 'Let's hear it for Choo-Choo Trainer!' She hiked her skirt and dropped into her cheerleader's squat, one arm out stiffly in front of her, the other cocked behind, and slowly, as Patrick and Jim took a grip on Charley's fat knees, got the old school locomotive going again. '*CHOO-oo-oo!*' Pause. '*CHOO-oo-oo!*' Yes, I thought as I watched Jim and Patrick, grunting, press Charley's knees back against his chest, the crowd in the hall all joining Janny now as she started to get up steam – 'Come on, everybody! *Choo-oo! Choo-oo!* That's it! *Choo-oo! Choo-oo!*' – time may or may not be passing, who's to say, but damn it, *something* is. '*Choo! Choo! Choo! Choo!*' Above us, Woody and Cynthia were kissing now, Woody holding her hips firmly yet somehow chastely in his square hairy hands, her hands resting on his shoulders as though knighting him with all her rings and bangles, and though there was an undeniable tenderness in their embrace and even a certain touching vulnerability in the plainness of their underwear, the neatness of their carefully combed hair, the very narrowness of the step on which they stood, there above the chugging Choo-Choo Trainer locomotive – '*CHOO-choo! CHOO-choo! CHOO-choo! CHOO-choo!*' – Charley himself now out of sight behind his upraised rump, Dolph helping out, lending his weight – '*CHOO-choo-CHOO-choo! CHOO-choo-CHOO-choo!*' – there was also something disturbing, almost shocking, about their imperturbable composure as they kissed so discreetly, so properly, that seemed suddenly to make Ros's death (*Oh! Oh! Oh!* I was thinking to the cheer's beat, *what have we lost— ?!*) all the more poignant and immediate, and I might well have started to get, joining red-nosed Charley, truly maudlin, had I not spied Naomi's cock sock on Alison's middle finger, beckoning me from the dining room doorway. '*CHOO-choo-CHOO-choo CHOO-CHOO-CHOO-CHOO!*' the crowd roared, Janny's arm working like a flying piston. 'Oh god, it hurts!' Charley cried, farting explosively ('Naughty boy!' exclaimed Patrick to everyone's delight) – and then in the sudden momentary silence that followed there was a hollow

KRR-POP!, a burst of cheers and laughter, and from Charley as they lowered his mass to the floor and covered him up with the robe, a grateful 'Oh, *yeah* . . . !' *'WHEE-EE-EE-ee-oo-OO-OO!'* the crowd shrilled in imitation of a train whistle, as Janny spun around then dropped into a still fairly passable split: *'CHOO-CHOO TRAINER!'*

While the crowd around Charley whistled and clapped, I slipped away toward the back, nearly bumping into Steve the plumber coming up from the basement with a big monkey wrench in his hand. 'Hold on, hold on!' Inspector Pardew demanded behind me. 'Is that someone having a game of darts down there?'

'A couple of women, sir,' said Steve, 'if you can call it a game.'

'Hey, there,' breathed Alison ('One of them's probably her, all right,' Bob was saying in back of me, while at our feet, Anatole, squatting down, asked: 'You all right, Uncle Howard?'), 'I've been looking for you, Superlover!'

'Ah, that must be my son you want.'

'I assumed it ran in the family.' The crowd around Charley was breaking up, many of them headed past us into the dining room ('No, no, no, no, *no!*' Howard blurted out petulantly, as though waking suddenly from a bad dream, or perhaps just talking in his sleep – Iris Draper was there, trying to feed him some soup), where Jim's wife Mavis was holding court, seemingly her old self once more. I could see people slipping in and out of the TV room with big grins on their faces and pausing, as they passed, to hear what Mavis had to say. Soapie was filling a brown bag with food from the table.

'Hey, Prissy Loo! I thought you took the veil!'

'No, some guy held me in escrow a while, that's all. Where'd you find the bug broth?'

'Yup,' said Bob. 'We're all set up for her.'

'In here, there's buckets of it . . .'

Alison drilled my chest with her stiffened peckersweatered finger, parodying recruitment posters: 'I want *you*, Gerald!' she declared throatily, clutching my belt with her free hand and knocking her pubes on mine. Which seemed to set off the phone: Regina answered it, Pardew saying: 'Very well, you'd best get on with it then.' 'It's *show* time, Mister Bones! When do we open?'

'As soon as we can get off centerstage.' I lifted the pointing finger to my mouth to tongue the base of it, under the sweater. I realized it had the same pattern as one of my ski caps. She spread her fingers and her breasts rose and fell in their silk pockets, as her eyes, sparkling, searched mine. 'Hey, what's goin' down here, Vagina?' cried someone, banging in through the front door behind us, his voice small and squeaky. 'Show me the card!' 'In the living room, Vachel! It's Ros!' '*Ros—* ?' 'Only one problem,' I murmured through her fingers, 'I have to use the bathroom so badly my teeth are chiming!'

'Me, too,' she admitted, letting go my belt to give her crotch a demonstrative little squeeze, 'but they've turned this one into a darkroom, and upstairs . . .'

'Hey, that's cute,' said Soapie, taking the sock off Alison's finger and peeking inside, then handing it back. 'I could use one of those to keep my pencils warm.' He was cradling a greasy paper sack full of food and an unopened bottle of scotch. Alison had curled round under my far arm, and now ran her hand up my back under my shirt (*'We can go out back,'* I whispered: '*Yes, let's!*' she urged), as Soapie poked his nose down the basement steps and asked: 'What's going on down below, d'you suppose?'

But we were already away, slipping through the kitchen door, Alison snatching up some paper cocktail napkins en route ('I always like something to read,' she smiled), Woody saying something as we passed about 'a lesson.' 'Yeah? Don't you believe it!' growled Vic, as the door whumped to behind us.

The kitchen seemed closed down for the night: things put away, counters clean, lights off and the room in shadows except for the nightlight on the oven and the fluorescent over the butcherblock table, pots and pans hung up, appliances set back under the cabinets. 'Your wife's such a great housekeeper,' Alison said, still whispering. 'I really envy her!' 'Well, this is a bit unusual,' I allowed. The general tidiness of the place was marred somewhat by the muddy tracks in and out of the back door: we were not the first, it seemed, to think of using the backyard. Also, now that I looked more closely, I could see that there was a pot simmering on a burner in the shadows, something cooking in the oven, some boiled eggs cooling on the counter near the sink, knives and tools laid out on the butcherblock, an apron – oilcloth, imprinted with foreign baggage stickers – draped over the breakfast bench. 'It's strange,' Alison murmured, turning to me as I paused, touched by some distant memory (but not of my wife, no – waiting for Ros in the wings during a performance of that toyland play, the toybox spotlit centerstage into which the other toys were all vanishing, Ros left on the floor outside, arms akimbo, as though forgotten . . .), 'but I feel as though I were standing at some crossroads – or, rather, that I *am* a crossroads in some odd way, through which the world is passing. Does that sound silly?' She put her arms around my neck. 'No.' I took her small silken waist in my hands. Blinking, she tongued her lips, which seemed to have swollen. There was a soft blush on her skin, a warm fragrance, and her breath came in quick little gasps. 'In fact, it's funny, but I was just thinking . . .' I let my hands slide down over her hips – then took them away again as her husband came in through the door behind her.

'Ah!' I said and cleared my throat. 'We were just, eh . . .'

'You've found your earring,' he said tersely, ignoring me.

'Yes, that nice man in the white pants discovered it for me,' she replied, turning dreamily toward him. 'On the living room floor – wasn't that lucky?' She smiled, touching the earring as though to show it to him, her free hand slipping into my back pocket to scratch subtly at my buttock, as though to sign her name there. 'We're just going out for some fresh air.'

'Yes, of course,' he said with an abrupt pinched smile, glancing at me, then away again. He seemed to want to look back over his shoulder, but restrained himself, pushing his hands into his jacket pockets, biting briefly at his beard. 'Watch where you step,' he added as he marched past us.

Alison took my hand and pulled me out into the darkness of the back porch. '*Hurry—!*' She tore my wrap-tie shirt open, flung her arms around my bare back. '*Kiss me!*' she begged, pulling herself upward to meet my mouth with hers. Her mouth was open, her tongue pushing between my teeth as though to mate there, her perfumed breath mingling with the nostalgic country odors of the backyard and the sweet scents sweeping up from within her dress. I clutched her body tight to mine – it was the right thing to do, I knew, the timing perfect! – and kissed her eyes, her cheeks, her mouth, her throat, my hands burrowing up under the whispering charmeuse skirt, childhood memories of camping trips, midnight hikes, forest dew, Inspiration Points filling my mind (it was a damp night, chilly, dense), and, her sash loosening, down into her tights. *'Oh Gerald!'* she gasped (her flesh down there was cool, sleek, so smooth it felt powdered, maybe it was, the fluff between her wriggling cheeks as soft as swansdown), jamming her hands inside my waistband, trying to, finally in frustration scrabbling frantically over the outside of my trousers ('No more rehearsals, Superlover,' I seemed to hear her say, 'I want climax, *I want the weenie!*' – but her mouth was pressed on mine), digging, fumbling for openings. I slid one hand around the curve of her hip onto her soft belly, and down into the damp velvety thatch between her thighs which heaved up to meet it, her legs spreading as in my mind's eye (and thus in truth! in truth!) they'd been spreading since the night we met. Yet even bare skin is a kind of mask, I thought wistfully, pushing deeper, my fingertips meeting, fore and aft, in the syrupy depths of her amazing furrow, maybe in fact it was something she had said that night during intermission: that desperate but futile effort (but I was trying, I was trying) to touch what can never be touched. I had suggested that night that theater, like all art, was kind of a hallucination at the service of reality, and that full appreciation of it required total abject surrender – like religion. 'Yes,' she'd said, setting her coffee cup down. 'Or love . . .' *'Oh fuck!'* she whimpered now, tearing wildly at my trousers, clawing my back, tugging at my testicles, while thrusting violently (it was, yes, this incredible impression of wholeness, this impression of radiance, of universal truth, the seeming apprehension of it, that surrender made possible, I thought, almost unable to think at all, unable to breathe – what had I just said?) into the little orifice I'd created with my two fingers and the bent knuckle of my thumb – *'You're the most beautiful man I've ever met!'* 'Alison— !' I groaned, pushing deeper from behind. '(*Gasp!*) A little . . . more— !'

Someone squeezed my hand and I jerked it away. It was Dickie, his white suit glowing spectrally in the dim light. 'Wondered what she was growing back there,' he said, lifting Alison's skirt to peer closer, playing the heckler, the hick in the gallery. 'Anyhow, I'm glad to see that, as an artist, Ger, you've got a good grasp of your subject.' He slapped her behind as though blessing it. I started to squeak out something, some- thing stupid probably, but he had already turned away. 'Hey, Hot Pot!'

he laughed, stepping down off the porch. 'Whaddaya say we go get some grass stains back behind the bushes!'

'It's filthy back there,' Sally Ann retorted. 'Like you, you creep!'

'Gerald,' Alison gasped hoarsely – she lay collapsed against my chest now, breathing deeply, my arms around her shoulders, hers around my hips, 'where can we go?'

'I'll have to think. They've taken over my study and—'

'How about the green room upstairs?'

'Green room?' I was still struggling to find my voice. I felt weirdly suspended, not quite outside time but not in it either.

'Where you kissed me . . .'

'Yes, the sewing room, okay . . .' Sally Ann stood nearby, staring – or probably staring, it was hard to tell – seemingly taken aback at finding us here, and I worried that if we didn't move, she wouldn't. 'But first . . .' I unlocked my arms (a titter of laughter floated out and I noticed again the chill in the air) and led Alison down off the porch – we were both a bit unsteady, our bodies still making moves of their own, our legs more or less elsewhere.

'Woops!'

'Steady now!'

It was a little brighter in the yard, lit up from inside, and I saw that her dress hem was caught in her tights: I pulled it out, smoothed it down, reveling (I don't like silk) in the feel of silk, and she cuddled closer. 'Can I hold it for you, Gerald?' 'Sure.' Anyway, she already was, leaning on it like a cane. A swaggerstick. If she'd let go, she'd probably have fallen down. There were others out here, whispering, chatting quietly back in the bushes, grunting, and I felt once more – though not so intensely as a moment ago with my hands between Alison's legs – that nostalgic flush of country memories: campouts, bike hikes, an all-night picnic back in college (the girl who'd held it for me that night had stupidly pinched it, trying, she'd claimed, to dot an i), sweet harvest evenings along the Rhine and the Douro, our Alpine honeymoon, star-gazing with my father at my grandmother's place ('Look, Gerry! there by the Fishes: the Chained Lady!'): there even seemed to be a fragrance of apples in the air.

I led Alison over toward a shadowy corner near the toolshed (there were muddy tracks everywhere, puddles, wadded-up cocktail napkins, cigarette butts), and she knelt to undo my fly. 'God! it's *gorgeous!*' she exclaimed softly as she opened up my shorts and let it fall out, pale as a stone pillar, into the night. She stroked it gently. I felt nothing: it was all puffed up, numb with excitement and anticipation. Inside, somebody squealed, and I could hear what sounded like the clacking of spoons, someone blowing on a sweet potato. A tall man stood, shadowed, in one gaping window, looking out as though to mirror me. 'Where shall we point it?' 'Well, away from the flowerbeds –' But she was gone. 'Alison— ?'

'Hate to tinkle all over your wife's garden,' rumbled Lloyd Draper, standing beside me, 'but I'm an old man and I just can't hold it in anymore.' I thought I heard her whispering behind me – I couldn't be sure, it might have been anyone: 'Is there room . . . ?' 'Sure, honey, sit down, sit down . . .' I looked around, but it was too dark to see anything but a few bushes, squatting like luminous trigrams, black at the roots. 'What's the matter, son? For a young lad, you seem to be having trouble making water there,' Lloyd remarked, squinting down through his bifocals. 'Oh, I see.' He spurted briefly, stopped, spurted again. 'Well, that takes me back a bit . . .'

'I just hope there isn't any poison ivy back here . . .'

'You avvertisin' that ugly tally-whacker, Big G, or juss givin' direck-shuns?' asked Charley, leaning boozily over my shoulder, my wife's dustmop under his arm as a crutch, Jim helping him at the other elbow.

'Yup, vanished days and all that . . .'

'Don't laugh, Charley. It hurts.'

'Seen a lot of 'em like that in my day,' sighed Lloyd, still squirting from time to time. 'They weren't workin' too well either, of course . . .'

'Who's laughin'? I'll trayja even'n throw in m'new alligator golfshoes b'sides!'

'Whoo-*EEEE!* Jes' call me Pipi' 'cuz Ah'm all *your'n!*' hooted Earl Elstob, joining us ('Thieves' hangouts, we called 'em in the trade . . .'), shooting a stream out over the flowerbeds and – *thrummm!* – against the toolshed wall. Jim and Charley were already firing away at shorter range and I was able at last to join in as well. Our radiant streams gleamed in the pallid glow from the windows (the man who had been standing there had disappeared) like a row of footlights. Tania had once spent six months on a painting she'd called 'The Garden,' trying to capture this glow, this strange yearning (she'd related it to what she'd called 'the sleeping dragon, the hidden force of nature'), and what she'd ended up with, she'd

said, was a fair facsimile of an illustration from a children's book she'd
had as a little girl.

'Hey, Earl,' laughed Charley, 'didja hear the one about the guy who
takes his wife to the theater, 'n atta – ha ha! – innermission—'

'The thee-ater?'

'Move over, ladies,' said Fats, joining us, 'I gotta re-hearse the scenery
here!'

'Yeah, 'n atta innermission he's gotta take a leak, so he hurries off to
the can. But he goes through a wrong door somehow 'n ends up inna
goddamn garden!'

'Oh yeah? Huh huh,' snorted Elstob from under his overbite, still
managing to hit the wall but no longer threatening to drill a hole through
it, and Fats, crossing Earl's stream with one of his own, said: 'Too-chay!'

'Well, the garden's very fancy, y'know – inna *French* style, as y'might
say—'

'Yuh huh hee,' Earl sniggered, jiggling around. Lloyd had left us, but
his place was taken almost immediately by a guy in corduroys and a
tweed jacket with suede elbows: 'This the place?' he asked, smiling
apologetically around his bent briar pipe, and someone in the bushes
behind us, grunting, said: 'Well – *ungh!* – there goes a little bit of
eternity . . .'

'And in a fancy garden like 'at, Earl, he don' wanna weewee onna
lotuses nor leave no nasty puddles around, right? So, real careful-like, he
lifts a plant out of a flowerpot 'n unloads in 'at, 'n'en putsa plant back
'n – hoff! – tippytoes back to his seat—'

'Sounds like the one about the audience catharsis at the tragical farces,'
remarked Jim, winding down.

'Yes,' I said, meaning something else. Alison had made some remark
about intermissions that night at the theater, giving them an importance
that haunted me now. 'Exactly . . .'

'Onlya goddamn play's awready started up again when he gess back
to his seat, see—'

'My name's Gottfried,' the man beside me offered, extending his free
hand. I changed hands and took it.

'Oh yes – you came with Fiona.'

''N he leans over to his ole lady,' Charley rumbled, leaning over
toward Earl, ''n he says to her, he says ('Fiona— ?'): "Hey, sugarpuss,

whuzz happen so far iniss act?"' What Alison had said that night we met, smiling up at me over her fresh cup of coffee, was that perhaps without intermissions there could *be* no catharsis in modern theater – and only much later did it occur to me ('I feel like all my energy's just leaking away,' someone murmured behind us, 'and it gives me a very mystical feeling, like I'm in tune with the universe or something . . .') that what she'd really said was 'intromissions' . . . ' "You oughta know, you dumb shit," his wife says,' Charley was saying, 'all scrunched down 'n mad as a bear with a bee up its ass: *"you were in it!"* '

Earl staggered backward, yaw-hawing uncontrollably, making us all duck, just as Leonard skipped out from behind the toolshed in front of us and started popping photos: 'Help! I'm blind!' wailed Fats, shooting straight up in the air.

'Come on, Leonard, what're you doing?'

'This goin' in the sports pages or the church announcements?'

'God, all I see are spots!'

'The hard thing sometimes,' sighed Gottfried beside me sucking on his drooping pipe, 'is just letting go . . .'

'Obishuaries, mos' like . . .'

'Jesus, I thought those two yoyos left when they took Yvonne away!'

'*Yvonne—?*' cried Fats ('. . .And then, other times, there's nothing to it . . .'). '*Who* did?'

'Hurry!' Alison whispered urgently behind me, rushing past. 'I'm almost done!' I gasped, trying to blink away my momentary blindness, but she was already gone, vanished like an apparition. 'Wait!' Then Leonard's flashgun went off again and I saw her, running barefoot toward the back porch (how small she looked!), clutching her tights like a spare wrap, her green sash loose and fluttering behind, pursued by Dickie and that guy in the chalkstriped suit – '*Hey!*' I shouted, just as Dickie caught a toe in a croquet wicket and slapped into the mud. Leonard missed it, shooting instead at a confused and bedraggled Howard being helped down the porch steps by Daffie and Anatole ('Ugh! just don't look back,' someone muttered behind me), Noble following them out, holding his crotch, his glass eye lighting up with the pop of the flash. 'Oh Christ,' Dickie swore, brushing futilely at the dark stains on his bright white trousers, as Alison, with a desperate backward glance, crashed into Noble, 'not *shit—!*' 'Yvonne?' Fats was blubbering. 'I can't *believe* it!' Leonard's flashgun went

off again (Howard stuck his tongue out at it, Anatole threw his hand up):
Alison, Noble, and the guy in the chalkstripes had disappeared.

'Well, folks – *shlup!* – Godspeed!' announced Earl Elstob with a toothy
self-congratulating grin, doing himself up and wandering off. He headed
toward the porch, but seemed to lose his way, circling back into the bushes
behind us instead.

'No need for you guys to rush away on our account,' Daffie announced,
her tongue slurred with gin, as she and Anatole dragged Howard over
and propped him up beside us (Fats had just gone charging off, crying:
'*Bren! My god*, Bren! It's Yvonne! They've *took* our *Yvonne . . . !*' and Jim was
zipping up). 'Nothing going on in there but a goddamn funeral.'

''Ass pretty much whuzz goin' on out here,' remarked Charley,
shaking his member out. 'Well, anyway I won' be hard to find inna
dark . . .'

'Funeral?'

'. . . Juss feel around, it won' be hard . . .'

'Yeah, for Ros. Fucking ghost festival, they're calling it, talking to
spirits – they're outa their conks.' She opened up Howard's pants, fished
around inside. She was having trouble keeping her footing. Someone
shrieked back in the bushes, Elstob sniggered giddily, there was a thump,
and Earl reappeared, doubled over, making his way once more toward
the back porch. 'Jesus, Howard, where *is* the damned thing – ?'

'Can I help?' offered Jim.

'I c'n do't *myself!*' Howard cried out, but it was all bravado, he was
helpless. Distantly there were squeals and laughter coming from the
upstairs bedroom, largely drowned out by the squeals and laughter
behind us as Leonard's flash went off in the bushes.

'By the way, Ger, that guy with the French tickler on his chin said he
had something he wanted to tell you. He – no, stop, Howard! *Wait'll I
get it out!*'

'Cyril?'

'He probably wanted to tell you about the body in the basement,' Jim
said. 'You about ready, Charley?'

'Body? What body— ?!'

'Goddamn it, Howard . . . now see what you've done . . .'

'Down in the rec room, you mean,' said Dolph, joining us as Gottfried
strolled away ('Whuzzat guy got a tape recorder for?' Charley asked),

and lifting his stream into a wheelbarrow back beside the toolshed. 'I wondered about that. I saw the feet sticking out behind the ping-pong table, but I didn't look closer – thought I might be interrupting something.'

'Just as well you didn't,' Jim said. 'It wasn't a pleasant sight.'

'I think he's a sociologist . . .'

'But what are you saying – *the rec room* – ?'

'That's right. The dart pierced the back of the head and penetrated the medulla, and that always makes for a rather pathetic disorganized death, I'm afraid. Probably just an accident but –'

'But – my wife was— !'

'Your wife's all right!' Dolph assured me. 'She's in there in the kitchen. The cops are, uh, with her . . .'

'Assholes!' Anatole muttered under his breath, as I hurried away (she'd been trying to tell me something about an interview, I remembered this now, I hadn't been listening), and Howard whined: 'My panz're all wet!'

'Of course they are, Howard – what do you expect?'

At the steps I caught a glimpse of something glittering in the grass, a little ring of light: Ah, she's dropped it again, I thought as I reached down to pick it up, this time just for me perhaps. I smiled. Or had Noble— ? Someone cried out – I thought it might have been Alison, or else my wife, and I rushed forward (that bastard! I was thinking, meaning no one in particular), but at the kitchen door a man was blocking my way. 'Excuse me— !'

'My wife,' the man said stonily. It was Alison's husband. He stood rigidly in the open doorway, silhouetted against the kitchen lights (yes, my wife was in there, I saw her, the two policemen as well, both looking flushed and sweaty, their clothes disheveled, Fred still in his bulky neckbrace, Bob's tie undone), one hand in his jacket pocket, the other gripping the carved bowl of his meerschaum. 'Where is she?'

'I don't know,' I gasped. 'Inside someplace, I think, I was just—'

'No.'

I couldn't see his face at all, and it made his voice, cold, uncompromising, seem alarmingly disembodied. It was important that I reach my wife ('We better get some blood, too, Fred,' the tall cop was muttering, and Fred, struggling with some pulleys above the butcherblock table, nodded stiffly), but I knew better than to try to push past him.

'You came out here together.'

'Yes, we, uh, sort of ran into each other – but then of course we separated—'

'You touched her breasts—'

'No—'

'And other parts.' It was like a recitation, an arraignment, distant, mechanical, menacing. And utterly (I thought, chilled by it) insane.

'Listen, you've got it all wrong,' I explained, tried to, 'it's only a party—'

'Yes, I know about parties.' I could hear Charley clambering heavily up the steps behind me, assisted by Dolph and Jim. 'You brought her out here – now what have you done with her?'

'I told you—'

'Have you raped her?'

'*No—!*'

'Raped who?' wheezed Charley at my shoulder.

'Whom,' Dolph corrected.

'I can smell her on you,' said Alison's husband.

'We *all* can,' said Dolph. 'Worse than a damn barnyard. No accounting for some people's tastes!'

'Say,' Charley yuff-huffed amiably, 'speakin' a that, didja heara one 'bout the two actors out inna sticks playin' the front 'n back end of a cow— ?'

'Are you in love with her?'

'What?'

'They get chased offa goddamn stage, see, 'n – haw haw! – they get separated—'

'I asked you—'

'C'mon, Charley,' said Dolph, leading him away. 'I think Ger's about to get the punchline without our help.'

'Awright, awright,' sighed Charley, limping. 'Foo! I'm feelin' awful! Whereza booze? I think I got too much blood'n my alcohol stream!'

'Very funny,' Jim said, keeping Charley from tipping over onto Alison's husband, 'but the truth is, you've had enough.' I started to follow them, but the space through which they moved seemed to close up behind them. 'You ought to take it easy. It's slow poison, you know.'

''Ass okay, Jim, I'm in no hurry . . .'

'I asked you if you were in love with her.'

His silhouette, which had dissolved momentarily into the larger mass of the others, now came into sharp focus once more as the light filled in behind him. As though he were honing it, I thought. 'Don't you think you're, well, letting your imagination— ?'

'Believe me, I know what it is to be a victim of love.' Through all of this he hadn't moved. Not even when Charley and the others had jostled past him (they were in there talking to my wife and the short cop now, Charley shaking his big head and saying something about growing older, or colder, Jim examining a small tool Bob was using) – he could have been a cardboard cutout posted at the kitchen door with a recorded message. He sighed. 'It's a kind of madness . . .'

'Yes, well – I don't know what you saw, or thought you saw, but in reality—'

'I know, it's the chemistry of it that most disturbs me. How it warps everything so you can't trust your senses. It's like some kind of powerful hallucinogen, transforming our conventional reality into something stark and dangerous – I always feel as though a hole is being opened up in the universe and I'm being pitched into it. Is that what you feel?'

'Well, ah, something like that . . .' I didn't like conversations like this, and felt unfairly singled out. 'But, honestly, as far as Alison – your wife – is concerned—'

'Inhumane. Utterly amoral. Atavistic. Yet transcendent. I sometimes wonder if it's what atoms feel as they're drawn together in molecules – or stars as they burst and implode . . .'

I could hear Wilma chatting with someone on the steps behind me, complaining about the discomfort of wet garter belts. Woody and Cynthia came out, still in their underwear, and Woody, sizing things up quickly, nodded back over his shoulder and said: 'Your wife needs you, Gerry, you'd better get in there.' 'I know . . .' Fred was attaching something to her ankle; Bob stood by with a pot of Dijonais mustard in his hands.

'Certainly it has nothing to do with marriage, I know that, you can't tame it, you can't institutionalize it – the raw force of it just smashes through all that.' For the first time he moved: he put his pipe – a pale hovering presence between us – in his mouth, drew on it, took it out again. I didn't know whether to be encouraged by this or not.

'Look, I know what you're trying to say, and your wife's very attractive of course, but—'

'I thought at first that marriage might be a way to isolate it, contain it, to give it a time and place, so that at least I could get ahold of the rest of my life – but I was wrong . . .'

Behind me, Wilma was expressing her condolences to Woody: 'She was so *brave!*' 'Yes, I know.' I had faced situations like this before, of course. All too often perhaps. Always there were misunderstandings . . . 'I would have just fallen to pieces!' 'We all have to make adjustments. Eh, where's the best place?' 'Well, *not* where *I* went!' The important thing was to keep them talking. 'You might try back by the swing set.'

'I've known all along, I suppose, but it finally came home to me just tonight, watching you and Alison . . .'

'Hi, Gerry, getting a bit of fresh air?'

'Actually, Wilma, I was just—'

'Say, that's a smashing shirt! Maybe I could get one of those for Talbot – not that it'd look as good on him as it does on you! By the way, do you know Peg's sister Teresa?'

'No,' it was the woman in the yellow dress, 'but—'

'Pleased, I'm sure!'

'There was a kind of awe, a kind of electricity in the way you looked at each other – especially when you were stroking her inside her tights . . .'

'Who did?' Wilma asked.

'No one,' I said. Maybe if I linked arms with these two, sandwiched myself between them . . . 'It's a . . . story . . .'

'Oh, I *like* stories,' gushed Teresa. 'And I like *parties!*'

'And then, later, when she knelt down to put your member in her mouth—'

'That's not what—'

'It was like a revelation . . .'

'Some people have all the fun,' Wilma sighed, patting her hair. 'If I knelt down, I'd just pop all my stays.'

'. . . Like the end of something, innocence for example – and at first I didn't know what to do with it . . .'

'And is that your wife in there on the butcherblock?'

'Yes, in fact I was about to—'

'Come on, Teresa,' said Wilma. 'I'll introduce you.'

'I thought of a lot of things I might do – violent things mostly . . .'
They were gone, I was alone with him again, the chance lost – almost as
though I'd never had it. I heard soft mutterings behind me, near the
porch, something about being afraid of the dark. Or the dart. I'd caught
the word 'violent' – it had seemed to key a new tension in his voice, a
slightly higher pitch. 'The worst part, I realized, was not the way you
played with each other's genitals – a mere appetite, after all, we all go
through that – but rather the peculiar rapport between you, that strange
intense *sympathy* you seem to share. I sensed this already that night we
met at the theater. It was as though, when you spoke to each other, the
very geography of the world had shifted, moving her to a place I could
not reach.'

He was completely mad, that was obvious. It was dangerous, I knew,
to ignore him – impossible in fact ('Come along, Teresa,' Wilma was
saying in the kitchen, 'it's best not to interfere . . .') – but you couldn't
reason with him either. 'All right,' I said ('Well, what I'm saying,' Teresa
argued – all I could see of my wife were her feet above Teresa's head –
as Bob frowned and slid a knife back and forth through our electric
sharpener, 'is that it seems a silly way to go about it!'), 'what do you want
me to do?'

'I hate these destructive feelings. They're completely contrary to my
life's work. I want you to help me free myself from them.' I wasn't sure
what he meant, but I didn't like the sound of it. In the kitchen Peg's sister
Teresa leaned down to my wife and said: 'Anyway, I'm delighted to meet
you! It's a wonderful party!' I couldn't hear my wife's reply, if there was
one, but I was thinking, maybe Vic was right, maybe these parties were
a mistake. Perhaps we should travel more instead, or take up some
hobby . . . 'I want you to give Alison what she wants,' her husband said.
'Or thinks she wants . . .'

'But I—'

'On one condition.' I settled back on my heels. He'd startled me at
first, but I knew where I was now. There was always a condition . . . 'I
want you to teach me about theater,' he said.

'I see . . .' I had been right of course, but not in the way I'd imagined.
'The theater, you say.' Ros, I recalled, had once, while sucking me off,
paused for a moment, looked up, and asked me to teach her ('There must
be an easier way to make a living,' Fred was complaining in the kitchen,

as he wiped his flushed brow with a dishtowel) about marriage, and I had felt as inadequate then as I did now. 'It's . . . it's a complicated subject.'

'I want to find my way back to her,' he said simply. 'And I feel somehow it's the key to it all.' He had pivoted slightly and light from the kitchen now fell on half his face. I could see the worry and fatigue in his eyes as he studied me. 'From what I've heard about you,' he added, stepping aside to allow me to enter, 'I'm sure you will help.'

It seemed to me, as I stepped over the threshold, that an age had passed since I'd crossed it going the other way, and for some reason I thought of that phrase that Tania had been so fond of and had concealed in several of her paintings – in 'Orthodoxy,' for example, and in (or on) 'Gulliver's Peter': '*What was without's within, within, without.*' 'Awright, ma'am, try to be a little more helpful if you can,' Fred was saying, more or less echoing Alison's husband (I felt him close behind me like an arbiter, a referee), and I thought: Tania was right, everything – even going out for a pee in the garden – was full of mystery. 'We'd hate to have to bring in the old exploding sausage . . .'

'Just a moment,' I protested. 'This really isn't necessary. My wife had nothing to do with—'

'It's all right, Gerald,' she said weakly, craning her head around under the bright fluorescent lamp. 'It's only a routine—'

'That's right, so just move along now, fella—'

'But I tell you, you're wasting your time! She doesn't know anything!'

'She knows more than you think, sir,' Bob said, pulling on rubber gloves from the sink, and my wife whispered: 'Your fly's undone, Gerald.'

'Ah! Sorry . . .'

'What's that . . . in your hand?'

'What— ? Oh yes, nothing . . .' I'd almost forgotten it was there. I realized I must have been rubbing it like a talisman throughout my encounter with Alison's husband, who now leaned closer to see what it was. 'Just something I, uh, found outside—'

'Looks like one of my buttons,' said Fred. We all looked: indeed it was. He searched his jacket, which gaped still around his bloodstained belly. 'Yeah, there it is. Musta come off when I was trying to button up out there in the dark . . .'

'Outside . . . ?' my wife asked faintly, her face puffy. Bob was holding a damp tab of litmus paper up to the light. 'Are my . . . flowers all right?'

'Well . . .'

'I guess I owe you one,' Fred acknowledged, pocketing the button. Alison's husband had pulled back, but I could smell his pipe still (I was thinking about hidden fortunes, something a woman had once said to me down in some catacombs: 'All these bones – like buried pearls, dried semen . . .' – whatever happened to that woman?), its aroma hovering like a subtle doubt. 'The Old Man woulda raised hell with me if I'd lost it!'

'You could start,' I suggested, 'by letting her down.'

Fred hesitated, glancing at his partner. Bob shrugged, nodded: Fred loosened the ropes and eased her down, though he kept her legs still in their shackles, a foot or so off the table. My wife looked greatly relieved and exchanged a tender glance with me. How tired she looked! 'Some more people have arrived,' she said with a pained sigh.

'Yes.' I could hear them wailing in the next room. 'Ros's friends mostly.' The blood, which had before rushed to her head, now drained away, and the old pallor returned, making the bruises there seem darker. Or maybe it was just the cold light of the fluorescent lamp. 'Listen, love, when this is all over, let's take a few days off, have an old-fashioned holiday – we can go away somewhere, somewhere where there's sun – even Mrs Draper said . . .' She smiled faintly.

'Sounds good to me,' said Fred, rigging up a lamp with an odd-shaped bulb ('Ultraviolet,' he added when he saw me staring: 'certain, um, substances usually always fluoresce . . .'), while his partner fiddled with a little rubber tube of some sort.

Eileen came in for some ice: For Vic,' she said. The bruises on her face made her seem wistful and sullen at the same time. 'He's just been down to the rec room, he *needs* a drink.'

'That sonuvabitch,' Fred muttered, touching his neckbrace, and Bob grunted: 'Don't worry, pardner. We'll get him.'

'Have you been up . . . to see Tania?' my wife asked, as though to change the subject.

It was strange. As I started to speak, I felt everything that had happened during the evening roll up behind me to feed my reply – and then, even before I got the words out, it faded . . . 'Not . . . not—'

'It's like . . . she was trying to . . . to put the fire out,' she added. I felt as though something were unfinished, like an interrupted sneeze. As though (*'Ouch!'* she cried, wincing, and I felt my own eyes screw up in sympathy) I'd been preparing all night to do something – and then forgot what it was. My wife closed her eyes for a moment while Bob put his mouth to one end of the tube. 'It must have been happening – *ngh!* – all night. I don't know why I . . . didn't notice . . .'

'Well, we all see only what we want to see . . .'

'Maybe she just got tired of waiting,' said Eileen wearily.

'I . . . I let the water . . . out of the tub . . .' Her knuckles, clenched tight, were white as burnished salt. Eileen had left. 'If you do go up, Gerald . . .' she added, then gasped and held her breath a moment, 'could you – *oh!* . . . check on Mark? He . . . can't seem to settle down.'

'Of course . . .' Iris Draper pushed through the dining room door now with Michelle, the chants from the other side augmenting momentarily. They seemed to be parading around the table in there. 'It was the same day,' Michelle was saying, 'that Roger had that dream about the old hunchback with her drawers full of gold.' 'Was that a dream?'

'He dropped a bag of water on Louise's head. It . . .' She gulped for air. I stared down at the bald spot on the top of Bob's head and thought about the Inspector's view of time and what he called – how did he put it? – the specious present . . .

'Yes, and apparently what happened, you see, is that Ros just opened the door and stepped out.'

'It . . . made her cry . . .'

'Really!' Iris exclaimed, as they stepped outside. 'She might have been killed!'

. . . The mysterious spread toward futurity . . .

'Well, she was on acid or something . . .'

'Perhaps, in the end, all self-gratification leads to tragedy,' Alison's husband murmured behind my shoulder. Fred was looking for a wall plug. 'We'll have to use an extension cord,' he muttered, and Bob, peering closely at a little bottle, wiped his mouth and grunted. 'But then, what doesn't . . . ?'

'It was so sad. In the old days, I'm sure . . . she would have laughed.' She opened her eyes again. There were tears in them. 'Do you remember that big jolly laugh Louise used to have . . . ?'

'That was a long time ago.'

'I don't think you want to watch this,' Fred said, uncoiling the cord. 'We'll let you know—'

'No, I'm not leaving,' I insisted, but just then Alison came through from the back, barefoot and unbuttoned, hair loose, eyes dilated from the darkness. She shot me a glance full of – love? betrayal? desire? fear? ('And Dolph was so funny,' my wife was saying, 'we always had . . . such good times then . . .') – then padded hastily on into the dining room, Noble and the man in the chalkstriped suit banging in behind her, their shirttails out: 'Where'd she go?' they laughed.

'You must hurry!' whispered Alison's husband, clearly shaken (we shared this), and my wife reached out to touch my hand. 'Yes, Gerald,' she sighed, 'it's all right . . . you might be needed . . .'

'I'll – I'll go find the Inspector!' I declared (Noble, lumbering through the dining room door, had glanced back to smirk one-eyed at me, a streak of red down one cheek, Alison's green tights tied round his thick neck like a superhero's cape). 'He'll put a stop to this!'

'Now, now,' admonished Fred, peering round at me past his neckbrace (I was already at the door), 'none of that . . . !'

'Wait, Gerald!' my wife called out faintly. 'I nearly forgot . . . !' Maybe, I was thinking, I should say something to the Inspector about Noble, the hairbrush and all that – he's capable of anything. 'I've made some nachos. They're . . . they're on a cookie tray in the oven . . . Could you . . . ?' 'Nachos! But— ?!'

'These what you're looking for?' Steve the plumber asked, bumping in behind me with an assortment of small red-handled pliers in his callused hands, and Bob, setting down a can of hairspray, said: 'That's them.'

'Please, Gerald . . . they've been in there . . . too long already!'

'I changed the washers on the downstairs taps and reset the drum on your dryer,' Steve said, moving over to the foot of the table, 'but I haven't been able to do anything yet about the stool upstairs.'

'Please . . .'

From this angle I couldn't see my wife's face – my view was blocked by Fred and Steve between her legs – but I knew she must be near to tears. I hurried over to the stove, stuffed my hands impatiently into oven mitts (Alison's husband was chewing on his beard again), and opened the oven door. 'Good god!' I exclaimed as I pulled the tray of nachos out. 'There's a *turkey* in here!'

'Yes . . . it's from the freezer,' she gasped. Steve looked up and said: 'I've rung my partner. He'll bring the tools we need for the biffy.' 'It could use another . . . twenty minutes or so . . .'

'But—!'

'Don't worry, we'll watch the timer,' Fred assured me, and went over to open the dining room door for me, seemingly eager to get me out of there. I heard the chants still, but more distantly, interspersed with waves of silence: they'd moved off to some other part of the house. 'And don't you be bothering the Inspector,' he added, snatching up a couple of hot nachos and juggling them in his hands (Steve was watching closely as the tall cop plugged in his vacuum cleaner and limped toward my wife with the suction hose), then popping one in his mouth. 'He's got a lot on his mind right now.'

His warning seemed almost a challenge, a dare, and as I carried the tray of nachos into the dining room (Dolph was there at the table, scraping at the remains of a bowl of moussaka, Dickie using a candle to light up a joint), I thought: It's clear, I've got to meet Pardew head-on right now. In fact, hadn't I already made this decision before coming back in from outside? 'Dolph, could you move that bowl so I can use the hot plate?'

'Hey, nachos! Your wife finally remembered us beer drinkers!'

Across the room, Mavis, surrounded by those stragglers not interested in Quagg's funeral parade in the next room, stretched her arms up, palms out flat, as though pressing them against some unseen wall: I sympathized with this. 'And that's coriander she's traipsing through, if I'm not mistaken, and there's sweet calamus,' Iris Draper was saying nearby, identifying the plants in Tania's painting for Eileen, who stood leaning against a wall, staring puffily into space. 'And those look like jujube trees, which the ancients got mixed up with something else, and this is probably sandalwood . . .' Between them, Vic, looking battered and unsteady but still strong, poured himself another drink. 'Looks like you stepped pretty deep in the dew, Gerry,' Dolph remarked around a mouthful of half-chewed nacho. 'It's halfway up your pantleg there . . .'

'A fucking mess,' Dickie agreed, taking a swift drag on his joint and handing it to me: I pulled off the oven mitts and joined him ('I wonder if all that adds up to something . . . ?' Iris mused, and Vic grunted: 'The question to ask is, what's she selling?'), sucking the sweet smoke deep

into my lungs as though, I felt, to mark some turning, the completion
of something, or the beginning, something perhaps not quite present
yet nearby . . . 'All the style's gone out of your parties, Ger' ('That's not
a very generous view of art,' Iris remarked, peering over her spectacles),
'there's too much shit and blood.'

'Maybe you're just growing up,' Vic growled, wheeling around slowly.
'Unlikely as that seems.' I caught a glimpse of Ros, her extremities concealed in translucent bags, being carried around on a kind of litter made
of one of our living room drapes tied at the corners to three croquet
mallets and a golfclub (it looked like a five-iron), held high, Hoo-Sin in
her kimono wheeling around below, eyes closed, keening rhythmically.
'Ritualized lives need ritualized forms of release. Parties were invented
by priests, after all – just another power gimmick in the end.'

'Not for me, old man,' said Dickie with a cold smile, taking the joint
back. 'For me, they're like solving a puzzle – I keep thinking each time
I'll find just the little piece I'm looking for.' Vic's jaw tightened – Dickie
turned toward me and winked, then glanced back over his shoulder
toward the living room, seeing what I saw: Alison among the mourners,
looking frightened, hemmed in by Noble and that guy in the chalkstriped
suit and some of Zack Quagg's crowd – Vachel the dwarf, that actor who
played the wooden soldier, Hilario the Panamanian tapdancer – 'Speaking
of which,' Dickie murmured ('Please, Vic,' Eileen whispered), moving
away, hand fluttering at his bald spot once more. 'Like so many open but
unenterable doors,' I thought I heard Mavis say, just as Dolph, scratching
now with both hands, said: 'The top cop's there in the TV room, Gerry,
if that's who you're looking for.'

'Yes . . .' I'd lost sight of her. Fats was doing a kind of dance in the
front room around Hoo-Sin, who was down on her knees now, twisting
her torso round and round, moaning ecstatically, some guy with a camera
circling around her, getting it all on videotape. They'd lowered Ros to
the floor and Hoo-Sin swept the corpse with her long shiny hair, back
and forth, wailing something repetitive through her nose, while the others
chanted and clapped or slapped the walls and furniture. Hilario banged
a tambourine, Vachel clacked spoons, Fats danced, eyes closed, smiling
toothily, his big body bobbing around the room above the others as
though afloat on the rhythms.

*

While Quagg – directing the camera crew, shifting the lights, calling the angles – pulled the others into a circle around Ros, Regina swooped into the center, eyes and hands raised as though in supplication. She called out Ros's name in a hollow stage whisper, and the others picked it up as a kind of chant. Alison (I saw her now) made a move in my direction, but Quagg stopped her, led her back into the circle, in a gap between Dickie and that wooden soldier actor. I tried to catch her eye, but she was peering anxiously back over her shoulder, where Noble and Talbot, digging at his crotch as though looking for the switch, were squeezing up behind her.

Malcolm Mee appeared then, as if from nowhere, in his ragged jeans and striped sailor shirt: he knelt solemnly beside Ros's body, bent stiffly forward, and pressed his head against her breast. When he staightened up there was fresh blood dripping down his forehead between his eyes. Regina let out a shriek and fell to the floor, her eyes rolled back (I'd seen her do this as 'Tendresse' in *The Lover's Lexicon*), Fats paused, the music stopped. 'Ros!' Fats whispered, and the others picked it up once more, chanting airily as though taking deep breaths together.

'What's all this supposed to mean?' asked Alison's husband, who'd stepped up unnoticed beside me, but Quagg shushed him angrily, pointing at the camera.

All eyes were on Mee, who knelt beside Ros still, back arched, staring up at the ceiling as though in a trance. His pants seemed to have opened up by themselves, and now his penis crept out like a worm, looking one way, then the other, finally rearing up in the lights like a flower opening to the sun. There were gasps mingled with the whispered chants *of 'Ros! Ros! Ros!'* Mee's eyes closed and his lips drew back as though in pain. The head of his penis began to move in and out of its foreskin like a piston, plunging faster and faster – or perhaps it was the foreskin that was moving. 'Look!' someone rasped. 'It's getting wet!' This was true: it was glistening now as though with sweat. Or saliva. Mee's hips were jerking uncontrollably, his head thrown back, bloodstreaked face contorted, the scar on his cheek livid, his penis pumping. The others, still chanting, pressed round – I too found myself squeezing closer to watch. Suddenly Malcolm bucked forward, went rigid: the swollen head of his member, now wet and empurpled, thrust up out of its fleshy sleeve at full stretch, seemed to pucker up, and then let fly – but even as his sperm spewed forth (we all shrank back) it seemed to disappear into thin air. There were gasps of amazement and people fell to the floor. Regina, emerging from her own trance, searched her dress: it was dry. The carpet too. It had been like an explosion of yoghurt and now we couldn't see a trace of it. Mee lay there, gasping, quivering, his eyes squeezed shut, the blood dripping down between them. Regina, with gestures grand and devotional, tucked his penis away and zipped his jeans up. 'All right!' exclaimed Zack Quagg, beaming, and he slapped the cameraman on the shoulder. 'All *right!*'

'I may be thick or insensitive or something,' sighed Alison's husband, 'but I just don't get it. I mean, is that what theater's supposed to be about, communication with the dead?'

She was gone. Mee had distracted me. And Noble as well, Talbot, that guy in the lilac shirt and gray chalkstripes, they'd all vanished. Dickie was still there: he'd spied Sally Ann nearby, staring at me, one hand in her blue jeans as though playing with herself. Holding my gaze, she withdrew her hand, held her fingertips in front of her lips, and blew – Dickie reached out as though to intercept her dispatch, closing his hand around it and drawing it, grinning, toward his nose. She made a face, pushed around him, and came toward me. 'Whoa there, Greased Crease!' he laughed, and caught her by a back pocket. 'At heart, theater doesn't entertain *or* instruct, goddamn it – it's an atavistic folk rite,' Quagg was explaining, somewhat irritably. 'Oh, I see,' said Alison's husband, adding in a whisper to me: 'She went out through that door to the dining room . . .' 'Ah . . .' It was over on the other side of the room. How had I wandered so far away from it? It was as though the room itself had circled around me. 'Jesus, Cyril and Peg shoulda seen that one!' 'Weren't they just here?' Regina was mopping the blood from Malcolm's forehead and nose with a white scarf. '*That*, bison gulls, is what you call ad-*lipping* it!' Vachel squeaked, drawing tense laughter ('Off the *elbow*, man!' 'No, haven't you heard?'), and Fats, his bald dome shiny with sweat, stopped me in the doorway: 'Doggone! What happened, Ger? I had my eyes closed!'

But she wasn't in the dining room either. There were some people in there eating and drinking, and Mavis was carrying on still in her hollow and melancholic way, but neither Alison nor the guys chasing her around

were to be seen. 'Death came to me there as a woman,' Mavis was saying
– some of her audience had drifted to the doorway to catch Malcolm's
act, but were now drifting back – while behind me, Wilma sighed and
said: 'Dear me, what a waste!'

'Ah well, spunk's cheap,' someone answered her, and Mavis said: 'Her
hair seemed to float around her head as though caught in a wind. She
had a large fleshy mouth, and when she opened it the inside glowed with
a strange fluorescent light.' I turned back, but Alison's husband was
standing in the doorway, also looking puzzled. 'Her breath smelled of
wormwood and gentian root and her eyes were shriveled like dried
mushrooms. Bruised fruit. She looked . . . like my mother . . .'

'*What— ?!*' bellowed Vic, whirling around and staring fiercely past
my shoulder, just as the man in the chalkstriped suit came, grinning, out
of the TV room.

'She was blind and clumsy and the labyrinth of ice was impenetrable
even for one who could see – it was easy to lose her—'

'*That goddamn sonuvabitch— !*'

'You got buried treasure down there, Dolph?'

'Look at him go! Moves like a man half his age!'

'He's ripe for a coronary . . .'

'I think I musta caught something . . .'

'But then, after I'd escaped from her, I grew lonely and longed, even
in my awful fright, to see her again . . .'

Nor in the TV room, where Jim sat facing the Inspector across the
games table ('It's a problem of dynamics, a subject–object relation,'
Pardew was saying, 'for in a sense it is the victim who shapes and molds
the criminal . . .'), Patrick just behind him, old Lloyd Draper over in the
easy chair, sleepily watching the TV screen, Knud snoring on the sofa.
There was a technician working behind the set, rigging up some kind of
switcher between the cassette recorder on top, a lot of gear strewn around
on the floor, and the tube itself, where now Mavis appeared in extreme
close-up as though being interviewed, saying: 'I went searching for her
but I couldn't find her . . .' The technician flicked a switch and the image
of Mavis gave way to a static wide-angle shot of a man in high-heeled
boots, a leather vest, and a thick black beard, coming through the front
door with a tripod over his shoulder: it was the technician himself, I

realized, as humorless on the screen as he was at his work. 'Did the victim suffer perhaps from extreme sensibility?' the Inspector asked.

Jim smiled, glanced up at me – 'Hardly,' he said with a wink – and the Inspector peered around. 'Ah,' he exclaimed, waving at me with what looked like a knitting needle, 'perhaps you can help!'

'Well, I was just looking for—'

'The good doctor here seems reluctant to provide us with the full medical history of the victim on the rather unprofessional grounds that it is not relevant,' he went on snappishly. Some of Mark's toy soldiers had been set up on the table in front of him, apparently to illustrate some theory or other, and it occurred to me suddenly what those 'marbles' were I'd found in my pocket. There was also another of Mark's drawings there – the one Mark said was of Santa Claus killing the Indians – as well as Peedie, his stuffed bunny. 'And I am trying to persuade him that there is a definite mutuality here, that the criminal and his prey are working on each other constantly, long before the moment of disaster, before they've even met each other, and that, in the war against crime, to know the one,' here he pointed with the knitting needle at one of the little soldiers, 'we must know the other!' He pointed at another soldier, then gave a sharp little thrust and tipped it over. 'By the way, why are all the heads gone off these things?'

'I don't know . . .'

'All that may be very well with wolves and tigers,' Jim said, 'but it has nothing whatsoever to do with human beings.'

'I can see that you have a higher – and a lower – estimation of humanity than I have,' replied the Inspector, setting the needle down and lighting his pipe. Without the scarf, the back of his neck looked raw and naked. I caught a glimpse now of Janny Trainer behind the open closet door, her pink skirt hiked above her waist, some guy's hand in her heart-shaped bikini panties. On the TV screen there was a wide-angle shot of my study with Roger's lifeless body upside down in the far corner. Nothing moved. Yet the relentless intensity of the unblinking shot was almost unbearable. Pardew turned around to look at me, holding up the needle. 'Does your boy *knit*, by the way?'

'No— !'

'There he is,' Wilma said, leading Peg's sister Teresa into the room and over to the sofa.

'We found it in his room.'

'Oh my! I'd like to be in *his* dreams!'

'Kitty says you probably *wouldn't* like it.'

'It's probably his grandmother's, my wife's—'

'Who was the *victim's* mother?'

'Look, Wilma!' exclaimed Teresa, pointing. 'There's Talbot on the TV!'

'Ros? She was an orphan—'

'Aha!' He banged the table with the needle, sending the little soldiers flying. Jim looked pained and shook his head at me (my wife, I recalled, had been trying to tell me something about Mark), and Wilma said: 'I wish at least the ninny'd stop scratching his pants!' 'An orphan! Now it's all coming *clear!*'

Charley entered, groaning lugubriously with each slow step, and the guy with Janny – it was Steve the plumber – hurried over to help the bearded technician behind the TV, fumbling abashedly with his overall buttons. What was Teresa saying? Something about a 'little boy' or 'little boys.' ''Sno good, Janny! I'm all – I'm all washed up . . . !'

'Oh, Charley, stop blubbering! Why don't you just push a cocktail stirrer in it or something?'

The camera, which had followed Talbot and Dolph and the others (Talbot, in response to an interviewer's question, had been describing his appetite for reflected sex) to the door of our master bedroom, now panned back down the hallway to the bathroom, and I saw as it slid past my son's door that it was ajar: the room was apparently empty, toys and bedclothes flung violently about – and was that a foot stretched out behind the closet door? 'Now about the hole in this stuffed rabbit,' Pardew was saying and the TV camera had entered the bathroom, where the shower curtain was being pulled aside, but I was already on my way out of the room: I remembered now, there'd been a bloody handprint on Mark's door when I'd passed it before – how had I failed to register it at the time?! – *there was not a moment to lose!*

I bumped up against Hilario in the doorway – '*Oops!*' '*Perdón!*' he exclaimed. 'I am all left *foots!*' – and over his shoulder ruffles I spied Alison in the group around Mavis: Noble was there, too, Earl Elstob, Dolph . . . 'I saw her at last,' Mavis was saying, 'but she was trapped behind a high wall of shimmering ice – she was hideous, yet pathetic, and I felt a terrible closeness and a terrible distance at the same time.' Alison mouthed something with a questioning look on her face – it looked like 'the green room?' – and pointed down at her crotch. '(*Just be a minute!*)' I mouthed in return, and Dolph, cupping a hand to his ear (the other hand was out of sight), mouthed back: (*What?*) 'And then, *suddenly*,' Mavis intoned as Alison, wincing, lurched slightly and cast me a panicked glance – but what could I do? there was the bloody handprint, my son's torn-up room ('*What*— ?! Down in the *rec room?*' cried Brenda. 'Oh *no!*') – '*everything began to melt . . . !*'

'Wasn't Malcolm's number something else?' someone at the table remarked as I pushed past it – Quagg's crowd were all in here pressing around the food now – and Hoo-Sin replied ('Fats! *Fats!*'): 'It was like the meeting of clouds and rain, tall mountains piercing the soft mist of the valley!'

'I tell you she was *there*, man!' It was the guy who'd played the wooden soldier, standing near the telephone: 'Didn't you catch her *smell?* That could *only* be Ros!'

'You'll never *believe* it, Fats . . . !'

'I didn't smell anything, but I could *feel* her,' sighed Michelle below me as I took the steps three at a time. 'It was like she was blowing through my clothes!'

'But I thought Mee's cock was tattooed like a serpent . . . ?'

Just as I hit the top, Ginger came wobbling out of the bathroom, looking unwell. She glanced up, met wide-eyed my startled gaze, and, as though in shock, all the stiff little pigtails ringing her face went limp. She snatched a kerchief away from one breast, clutched it to her mouth, covering her breast with her other hand, and went clattering down the stairs.

When I reached my son's room, I found there was no blood on the door after all, maybe I'd been mistaken – but inside, the room was, as I'd seen it on the TV, all torn up. And the bed was empty, there were stains—! '*Mark*— ?!'

'Stick 'em up, Daddy! It's the Red Pimple!' he cried, jumping out from behind the closet door.

'Hey— !'

'Did I scare you, Daddy?' he giggled, as my mother-in-law came in with a glass of milk. His face was painted bright red and he had a towel tied around his neck for a cape. My heart was pounding.

'Boy, you sure *did!*'

'The police were in here,' his grandmother said without looking at me. The room was a mess, things strewn about everywhere, books, toys, bedding, unwound balls of yarn.

'I'm sorry . . .'

'They took Peedie away!'

'They'll bring him back, son.' What had I been afraid of? I didn't want to think about it.

'They better! That's *my* Peedie!'

'Now they are in the kitchen.' She seemed to be talking to the closet. She handed Mark his milk.

'I know. I've just come from—'

'That towel is filthy, Mark. And what have you done to your face?'

'Yuck! This stuff tastes like soap!' He now had a white moustache on his crimson face.

His grandmother gathered up the sheets and blankets, spread them on the bed, her movements slow and forced, as if causing her physical pain. 'I'll get a washcloth,' she said, taking the towel with her as she went.

'Why did the policemen throw all my things on the floor?'

'They were probably looking for something. It's part of their job.'

'Are they the ones who broke my soldiers?'

'I don't think so. Crawl in here now, it's late and Grandma's getting upset.'

'Not without Peedie! I can't sleep without Peedie!'

I knew this. He curled round it and put his finger in a hole he'd dug. We had to take the rabbit everywhere we went. 'Maybe if I told you a story . . .'

'Gramma already told me one. About a bad man who cut ladies' heads off. Daddy, what's "happy the other laughter"?'

'Happily ever after? Nothing, just a way to end a story.'

'Why don't they just say "the end"?'

'Sometimes they do.'

'Or "hugs and kisses," like on a letter?'

I smiled. His grandmother began working on his paint job with the washcloth, and he screwed his face up in disgust: 'Oww!' My grandmother used to sign her letters: 'Please don't forget me.' My father: 'Be brave.' My mother never wrote. 'What's a French letter, Daddy?'

'I suppose, uh, that's a letter from France.'

'No, it isn't, it's a balloon. That girl told me.'

'Well, all right, a balloon.' I gazed down at him as he sucked his thumb there on the pillow (his grandmother had retired to her rocking chair and was staring furiously at the blank screen of the drawn window shade), recalling a young girl I'd known in Schleswig-Holstein, an afternoon in a wildlife preserve, lying naked in the tall grass out of sight, more or less out of sight (what did it matter, we were young and one with the wildness around us, flesh then was *truth*, this was a long time ago), teaching each other all the sex words of our respective languages. That day, I'd lost my condom inside her, and she'd exclaimed irritably, fishing for it: 'Ach, die miserable Franch Post! Fot can you hexpect?' 'Well, anyway the delivery's been made,' I'd muttered lamely, feeling guilty (the truth of flesh is complex and disturbing and never quite enough, that beautiful oneness with nature ultimately a bed with stones and ants that bit: perhaps, there in the sun, I was beginning to think about this), and she'd shot back: 'Ja, gut, only zo zere ist no postage due!'

'But it isn't, is it, Daddy? Ever . . .'

'What's that, son?' As he sucked, he pulled his nose down with his index finger.

'The end.'

I hesitated. There was such a sadness in his little eyes, his stretched-down nose. I wanted to relieve it with a little joke, but I couldn't demean his question, even though it meant, I knew, a kind of betrayal. His eyes seemed to widen, then they went dull. 'Ask Mommy to come up and kiss me good night,' he said around his thumb.

'Well, she's . . . busy, but she'll—'

'Now,' said my mother-in-law coldly from her chair.

'Yes, right *now*, Daddy,' Mark repeated.

'Of course.' I could understand her feelings – I hated the police, after all, even more than she hated my guests – but it seemed to me that her expectations of me were not all that different from Mark's: I'd become in her eyes, as I was naturally in his, a kind of generalized cause.

'*And get my Peedie!*'

The sewing room as I passed it was darkened, the door half-closed. '*Hold on to it!*' someone gasped from behind the door – or '*to her*' – and there was a muffled sound as though someone were struggling. I stopped short. But then I caught a glimpse of my mother-in-law out of her chair and watching me sternly from Mark's doorway. 'I'll be right back!' I said to her – and to anyone else who might be listening – and as though in reply, someone whispered from in there: '*Do you know what you're doing?*'

In front of the mirror at the foot of the stairs (on the landing, Wilma, showing Teresa Tania's painting, said: 'Well, as you can see, she never really tried to flatter herself – but I *do* think she always looked better with her clothes on . . .'), Jim was treating Eileen's left eye, which, puffy and red, now matched the right. 'Not again!' I exclaimed, stepping down, and Jim shrugged. 'She told Vic he was nothing but a utopian sentimentalist, something like that, and he proved it by belting her one.'

'My father's out of control,' Sally Ann said, then smiled up at me, her throat coloring.

'It's going to get worse,' Eileen muttered. Nearby, Ginger was diapering herself in Pardew's silk scarf, pinning it front and back to a kind of serape she'd fashioned out of what remained of her kerchiefs. 'I tried to tell him, to get him to go before it's too late, but he won't listen.'

'Mmm. By the way, I tried in the kitchen,' Jim remarked, glancing up at me, 'but they won't listen either.'

'I know. I've had enough. I'm going to do something about it right now.'

'If you need any help . . .'

'Thanks, Jim. I'll let you know.'

Ginger, Pardew's fedora perched on her wiry pigtails, her fingertips at the brim to keep it from falling off, went tottering into the front room on her high red heels, watched leeringly by Vachel the dwarf. Vachel was chewing a fat black cigar nearly as big as he was. '*Gudjus!*' he piped.

'God! it's awful!' Brenda was saying. She was nearly crying. She and Fats had apparently just come up from the basement. They were leaning on each other and Fats was blinking still in the bright light of the hallway.

'Just *look*, Gerry!' She showed me a photograph: it was Ros on her hands and knees, looking over her shoulder at her raised bum – or rather, not a bum at all, but a rich banker, a snowman capitalist with greedy black-button eyes on each pale cheek, a carrot-nose stuck in her anus, top hat perched on top, and a wet bearded mouth about to ingest a shining gold rod. The photograph was full of holes. 'They've been throwing *darts* at it, Gerry! Who'd ever *do* such a thing?'

'It's somethin' else down there, man!' said Fats, wiping his face with a big bandanna.

Daffie, wandering in from the back with a somewhat dazed Anatole, guiding him toward the stairs, took the photo away and said: 'That popsicle looks familiar – I think I've seen one somewhere just like it.' She winked at me drunkenly and immediately, as though cued, the telephone rang. I turned to answer it and nearly bumped into Louise, moving heavily toward the back of the house with a fresh bathtowel. Her glance was withering. 'Have you been out on the mall communing with nature, sweetie?' Brenda asked, making Anatole blush, and the actor who played the wooden soldier in the toyland melo picked up the phone and said: 'Hullo? No, Horner's the name.'

'If it's a man, it's for me,' called Peg's sister Teresa, leaning over the railing.

'No, there's nobody here named Gerald, fuckface – you must have the wrong number.' 'Wait— !' But he'd already hung up. 'I could tell right away that shit-for-brains didn't have your class, baby!' he said, grinning at Teresa, who, as though in reflex, pushed one knee through the railings ('I – I've already been,' Anatole was stammering as Brenda hooked her arm in his: 'Well, you can help *me*, honey . . .'), and in the dining room there was a burst of applause.

But then I saw her, free at last, in by the table with Janny Trainer and Hoo-Sin—

'Hey!' I exclaimed softly, hugging her from behind.

'Why, Gerry, what a nice surprise!' It was Knud's wife Kitty, her mouth packed with bread and salami.

'Oh, I'm sorry – I thought it was my wife . . . !'

'What's to be sorry?' she laughed, spewing food. 'Oops! See how excited you got me?' She wiped her chin with a cocktail napkin, examined her front. Though my wife had a dress something like that and they were both about the same size, I was nevertheless amazed that I could have confused the two of them. Alison was gone, as I'd known she would be – Mavis, seated now in a captain's chair, was surrounded mostly by women. Only Talbot was there among them, his ear bandage dirty and unraveling now like some kind of primitive headdress. 'I borrowed some of your wife's clothes, I hope she won't mind, mine were all . . .' Kitty's chirpy manner faded. She swallowed. 'Once, at a party, when he was, you know, in one of his moods,' she said, staring off at Mavis (Janny sighed, Hoo-Sin nodded, Brenda came through from the front, popping gum, a reluctant Anatole in tow), 'I tried to cheer him up by saying, "Relax, Roger, it's all just a game, what the hell." Without taking his eyes off me, Gerry, he bit right through the glass he was drinking from and started chewing up the pieces – God! I nearly fainted!'

'When the lotus blooms in the midst of a fire, it is never destroyed,' Hoo-Sin said solemnly.

'Oh no!' cried Janny. Brenda and Anatole, trying to push out through the kitchen door, had got stopped by someone trying to push in ('But I'm in a bigger *hurry* than you are!' Brenda laughed, shouting through the door). 'Don't *tell* me there's going to be a *fire!*'

'Only in my heart,' crooned Fats, putting his arms around them both: Hoo-Sin elbowed him sharply in the gut and he backed off goggle-eyed and wheezing, bumping into Hilario, just emerging from the TV room, who exclaimed: 'Eh! Fats! You muss learn to not fock yourself aroun' weeth the moveeng force off nature!'

As Brenda got her way and, laughing, dragged Anatole on through to the kitchen ('I think Uncle Howard needs me!' he was pleading, trying to hang back), I felt suddenly overtaken by a terrible sadness – I don't know what it was that brought it on, that image of Roger chewing glass maybe, or Hoo-Sin knocking the wind out of Fats, or perhaps it was just an accumulation of everything that had happened all night, Ros and Roger, Eileen, Tania kneeling at the tub with pink soap scum up to her elbows, the police and all their gear and Ros's rolled-down stockings, my wife boiling eggs, all these people, my torn-up study, the food mashed in the carpet, the mess in the rec room, the look on Yvonne's face as she vanished through the front door or on my son's face just now when I left him or on Daffie's right this minute – whatever it was, it stopped me cold for a moment, such that when Woody came in from the kitchen with Cynthia ('Technically maybe,' she was saying, fingering her medallion at the cross-strap of her bra, 'but, I don't know, somehow it just doesn't seem—'), a sudden look of concern crossed his face and he interrupted her to ask: 'Is everything all right, Gerry?'

'You know it's not,' I said, my voice catching. 'You know what they're doing.' The door behind him was moving still, chafing subtly the door-jamb. 'Can you help?'

He observed me closely, one hand gripping a strap of his ribbed undershirt. His counselor's deadpan calm returned. 'Sure, Gerry. I can at least try. Don't worry, there are laws, precedents – things will work out. Why don't you get Cynthia a drink meanwhile?'

'Yes, you've been neglecting me,' she said, gazing at me with that same worried look she'd been giving Yvonne earlier. She took my arm and led me like an invalid toward the sideboard. 'What was that special drink you fixed for me earlier tonight?'

'An old-fashioned, I think.'

'No, it had gin in it. It was a funny color.' Fats, with a pained grin on his face, was moving in on Hoo-Sin once more, Hilario cautioning him from the sidelines: 'Theenk two times wut you do, my frien'.'

'A blue moon?'

'That's it.'

People seemed to be drifting about without focus. We pushed through them. It was like happy hour back at the ski lodge. Maybe the last play in the world would be like this: an endless intermission. Above us, Susanna stepped out into nothing. No, I was mistaken: there were no gold loops in her ears.

'All we got is love, baby, in this crazy mazy world,' Fats rumbled at Hoo-Sin's back, doing a hopeful little shuffle, and Kitty, joining the crowd gathering now around Mavis (Michelle glanced back over her shoulder at me: the resemblance was still there but she and Susanna had grown apart, the one toward mystery, or the fear of it, the other toward sorrow), said: 'Tell us again, Mavis, about how you first met Ros . . .' We ducked as Fats arched slowly, almost gracefully, into the air over Hoo-Sin and crashed to the floor behind us, and I thought ('Are those back in fashion?' Iris Draper inquired, bending down and adjusting her spectacles. 'I wonder if I threw all mine away . . . ?'), Vic was right, who was I to mix drinks and answer doorbells? I wished I could just go home.

'I know,' Cynthia said, patting my arm with a ring-laden hand. Had I been talking out loud? 'We all feel that way sometimes.'

'It all began one day when Jim was called to an orphanage to deal with a peculiar medical emergency,' Mavis said in a hollow portentous tone, and Iris, turning away, whispered: 'Ah! I don't want to miss this!' I dug out the crème Yvette, checked the ice bucket: three cubes, a puddle of discolored water, some soggy cigarette butts . . . and the wooden-handled pick. 'He was often called in, of course, for circumcisions, hot douches, infibulations, and the like, when the girls reached puberty, but in this case the child was only ten years old – yet so precocious that they had already lost, through scandal, three tutors, a handyman, and two members of the board of trustees. As for the other girls . . .'

'Here,' I said, straining the drink into a cocktail glass and handing it to her. My hand was shaking. I glanced past her shoulder, creased by its heavy strap, into the TV room, where Charley had Steve the plumber in a huddle, apparently trying to sell him something. The Inspector stood just behind them, watching the television, his back to the door. Well, I thought, if things seemed out of focus, I could do something about it. I reached into the ice bucket for the pick. The handle felt worn and comfortable in my grip. 'Now if you don't mind, my son asked me . . .'

'I'll go in with you.' She didn't seem to want to let go of me.

Charley passed us in the doorway, giving the thumbs-up sign. 'I may get group outa this,' he growled happily, 'if I c'n juss fine – hah, *there* she is!'

As though this were an announcement, Pardew turned around and said: 'Good, our engineer! Perhaps she can help!'

Steve was squatting behind the TV set once again, assisting the bearded technician. Images were flickering intermittently on the screen, and sometimes in montage, as though the switching cables had somehow fused. 'Such commotions had a way of flarin' up at public executions in olden times – and recent ones, too, y'know,' Lloyd Draper remarked, peering down his nose at the set (I caught fleeting glimpses there of the back of Jim's head, Noble doing an obscene handkerchief trick, Fats on the floor, the stopped-up toilet, Elstob yipping and snorting, Mee testing a razorblade across the palm of his hand, a patch on Sally Ann's fly that said 'OPEN CAREFULLY AND INSERT TAB HERE,' Horner with her, getting a message in his ear, someone's fist in a bowl of peanuts, bright lights, out of focus), and Pardew said: 'I know. Contagious hysteroid reactions of this sort are typical wherever masses are assembled – it's an imitative ritualization of the bizarre and hallucinatory tendencies of the odd few, and always, I've noted, with a tinge of the burlesque. Frankly, it's the sort of thing I see too much of.' Patrick, not far from the Inspector's elbow, gave a sympathetic little sigh.

'I think we've got it now,' Cynthia said, detaching some cables, plugging in others. The image had stabilized on Mavis (' – determined that it was best for all concerned to bring the child home to live with my husband and me for a while,' she was saying into the camera, her gaze intent yet misty, 'in order to keep her under daily observation, and perhaps to assist her – through close personal guidance and a more precise education – to transcend her singular and somewhat—') and they switched it now to Quagg, being interviewed, or perhaps interviewing himself.

'Okay,' said the technician, crawling out from behind the set, adjusting slightly the color. 'I'll go pick up the camera.'

'That's right,' Quagg was saying, 'Ros had just got the lead in our new feature spasm, *Socialist Head*. It's a radical and theatrically mind-blowing miracle play that examines the modes and variations of oral sex in a revolutionary society – dynamite stuff really, and of course Ros was like handmade for the part. Howzat? Something special? You betcher ass, baby! We'd really hoped to hit the nut on this one, get our tokus outa the tub, but now . . . with poor Ros on ice . . .' His voice broke. 'Aw shit . . .'

As the camera, hand-held, began to move away from Zack past Vic and Daffie, Eileen, Scarborough in a gloomy hangdog slump, Alison's husband, the crowd around Mavis (' – but little did we imagine –' I heard her say), and on out into the hall, where Horner and the man in the chalkstriped suit could be seen racing each other for the basement stairs, Teresa peeking into the downstairs toilet (the camera seemed to be headed either out or up: now the front door came into view), the Inspector, clutching my son's stuffed rabbit in his arms, his finger in its hole, continued his angry harangue about what he called 'this compulsive attraction for the new, for sensations, thrills, overloaded circuits, the human imagination unchecked by the proper and necessary intervention of sober critical faculties, and so laid open to all manner of excess and delirium.' Patrick punctuated this monologue with his infatuated yea-saying ('Oh yes! Absolutely! Dreadful! Utterly insane!' – his split lip had made his lisp worse), all the while trying to touch the bunny in Pardew's arms. Staring at the glass eyes of the stuffed bunny, I seemed to see my mother-in-law's stern demanding gaze. Right *now*, she'd said. I cleared my throat. 'Excuse me, Inspector, I—'

'*Sshh!*' Pardew hissed, squinting at the set, and Patrick snapped: 'Yes, Gerald, don't interrupt!'

'But you *must* – the police – your two officers – in the kitchen, *my*—!'

'Not now, damn you!'

'*But*—!' My throat was all knotted up, I could hardly speak. 'My son *needs* her! It's not *fair!*' I might as well have been shouting into the wind. I held up the ice pick in my trembling fist: '*Look!*' Cynthia glanced up in alarm. '*Here's* what you've been—!'

'*There! You see?!*' Pardew was pointing excitedly at the TV, where Ginger, seemingly in a state of shock, her pigtails collapsed, wavered at the top of the stairs. 'Who was that man with her just then?' 'I didn't see, we'll get it on playback . . .' Clutching a kerchief to her mouth and a hand to her bared breast, she wobbled forward, but as if unaware of the stairs in front of her: she hovered there a moment with one foot out in space like a divining rod, then came down hard, striking the edge of the first step with her thin stiletto heel, her ankle warping, knee buckling, and down she pitched, looping arse over elbow, kerchiefs flying, limbs outflung in all directions, all of it slowed down and thus mockingly balletic in its effects, like someone tumbling on the moon. '*A redhead! Of course . . . !*' Somehow she hit the landing on her feet, sinking softly into a kind of frog squat, her back to the camera, which was slowly zooming in – but not for long: her narrow bottom bounced in slow motion off the floor like the head of a twin-peened hammer and she began to rise again, floating up into space once more, arcing head-first and heels high toward the camera. 'It should have been obvious to me!'

'In Greek theater, you know,' Patrick confided at his elbow, 'they put these lovely red wigs—'

'*What's happened*— ?!' Pardew cried, so startling Patrick that he fell backward onto Knud, who grunted irritably and rolled over. The screen had gone blank just as Ginger in full tilt was revolving feet-first toward the in-zooming camera, and now the Inspector beat on it with his fists: '*Come on, damn you!*'

'I don't think it's the CRT,' Cynthia said. She worked the switches, picked up Mavis ('"– is what it's *for*, Aunty May," the sweet child explained, touching me. I . . . I didn't even know I *had* one . . . !'), then Daffie tapping her gleaming teeth with a spoon, Noble with a straw up his nose, but only a blank screen where Ginger should be. I lowered my arm, which ached now with its dull news.

'*It's a plot!*' Pardew raged, kicking the set and swatting it with Peedie so hard one of the ears flew off.

'Uh . . . I'll go check the camera,' Steve the plumber mumbled, slipping away.

'*Where are my officers— ?!*'

'*That's what I've been trying to tell you!*' I cried, pointing past his shoulder with the weapon in my hand. But I was pointing in the wrong direction. The two of them were in the doorway behind me.

'Uh, Chief, we got a bit of trouble . . .'

'*Trouble? You don't know the half of it!*' the Inspector roared. They glanced at me uneasily. Or maybe respectfully, I couldn't tell. '*If I don't get this picture back— !*'

Fred turned to Bob, who shrugged, and they came forward into the room.

'*It's not the set, you imbeciles!*' the Inspector cried, shaking the stuffed rabbit at them. '*It's the camera! Out in the hall! MOVE, damn you! We're missing everything!*'

'Yes, sir,' Fred said and they lumbered out, Bob muttering something sullenly under his breath. On the television, Regina clutched her shoulders and stared. Then Mavis, filling the screen, said something about Jim's tongue. Vic belched, Prissy Loo lifted her toga to show Dolph her military longjohns. 'I think you were looking for this,' I insisted, offering Pardew the pick.

'We've got it now!' cried Cynthia.

'Aha . . . !'

The fall was over. The camera seemed to be in the living room now. Ginger, wearing the Inspector's white scarf as a kind of diaper or loincloth beneath what kerchiefs remained, was standing, knees out, in the doorway, trying on his crushed fedora.

'*Now* what?!'

'I'll take that,' Cynthia said, coming over.

'It really doesn't matter,' I sighed. 'I don't know where it came from anyway.'

'I know. We'll let Woody handle it.'

'They got the camera going again,' Fred said in the doorway.

'You think I'm blind?' the Inspector growled, chewing his lip and digging irritably in Peedie's hole. '*Damn* her!'

The fedora lay springily on top of Ginger's revived pigtails, bobbing above her head as she walked. When she stopped, the hat leaned forward over her eyes, then rocked back. When she stepped forward, it seemed to hesitate a moment before following her.

'Most places I've been,' Lloyd Draper put in, 'red hair's pretty unlucky. Folks have a way of choppin' it off, don't y'know, head and all . . .'

'*What's happened to my overcoat— ?!*' the Inspector bellowed. Ginger was pulling it on now, her thin arms lost in its long floppy sleeves. It was wrinkled, misshapen, and had huge dark blotches all over it. It seemed to weigh her down, and her knees bowed out another couple of inches.

'You ask any Hindoo, he'll tell you that red, heh heh, is just bad news. Once when we were up in India, Iris and me, we got tickets to a—'

'They been using it,' Bob said (Ginger was now staggering about in the coat's bulk, the fedora bouncing on her head, peering at everything through an oversized magnifying glass that stuck out of one sleeve like an artificial claw), 'to catch the drip from the upstairs crapper.'

'What— ?!'

'I said, when Iris and me were in India—'

'*Enough!*' barked Pardew, twisting Peedie's other ear off. He pointed with it toward the front of the house, and the two officers, unsheathing their clubs, disappeared.

Ginger had now discovered Ros's body (the wake seemed to have started up around her again) and was down on her bony knees with her head under the skirt. She emerged with a look of triumph on her face and the fedora squashed down around her ears. She pushed a thick sleeve back, reached in and fished about, her eyes rolling, then began to pull on something: she tugged, strained, her eyes crossed – it gave way and she tumbled backward. She held it up: it was the Inspector's briar pipe. 'Damn!' he muttered, slapping his pockets. Ginger gazed at it curiously, sniffed it, then prepared to fit it into the pucker of her mouth – but something over her shoulder alarmed her: she staggered to her feet and went stumbling and tripping through the mourners off-camera, dragging the tail of her thick checkered coat behind her. Bob and Fred appeared on the screen. They looked around in confusion – then, swinging their nightsticks, charged off in pursuit. My heart leaped to my throat. The camera, following the cops' exit, had come to rest on Alison. Slowly it zoomed in, Alison staring straight at it with that same look of terror and supplication I'd last seen in the dining room. Noble, Dickie, Horner, the man in the chalkstripes, all crowded around her – and beneath her charmeuse skirt there were not two legs but four – Vachel! 'Now what was it,' the Inspector asked, turning toward me, 'that you wanted to— ?'

But I was already out the door, pushing through the pack-up in the dining room (' – watching the child's astonishing performance through the two-way mirror, as if art and life were somehow separate,' Mavis was saying, breathing heavily now and stroking her pale white thighs below her rucked-up skirt, 'but then, suddenly, overtaken by excitement and desire . . .'), fighting my way as though through a briary nightmare toward the living room – but to no purpose. Except for Vic, slumped in an armchair next to Ros, and Malcolm Mee in the sunroom, his head bent solemnly over a handmirror 'I've never done anything like this before,' some guy was crooning hollowly on the hi-fi), the room was empty. That must have been a tape replay on the TV. In fact, now that I thought about it for a moment, I'd just seen the cops in the dining room, setting out silverware and stacks of plates on the table, and the camera, of course, was on Mavis.

There were too many lights on in here. The wreckage, the debris, was all too visible. It was like a theater after the play is over, deserted and garish, its illusions exposed. I gathered up some crumpled napkins, fallen ashtrays, half a bun smeared with catsup, a shattered cigar butt, a couple of glasses and a roach holder – but then I didn't know what to do with them, so I set them down again. This time on the coffee table. There, by one foot, lay Alison's green silk sash. I picked it up, held it to my lips.

'Mustn't take it too hard,' Vic said, but I wasn't sure whether he was talking to me or to himself. He was staring down at Ros, unrecognizable now except for the tatters of her silvery frock. 'It's fucking sad, but what the hell, there's nothing tragic about it.'

'No . . .'

'Life's too horrible to be tragic. We all know that. That's for adolescents who still haven't adjusted to the shit.' He shook the ice around in his drink, watching it. 'Nonetheless . . .' He was struggling still with his sense of loss. I understood this. I'd said the same things many times, half-believing them. When I'd found my father, for example. In a room much like this one, his last hotel suite. The consoling overview: catastrophe as the mechanism that makes life possible, sorrow a morbid inflammation of the ego. A line, like any other . . . 'You know, I've been thinking about that play Ros was in, the pillar of salt thing . . .'

'You went to that?'

'Yeah. I wasn't about to make a fool of myself down there on stage, if that's what you're wondering, crazy as I was about her, but I watched the others who did. And it gave me time to think about that story. God saved Lot, you'll remember, so Lot afterward could fuck his daughters, but he froze the wife for looking back. On the surface, that doesn't make a lot of sense. But the radical message of that legend is that incest, sodomy, betrayal and all that are not crimes – only turning back is: rigidified memory, attachment to the past. That play was one attempt to subvert the legend, unfreeze the memory, reconnect to the here and now.' He scowled into his glass. I was thinking of Ros, salted blue, warming to rose under all those tongues. Ros, who never looked back, not even for a soft place to fall. 'And maybe . . . maybe her murder was another . . .'

'How's that?'

'Or maybe . . .' He grunted, sighed, drank deeply. 'Who knows?' He shuddered slightly. 'Why can't I shake this off, Gerry?'

'Well, perhaps,' I suggested, recalling the feel, on the back porch, of Alison's sash giving way, thinking then of love as a kind of affectionate surrender, an alternative to both resignation and confrontation (Mee floated past us on his way to the dining room, wearing my soggy ascot now as a headband), 'you should stop fighting it.'

'Hmpf, you're as bad as that dead battery I'm with tonight,' he grumped. 'Know what she called me? A fucking sentimental humanist! Hah! A goddamn affront to the universe, she said!' The faint trace of a wry smile flickered across his craggy features. 'That's not bad, I have to admit . . . but goddamn it, Gerry, I *hate* sentimentality! I *hate* fantasy, mooning around – *I hate confused emotions!*'

'Too bad,' said Jim, coming in from the hallway, his jacket on once more, a drink in his hand, 'that's probably the only kind there are.' My own now were mixed with guilt: that terrified appeal on her face on the TV screen just moments ago, and then before that in the dining room – or was it in here? – and in the kitchen . . . 'How's your wife, Gerry?'

'What? Oh, I don't know, Jim. The police . . .'

'The police what?' Vic wanted to know, looking up.

'You know, their inquiries, a while ago they were—'

'What – your wife? Those goddamn fucking – what have you *done* about it?'

'Well, I spoke to Woody—'

'Ah. Good . . .' He seemed lost again in his own thoughts, his elbows on his knees, staring into his glass. Jim watched him with concern. I was thinking of something my father said; it was the last time I saw him alive, about six months before he'd, as he liked to put it, reached for the inevitable. 'Why don't you let me check your blood pressure, Vic?'

'What – with that gizmo they were blowing up around Ros's neck a while ago? No, thanks!'

'They were just getting a fingerprint. Trying to. They had to use it to clamp the X-ray film cassette to the skin, that's all.' He smiled. 'What's the problem? Figure it might be catching?'

'It's not that . . .'

'Yneh!' groaned Regina, sweeping into the room in her wispy gown, her hands upraised as though in protest. 'That lady in there is too much!'

'Lady— ?'

'That – that child molester! That geed-up dip with her fat hands in her pants! I can't *believe* it!' Time is hard and full of calamities, my father had said, but man is soft and malleable. If he chooses to endure, then he also chooses metamorphosis, perhaps of an unexpected and even unimaginable nature, such that choice itself may no longer be part of his condition. A signal, of course, which I hadn't heeded. I draped the sash around my neck, thinking about my own metamorphoses, my diffluent condition. 'She's giving a blow-by-blow description – and I choose my *mots* carefully! – of a frantic three-way grope, featuring her, her old man, and Ros when she wasn't ten years old yet and hadn't even got her *hair!* Oh my God! *Poor Ros!*'

'It didn't seem to do her any harm,' Jim said quietly. Lloyd Draper came in with a screen and slide projector and started setting up in the sunroom. 'Oh yes, many children,' he was saying. 'One feller strung ten of 'em up at a time, called it a warnin' to men and a – heh heh – spectacle for the angels! I got pictures here, you'll see!' 'We're probably too emotional about pedophilia. In a lot of societies, children have sex with their parents, grandparents, brothers and sisters, aunts and uncles, all the time, and as far as we can tell they don't seem adversely affected.'

'I believe it,' said Vic, his temples throbbing, hand squeezing his glass as though to crush it like one of Dolph's beer cans, 'but I don't believe it.'

'In fact, sex with their grandparents is probably *good* for them.'

'Blah! Mine would've given me the clap!' Regina retorted, crossing her hands over her breast. 'I gotta admit, though, that little kid in there is sure eating it up!' The telephone rang. 'I'll get it, it may be Beni!'

'What little kid?' I called after her.

'I think she means Mark,' Jim said, sipping at his drink. 'He came down looking for his rabbit, he said.'

'What— ?!'

At the door (how many times had I been through here? I felt like I was chasing after lost luggage in an airport or something) I bumped into Alison's husband, who turned pale when he saw the silk sash around my neck. 'Is it . . . over?'

'Not yet,' I said and sneezed. 'I haven't even—'

'*Sshh!*' someone scolded.

He frowned and looked about, pipe clamped in his teeth, craning his head. She wasn't in here but Mark was: right up front in his SUPERLOVER sweatshirt, sitting on the prie-dieu next to Vachel the dwarf. I had the impression Vachel might have his hands on him, but my view was blocked by all the others pressing around, I couldn't be sure. Mavis, her skirts dragged up past her marbled thighs now, both hands digging frantically inside her shiny balloon-like drawers, was apparently describing Ros's childish body (' – like cherries, and – *unf!* – her little cheeks were – *ooh!* – suffused with the – *ah!* – tint of roses . . . !') as she squatted over Mavis's face while manipulating her with one hand and stroking Jim with the other, sucking one of them – I couldn't tell which, maybe both, it didn't matter – I just wanted to get Mark out of there.

'Hey, come on! Stop pushing!'

'We were here first!'

'*Psst! Mark!*'

'Ouch!'

'– With her velvety tongue and with her – *gasp!* – fingers in me like the feet of – *oh!* – little birds, I felt my mind just explode and spread through my – *whoof!* – whole body, surrendering, ah – abjectly – an incredible – *grunt!* – radiance and – and *truth!*—'

Vachel leered at me over his shoulder as I pulled on Mark. Mavis was now hauling at her vulva as though scrubbing clothes at a washboard, her hips slapping the chair, head lolling, eyes glazed over, mouth bubbly with drool. 'I don't *wanna*— !' Mark whined, and some of Quagg's crowd hissed and booed me playfully, grinning the while in open-faced admiration of Mavis's mounting orgasm. '*Go! Go!*' some of them chanted. '*No*, Daddy! I wanna hear the *story!*'

'It's all over,' I insisted, dragging him away as though out of a dense thicket. All but anyway: nothing now but yelps, groans, squeals, a few blurted phrases (something about 'miracles' and 'sweet vapors' and 'groves of wild angels' or 'dangers' – Ros, apparently, had changed positions), and the rhythmical whoppety-whop of her huge soft buttocks against the seat of her chair. 'Hang on to your pajamas!'

Too late, he'd lost them. He dropped to his hands and knees and went scuttling back in after them, but I pulled him out again – and in the nick of time, for Mavis suddenly shrieked rapturously and fell out of her chair, sending all the people around her staggering backward and all over each other – 'You might have been stepped on, son!' I scolded as the others choked and giggled, muttered apologies ('But my *jamapants*, Daddy— !' 'You've got others . . .'), or caught their breath. '*Wow*— !'

'And then . . . !' Mavis gasped from the floor, and the crowd fell silent again. Her breathing was labored, her voice raw and as though miles away. 'And then . . . Jim . . . Jim *kissed* me!'

Her audience, some of them still picking themselves up, whooped and whistled, giving her a big hand. 'God, that was one helluva moving story!' someone exclaimed. 'Wild – but *real!*'

'Why doesn't Gramma read me stories like that?' Mark wanted to know.

'Style, man – some people got it, some don't.'

'Where is Grandma anyway?'

'She's with some man.'

'She on the spike, you think?'

'Grandma— ?'

'Didn't you notice when her skirt was up?'

'These yours, Mark?' Kitty asked, emerging from the crowd now milling about. She held them up in front of her like an apron. 'One thing for sure, you can tell they're not mine!'

Mark laughed, and Kitty knelt to help him put them on, a bit flushed still from Mavis's tale and none too steady. 'Been in to see your old man, Kitty?' Talbot asked, tilting his head toward his good ear.

'What's there to see?' The bearded technician in cowboy boots now crouched behind her shoulder, his camera focused on Mark and Kitty's fumbling hands – I stepped forward to block his view, but just then the two police officers came staggering in from the kitchen, supporting a huge turkey between them, shouting at me: 'Hey, *you!* Move that empty tray, will ya? *Hurry!*' 'Just appearance, Talbot – believe me, dreams are never as good as the real thing! Isn't that right, Mark?'

'What real thing?'

'Hey! Look at the little birdie!'

'Easy!' grunted Fred as they lowered the turkey gingerly onto the hot plate, the others in the room beginning to press around the table. 'Here, gimme that rag!' he cried, snatching the sash from around my neck.

'Wait!'

'Back off now!'

'Jesus, whoever lives here really opens up his pockets!'

'You shoulda been here earlier, Gudrun – there was a curried shrimp dip you wouldn't believe!'

'Say,' Zack Quagg whispered in my ear, nodding toward Alison's husband in the doorway ('But I heard him *say* he was going to do it,' Janny Trainer was insisting with tears in her eyes, 'right in her chest like that!'), 'that bearded dude got any green?'

'And mushroom turnovers!'

'He does all right, I think.'

'He's so cute!'

'Thanks, man – that's what I wanted to hear.'

'I'll get a bowl for the stuffing,' Bob said, taking his oven gloves off, and Janice Trainer, beside me, gasped in disbelief, clutching her bosom: 'Oh no! You mean he sits right on their faces and— ?!' 'And that blade you just honed!' Fred called after him.

'That's right, you little dope,' said Daffie sourly, blowing smoke. 'And now you've driven him away with your nasty little rumors.'

'Well, I didn't know!'

'What? Has Dickie gone?'

'He's just leaving,' said Dolph, wandering in ('Is it . . . is it fun?'), a boozy smile on his face. He winked at Talbot, nodded back over his shoulder toward the hallway. 'H'lo, Mark. Say, you're on a real toot tonight, aren't you?'

'It can be felt,' Hoo-Sin explained at Janny's shoulder, 'but it cannot be grasped.'

'Yeah? Try telling Dolph that!' groaned Kitty, slapping his hand away, as I took Mark's. 'Uncle Dolph's got ants in his pants, Daddy.'

'Hey, what's Mavis doing down there on the floor?'

'Whatever it is,' Regina declared, fluttering in from the living room, 'you can bet it's something *dirty!*'

'It has no surface . . .'

'Trouble with Dolph is, he starts at the bottom but never works his way up!'

'Don't put the act down, Vadge, the big lady's got talent,' admonished Zack Quagg, working his way away from the table with a thick slab of breast, just as Fats came waddling up behind Regina, crooning: 'Ruh-gina! Won't you be my Valentine-a!' She grimaced and shrank away.

'. . . No inside . . .'

'Man, this turkey's a fuckin' flyer!' Quagg had apparently dunked it in the mustard; it was running down his chin and dripping on his unitard. Regina pushed Fats' hands away, glowering toward Hoo-Sin ('Gee, it sounds *nice*,' Janny was saying, and Hoo-Sin, smiling enigmatically, left her). 'Did you get hold of Benedetto?'

'He's coming as soon as his show's over,' said Regina. Hoo-Sin now had Fats in a half-nelson. 'Wait— ! Have a heart!' he gasped. 'To have mercy on wolves is to be tyrannical toward sheep,' Hoo-Sin replied, as though intoning Scripture. 'He'll be bringing some of the cast.' Fats was in the air again.

'Terrific! Hey, we got the goods – let's frame a show here! Malcolm—?'

I realized too late we should have gone the other way. We'd made it as far as the hall door, but were blocked there by incoming traffic. 'Malcolm may be down in the dungeon, Zack – something's on the boards down there . . .' Mark pulled back so I took him up in my arms. 'Is that little man a dorf, Daddy?' 'Yes.' 'A real one?' It was like having to go the wrong way in a train station at rush hour. 'Lemme at that roast canary, boys! I gotta round out my saggin' career!' But there was no turning back either, people were pushing toward the table and away from it at the same time. Fred backed off, gingerly holding his neckbrace: they were tearing the bird apart in there with their bare hands, it was as though we hadn't put anything out to eat all night.

'Are real dorfs naughty?'

It was the tall cop, Bob, limping through with the butcher knife, who finally opened up a gap we could slip through. He scowled angrily at us as he squeezed past, and, glancing up, I saw that Mark was sticking his tongue out at him. 'Hey, Mark! That's not nice!'

'I don't like him, Daddy. He *pinched* me.'

'The policeman pinched you—?'

'Whaddaya say, Mark?' grinned Charley on his way in. 'How's yer ole rusty dusty?'

'How's your ole boo-boo, Unca Charley!' Mark replied, giggling. Charley rolled his eyes and did a sad little flat-footed dance around us. 'My ole boo-boo's gone blooey!' he declared mournfully. There were people piling up and down the basement stairs ('Whoo! game, set and *snatch!*' 'Ha ha! you goin' down again?' 'Yeah, man, one more time . . .'), but it was less crowded out here. 'It's bye-bye, boo-boo, Mark, ole buddy!' Charley called. Mark laughed and jumped up and down in my arms as I carried him toward the stairs. My study door had been pulled to, but the toilet door was open, the darkroom light still on. It glowed from the inside like hell in a melodrama. 'Boo-hoo-*hoo*-hoo!' Quagg had used just such a scene in *The Naughty Dollies' Nightmare*, when the wooden soldier sold his soul to the golliwog. 'How's your ole *poo-poo*, Unca Charley!' Mark squealed.

'That's enough, Mark. You're getting overexcited—'

'Wait, Daddy!'

'No, Uncle Charley's gone now, it's time—'

'But *Peedie!*' he wailed. '*I want my Peedie!*'

'Ah.' This was a different matter. In fact, if I wanted any peace, I had no choice. But the TV room was impossibly distant, I didn't know if I had the strength to go all the way back through there again. I felt as though I'd crossed one border too many: I just wanted to book in somewhere. Sit back and use room service. What made me think we wanted to go traveling again? 'Do you think you really need it, Mark? Maybe we should try to go to sleep once with – all right, all right, stop crying.' He was heavy, or seemed so suddenly. I set him down. The front room looked empty but there was music playing. A dance tune, 'Learning About Love' – it sounded tinny and hollow. 'Wait here, I'll go get it.'

But when I turned around, there was Cynthia holding the rabbit up, waving it like a flag. Mark ran to her, arms outstretched, and I followed. It even had its ears on again. 'Thanks, you saved my life,' I said.

'His ears are all funny!' Mark exclaimed. She'd pinned them on backward.

'Oh, I'm sorry – I guess I don't know much about rabbits!'

'He's wearing them that way for the party,' I suggested. 'You know Peedie – anything for a laugh.' I winked wearily and Cynthia smiled. There was a faint blush on her skin from the darkroom light. 'We'll fix them back tomorrow.'

'Naughty Peedie!' Mark scolded, giving the thing a thump. Then he hugged it close, pushing a finger up its hole, a thumb in his mouth.

'You're so good with children,' Cynthia said.

'Did you get into the TV room?' Woody asked her, coming up from the cellar stairs as I was leading Mark away.

'Yes. It was a disappointment.' Someone behind us laughed at that: 'It always is!' Woody, I'd noticed, was still in his underwear, but his shorts were on backward now. His hair was mussed, his eyes dilated from the cellar dark. 'They're in there now watching slow-motion replays of the doctor's wife.'

'Mavis . . . ?'

'. . . A story . . .'

My grandmother used to tell me a story about a man who had to climb a staircase with a thousand steps to get to heaven. She'd start at the bottom and take them one by one, and I'd always fall asleep, of course, before the man reached the top. I remembered – would always remember – the terrible ordeal of that climb, as I struggled desperately to keep my eyes open to the end, and I still had dreams about it: poised halfway up an infinite staircase, my legs gone to lead. For a while I even supposed a thousand might *be* an infinite number, but I tried counting it in the daytime and found it only took me ten or fifteen minutes. In fact, as I learned on mountain holidays with my father, it's not even that high a climb. Of course my grandmother always counted slower than I did, but that still didn't explain why I always fell asleep halfway up and usually sooner. I thought it might be the sleepy rhythm of the counting itself, so to counteract it I tried to distract myself with puzzles and memories and silent stories of my own. This was even less successful than concentrating on the counting, and what was worse, I seemed to lose the stories and memories I used that way. It was as if they were getting sucked up into the counting and there erased. Not that I wouldn't have sacrificed them willingly to reach the top, to be able to see what the man saw, but clearly they were not the route. It seemed that nothing was, and I even began to worry that there might be something wrong with me, something having to do with words I'd been learning about like 'souls' and 'corruption' and 'predestination.' I remembered startling my parents one day on a drive to my grandmother's house by asking them what was original sin. 'Not being able to read a roadmap,' my mother said drily, and my father laughed and said: 'Being born.' Then one day I suddenly discovered my grandmother's secret. It was simple. There was always a preamble to the climb, a story about who the man was or how he'd died – often she claimed it was a relative or someone who'd lived there in town – and then a more or less elaborate account of his travels through the next world before he finally reached the stairs. And of course my grandmother was tailoring the length of this prologue to my own apparent sleepiness and the lateness of the hour. So I laid a trap for her, curling up in a corner early as though exhausted, pretending to fall asleep on her shoulder as she put my pajamas on, yawning and dozing through her preliminary tale until she got the man to the bottom step, letting him climb the first dozen or so, so there'd be no turning back. During these first ponderous footfalls, as I lay there with my eyes closed, I felt a momentary rush of guilt for having done this to my grandmother, and I nearly chose to carry the deception right on into feigned sleep – or real sleep, it might have got mixed up. But curiosity got the best of me, I'd waited too long for this: before I even knew it, I was sitting bolt upright in bed, hugging my knees, my eyes wide open, watching her intently. She gave no sign that anything was different, proceeding resolutely, step by step, toward the top, as though this was the way she'd always told it – and how could I be sure she hadn't? The first four hundred steps or so were excruciatingly difficult – I was partly right about the incantatory powers of the slow ascent, and in spite of all my preparations, they nearly did me in. I perked up a bit after that, animated by the challenge of getting at least halfway, but then faded again around seven hundred, even losing a number of steps altogether – or perhaps my grandmother, seeing my eyes cross and my head dip, skipped a few. As the man started up the last hundred steps, I felt a surge of excitement – suddenly it was the best story I'd ever heard and I was wide awake. At last! But, typically, I'd peaked too early. Fifty steps later I was sinking again, overwhelmed by a thick numbing stupor. I couldn't believe it. What was the matter, I asked myself fiercely, didn't I want to see it? Didn't I want to know what it was like? I pinched myself, shook my head, bugged my eyes, tried to bob up and down in the bed, but I couldn't shake it off. Each step the man took fell like lead in my brain. It was as though my whole body had turned against me, refusing me at the last moment all I'd struggled for. I couldn't see my grandmother, just the steps, looming high above me. The numbers tolled hollowly in the back of my head like heavy bells. It was my first true test of will, if there is such a thing, and as the man climbed the last steps up through the clouds, I must have looked a bit like him – largely lifeless, staring rigidly, teeth bared, grimly hanging in. Amazingly, we both made it. When he pulled himself up that final step, I was paralyzed with fatigue and anxiety, but I was at least able to see my grandmother again. 'And what do you think he found?' she asked. Her expression was the same as when she'd begun. 'What?' I responded hoarsely, almost afraid. 'You tell me,' she said. I thought it might be a riddle, a final test, or her way of helping me wake up enough to hear the end. 'Angels,' I said. The back of my neck ached from trying to hold my head up. 'And lots of toys and candy and things.' This didn't seem serious enough. I was trying to remember things I'd read or been told. 'God – and his own father and mother. And grandmother.' 'Yes . . .' She seemed to want something more. I sank back on the pillow, trying to think. 'Streets made of gold. Flowers that taste good, and . . . and happiness . . .' 'That's right.' I hesitated. My tongue was sore where I'd been biting. And my eyes, which hurt from holding them open, wouldn't close now. 'Is that . . . is that all?' She tucked me in and gave me a kiss. 'He found everything he wanted,' she said and left me. It was a terrible disappointment. I stayed awake for hours thinking about it and it made my head ache for days after. I couldn't quite think what it was, but I felt I'd lost something valuable – the story for one thing, of course: that special bond, while it remained unfinished, between my grandmother and me, now gone forever. And especially those preambles about the different climbers and how they'd died and then their travels in the afterlife – I found I'd enjoyed them more than I'd realized at the time, obsessed then by the need for denouement, and I wanted them back, but they'd lost their footing, as it were. No stairs at the end now, just an abyss. I kept wondering for a long time afterward if I'd missed something, if I'd maybe dozed off at the wrong moment after all or failed to understand a vital clue. Only years later, about the time my grandmother died and began her own climb – or rather, vice versa – did I finally understand that there was nothing more to search for, that I had indeed got the point. It was, as my grandmother had intended from the first step on, her principal legacy to me . . .

Mark was right, there *was* someone in there with her. I could hear them talking. My mother-in-law was saying something in that flat moralistic tone of hers about 'sucking the mother's finger.' A euphemism, I supposed, leaning toward the door: I hadn't heard her speak like that before. 'So he was married, then,' the man said, his voice muffled, 'and raped a woman who was as well as dead.'

'Yes. And then he left her and forgot her, as you might expect. Though later, he went back and prolonged his illicit amours, it being his dissolute nature.'

'I see. So it's not true about the mother-in-law, the accusations, I mean, that she murdered – or at least tried—'

'How could it be? It's impossible when you think about it. No, it was his wife, who, with good reason, put in execution those so-called horrible desires . . .'

'That's a very serious accusation, m'um. Yet my own experience tells me it must be so. Funny how, with repetition, it gets all turned around.'

'What are we waiting *outside* for, Daddy?'

'Sshh! Don't bother Grandma!' I whispered and eased the door on open.

I was sure they'd heard us, but if so, they gave no indication. She was in her rocking chair and the man was on the floor at her feet, his head in her lap. 'You've been so much help to me,' he said. It was Inspector Pardew. She seemed to be stroking his temples. 'I'd always thought of that story as a parable on time – the hundred years compressed to a dream, the bastard birth of chronology, then our irrational fear of losing it. The destruction of dawn and all our days, our sun, our moon, seemed so horrible that only something beyond our imagination, like a demon or an ogre, could be responsible. But, of course, all it takes is a jealous wife . . .'

'Yes, but one mustn't forget the prior crime, the one that set the rest in motion—'

'Daddy? There's something *hard* inside Peedie.'

'Yes, all right . . .'

'Why are we whispering?'

The Inspector looked up. 'Come in, come in,' he said irritably, and put his head back down in her lap. He was wearing his scarf again, clasping the ends with one hand. I pushed the door shut behind us. 'You were saying, m'um, the original— ?'

'You know, the party, the disgruntled guest, the curse. The stabbing . . .'

'Ah yes – but was it really a crime? Or only a sort of prior condition?'

'Get it *out*, Daddy!'

'All right, all right.' I laid him in his bed and drew a loose sheet up over him (he kicked it off), took up the stuffed bunny. I knew, even before I'd pushed my finger in the hole and touched it, what it was. 'It makes him stronger, Mark, like a backbone – you sure you don't want to leave it in there— ?'

'I want it *out!* It *hurts* him!' The Inspector sighed impatiently and closed his eyes. Mark was tired and on edge from all the excitement – the least thing and he could break into one of his tantrums. I reached in with two fingers, clamping the handle, pushing down on the point from the outside.

'Perhaps, like you say, I've been struggling with this problem too long,' Pardew brooded. 'I feel as I circle around it, groping, scrutinizing, probing, that something *is* trying to be born here – but that, unfortunately, it might already be dead.' My mother-in-law flinched at this. 'I'm sorry, did I— ?'

'No . . . a memory . . .'

The end of the handle was protruding now: I drew it out, remembering something my wife had said, shortly after she came home from the hospital: 'It's not the loss, Gerald, there are others waiting to be born, but rather . . .'

'Daddy, I'm afraid of the dark.'

I stooped to kiss him and tuck him in. 'Rather,' my wife had said, 'it's the way it *hated* me at the end, I knew everything it was thinking, the terrible bitterness and rage it felt, it would have *killed* me if it could – and what was worse, I agreed with it . . .' 'Well, it's not dark now.'

'When I go to sleep, it *gets* dark.'

'I only meant that truth, when it is no longer pertinent, is not in the same sense truth any longer, do you follow, m'um? I may solve the crime, you see, only to discover that its very definition has moved on to another plane.' The Inspector seemed not to want to be interrupted, so I set the ice pick on the emptied shelves near him, where he could find it later. My mother-in-law frowned at it, glanced sharply up at me. I shrugged. 'It's as if that prince of yours were to hack his way through his thicket of briars and brambles, only to arouse a creature suffering from a fatal disease, as it were, or one who's lost her wits.'

'Or perhaps to find a host of competing Beauties,' she suggested, turning back to the Inspector, her face dark with consternation, 'each seemingly fairer than the rest, and then what's he to do? Awaken only one and condemn the rest to death in life? No, yet if he should kiss them all, their multitudinous awakenings would reduce his own life to chaos and madness . . .'

'Yes! Strange! I – I was just thinking the same . . . !'

'I know,' she sighed and stroked his head.

'It all goes round and round,' the Inspector said, his voice quavering slightly. 'Sometimes I . . . I don't know where I am!'

'Yes, yes . . . it's all right . . .'

I turned to leave, but I heard a lot of people outside the door – Wilma,

Patrick, Vachel, Kitty, Cyril perhaps ('Fiona— ?' someone asked), Teresa, others – and I didn't feel up to facing them. Anyway, Mark was settling down at last, his eyelids fluttering, it seemed best not to let anything or anyone disturb that.

'May I . . . may I tell you a story, m'um? It's been bothering me and I—'

'Certainly.' My mother-in-law had stacked some dirty plates and glasses on the chest of drawers near the door – I found half a warm old-fashioned and something else with ice and mixed them.

'Well, many years ago, you see, when I was just getting started in the force, I was called in to assist on a strange case that had utterly baffled the shrewdest and most experienced minds in our division. A famous historian – his field was actually prehistory, I believe: would that have made him a prehistorian? no, it doesn't sound right – at any rate, this historian was found in his library one morning, bound hand and foot, and strangled to death with a garrote believed to have been of ancient Iberian origin. At first it had seemed a case of simple robbery – several gold and silver artifacts were reported missing, the windows had been jimmied, there were footprints in the garden – but in fact it had seemed *too* simple, too *self-referential*, if you take my meaning. A careful examination of the impression made in the window frame by the jimmy revealed it to have been an exotic Iron Age relic, and that plus the murder weapon itself pointed to someone familiar with the victim's scholarly field. This suspicion was soon confirmed by a laboratory analysis of certain fibers the dead man was clutching in one closed fist and a lone fingerprint on the garrote itself, which turned out in both cases to belong to the historian's young assistant, a man known for his adventurism and unbridled ambition. But before the arrest could be made, the suspect died suddenly of a rare subtropical disease. Poetic justice, one might say. Some of the missing artifacts were found in the young man's quarters and – even more damning – the exotic jimmy. The case seemed closed – until a meticulous autopsy revealed, about three inches inside the young man's rectum, the remains of a suppository containing traces of a deadly bacterial toxin. Intimacy with his assailant was assumed, needless to say, leading the Inspector on the case to suspect the historian's daughter, who, according to the family butler, had once been ravished by the young man and had subsequently become, though engaged to another man, his slave and paramour – I quote the butler, of course, m'um, who, as a native of the Andes, spoke with a certain quaint frankness. It is true, other suppositories of a more innocent nature were found in the man's medicine cabinet, such that theoretically the murder weapon could have been, as it were, self-administered, but there were other reasons that the daughter fell under the strong shadow of suspicion, not only for his murder, but for her father's as well. With the young assistant out of the way, she was now the sole heiress to her father's works, published and unpublished, together with all the research materials gathered by both of them. Her public rivalry with the young man was well known, as well as her violent amatory relationship, which no doubt exacerbated what hostile feelings she might have harbored, and it was also no secret that she bore no natural affection for her father, a man so hermetically enclosed in his work, he had paid her, throughout her life, scant attention. I hardly need point out to you, m'um, the dismal consequences that so often attend the negligence of one's paternal duties. Morever, it was she who had found her father's body, in all crimes a suspicious circumstance, and it was now remembered that she had been wearing white gloves at the time, the sort worn by museum personnel when moving valuable displays, or by technicians handling film. It was altogether possible that the butler had surprised her at the conclusion of her murderous act such that she had had to, quote, discover the body sooner than she had intended, if you follow my drift. When, finally, one of her personal hairs was found embedded in the, admittedly, minuscule remains of the suppository inside the young man's lower anatomy, the evidence against her, as you can imagine, was irresistible. Of course, it was possible the young man might somehow have swallowed the hair, but the means of doing so, in those days anyway and in such august circles, seemed quite beyond the imagination – as perhaps it is beyond your imagination now, m'um, in spite of the depraved times in which we live. At any rate, the Inspector gathered all the suspects together in the father's library, scene of the prior and, as it were, primal murder, and – with the appropriate dramaturgical preliminaries – announced his suspicions. The young woman looked shocked, pained – but it was real pain as it happened, for in fact she was dying, poisoned it would seem by someone in that very room, her glass of cascarilla, as we soon discovered, having been laced with deadly aconite. It was at this point that I was brought into the case, a young lieutenant with a specialization at that time in forensic anthropology. I needn't go into the details. The butler, who had been near the scene of the crime on all three occasions and who, by virtue of his service, had left traces of himself everywhere, including, as it turned out, his telltale footprints in the garden, seemed clearly to have been the ingenious perpetrator of this baffling triple murder, motivated evidently by a desire to revenge the ruthless pillaging of his nation's treasures by these foreign intellectuals and perhaps to create thereby the legend of a curse upon these artifacts in order to encourage their eventual return to his people – but no sooner did we seem to have the goods on him than he too was suddenly done away with, in this instance by particularly brutal means: he was savaged, m'um, by the family's pet lynx, believed to have been crazed by a fagot of rare tropical herbs tossed into its pen. And so it went, from one suspect to another – the historian's semi-invalid wife, the young creole maid, a former student of the historian suspected of ties with an unfriendly foreign government, an elder colleague at the historical society – each in his turn found, a suspected murderer, murdered.' The Inspector paused in his story. Mark, snuggled up around Peedie, was asleep at last and the traffic outside the door had subsided. It was a good moment to slip away, but I really didn't know where to go – like Mark, I was feeling lulled by all this genteel violence and hesitated to make any move that might break the spell. 'It was my first challenge, m'um, and I was failing. I'd . . . I'd even begun to wonder if our efforts were, in some bizarre way . . . well . . . I mean, it was almost as if we were selecting the victims . . .' His voice broke slightly.

'It was like a trial,' she said. 'You were being tested.'

'That's true . . . those were dark days, m'um . . .'

'But you won through in the end . . .'

'Well, I did. But not as I might have foreseen. As a young criminalistician, I was committed to the classical empirical tradition, to pure scientific analysis and the deductive enterprise. But, in the end, the solution came to me, I must tell you . . . in a dream . . .' He heaved a tremulous sigh that shook his chest. 'A . . . a young woman . . .'

'I see . . .'

'She was so . . . so . . .' He clutched his face in his hands, his shoulders quaking.

'There, there,' my mother-in-law said, patting his pate.

There was a pause. His trembling subsided. When he took up his story again, he had regained his composure, but there was a quaver yet in his voice, the cords tensed. 'She ... she came to me across a vast expanse of what in the dream seemed more like time than space. A barren wasteland – like truth itself, I thought when I awoke.'

'Yes ...'

'There was something before this about a city, or more than one perhaps – I'd been traveling, I think, through ancient iniquitous realms, dream representations no doubt of those deplorable consequences of man's incorrigible nature which it had become my lot to study, to live among – but now we were alone together in this infinite desolation. She wore a pure white tunic, a girdle at her waist, her head and shoulders bare, her feet too perhaps, I don't remember. A common stereotype, you will say, a storybook cliché – and it is true, as I watched her glide toward me across the flats with a grace that was itself archetypal, I felt reduced to a certain helpless innocence, simplified, stripped of all my pretensions, my professional habits, my learning – literally stripped perhaps, for I felt a certain unwonted vulnerability, not unlike nakedness, though of a spiritual sort, I'm sure you'll appreciate ...'

'I know ...'

'But she was not as she seemed. Oh no! It was as though she had dressed herself up as a commonplace, the more to set off her very uniqueness, her extraordinary, her special – what can I say? – her profound *selfness*. Instinctively, I understood: she was the *truth*. The rest of my life seemed like those ruined cities I had just visited, teeming with congested activity and feverish aspirations, but inwardly empty and aimless. And utterly condemned. So you can imagine how I felt, standing transfixed there in that boundless space – or time – feeling naked and unworthy, yet flushed with a kind of bewildered awe that I should have been singled out, chosen among all men, to receive her. Nothing like this had ever happened to me, in or out of dreams. I was struck dumb with wonder. As she drew near, the very barrenness around me seemed to glow, to pulsate with an inner frenzy. And then she stopped. Not near enough to touch, but I wouldn't have touched her had I been able, m'um, I couldn't even move. She smiled – or rather, the serene smile she bore by nature deepened – and she spoke. What she said was: "The victim is the killer."' He paused as though redigesting this news. The hand clutching the scarf at his throat trembled slightly. 'Even now I can hear her voice . . .'

'A riddle . . .'

'So I thought, though later I was to learn otherwise. Now, in fear and trembling, I asked her to repeat herself, but she would not, she only smiled. I begged for another word, some understanding, had I heard her right? But she only continued to smile. Or rather, the smile seemed locked onto her face, for she no longer seemed quite real, an image rather, a kind of statue, but slowly fading – my heart leaped to my throat! I was about to lose her, lose everything! I reached out at last toward that silvery presence – but into nothing, she was turning into thin air! In fact, she *was* thin air – I was sitting up in my bed, groping in the dawn light, and staring at a pale frozen figure across the room: myself in the floor-length mirror on the far wall.' So he stared now, his face drawn, his moustaches hanging heavy as anchors, seeming to drag the flesh down after them.

My mother-in-law drew his head into her lap once more, caressed his temples. 'It was not a riddle?'

'No.' His voice was muffled now, shaken, but, when he resumed, resigned. 'I wrestled with it as though it were, alone of course, reluctant to mention it to my dour and earnest colleagues – they would have thought me mad, as I thought myself at times. But then another suspect died – a former lover of the historian, a teacher of Hellenic romances who fell, or was pushed, down a pothole in the Pindus Mountains whereto she'd evidently fled – and suddenly the whole sinister pattern of this bizarre case became clear to me. Without explaining myself but hinting at my suspicions, I asked that the historian's private diaries be unlocked. My colleagues scoffed – "Audacity don't win no medals around here, son," the Inspector on the case said, being as he was from the old school, you see – but I warned them that if we didn't act quickly other victims would almost certainly be caught up in this deadly chain. Reluctantly, they let me have my way – and sure enough, hidden away in the more recent entries, encoded to appear nothing more than notations on an ancient Mayan calendric stela, lay the historian's ingenious plan to set into motion, with his own suicide, an infinite and ineluctable series of murders. Some he had merely foreseen, others he had himself committed – the poisoning of his daughter, for example: with his profound know-ledge of historical – and prehistorical – theatrics, he had foreseen our gathering there in his library that night, known of his daughter's singular weakness for cascarilla, and so on, obtaining in advance the unsuspecting butler's fingerprints on the decanter. The lover in the pothole had been found clutching what looked like an old-fashioned treasure map drawn with vegetable inks, and these too were found in the historian's safe. The elder colleague at the historical society had sat on a poisoned tack in the very room in which the police interviewed him, a room kept locked except for occasions, as the prehistorian was well aware, when extreme privacy was required. On the other hand, it was fairly likely the former student *had* shot the creole maid, a necessary link in the chain, but hardly less inevitable than the others.'

'It's quite extraordinary!'

'Yes, m'um, the fatal series might have run on forever had we not, upon deciphering the encoded plot, stopped the historian's brother-in-law from taking the late daughter's fiancé out hunting. And in the nick of time. It was a celebrated case, the turning point of my career. With it I won advancement, fame, the respect of my colleagues.' He sighed. 'But . . .'

'It's not why you've told me the story.'

'No . . .' The Inspector withdrew one of Ginger's kerchiefs and blew his nose in it. 'Are you sure you want to hear all this?'

'Of course . . .'

'I . . . I'm not married, you see . . .'

'The young woman in the dream . . .'

'Yes. I thought you'd . . . you'd understand. I've needed to tell someone about it for a very long time. I've kept it . . . kept it bottled up all these years. It was a very strange period in my life . . .' He lay his head back again. 'An intermingling of life and dream that was very much like madness . . .'

'Was that the only time— ?'

'No, over the next few years, she reappeared every now and then in my dreams, often to assist me in a case, sometimes to bring me consolation or courage, once to provide, if you'll pardon my opening my heart to you in this way, m'um, a kind of pleasure – the only pleasure of, well, that sort I've ever known or wish to know, unless it should come from her lips, her hands . . . and so forth.'

'It's very rare. To fall in love in a dream, I mean . . .'

'I know. And you can take my word for it, it's a very dangerous sort of love. A kind of possession, really. Like all lovers everywhere, I was given to violent extremes of passion and desire, but they had no living object. Though my beloved was less even than a phantom, I loved her more than life itself, which without her was unbearable, and more phantasmal than my dreams. My appetite declined, I was easily distracted, easily enraged. Never more so than when awakened from sleep. It was, at that time, all I longed for: the chance – the *only* chance – to be with her again. I spent more and more of my life in bed, forcing sleep, searching for her through half-real, half-nightmarish landscapes, begging her to reappear. She did so only rarely but often with a certain timeliness: without her insights I probably would have failed utterly at my neglected work and lost my position on the force. She rescued me from that. But not from my mad passion, as boundless and ultimately as barren as that vast plain where first we met. I once asked her whence she came. "From far away, in another place," she replied, and again I was sure she meant "time." I never dared to try to touch her after what had happened that first time, though once she . . .' Again a racking sigh broke from the Inspector's chest, and his face seemed momentarily flushed and swollen, his eyes feverish.

'I understand . . .'

'Finally, fearing for my sanity, I consulted a specialist, a psychiatrist who had often assisted us in cases requiring the interpretation of dreams. He convinced me that my original insight had been the correct one: she was indeed the truth. Only not an abstract external truth, mysteriously turning up from nowhere, but the more complex and profound truths I carried within. I had to admit that everything she had said I had probably intuited myself, in some form or another, but, through timidity or professional caution, or even fear or shame perhaps, I had hidden these thoughts away in some deep recess of my inner self: she was the figurative representation of the beauty, the serenity, that attends their release from what he in his profession called repression. Once I had been able to accept that, though I loved her still and would never love another, she at least and at last disappeared from my dreams, allowing me to return to the waking world, and I never . . . saw her . . . again.' He was beginning to choke up. He pressed his trembling fingers to his brows, as though trying to stop his head from splitting open there, took a deep rasping breath. 'Until . . . until tonight . . . !'

'Oh dear!'

'That girl . . . down there!' She reached for him as he began to sob. 'In the – *gasp!* – the *silvery frock!*'

'Now, now . . .'

'It was *her!* I *know* it was!' he wept. *'I've missed her so! Boo hoo! And now . . . !'*

'That's right, let the tears come, you'll feel better.'

'Oh m'um— !' His chest heaved and he pitched forward into her lap, burying his face there, just as someone or something hit the door with tremendous force, making us all jump.

My mother-in-law swung round to glower at me – then they hit it again. The whole room shook, a string of pennants fell, a crack appeared above the door. *'Stand back!'* someone shouted – it sounded like the tall cop, Bob.

'It's not locked!' I yelled, lurching for the knob – but too late, the door gave way with a splintering crash, and Bob and Fred tumbled head over heels into the room. They leaped up and sprang at the bed, pitching the mattress over, Mark and all. *'Hey, wait— !!'*

'We can't wait, we got a hot tip!' hollered Fred, scrabbling through the bedclothes and under the bed. I rushed over to help my mother-in-law pull Mark out from under the mattress – his eyes were wide open but so far he hadn't let out a peep. He didn't even seem to know where he was. Or who I was as I picked him up. *'There it is!'* cried Bob.

They ripped Peedie out of his arms and tore it apart, flinging the stuffing into the air like snow. Now Mark did open up: he began to scream at the top of his lungs. The Inspector was on his feet, his back to us, cleaning out his nose with Ginger's kerchief; he turned to scowl over his shoulder at Mark with reddened eyes. My mother-in-law took him, still howling, from my arms: *'Now* see what you've done!' she fumed.

'It ain't in there,' said Fred; not on the bookshelf now either, I noticed. All that was left of the rabbit was a limp rag. Fred looked up at the people crowding into the room behind me ('What's happening?' a woman called from out in the hall – 'They're beating up the kid!'), then shrugged: 'Ah well, win a few, lose a few. Here, boy.' He handed the empty pelt back to Mark, who shrank away ('Yeah? Let *me* see!'), shrieking in terror.

There was no turning him off now, he was completely out of control. My mother-in-law, in an ice-cold rage, snatched the rag out of the cop's hands and started gathering up the stuffing, Mark ('I *love* it!' someone exclaimed) still kicking and squalling madly in her arms. 'Before you go, you can put that mattress back!' she ordered, and with a murmur of sullen 'Yes'm's,' the two officers dutifully heaved it back on its box springs again.

'What's the matter with that damned child?' Inspector Pardew complained, brushing irritably at his gray suit.

'I'll go get his mother,' I offered, not knowing what else to do. Mark, I knew, could scream like that for hours. Fred looked up at me with raised brows, glanced at Bob, who looked away. '*And* the bedding!' my mother-in-law commanded. 'We ain't housemaids,' Bob grumbled, but they did as they were told.

'That young man needs a little discipline,' remarked Pardew gruffly, nodding at his cops.

I pushed out through the jam-up in the splintered doorway (Patrick was out there, pacing nervously: 'Do you think I can go in now?' he asked Woody), thinking that what *I* needed right now was a long cold drink. It was what my mother always said whenever my father began to wax philosophical. He was never very happy on such occasions; that always made him feel a lot worse. She tried it on me once when I started to tell her what I wanted to be when I grew up; I could imagine how he felt. Of course, an excess of philosophy was not exactly my problem right now ('Oops! excuse me, Gerry,' said Wilma, catching me in the ribs with her elbow, 'is Talbot in there?'), but something of the rotten moods that always attended my father's disquisitions was working its way deep inside me – sometimes on long family drives it got almost unbearable, and (Mark was still shrieking, Pardew was shouting, his assistants shouting back, I was surrounded by drunk and irascible guests, sour boozy breaths, total strangers, the guy with the TV camera shoved past me like he owned the place, my house was coming down around my ears) it was almost unbearable now, such that when Kitty touched my forearm at the head of the stairs, I nearly threw her down them. 'There's someone,' she whispered. '*What*— ?!' I bellowed angrily. 'In there,' she said, shying from my outburst and ('Oh, get off your high horse,' my mother would say, my father having just remarked that 'Beauty is like the rescue of an enchained maiden from some monster from the deeps – but Truth is that poor damned beast,' 'and fix me a

cold drink!') nodding toward the sewing room. 'Waiting for you.'
'Ah . . . ! Sorry . . .'

I could hardly move. I'd all but given up and now, suddenly . . . No,
no, it's often like that, I reminded myself, my heart pounding: Don't be
afraid. But I was afraid. I'd waited too long: now ('And Goodness is the
reckless stupidity of the maiden,' he'd add, turning to me with the
cocktail shaker in his hands, 'the beast's wistful surrender . . .') it seemed
unreal. And just an arm's reach away. I stepped toward the door, ordering
my legs to move. The air was heavy near the bathroom, it was almost
like swimming. 'Alison— ?' I whispered. The door was a couple of inches
ajar: the lights were out, it was dark inside. I saw the peckersweater on
her finger then and, after a quick glance down at the landing (it was
empty), followed it in.

'Hey, keep the door closed,' someone muttered from across the room.
'Alison!' She pulled me inside and threw her arms around me with a
whimper almost of pain. I felt it too: a constriction in my chest (the
peckersweater was what she was dressed in!) that took my breath away.
'At last!' I cried, clasping her flesh in my arms, flooding over with the joy
of it, the familiarity, the suppleness – 'I can't believe it! I thought you'd— !'
'*Sshh!*' she hissed, and pressed her mouth against mine, running her hands
up inside my shirt, loosening the tie, fumbling with the belt, her
excitement making her almost childish in her clumsiness: I was clumsy,
too, my hands trembling, my breath coming in short gulps – this was it
then! it was happening! '*Hurry!*' she whispered, dragging me toward the
sewing area (the studio couch in the corner was taken, I could hear
rustlings and mumblings: 'Well, it's *different*,' someone acknowledged)
where pillows had been tossed down and heaped with clean laundry. I
was shackled by my trousers: I managed to kick one canvas shoe off and
free a leg. I felt rushed, as though something important (distantly Mark
was screaming, I didn't hear him) had been passed over, but I understood
it – it was like what Tania used to say about painting: you plan and you
plan, but when it happens, it's a total shock, sudden and overwhelming,
and you have to take it as it comes, trust your craft and surrender to the
unexpected. She held my penis with her bare hand (I surrendered it, not
at all wistfully, the unexpected encasing me like a condom), stroking my
testicles with the furry cock sock, her mouth at my throat. I buried my

face in her hair which was almost crackly with excitement, its sweet smell mingling with the deeper aroma now wafting up between her legs, she was spending freely, if that was the word, it sounded too commercial, my hands wallowed there, reaching as it were for that magic moment on the back porch, though everything was harder now, more real, no, for all the familiarity of it, this had *not* happened before, this was new – and *now*: the comings and goings were over, *it was on!*' 'Oh yes! *good* boy!' gasped some woman in the corner. 'That's not him, it's me,' another woman said, her voice muffled. I knelt, sliding my mouth (Craft! *Craft!* I was shouting at my exploding mind) down her taut trembling body toward that sweet flow below, but she pulled away, sinking back onto the pile of pillows and laundry and dragging me with her. Yes, true, it was not to be wasted – she was coming, her whole body was shaking as I rolled between her legs, and my own excitement was surging toward hers – we were rushing pell-mell toward that denouement we'd share, the cracker, as Quagg would say, the blow-off, the final spasm. Which in the end is achieved, as I might have said that night at the theater and perhaps did, neither by art nor by nature, but by a perfect synthesis (I could still remember such words: synthesis) of both. There was such an abundance of secretions between her legs that I slipped right past the entry, squeezing down the greasy aisle between the cheeks of her behind: she reached under (she was clutching my neck tightly with her other hand, her mouth at my ear, the fragrant laundry billowing around us like some kind of magical cloud) and guided me in: she was amazingly tight as though resisting her own mounting excitement, holding back, waiting for me. I thrust fiercely at her (the people on the studio couch were climaxing, too, I could hear them gasping and grunting – 'God, I'm hot!' one of them wheezed), just as she pitched upward to meet me, driving her thighs up under my arms, whimpering: 'Oh, I *love* you, Gerry! I *love* you!' in my ear.

'*Sally Ann— !!*' I bellowed, with such a shout that, startled, her whole body constricted in a violent spasm, locking me into her, my penis gripped just under the crown by the knifelike edge of her half-ruptured hymen. '*For god's sake, let go!*' I cried.

'*I can't!*' she wailed. '*Owww!!*'

'*Damn* you, Sally Ann! You're *hurting* me!'

'What's going on?' asked one of the women on the studio couch.

'Are you all the way in, Gerry?' Sally Ann choked, her voice squeaky with shock and pain.

'No – *ow!* – I'm not in *or* out, it's much *worse* than that!'

'That's all right, I'm all done anyway,' a man said. 'I'll go splash 'em.' I could hear him padding across the room toward the door.

'*Please*, Gerry! Don't stop now! I don't care *how* it hurts!'

The lights came on, blinding us for a moment. Sally Ann, in anguish, continued to pump away, hugging me tight, trying to lodge me deeper, but I'd long since gone limp with pain.

'Well, well, what have we here?' It was Horner, that wooden soldier, at the light switch, one hand holding his pants up. Teresa was frantically pulling on her yellow knit dress, Daffie stretched out naked on the studio couch beside her, legs wearily aspraddle. 'You could have waited a minute!' Teresa called out from inside the dress, jerking the hem down past the swell of her midriff.

I had torn Sally Ann's hands away and was trying to extricate myself, but the door, as they say, had swung shut on that domain. 'I didn't know it would *be* like this, Gerry! I'm *sorry!*' she groaned, her eye paint-smudged, making her look like some theatrical parody of the living dead. I drew my knees up under her thrashing rear and leaned back on my haunches – not very comfortable, but I could hold her down that way, keep her from scissoring the thing off.

The door opened and Zack Quagg poked his nose in from the hall – 'Hey, Horn, I been looking for you, what's going on?' – followed by Woody and Cynthia (Horner, winking, licked his thumb as though to turn a page), holding hands: 'Oh no,' Woody said, his eyes crinkling up with compassion when he saw me. 'I'll go get Jim.'

'Yes, please!' I gasped. '*Hurry!*' I could hear Mark again – his wailing was now sleepy and rhythmical, dirgelike. 'Stay still, Sally Ann!'

'I *want* to – but it's all moving by *itself!*'

'For goodness' sake! What have you been *doing?!*' asked Wilma, arriving short of breath as though after a run. 'Lloyd Draper's giving a slide show downstairs, Teresa, and we've been *waiting* for you!' Cynthia knelt beside us, holding back my pubic hairs to have a closer look. 'Can you relax a bit?' she asked, and Sally Ann wailed: 'I *am* relaxing!' Quagg was pulling Horner ('This place looks too busy,' said Janny Trainer, peeping in, our plumber Steve in tow), still blowing kisses back over his shoulder, out the door: 'Come on, we got something on the boil, man – something *great!*' 'Yeah, okay, Zack, but first lemme get something to eat . . .'

'He *said* he was casting me for a part,' explained Teresa, smoothing down her skirt, looking around on the floor for something more, and Wilma said: 'Well, just try telling that to Peg!' 'What? Is my sister still here?' Cynthia was wriggling my member back and forth as though trying to free a key from a broken lock: 'Ow, don't!' I cried. 'That's not helping!'

'You're bleeding, Sally Ann,' Cynthia observed, looking at her fingers. 'Am I?' Sally Ann lifted herself up on her elbows to see for herself. 'Yeah!' she gasped, and lay back smiling, her face wet with sweat. 'God! I'm bleeding!'

'It may be *me!*' I whimpered.

'And this is our sewing room,' my wife said. 'Soyng?' She stood in the doorway with Iris Draper, Alison's husband, Hilario the Panamanian tapdancer ('Ah! Zo-eeng! Weeth the leetle, how you say, pointed theeng!'), that guy with the elbow patches I'd met out in the backyard, and two people I'd never seen before. 'It hasn't been redecorated for a few years, I'm afraid.'

'It's very nice,' said Iris, and my wife sighed and said: 'It serves its purpose, I guess.' Alison's husband frowned when he saw me; what's-his-name (Geoffrey?) from outside smiled and waved. 'Do you need any help, Gerald?'

'Jim's coming,' I gasped, gritting my teeth, and Wilma, buttoning Teresa up the back, said: 'You should have seen Cyril just now on television! You really missed it! He's a natural!' 'He's a pig.' 'How can you say that?' 'Haven't you heard?' Gottfried, that was his name ('Fiona? Really – ?'), I could hardly think. My head seemed to be full of little sparks. 'But you're . . . all right— ?'

'All right?'

'The – *gasp!* – interview . . .'

'Oh yes, Woody was very helpful. Some of the things they were doing were apparently illegal.' She was wearing that plasticky apron with the old soap ad on it, and it made her look stiff and mechanical somehow. 'He made them take the candle out, for example.' Iris came by, evidently studying the paintwork, or maybe all the childish decals on everything. 'Goodness, I suppose it was a mistake to do all that laundry . . .'

The bearded guy with the video camera on his shoulder pushed in behind the others, viewfinder to his eye, one hand working the zoom. I tried to turn my back to him, but it hurt too much to move. Iris spied the fallen peckersweater and picked it up: 'Interesting!' she said, adjusting her spectacles. Sally Ann reached up and covered herself as the cameraman closed in. 'If you haven't really done it, Gerry, don't let him see.'

'Wait for me!' called Teresa (Wilma was in the doorway, introducing herself to the two strangers, a stout man in a brown three-piece suit and a white-haired lady in lime slacks, a pink-and-lemon shirt, Iris saying something about having to go through her catalogues when she got home, see if she could find one, Lloyd was always getting a chill). 'My other shoe . . .'

'I think I'm lying on it,' Daffie grumbled, and Hilario, turning to go, asked: 'Ees peenk woe-man, no?'

'Any color you can get, lover.'

'The only trouble,' Iris decided, after a stroll through the room ('What's she trying to hide?' the cameraman wanted to know, and Cynthia tugged Sally Ann's hands away: 'Don't worry, dear, it's all right . . .'), 'is that there's not enough light.'

'I know, it's on the north side.'

'No, I meant the wallpaper.'

'Well, now, let's see what we have here,' Jim said, announcing himself, and the cameraman moved on ('It's called "Paintbox Green,"' my wife was saying) to pick up Daffie. 'What do you think about the breakdown of law and order in our society?' he asked as he zoomed in. 'She seized up on him,' Cynthia explained quietly, lifting the root of my penis. 'Just here at the neck.' Jim set his bag down and knelt beside us. 'Hmmm,' he said, probing Sally Ann's thighs and the muscles around her anus. 'All this handcream she has packed in here might've helped if she'd put it in the right place . . .'

'That's the sort of sewing machine I've been telling you about, honey,' the lady in the lime slacks said.

'Ah, yes . . .'

'These are our new neighbors from down the street, Gerald. Mr and Mrs Waddilow.'

I craned around to look at them. 'We heard the music and just stopped in to say hello,' Mr Waddilow smiled. 'Hope you don't mind.' Alison's husband had disappeared, Hilario as well, but Howard was in the room now, over in the far corner near the ironingboard closet, wearing Tania's half-lens reading glasses on the fat part of his nose, watching the cameraman as he panned the horizon of Daffie's body. 'You've got a nice place here,' said Mr Waddilow.

'Why don't you stuff that ray gun up your ass, cowboy?' Daffie suggested.

'It's lightweight and almost entirely automatic, with a special attachment for lace edging,' Mrs Waddilow called from across the room.

'What?' her husband toddled over to look at it, his pantcuffs riding an inch or two above his white socks and two-toned shoes, crossing paths with Howard, who floated out now without saying a word, hands clapped decorously over his brassiere cups. 'Oh yes, I see. Very good.'

'Mr Waddilow is an airline pilot, Gerald.' 'Does this hurt?' asked Jim. '*Yes!*' cried Sally Ann, and I yelped as well. 'I don't think we've ever had a real pilot in our neighborhood before, have we?'

'No . . . but – *ow!* – if you don't mind . . .'

'Retired, actually,' Mr Waddilow said, hooking his thumbs in the pockets of his brown vest. 'I'm in travel now.'

'This old sewing basket is nice, too,' Mrs Waddilow added.

'You should check on Mark,' I gasped, 'they broke the door down—'

'I know, I was just in there. Mother's fixing Peedie.' That's right, I noticed now, I couldn't hear him anymore. 'Someone put the ears on backward.'

'I'm afraid that was my fault,' smiled Cynthia, looking up over her shoulder. 'I don't know much about rabbits.'

'*Wah—!*'

'Sorry . . .'

'If I can be of any help,' Mr Waddilow said. 'I used to raise rabbits.'

'You can feel here the adductor muscles,' Jim was explaining (Woody had returned and now squatted by Cynthia, pursing his lips thoughtfully), 'the so-called "pillars of virginity," how tense they are, right up into the vagina.' 'Oh yes . . .' He searched through his bag, watched closely by the cameraman, who, kneeling beside us, focused now on Jim's hands. 'What are you going to do?' Sally Ann asked apprehensively, propping herself up on her elbows.

'Take your tonsils out,' Jim smiled. 'Now just settle back . . .'

'I haven't seen one of these things in years,' Woody murmured. His shorts, still on backward, bagged up oddly above his thighs.

'Come, I'll show you our guest room,' said my wife.

'When you think about it,' Cynthia whispered, gently separating with ringed fingers Sally Ann's spongy outer lips, 'it's really a kind of packaging problem.'

'Though actually right now it's being used by my mother.'

'Catch you later,' Mr Waddilow called, following my wife out, and Gottfried tucked his long bent pipe in his mouth and waved again. 'Oh, do you have your mother staying with you?' someone said out in the hall. 'You're very fortunate!'

'I'm going to make a very tiny incision,' Jim explained, and I felt her flinch again. 'And then you can do the rest with your fingers.'

'Won't it hurt . . . ?'

'Only a little.' He pulled a stick of gum out of his pocket and handed it to her. 'Here, this will take your mind off it.'

Sally Ann lay back and unwrapped the gum, her eyes dark with worry and smeared makeup. 'Is she no longer a virgin then?' the cameraman asked, zooming in as Jim leaned forward.

'Who can say? Technically, she's neither one thing nor the other, but—'

'*Yow!!*' I cried.

'Sorry, Gerry.'

Woody cleared his throat. 'Well, legally—'

'Something *stabbed* me!'

'I know. Here, hold this up for me, will you?' he said to Cynthia, pincering the shaft gently between thumb and forefinger. 'Don't let it sag . . .' Sally Ann's jaws snapped at the gum as though trying to speed up time, and for a brief moment I felt a certain empathy with the child, roughly but intimately linked with her as I was, as though I'd been giving birth to her and the navel string had knotted up and needed cutting. Not (I shuddered, and Cynthia patted my member gently: 'Won't be long now . . .') that the image was a comforting one.

'A little more . . .'

Sally Ann groaned. Her jaws were clamped now, her teeth bared, a little bubble of gum sticking up between them like a fleshy growth: she gasped as Jim broke through and the gum disappeared. 'Oh my gosh,' she choked, 'I think I *swallowed* it!'

'You're doing fine,' Jim said, guiding her hands down. 'Now just take hold here and slowly stretch yourself apart . . .'

'I thought this was supposed to be fun,' she whimpered. Over on the couch, Daffie laughed and said: 'You been going to the wrong church, kiddo.'

Our midwife Cynthia, jiggling the key again, gave a quick tug and I was free, sliding out through Sally Ann's clenched knuckles as though on rails. I fell back, struggling to unbend my legs. One of them was still tangled in my trousers: Cynthia pulled my shoe off and stripped the rest away. I stretched out, ignoring the cameraman who hovered above me, thinking: So this is what it comes to, all the artful preparations, all the garnering of experience and sensual fine-tuning, and you're just another curiosity, a kind of decorous monster who pees on his wife's flowers and hurts children.

Sally Ann was crying, curled up on her side with her hands between her thighs, the cameraman moving in over her blood-streaked buttocks onto her tear-streaked face, then switching off. He unbelted the camera, took the weight off his shoulder: 'Good show,' he grunted, and put a lens cap on. 'I don't really think that's necessary, Woody,' Jim was saying, and Woody, holding hands with Cynthia above me, said: 'Perhaps not, but he's a client. I have an ethical responsibility to let him know.'

Jim shook his head as they left, then stooped to put his gear back in the bag. 'Here, put this between your legs,' he said, handing Sally Ann one of our kitchen curtains. 'If you'll come to see me, I'll teach you how to pass graduated heated pneumatic dilators up to half a foot or so, then you won't have any more problems.' Sally Ann only moaned, doubled up there in her nest of laundry and clutching the curtain to her fork like a child its security blanket, but the cameraman said: 'I wonder if you'd look at this cut on my face, Doc.'

'Hmm. I hadn't noticed it there, under the beard. It's quite deep—'

'Yeah, stiletto heels. Very sharp.'

'I think there's some antibacterial cream in the bathroom.'

'Too bad she didn't get him in the eye,' Daffie grumbled, as Jim led the cameraman out. 'If it hadn't been for him, Dickie and the others'd still be here.' I was searching around for my clothes, but all I could find were my shirt and socks. 'Your pants are over here, Ger.'

I struggled to my feet and crossed the room, but my knees were so weak I could hardly walk. 'Do you mind?'

'Sit down, sit down . . .'

My trousers were all knotted up and inside out. It was as if someone had tried to make a cat's cradle out of them. Just getting the underwear separated from the pants was like a Chinese puzzle. 'Dickie's gone then, it's true,' I said.

'Yeah. Between the cops, the mess his pretty clothes were in, and little young bung's maniacal old man . . .' She took a pull on her cheroot and then sighed, expelling the dark smoke past my hip. Sally Ann was also beginning to stir, pushing up on one elbow to examine the curtains between her legs, the three of us alone now in the room.

'Why didn't you go along?'

'He had a full load.' So that was it then. No point in asking who he'd taken in her place. I sighed, surrendering to the inevitable as though learning a new habit. 'Why all these *preparations?*' Ros had once asked me. 'What are we *waiting* for?' I should have been listening. Sally Ann, waddling about now in her bikini underpants with extra padding in the crotch, had discovered a mirror (the frame was a cartoonish clown's face, the mirror his laughing – or gaping – mouth: little Gerald, I thought, was with us still) and was wiping the eye paint out of her eyes with a pillow-case. 'You wanna know the truth, Ger?' Daffie said, her voice constricted. 'I hate this fucking piece of meat. It makes me a lot of money, but I hate it.' She stubbed her glowing cigar out on her pubis.

'Daffie—! *Hey!*' I pushed her hand away. There was a fresh pink wound just above her mound, and in the air the faint aroma of burnt hair and flesh. There were a lot of scars there, I saw. 'I . . . I wondered why you never did full frontal poses,' I said, touching them. They were glossy and unyielding, nubbly, rippling across her abdomen like faults, as though the flesh had been strip-mined. Her navel was blurred with overlaid scar tissue like the scratched-out face in Tania's painting.

'I wanna believe that the mind is something unique, Ger, that there's something called spirit or soul in me that's all my own and different from the body, and that someday it can somehow get out of it: it's my main desire. And it's all just a fucking fairy tale, isn't it? Her old man is right.

And poor dumb Roger. Body is what we got. A bag of worms . . .'

Her act had sent a chill through me. It was as though she were trying to turn her flesh to stone. Tania liked to say that the idea of emptiness consoled her. Which I took as an ultimate form of madness: the mind rising to its nadir. I squeezed Daffie's hand. 'Maybe,' I said, the tears starting. 'But yours is more beautiful than most. For our sake, you should keep it that way.'

Sally Ann, standing beside us, also had a glitter in her eyes, though maybe it was just from scrubbing the paint away. She had a patch on the thigh of her jeans now that said 'OPEN FOR BUSINESS' – probably she'd been saving it. 'Thank you, Gerry,' she said tenderly, knotting her shirttails. 'It was beautiful. It was the most beautiful moment of my life.' She stared charitably down at my limp organ. 'And don't try to explain. I understand. Honest, Gerry, I wasn't at all disappointed, it was more than—'

'It was a cheap trick, Sally Ann. I ought to tan your britches!'

'Oh groan,' she said, unwrapping another stick of gum, 'all you dirty old men are just alike! Well, go ahead then!' She folded the gum into her mouth, switched around and arched her fanny up in front of my face: I couldn't resist. I reared back and cracked it with all my might. She yelped in surprise, then started gagging. 'Oh *pee*, Gerry!' she wailed. *'You made me swallow my gum again!'* She took a wild swing at me, which I parried, then she went running, bawling, out of the room. 'Boy, that felt good!' I said.

Daffie laughed, then raised herself up on one elbow and picked up my penis to have a look. 'Anyway, it hasn't been husked.' She slid the foreskin back with a deft finger.

'Ouch!'

'Oh yeah, I see. It's all raw there under the nub as if somebody'd tried to bite the nozzle off. Well, it's pretty, Ger, you know that, but it's just not callused enough.' She dropped it and pushed herself up off the couch, stood there weaving, her feet planted wide apart. I'd got one pantleg free from the shorts, but the other was bound up in some kind of hitch knot. I untied it and turned the pantlegs rightside out. 'You got anything here I can wear? My rig's all assed up.'

'Whatever you find, help yourself.' I pulled the shorts on, watching her stagger through the clutter (she dipped to one knee briefly, but got back up again), remembering the time we first fixed this room up as a nursery: everything in its place then like stage props. So long ago. And so much had happened. But then, I thought, recalling my wife in the doorway just now (she'd seemed her old self, hardly affected by all I'd seen her having to go through in the kitchen – that was coming back to me now, as I drew my trousers on, as though from some circuitous journey: the dark bruises on the backs of her thighs, for example, her tummy fanfolding, the faint trickle of blood radiating across her pale nether cheeks – like cracked porcelain, I'd thought at the time, over-whelmed just then by an inexpressible compassion . . . or at least it had seemed inexpressible, and probably it was), not so much. What had Pardew said? Change is an illusion of the human condition, something like that. The passing images our senses delivered to us on our obligatory exploration of the space–time continuum, pieced together like film frames to create the fiction of movement and change, thereby inventing motive. Like this frame in front of me now of Daffie's internationally famous derrière, glittering with perspiration, as she bent drunkenly from the waist to muddle about in the scattered laundry: a way-station on the trajectory like any other. Just the same, I was glad not to have missed it.

She held up a pair of my pale blue stretch denims that my wife had up here for mending. 'These okay?'

'Sure.'

She got one foot on all right, but had trouble managing the other, stumbling and loping through the pillows and laundry until she hit a wall that propped her up. 'Tell me something, Ger,' she panted, 'that *was* your joystick in the photos with Ros, wasn't it?' I nodded, feeling a prickling in my eyes again. 'I thought I recognized it when you were outside hosing down the roses. Who took the shots?'

'Some guy. We spent all afternoon at it.' Daffie had the jeans up past her thighs but was having difficulty, in spite of the give in the material, squeezing the rest in. 'A funny thing, there was a matinee on that after-noon, and Ros was supposed to make a final brief appearance as one of a group of resistance fighters, which she forgot about until she heard them shouting for her. She went drifting dreamily away from us and, through the wrong entrance, out onto the set, wearing luminous green paint, some feathers on her tail, and a golden crown, which of course brought the house down. Then, apropos of nothing happening on stage, she delivered her one line: '*Follow me, brothers, we have lost the battle, but we have not lost the war!'* Daffie laughed, but she was crying too. I wiped at my own eyes with my shirtsleeves. 'Probably her finest hour . . .'

Daffie took my arm. The jeans were stretched so tightly around her hips they seemed almost to glow, but the waistband gaped above like an open barrel. 'Come on, Ger, stop your snuffling, let's go get juiced.'

'Do you want a shirt?'

'Nah, it's too hot . . .'

Earl Elstob came dragging a dazed Michelle into the room as we left it. 'Huh!' he slobbered, weaving a bit, his eyes crossing. 'Yuh know how tuh – shlup! – make a gal's eyes light up?'

'Listen, Michelle,' Daffie said, reaching for her free hand, 'let's go suck a turkey leg.'

'It's all right,' Michelle murmured, 'I don't mind.'

'Yeah, but come *on*, honey, *this* birdseed?'

'*Yuh plug her in!*' Elstob hollered, falling back against the doorjamb. Steve the plumber and some older guy, I saw, were trying to repair the door into my son's room, watched grimly by my mother-in-law; Janny stood by, looking bored, chatting with Hoo-Sin.

'I know how he feels,' Michelle said gently. 'I had a dream once that I had teeth like that in my vagina.' Hoo-Sin was sweeping her hands about as though describing a vast space: 'In the West you think of it as a river, but in the East it is a placid silent pool,' she said. Mark seemed to have settled down at last. 'Everybody laughed at me and pushed awful things up me to watch me chew. My Daddy took me to an orthodontist, but when he pointed to the problem, I ate my Daddy's finger off.' She sighed. 'Yuh huh huh!' Earl snorted, slapping his knee, and Janny said: 'I guess I mostly think of it as a leaky faucet.' 'After that, the teeth weren't there anymore, it was a different dream . . .'

'Hey – *huh!* – yuh know what a bedspring is?'

'Spare me!' begged Daffie, pulling me toward the stairs, where we nearly crashed into our new neighbor, Mrs Waddilow, stumbling pale-faced out of the bathroom, her eyes popping from their sockets: 'For the love of God, why didn't somebody *tell* me— ?!' she croaked, and went clambering weak-kneed down the stairs ahead of us. 'I know what a buzz you get outa your wonky guest lists, Ger, but where'd you ever dig up *that* squirrelly suck-egg?'

'Charley brought him . . .'

The porch door flew open at the foot of the stairs and in strode Benedetto and four or five friends, all dressed up still in their Renaissance theater costumes. Discovering me on the landing, Beni flung his arms wide and cried: 'Sir! What sort of affair *is* this? There's a *body* out there in the bushes!'

'What—?'

Daffie seemed to stumble and she clutched my arm. 'Was he . . . dressed in white?'

'Madame, I am not even certain it was a *he!* Which is not, I hasten to add, a *present* dilemma . . . !' He twirled the tip of his false moustache, ogling her bosom grandly, then swept off his plumed hat and bowed.

'I'll give him a call,' I said, pulling away. Hilario, standing at the foot with two drinks in his hands – a highball and what looked like dregs from the bottom of a mop bucket – said: 'Beni, you haff see anytheeng yet, I theenk!'

I remembered a play I'd seen, Ros wasn't in it, in which the actors, once on stage – it was ostensibly some sort of conventional drawing-room comedy – couldn't seem to get off again. The old pros in the cast had tried to carry on, but the stage had soon got jammed up with bit actors – messengers, butlers, maids and the like – who, trapped and without lines, had become increasingly panic-stricken. In the commotion, the principal actors had got pushed upstage and out of sight, only a few scattered lines coming through as testimony to their professionalism. Some had tried to save the show, some each other, most just themselves. It was intended to produce a kind of gathering terror, but though I hadn't felt it then (a stage is finally just a stage), I was suddenly feeling it now.

I dialed the number, turned to Daffie, who'd been stopped by Hilario: 'I cannot find peenk, so I meex violent and green – hokay?'

'Hello?'

'Benedetto!' cried Quagg, brushing past me, his cape flying.

'Zachariah! My friend!'

'Hello? Is that you, Dickie?' Daffie, without looking at the drink, tossed half of it back – then, wheezing, held it out at arm's length, bugging her eyes at it. Zack was carrying on noisily about the act he was getting up ('We got this wild frame, man, about a jealous old hag who spooked Roger and cast a spell on Ros – a kind of fairy godmother, ancient sex queen, and death-demon all in one, see . . .'), Beni approving exclamatorily and booming out introductions, while behind me people were clambering up and down the cellar stairs, or coming in from the backyard, there was music pouring out of the living room – I couldn't hear a thing. 'Dickie— ?'

'Who is this? Ger?'

'Benedetto!' cried Regina, sweeping past.

'Dickie! Are you all right?' I shouted. Daffie, her damp breasts drooping with relief, slumped back against the stairway and, wrinkling her nose up ('Regina! My little dumpling!'), carried on with her drinking.

'Hell, I dunno, I think I drank too much. Listen, Ger, call me in the morning when I'm feeling better, okay?'

'Ach! Regina!'

'Olga!'

'I'm sorry, Dickie, there's a . . . a body outside – and we thought—'

'Yeah, I saw it. Hey, what did you *do* to my little Nay, Ger?'

'What do you mean?' I glanced at the traffic on the basement stairs. Noble came up holding his crotch, his good eye dilated from the dark, the mock one apparently having fallen out. 'Christ!' he groaned happily, 'I think my goddamn balls are turning blue!' He was wearing my new herringbone shirt – I hadn't even taken the pins out yet; it was stretched out of shape and already sweaty in the armpits. I turned away.

'Well, she's over the moon, Ger, you're all she talks about.'

'She's there with you?' Vic had appeared in the living room doorway, looking rumpled and tired, ready to go home probably. The song on the hi-fi was a melancholic old showtune, 'It's All Happened Before,' a song from one of Ros's plays, *The Lover's Lexicon*.

'Yeah, well, I admit I'm only second best. You've got the touch, Ger – she's taken a real *shine* to you, as you might say.' It was a relief to know she was all right. What had I been thinking? 'I don't know if it's over,' the vocalist was singing, 'or if it's just begun . . .' Quagg had found Alison's husband somewhere and now dragged him over to meet the newcomers. One of the women kissed him. Benedetto gave him a big hug and planted his floppy wide-brimmed hat on his head. He flushed and, pulling on his beard, grinned sheepishly underneath it. Vic watched benignly, seeming to hover at some empyrean remove. I felt his detachment like a kind of balm and began, myself ('. . . but tonight,' came the song, 'you're the only one . . .'), to disengage. After all, I thought, what else was there to do? 'She says you're the kindest sweetest man she's ever known.'

'All I did was oil her behind, Dickie.'

'Well, you know what they say in showbiz, Ger, it's not the egg—'

'I know . . .' It's how you lay it. Or crack it. But sometimes, as my wife would say ('It's how you scramble it,' Dickie was saying distantly, not to me but, off-mike as it were, to someone there in the room with him), it *is* the egg. Woody had joined Vic in the living room doorway, watching me over Vic's shoulder. I smiled and nodded, but he didn't return it. Vic was toying wistfully with a fork in his hand, looking as resigned and serene as I'd seen him all night. I remembered something he'd told me about so-called 'waves of silence' in the brain – perceived by some apparently as a kind of local conspiracy at the cellular level to shut down briefly and rest up – which he'd denounced as an example of 'ideological biology,' but which I saw, having more faith in chemistry than in will, as fundamentally applicable to all behavior, human and otherwise. I felt momentarily suspended in such a wave right now, in fact, as though this quiescent mood were not in me but in the hall itself, maybe the whole house, a conspiratorial nourishing, as it were, of the appetite for tranquility.

'Hold on a sec, Ger! I got another beautiful lady here who wants to say hello!' I could hear her shushing him. I'd supposed he'd have to rub it in. Her husband, Benedetto's plumed hat down around his ears and a look of flushed infatuation on his face, was now preening for Quagg, who was peering at him through a circle of thumb and index finger as though giving him a screen test. I saw this as though peering through a lens myself, as though watching it on an editing table or in some darkened theater. 'So, for the skeet, we use the faht lady, no?' 'She's been holding out on us, Ger.'

'The Arctic explorer? Nah, she's in there purring like a cat, Hilly, but we can work in her crazy story – a kind of initiation bit, the sacred cave—'

'She's terrific . . .'

'I'm sure,' I said and swallowed. 'Sacred cave?' her husband asked from under the brim of Beni's hat. He didn't seem to know. Or if he did, he accepted it. Maybe I wasn't the only one he'd struck a deal with. My head was starting to ache. 'Yeah, it's a symbol for the unconscious,' Quagg was explaining to him. He looked pained. 'You know, where all the action takes place.' I closed my eyes. 'Give her . . . my love,' I whispered, remembering something she'd said that night we met: beauty in the theater is not a question of language *or* action, she'd insisted (I'd tried to argue it was a balance of both), but of the *hidden* voice and the mysterious illusion of *crossed destinies*. Yes (I opened my eyes), I could see that . . . Vic, his gray head tilted toward Woody (he was still peering at me, past Vic's hunched shoulder), seemed to be boiling up again: perhaps the wave was passing. I turned to look into the dining room ('You won't believe what she's got tattooed on her handsome little ass, Ger!'), but caught a glimpse of ('*What?!*' Vic roared – '*With Sally Ann—?!*') Horner, mouth agape, eyes startled: '*Duck!*' he yelped.

'*You! You goddamn traitorous sonuvabitch – YOU were the one!*'

I whirled around just in time to see Vic lunging toward me, a terrible look on his ravaged face I'd never seen before, not frontally like this, his bloodshot eyes ablaze, lips drawn back, fist clenched around the fork, raised to strike – '*Vic! Wait—!*'

Two shots rang out, something hit me in the shoulder, there was a shriek and a tumble, people falling all around me – Vic slumped to one knee, a look of awe and wonder erasing his rage, then pitched forward and fell into my arms. The tall cop, Bob, crouched in the living room doorway (Woody had vanished), the smoking barrel of his revolver staring me in the face. 'Oh my god! *Vic—!*'

I felt something warm and wet on my hands. Vic groaned, his shaggy head heavy on my chest. The cop limped toward us, keeping his gun on him. 'What have you *done—?*', I cried.

'He was going for you, so I shot him.'

'But – he was my best *friend!*' The cop grabbed Vic by the collar, threw him backward to the floor. There was a big hole in his chest. 'All he had was a damned *fork!*' I was nearly screaming.

'I missed him once – this time I made fucking sure.' He kicked Vic but got no response. Vic was breathing in short gasps, his eyelids fluttering.

The others started picking themselves up. 'What happened?' asked Teresa, coming in from the dining room with a dessert plate heaped with turkey stuffing, cheese balls, and pickles. I stared at my bloody hands, my eyes watering, then knelt by Vic. It had all happened so fast . . . 'Hey, old man . . . ?' There was no reply: his head lolled, his mouth gaped. 'So that's it,' Eileen said stonily, standing framed in the living room doorway. 'I knew it'd end like this.' Perhaps she had known. I recalled her oracle on the toilet and even before that I remembered thinking, when she was lying on the couch in the living room, Vic having just struck her, that she had glimpsed something that none of the rest of us were aware of yet. Maybe Vic had seen it, too, and had merely been swinging blindly at a truth that enraged him. 'I tried to warn him, and the sonuvabitch beat me up.'

Cynthia eased past her, squatted by Vic ('You can come on back now, tiger,' Daffie was saying, having picked up the fallen phone receiver, 'they just shot that little girl's old man . . .'), touched his throat. This seemed to help for some reason: he closed his mouth, blinked, tried to focus. When he saw me, a pained look crossed his face, then faded. 'Get Sally Ann . . .' he whispered.

'Sure, Vic, but—'

'And a drink.'

'Listen, I'm sorry, but—'

'*Fuck* sorry! Get me a goddamn *drink!*' he croaked.

'Vic— ?'

'He won't listen to you,' Eileen said dully. The others watched us now at a distance, keeping a wary eye at the same time on the cop, who was reloading his revolver. 'He's a smart guy. He knows it all.'

'I'll get him something,' Teresa offered, sucking a pickle. 'What's his— ?'

'Bourbon.'

'The kid? Nah, last I saw, that chirpy fatassed welfare worker was taking him out on the back patch to get his stake tolled,' said Daffie glumly on the phone. 'I've had nothing but the goddamn losers, Dickie, I don't like it here.'

'Where the hell *am* I?' Vic wheezed. He groped weakly for his chest as though looking for something in his pocket there.

'You're at my house, Vic. A party—'

'Jesus Christ! I'm *bleeding!* Oh, shit, Gerry! What have you done . . . ?'

'Hey, maybe we can work this in,' mused Quagg, squinting down at Vic, as he slumped there against Cynthia ('Well, who knows . . . maybe it's the – *gasp!* – the way I wanted it . . .'), clutching his wound. 'I *like* the fast action!' Malcolm Mee, who'd joined him, nodded, then mimed the draw. '*Right!* Blue *lightning*, man!' laughed Quagg.

'Yeah, well, when you're done, you can kiss mine,' Daffie mumbled tearfully, and banged the receiver in its cradle.

'Only maybe the guy who gets his lights blown out is the one playing Roger on the stage, and it's Roger himself, out in the audience, who does the shooting!'

'Roger's dead, Zack.'

'Listen, I know, you think I'm crazy? I'm talking about the *play*, man!'

'Roger— ?'

'It's been a long night, Prissy Loo.'

Teresa returned with a tumbler of iced bourbon. 'Here,' she said and, bending over, spilled her plate of food in Vic's lap. 'Oops! Darn, that's all the stuffing there was left!'

Cynthia took the glass and held it to his lips – he slurped at it greedily, choking and spluttering, then knocked it to the floor; it rolled across the hall, the ice cubes scattering like thrown dice.

'Hey,' warned Bob, waggling his revolver.

'Do you mind?' asked Teresa, picking the food off his lap with her fingers and eating it. 'It's a shame to waste it.'

'The way I see it, we got Ros playing herself – we use the corpse, I mean – but the rest of the cast interacts with it like she's alive, you dig? The trick being to make the audience get the sense she really *is* alive!'

Vic peered up at us under his shaggy gray brows, his eyes crossing. '*Another one!*' he demanded, and broke into a fit of coughing.

'I don't like it,' Regina objected. 'It's like abusing the dead or something.'

'I think he's going . . .'

'We're not abusing Ros, baby, we're abusing death itself *through* Ros – really, it's an affirmation!'

'I dunno, Zack, somehow it's like that time you pulled that onstage autopsy—'

'He needs help,' said Cynthia. 'Is that doctor— ?'

Bob twirled the revolver on his index finger ('But that was *beautiful*, Vadge!'), slapped it into the holster. 'I think I seen him in the kitchen.'

'Yeah, if you could stop from throwing up.'

'I'll get him,' I said.

Before I could reach the kitchen door, though ('Say, where's that sewer hog?' Quagg turned to ask as I passed him. 'We could use him as an extra grip to help the Scar.' 'There's two of 'em here now, Zack,' said Horner, 'him and his partner . . .'), Talbot, Dolph, and the guy in the chalkstriped suit came whooping and hallooing through it, bearing Anatole on their shoulders. 'Ta-*DAHH!*' they cried. Anatole, half-dressed and grinning sheepishly, begged to be put down, but his porters only hooted the louder, parading him around the room, getting everyone to clap and join in on a chorus of 'Pop! Goes the Weasel!' The door whumped open behind them and Brenda came streaking through, holding her red pants in front of her face – '*Hip hip HIP!*' they shouted – and I slipped through behind her.

Jim was at the kitchen stove, sterilizing a needle in what looked like a sardine can. 'Jim!' I cried. The room had dimmed, things had been put away, a kind of calm had descended here. Or been imposed. But I did not feel calm. I made it to the butcherblock and leaned against it. Fred, the short cop, sat in his shirtsleeves and neckbrace at the breakfast bench, eating sausage with chilled vodka from the fridge, my wife on a chair nearby sewing the brass button on his coat. There was something incongruously domestic, almost emblematic, about the three of them – cooking, sewing, eating there in the stillness, the subdued light; behind me the others reveled as though at some other party. 'It's Vic! *He's been shot!*'

'All right,' he said wearily. 'Won't be a minute.'

'It's *urgent*, Jim!' I held up my bloody hands.

He glanced over at me. 'Yes, I know, it's always – say, what's the matter with your shoulder?'

My wife looked up in alarm. 'It's nothing, a scratch—'

'Come here, let me take a look at it.'

The other policeman stuck his head in the door behind me. 'Got him, Fred.'

'Yeah, thanks, I just heard.'

'Looks like you've been grazed by a bullet. Were you near Vic when— ?'

'Yes, I was on the phone, but— !'

'Mmm. That explains it.' He turned the fire off under the needle, knelt to search through the black bag at his feet. 'Do you need help, Jim?' my wife asked.

'No . . .'

'I do wish people wouldn't use guns in the house.' There was a tremor in her voice.

'Vic's been hit bad, Jim. I think you ought to—'

'First things first, Gerry. That's not a serious wound, but it should be cleaned up right away.' He came up with a bottle of iodine, a swab, and some bandages, and set them on the stove, then went to the sink and rinsed a gray dishrag out under hot water.

'If I had my way, I'd outlaw the things, ma'am,' said Fred around a mouthful of garlic sausage, 'but you might as well outlaw eating and sh – uh, shaving.' Louise stepped out from a dark corner – I hadn't noticed her there before – and, as though pursued, rushed on out of the room, watched sorrowfully by my wife. Fred washed the sausage down with vodka. 'I hope I didn't say nothing—'

'No . . .'

'Now let's see what we've got here,' said Jim, ripping my shirt away from the wound. 'This may sting a bit . . .'

'Yes – OW!'

'He's such a baby,' my wife smiled. This was true. I dreaded the iodine to come more than being shot again – just the gritty dishrag was bringing tears to my eyes.

'A millimeter more,' Jim said, the gray lock flopping over his brow, 'and you might have lost some bone.'

'You gave me a button like this once, Gerald. Do you remember?'

'No . . .' Instead I remembered, for some reason, Naomi bent over the toilet, Dickie looking frazzled, Tania saying something (and there was this strange sensation of having just completed some kind of anti-phonal figure, like a round of passed bids: echoes as it were of those shots still ringing in my ears) about cowardice and hysteria. Maybe it was the musty-smelling rag in Jim's hand . . .

'You know, you should stop worrying about others so much, Gerry,' he counseled now, 'and start thinking a little about yourself for a change.'

'My wages, you said.' She turned to Fred. 'He said if I gave him a good time I'd get a second one.' She sighed. 'But I never did.'

Fred chuckled, winking at me. Jim dipped the swab in the iodine. 'He got it in the chest, Jim. At least twice. I really think you ought to – *YOW!*'

'My goodness, Gerald – you're worse than Mark when he's having a sliver out!'

'Don't let him fool you, he's braver than you think, ma'am,' said Fred with another wink.

'Come *on*, Jim, *that's enough!*'

'Easy! A little more . . .'

'Did you see the look on Cyril's face when Peg told him she was leaving him?' my wife asked as though to distract me.

'I don't know if I've seen them all night,' I gasped, and Jim said: 'You're kidding! Not Cyril and Peg— ?!'

'Yes, I don't understand it at all, do you, Gerald?'

'What? No! Yes! *Ow!* I'm not sure!'

'What *are* you trying to say, Gerald?'

'I think Tania told me,' I explained, pushing the words out through gritted teeth. Was this true? It seemed unlikely, even as the words came to me. Cyril and Peg? 'Or was about to. *Oh! Ah!* It has something to do with Ros, the lines from some play and wanting to ad-lib or something, I don't know – *OUCH!*'

'Well, that certainly makes it all clear as pie,' my wife remarked wryly, raising her eyebrows at Fred, who laughed and forked another hunk of sausage in his mouth.

'I really find it hard to believe,' said Jim. He had stopped molesting the wound with his swab and was now unrolling a bandage. He pressed a fold of gauze to my shoulder. 'Hold that, Gerry.'

'Anyway, I guess that's one party we'll miss out on,' said my wife. She bit the thread off, pinned the needle in her calico apron, held the coat up. 'That must make you and Mavis the real veterans here tonight, Jim.'

'I think probably Charley and Janny . . .'

'Well, they may not be doing so well either,' she said, folding the coat gently and laying it on the bench across from the policeman. 'From what I've heard . . .'

'Thanks, ma'am.'

Jim was taping the bandage to my shoulder, muttering, 'It's strange, they were almost a legend . . .' I was staring out at the backyard, where a dark heavy hush had settled, pressing up against the back door as though to embrace us. Ah well . . . I recalled the soft furry V of her pubes as they thrust against my fingers out there, the nubbly caress of her tongue as it coiled between my teeth, her hands scrabbling over me like hungry little crabs – but it was not an erotic memory, no, it was more like a solemn meditation on memory itself: the warm slippery stuff of time, the dry but somehow radiant impressions that remained. Like the muddy tracks (the voices were stilled now, the traipsing in and out) on the kitchen floor.

'I cleaned it all up,' my wife said, following my gaze, 'but then Anatole and Brenda and all that crowd came through.'

'I know, I saw him on exhibit in there . . .'

'Yes, that was nice. I think he'd been feeling a bit lonely, especially since . . . since his aunt . . .' She stared at her hands, her eyes watering. Jim capped the iodine and fit it back in the bag, rolled up the bandage, snapped the protective metal ring around the tape. 'We should invite more young people next time.'

'Maybe it'll milk some of the piss and vinegar outa the little jerk,' grumped Fred, 'pardon the French, ma'am. He's been giving the Chief a lotta stick, and we're pretty darn tired of it.'

'He's still very young,' my wife reminded him.

'Yeah, but he don't appreciate the difficulties – it ain't an easy job.'

'I think the Inspector makes his own difficulties,' I said.

Fred bristled momentarily, but then, thinking it over, cut himself another hunk of sausage. 'Well, the Old Man's got his weaknesses, I admit. We all do. He spent all that time in there with them watches, for example, just to figure out the murder took place exactly thirty minutes after we *got* here. Huh huh!' Jim fit one of the sterilized needles in a syringe, put the others in a plastic box, emptied the little pan in the sink, then tossed it in the garbage. 'Bob and me bailed him outa that one by taking a temperature fix with that stabhole in the liver, but it ain't always so simple like that – he's a pretty ingenious fella, like you seen, and sometimes we don't have a clue how to clean things up after. Sometimes we don't even know what the hell he's talking about. But, listen, loopy as he may seem, old Nigel's solved a lotta crimes. He's got a special knack.' He poured himself a shot of vodka and tossed it down, smacked his lips, poured another. 'He does it by somehow sinking into the heart of the crime itself, making a kinda transmitter outa hisself, don't ask me how. As far as he's concerned, see, there ain't no such thing as a isolated crime, it's always part of something bigger, and he figures the only way to get at this bigger thing is to use, not just the brain, but the whole waterworks – it's what he calls "*seeing through*" a crime. He's a artist at it, best I ever seen!'

Jim had left us meanwhile with his syringe needle up like a pointing finger. My wife was rinsing out the bloody dishrag. 'So it's true what they've been saying about Mavis – that she's . . .'

'Yes, she's an epileptic, Gerald. I thought you knew.'

'Old Nigel once told me something pretty weird,' Fred continued, sipping thoughtfully at his vodka. Epileptic? 'He said if a fella could become fond of the *evil* in the world, he'd find hisself *embracing delight*. Them were the Chief's exact words: *embracing delight*. Of course, evil, that takes in death, disease, cruelty, crime, the whole toot and scramble – so not much chance, hunh?' He got up, brushed the crumbs from his lap, went over to the sink to wash his hands. 'In the end, though, it's gotta be said, for all his fancy talk, old Nigel still seems to suspect foreigners, perverts, freaks and bums, just like the rest of us.'

'That's not very charitable,' my wife remarked, wiping off the breakfast table with the damp rag Jim had used on my shoulder.

'By the way,' I said (I realized I'd been staring for some time at a little heart-shaped stain on the butcherblock next to the can of body spray: something someone had said . . . ?), 'it turns out that valentine Naomi had was one I once gave you—'

'Yes, I know. Dickie asked me to go through her bag before they left and it was in there. She had your electric razor as well, and somebody's scout knife, Mother's hairnet, a yellow ball painted with an eye, even Mark's old potty and a bunch of inky thumbprints.' Fred glanced up and winked at me over his neckbrace, shaking the water from his hands. 'But Cyril said she couldn't help it.'

'Cyril?'

'Yes, he was there to see Peg off, of course.' She put the vodka and leftover sausage back in the fridge, then stood staring into it as though watching a movie there. 'Now I wonder what I could—'

'Peg . . . !' It was slowly, very slowly, dawning on me . . .

'Yes, when she left with Dickie – why! what's the matter with you, Gerald? We were just talking about—'

'Right . . . !' I turned to gaze out once more on the back porch where the dense tide of night seemed suddenly to be falling back: of course, it was Peg who had gone with him, her tattooed bottom, Dickie had mentioned – it hit me now like a revelation: *Alison was still here then!*

'Maybe I could make some brandied stuffed eggs . . .'

'Exactly!' But where? 'What?'

'You were right about that sleazy bastard, by the way,' said Fred. 'Whisked his redheaded baggage right outa here just as we was bringing charges. Accessory after the – *wurr-RRP!*' He belched loudly, patting his stomach. 'Whoo, that's better!' He belched again, a kind of brief little afterclap (yes, I thought, hugging myself, even for artless fools there are second chances!), then asked: 'You ain't never thought of taking up police work, have you?'

'Not right now . . .' My mind was elsewhere, searching, as it were, the premises.

'Too bad. We could use a fella like you. You got the gourd for it. And a good eye.'

'What? Ah, well . . . but no stomach.' Those others were giving her a bad time; maybe she went outside to hide. I seemed to see someone on the back porch. But, no, all those guys had just come in from there . . .

'You get used to it. You got the right attitude and that's what counts. Of course, as a career, it ain't what it once was, I admit that, not since they legalized fornication, as we used to call it.' He pulled on his coat, exercising his shoulders against the seams, then buttoned up. My wife put some water on to boil (where had I last seen her? the living room? I couldn't remember, it seemed so long ago . . .), got some tomatoes and green beans out of the fridge, some cottage cheese and butter, a carton of brown eggs. 'I hope we still have some capers,' she said. 'Them were the days – crime everywhere and even them not guilty of fornication was all the more likely to be guilty of something else: fantasy or murder or virulent possession – an excess of sentiment, as the old statutes put it. The force was the place to be in them days, I'll never forget it, it had something special.' Maybe the first thing, I thought, is to see if there's any vermouth left, pick up somehow where we . . . 'Of course I was young then – but we had a lotta professional pride and enthusiasm, it was a kinda golden age for the old P.D., all the best brains was in it – that's when old Nigel joined up, for example – but now, well, most of them boys are gone. The new breed's got a whole different slant on things. It's all statistics now, stemming the tide like they like to say – in fact, fornication's a kinda police weapon these days to keep the citizens confused – these young fellas've got no time for dickprints or cuff debris or sussing out a hidden motive. And there's all this do-gooder crime now, bomb-throwing and food riots in the camps and computer-bashing and the like, most of it happening way over my head – though that don't mean I won't lose an arm or a leg from it. Just defending a poker game down at city hall these days can get you napooed.' He tucked his cap under his arm, adjusted the knot of his tie under the neckbrace, checked his weapons. Quiet deliberations, that's the important thing, I thought. No more impulsive leaps in the dark. Harmony and balance – I was very excited . . . ! 'No, the fun's mostly gone outa crime these days, what you might call the personal touch – I mean, it's a real kick for us to get an old-fashioned murder like this one, it sets us up for a week after, even if it *is* something of a luxury – you shoulda seen old Nigel on the way over, he was tickled pink.'

'That reminds me, Gerald,' said my wife, prying the lid off a flour tin, 'what *is* the way you find out if a girl is ticklish?'

'What's that?' The green room, we'd said. Right! But then . . . ?

'Mmm, looks good,' said Fred, staring into the boiling water.

'That man with the buckteeth,' she replied vaguely, fishing around now among the dishes in the sink. 'He was saying . . .'

'Earl's joke, you mean? You give her a couple of test tickles.'

'Well, that's what *he* said, but what does that prove?'

'Test-tickles. Testicles.' I pointed. They were stirring again. I smiled.

'Oh, I see.' She sighed and peered dismally into the empty pot of Dijonais mustard. 'What did you want to talk to Alison about?'

'Who— ?' She had an amazing way of juxtaposing things (the smile had become a wince: I touched my shoulder gingerly). Maybe it was the secret of her cooking.

'That woman we met at the theater. Louise overheard Sally Ann telling her you were waiting for her down in the rec room.'

For a moment I couldn't think. 'What?' What did she say? I was suddenly locked in somewhere, deep inside. And then something broke open, it felt like the police smashing in through Mark's bedroom door, a splintering crash, and I staggered back. Or perhaps I was already staggering. The rec room! I should have known: all those wisecracks, the traffic up and down the stairs (had somebody mentioned bondage?), Alison's husband staring fearfully down them as I was carrying Mark up to bed, Noble's sweaty armpits and insolent complaint – it all came together now, I saw things plainly, all too plainly, and it took my knees right out from under me. I slumped weakly against the butcherblock. Going down.

'Gerald? What's the matter— ?!'

'It's his wound, ma'am, He's probably in a bit of shock.'

What was worse, she'd suppose I'd set her up for it – she'd never been to one of our parties before, how could she know it wasn't a game we played with all our first-timers? I felt like crying. I *was* crying. Goddamn Sally Ann! The lights in the kitchen seemed to dim and a wave of nausea rippled through me.

'Maybe he should lie down.'

'It's usually better to try to walk it off.'

'Hey, Ger, what's wrong? You look terrible!'

'He's been wounded, sir, nothing serious.'

I realized we were in the dining room. I seemed to be making progress through it without any effort of my own, held up by Fred and my wife. I still felt lightheaded and queasy. All I could think of for the moment was Tania staring despairingly into the bathtub full of pink suds, over-come – this was clear to me now, it was the only thing that was clear to me – by a paroxysm of self-hatred.

'Here, try this.'

They were holding something alcoholic to my lips. It dribbled down my chin. Somehow I'd forgotten how to swallow.

Jim turned up then and said, no, I should be lying down, my feet higher than my head.

'That's what *I* thought,' said my wife.

'I've had 'em die on me like that,' Fred disagreed. 'We like to keep 'em moving around.'

They made some room for me in front of the sideboard, dragging Mavis out of the way, and stretched me out. Something was pounding in my ears. It might have been my heart. But it sounded more like feet thumping up and down the stairs. Someone brought our camel-saddle in from the TV room and propped it under my ankles. Fred made it clear that if I popped off, he wasn't to be blamed, and Wilma, standing nearby, said I reminded her of the last time she'd seen her third husband Archie. 'He had that same blue look in the face.'

'Open his shirt there, give him some air!'

'Loosen his belt!'

Heads dipped over me and bobbed away again like those little drinking birds sold in novelty shops. The ceiling, too, seemed to be throbbing, at times pressing down, at others vanishing into some vast distance, like the empty horizon of Pardew's dream. Shadows flickered across it like faint images on a cinema screen or a drawn windowshade. I remembered Alison saying: 'There *is* no audience, Gerald, that's what makes it so sad.' Or perhaps my wife had said that. In any case . . .

'Oh dear, look at that bruise under his navel,' she said now.

'He looks pretty tender all over.'

'Is there anything else we can do?'

'You might wet a washcloth with cold water,' Jim said.

'Has he been crying?'

'Well, Vic was his best friend, after all.'

'Listen,' said Fred, leaning close, 'I gotta go now, and I just wondered if you got any more hot tips for us?' His breath reeked of garlic and vodka. I turned my head away. I found myself looking up somebody's skirt and closed my eyes. 'You'd be doing us a real favor . . .'

'No . . .' I whispered faintly, or meant to – what I found myself saying was: 'No . . . ble . . .'

'I think he said something.'

'That's a good sign.'

'That ham wizard with the glass lamp, you mean?' murmured Fred in my ear. I shuddered. 'Hmm, pretty tricky – he's got that lawyer buddy, family of some sort. Still . . .'

'He seems to be getting some of his color back, too.'

'Gosh, it was *great*, Uncle Howard!' Anatole was saying somewhere just past my vision. 'I never realized doing it was so *easy!*'

'. . . I'll see what I can do.'

'No, that's probably just fever.'

'And now I'm going to be a playwright!'

'Gerry? Can you hear me?'

'Mr Quagg said I'm to be the brains for the show!'

'Wait—!' I whispered, turning back ('Don't be silly, he was with me,' I seemed to hear my wife say), but the policeman was gone. What I saw instead was Fats floating high above me, as though suspended in midair: he hung up there, startled, looking like he was about to sail off into distant space – then he came crashing down, making the whole room shake.

'What?'

'The more things change, the more they are the same,' said Hoo-Sin.

'It's gettin' rough in here, Scar – wanta go up and try on the county fair?'

'No, thanks, she's fulla fleas and I got this preem to mount. Anyhow I just been fannin' the rubber in the dungeon, man, I got no more snap.'

'What am I doin' wrong?' Fats groaned from the floor ('That opus still pullin' 'em in?'), and someone said: 'I love what you've done with the space in here, this delicate balance of old and new.'

'Yeah, but not for much longer – if you wanta catch her act, you better get on down there.'

'Hey, you come on like an ice wagon, Fats, you gonna get wrecked!'

'Material goin' a bit stale?'

'You're kidding—!'

'It's just terrible about Tania, Howard. Such a tragedy!'

'Pregnant?'

'Well, the tread's a bit worn – but what's really closin' the show down is this dyke out there at the head of the stairs, doin' a soapbox number on anybody with an honest bone-on . . .'

'I know how you must feel.'

'Do you indeed.'

'. . . I mean, man, she sorta takes the starch out . . .'

'I only meant . . .'

I closed my eyes again and found myself recalling ('So that's why Cyril . . .'), or trying to recall, something that woman in Istanbul had said to me. We were crossing an arched bridge, I remembered ('Eileen?' someone asked, this was very far away), there were overladen carts pulled by mules, a leaden sky, a certain spiciness in the air. 'This will soon be over,' she'd said. Yes. Tin cooking ware was clinking on the back of one of the carts, and there was a dull rumbling continuo underfoot. 'In a sense, it was over before it began. We have been living with the last moment ever since the first. That's been the magic of it all: experiencing the future with the sensual immediacy of the present and all the nostalgia of the past . . .'

But then . . .

'Papanash,' someone said. What? I heard ice tinkling in glasses, smelled hot food, or perhaps I *felt* these things: a chill, a flush . . . 'I've never felt *anything*,' Janny Trainer was saying, and someone asked: 'Vomedy?' Someone had placed a wet dishtowel on my forehead. 'Yum!' 'Quagg's casting!' 'Oh yeah?' 'I always did it because I thought I was *supposed* to, but suddenly I don't feel as *dumb* as I used to!' 'Oh, I see – I thought it was a vomit remedy!' This was Jim. I opened my eyes. There was a lot of excited activity around me. People preening, straightening stockings, tucking their shirttails in. Fats was on his feet again. 'Hey, man, can you use a good piana player?' 'Right now,' said Quagg, 'I need a coupla grips to help Scarborough skate the flats!' Maybe I'd dozed off. My head was thick and there was a metallic taste on my tongue. 'It's like letting men shove their thing in me all the time was making my brain all sticky and stupid . . .' 'Feeling better?' Jim was bending over me. 'Hot as a junked-up canary, man!' 'Hey, where you guys been?' 'Vot? Chunk?' 'Noble,' I murmured. 'I have to tell him . . .' 'He's all right. The police are talking to him. Do you want to try sitting up?' 'Down the well, Zack, you know – so what's on the menu, somethin' special?' What's on the menu. The line stuck in my head for a moment. As Quagg read it off ('Ach, yah, *zeks!*'), I seemed to see real menus, one-page books, tantalizing, yet unreadable, opening out before my eyes. Choices could be made, they said. They are always the same choices. 'Gerry . . . ?'

'Let one who knows your nature,' breathed Hoo-Sin soothingly, 'feel your pulse.'

'Well, it hasn't got a name, though the kid's working on that. But it's about time and memory and lost illusions . . .'

'Oh yeah! Is that the one where the director comes running in and says: "No, no, Ros! you're supposed to pick up the *clock* and—"?'

'Or how 'bout a little soft-shoe,' wheedled Fats. '*And* play the piana!'

'No, this is all new, man!'

'The way I heard it, she was – ha ha – supposed to pick up the jewels and run . . .'

'Both at the same time, Zack, both at the same *time!*'

Menus, my mother used to say, were fun's bait, misery's disguise. She could be epigrammatic like that. She'd sit over hot coffee, smoking nervously, thinking up these depressing little aphorisms. Happiness, she'd say, is a missed connection . . .

'Come on, Gerry . . .' Jim was slapping my cheeks gently. I felt very remote. The menus had become cue cards, curtains, candles, calendars, the white wakes of ocean liners (Regina said something about the 'last act' or maybe 'elastic,' and there was distant laughter like the sound of waterclocks), wet laundry . . .

'To experience perfect interfusion, let all the knots be dissolved.'

'Well, I *suppose* it's all right . . .,' said Janny.

'Here, we don't need every fucking "*i*" dotted, son – just give us the nub and a zinger or two and we can pong along on the rest.'

'. . . Though I'm a little bit ticklish there!'

'What's Scarborough *doing* in there?'

'Uh, what'd he say, Uncle Howard?'

'Has to do with some saint, he said.'

'Yeah? Well, it's *wild*, man!'

'I believe he wants you to prepare an outline.'

'You ever *seen* me bang the dogs, Zack?'

'Gerry . . . ?'

I opened my eyes again (this took effort) and found myself staring across the floor at Mavis, staring pitiably back. Her own eyes were glazed over ('Hoo! hah! Just – *puff!* – clamp your lamps on *this* move, man!') and she was grinning, but she didn't seem to be dead. Just listening. The pale rolls of flesh on her arms and legs lay spread out on the carpet as though deflated. Or deboned. I tried to flex my own arms, but couldn't.

'Jesus, he looks like he's fucking had it!' muttered Dolph.

'No, I'm all right,' I whispered. But he wasn't talking about me, he was looking at someone across the room.

'Whoo, all bets off on that one!'

I twisted my head around. Steve the plumber and an older guy were hauling Vic in feet first through the crowd, Hilario and Daffie clearing the way. The older guy had his name stitched over his overalls pocket like Steve, but I couldn't read it. He seemed to resent having to drag Vic in and bumped him along irritably, knocking his lolling head against the doorjamb and table leg, elbowing people (Fats was huffing out a nasal tune and bobbing about recklessly, making little Vachel duck and scowl, and Hoo-Sin, kneading Janny's kidneys – 'Ooh, that feels good, I was just itching there!' – backheeled him deftly in the crotch just as Dolph popped a beer can open) out of the way. With every step, blood bubbled out of Vic's chest wound, staining darkly his pale blue workshirt. 'What . . . what are you *doing*— *?!*' I gasped.

'In *drag?*' whimpered Fats, hobbling around, doubled over. '*Hunh*, Zack? Whaddaya say? And *falsies?*'

'We breeng the chackass to the reever,' Hilario smiled, helping the two workmen prop Vic up in the corner of sideboard and wall. He was still clutching the fork, but more like a standard than a weapon.

'He was asking for a fresh drink every five minutes,' Daffie panted, wiping the sweat off her breasts ('With *high heels?* Eh? And striped *longjohns?* How '*bout* it, Zack?'). 'He was getting to be a goddamn nuisance.'

Vic groaned and blood dribbled down his chin. 'Looks like his valves are shot, Goldy,' sighed Steve, digging at the blackened crotch of his overalls. 'Yeah, well, for that I *ain't* got the right tools.'

'Who the hell did that?' Dolph wanted to know.

'I dunno. Gerry ('Olga— ?') was there . . .'

'Vic— ?' I tried to sit up but ('Oh yah, annudder, bitte!') I was too lightheaded.

'Aw, Zack, c'mon – y'mean that lollypop who useta moon around Ros's door?' Vachel was whining. 'You gotta be kidding!'

'I'm sorry, Gerry,' Jim said. 'The second bullet apparently ('Dot's enuff!') ricocheted off a rib and lodged in his heart, there's nothing I can do.'

'Whaddaya mean? It's your kinda role, Vaych! Look at him, he's a real downstage sorta guy! And you can interpret it any way you—'

'In fact, probably lucky for you it did.'

'Tank you.'

'Wha— ? That bushwah tinpot? That fashion-mag foof?'

'That's the guy there, Goldy, the one with the blue belly hanging out. It's his spread.'

'Cheez, Zack! Have a *heart!*'

'All right, all right, I hear ya talking . . .'

'Hey, mister, is there anything else?' I opened my eyes again: it was the older plumber, standing over me, squat and jowly, wiping his hands on a greasy rag. He had a wad of something in one cheek, which now he shifted.

'I tell ya what, man, we'll make it the main speaking part, whaddaya say?'

'Come on, pal, I ain't got all fucking night, you know.'

'Okay, okay,' squeaked Vachel, 'just so you don't stick me in a robot suit like last time,' and Steve said: 'I think his wife said something about the dishwasher making a funny noise, Goldy.'

'Yeah? Where is it then? Let's get it over with, goddamn it – you took me out of a good movie on the box.'

My head was a sieve, everything just came rattling in. It was like a frequency scan. White noise. My shoulder was beginning to hurt again, though, which was probably a good sign.

'A *drink!*' burbled Vic.

'What do you think, Jim?'

'Sure, what harm can it do?'

'Poor Veek! He ees, how you say, crosseeng out, no?'

'Yeah. Does his daughter know?'

'What's that? Vic goin' out?' asked Fats, lumbering over. 'Don't step on Gerry,' someone said. 'Hey, can he bring back some fresh coronas?'

'I think Woody's breaking it to her.'

'No, no, Fats, I mean, he ees feenesh, all gone over, goode-uh-bahee!'

'Okay, now the actual murder scene, we're gonna do in the nude, so we need somebody who strips well.'

'Finished?' Fats, tottering above me, rocked back on his heels. 'Who, *Vic— ?!*'

'Great idea! What about the Vagina?'

'Oh no,' at least two people said at once, and Daffie, pouring out a tumbler of bourbon, murmured: 'That Woody's a busy little boy.' 'She's tripping over her bags these days and her goddamn cheeks (*'Bren!* It's *Vic!* Oh my *god*, Bren. He's been *shot!'*) 're hanging down behind her *knees!'*

'*Beautiful!*' rumbled Charley Trainer, hobbling up to the sideboard, as Fats staggered away. I seemed to hear people cheering in another room. 'Hullo, Dollfish, Howard – hey, I *like* the bra, Howard!' And booing. ''Ass cute!' I rose up on my elbows (there was another burst of cheering) and stared down at my exposed navel, trying to get my bearings. There *was* a bruise there – had Sally Ann kicked me? No, that's right, Roger . . . I fell back again. 'Whatcha call keepin' abreast a the times, hunh?'

And more boos: seemed to be coming from the TV room. It was like a kind of voting. Jim propped the camel-saddle under my head.

'Say, getcher paw outa Olga's muu-muu for jussa sec, Dolph ole pal, 'n pour yer ole dad one, wudja?'

'I got it, Zack! How about that ripe chunk in the yellow knittie?'

'So *dot's* vot it vass! I *tot* I haff *vorms* back dere!'

'Chunk?'

'*Sock it to him, gimpy!*' someone shouted from the other room. '*Put him on ice!*'

'You mean that suburban hausfrau of yours? C'mon, get serious!'

''Ass ole Dolfer, m'love – haw haw! – awways takin' a backseat!'

'*Yay!*'

'We're not doing farce here, Horn, we don't want any goddamn travesty!'

'Fartz?'

'No, wait, Zack, think about it. Anybody here would be a travesty of Ros, am I right? So all right, you *accept* that and you push on *through* into something *else!* You dig?'

'Make it a short one, Dolph,' Jim cautioned. 'Charley's had too much already.'

'*Send him up the country!*'

'*Boo!*'

'I mean, you're not just tryin' to give these people some cheap fantasy, are you?'

'What are they yelling about in there?'

'Okay, Horner, maybe you got something. Why not? See if she'll do it.'

'Hey! Wha' happena ressa my *drink*, Dolf-ball? 'Ass oney *half* of it!'

'They're watching old videotapes. Weird stuff. Full of sex and violence.'

'Sorry, Charley, Jim said—'

'What's weird about that?'

'What? *What?!*'

'It's so fucking *cold* . . . my legs . . .'

'I take 'iss drink as a *insult*, ole buddy!'

'Easy, Vic.'

'Did you catch the slow-mo sequence with the croquet mallets?'

'Yeah, hairy, man! All that squosh and splat – really shook me up!'

'Forshunately, bein' a easy-goin' fella, I can *swallow* a insult!'

'I still can't understand what caused them to break up,' Jim was saying ('But beautifully filmed!'), zipping up my fly. 'After all this time . . .'

'I don't know,' said Daffie. 'Maybe they thought people weren't paying enough attention to them.'

'*Daddy*— ?!'

'Woops, watch it, here she comes!'

'Oh, *Daddy!*' Sally Ann cried, her voice breaking. She stumbled over me, falling heavily into Vic's arms. 'What have you *done?*'

'Sally Ann? Is that . . . you?'

'Yes, Daddy. Don't try to talk . . . !'

'I've had it . . . this time, kid! It's the – *whoof! hack!* – the end!' He gasped for breath. ('He's not got much longer,' someone said, and Olga asked: 'Much longer don whoose?') 'I never really thought I'd . . . have to . . . have to die . . .'

'Is that all you can do, Olga, talk funny?'

'I – I've always known what life,' Vic spluttered, '. . .what life was about . . .'

'Yah, vell, it's *sum*-ing.'

'Mmm – goodness, what *is* this?'

'And I never kidded myself about – oh damn! it *hurts*, baby . . . ! – about death . . .'

'It's a sort of pilaf. With yoghurt sauce.'

'But I could never imagine . . . that moment . . .'

'Gee, I don't know,' Teresa was saying ('Well, it's *delicious!* I don't know how you do it!'), 'in front of everybody?'

'. . . In between . . .'

'Don't, Daddy. You scare me when you talk like that.'

'Come on, sweetheart! This is your *big chance!*'

'The truth's . . .'

'The break you been waiting for!'

'Just leftovers, I'm afraid.'

'. . . Always scary, girl . . .'

'Well, if it's art, I guess it's all right.'

'And in any case it's about all I've got left . . .'

'Atta girl!'

'. . . To give you,' Vic was mumbling ('So get *in* there and tear it *down*, baby!'). He seemed to be fading again. 'And what's inside these fan-*tas*-tic *eggs?*' 'I'll give you the recipe,' my wife said, and Quagg shouted out: 'Okay, all you lot, into the parlor! It's time for the apotheosis of Ros!'

'Tell Mom . . . I'm sorry, and . . .'

'Oh oh,' somebody cried out ('I already called her, Dad, and she said she didn't know who I was talking about . . .'), 'here comes that lady guerrilla again!' I felt someone's hands in my armpits. 'You'd better get out of her way, Gerry,' Jim was saying somewhere behind my ear ('And do me a favor, baby . . .') as I rose, lifted, from the floor: 'Could you – *ngh!* – give us a hand, please?' It was Eileen: she was wearing a trenchcoat with the collar turned up, her hands stuffed in the pockets, a scarf around her head.

'He's weak . . . and frivolous . . . confused . . .'

'Don't worry, Daddy, I won't . . .'

'Well, we meet again,' said Mr Waddilow. He was one of those holding me up. The other one ('. . . Anyway he's too old . . .') was the older plumber, Goldy; Jim, letting go, was getting dragged away by Quagg's set-builder Scarborough, who was explaining: 'We're using her as part of the scenery, you dig, and we need you to get her ready . . .'

'I don't know . . .'

'And hang on to the – *kaff! huff! hoo . . . !* – present, baby! It's all you've—'

'Oh, Daddy, stop it! You're spitting blood all over!'

'No, listen— !'

Eileen stepped up and kicked the glass out of his hands. 'What are you carrying that fork around for, greedyguts? Nobody's going to insist on good manners when you're eating cold mud.' Vic, grinning, wheezed appreciatively, his hand searching for the lost glass. I realized ('I've never *seen* Eileen like this before!') my whole right side had turned to stone. 'You liked that? Try this one!' She kicked him in the mouth: his head bounced off the wall, teeth flew.

'Jesus, that hurt!' Vic whimpered, laughing.

'Don't talk to her, Daddy.'

'Way to go, sister!' Goldy grinned, spitting thickly into a plastic cup he was holding in his free hand, and Charley, pushing out his thick soft mitt past my petrified elbow ('When Jim told her Vic had a bullet in his heart, you know what she said? She said, "Then why don't you just reach inside his asshole and pull it out!"'), said: 'Don' believe I've hadda pleasure. Trainer here, Mushual Life.'

'This is Mr Waddilow, Charley,' I gasped, trying to stand alone. 'New neighbors . . .'

'The next one in the goolies, tough guy!'

'Oh ha ha! *Spare* me!' Vic groaned.

'Neighbors, hunh?'

'I left your bill on the dishwasher, mister,' the plumber said around his chaw, squinting up at me. 'Easy, Eileen, he's dying,' Daffie cautioned, touching her forearm. Eileen shook her off. 'So? Who isn't? Some just have more fun at it than others, that's all.' 'Thank you,' I said, gripping the sideboard. 'You're welcome to stay . . . have a drink or something . . .' 'No, thanks.' He spat another oyster. 'I got no time for this shit.'

'In fact he looks good drooling blood like that – it's like the mask's finally off the bastard.'

'Steve's a young kid, it's all new to him, he can hang around if he wants to. Me, I seen it all. I got a job to do, that's it.' He turned to go. 'Can I give you a ride somewhere, sister?'

'No, thanks. I'll walk.'

'Hey,' Kitty asked, 'where *is* everybody?'

'Don't be stupid, girlie, it's dangerous out there.'

I looked around. Kitty was right ('Anatole has written a play,' Howard was explaining to her – he'd cleaned up some, wore Tania's glasses on a chain around his neck now, his red tie and the bra, but no shirt, and my white boating cap, 'you just missed the casting . . .'): the dining room had emptied out, there were only the few of us clustered around the drinks now like refugees, Mrs Waddilow alone over at the table, Mavis grinning up at us from the floor, Cynthia and Woody in the next room watching television.

'And relax, sister, I'm off fucking for life. I mean it, I'm into beer, old movies, and model trains. When I'm not unplugging rich guys' toilets.' His partner Steve came in with Scarborough and Horner and they commenced to move the dining table out from under Mrs Waddilow. "Scuse us, ma'am.' 'So whuzz your poison, Waterloo?' Charley asked, slumping heavily against the sideboard. 'You like model trains?'

'Just a bit of tonic, thank you. Not a drinking man myself.'

'I don't know,' Eileen said, staring down at Goldy, hands stuffed in her pockets, her face swollen and blue with bruises. 'I don't think so.'

'Gerry?' It was Sally Ann, her voice anxious. 'I think Dad's getting worse!'

'You oughta come and see my layout, I got everything, uses up half my basement, whole fucking county in miniature.'

So he was: his head, eyes rolled back, had fallen to one side, blood dribbled down his chin still ('Just like real life. Only without the horse-shit . . .'), his breath was coming in hoarse erratic gasps. There was a tooth lying loose on his chin like a beached castaway. 'Vic?' His lips were moving ('You're as bad as this guy,' Eileen was saying, 'just another closet idealist!' and Goldy said: 'Hey, you like horseshit? I'll put in horseshit!'), but only the odd word or two were getting out: '. . . nihilistic bastard . . . what? . . . and hope, shit . . . what I *hate* – kaff! foo! . . . so goddamn wet—' 'I'll go get Jim,' I said.

'Hurry . . . !'

It wasn't easy to hurry. I seemed to be carrying a hundred pounds of dead weight on my right side, and my knees were like jelly. I heaved myself to the doorway and leaned dizzily against it, staring into Scarborough's transformation of our living room. Nothing was in its place, except perhaps my wife, who was vacuuming the rug. It was like some kind of spectacular fusing of the familiar, the whole room tented in sheets, towels, bloody drapes and curtains, all meant to suggest some sort of cave, I supposed ('I won't be a moment, Zack,' my wife shouted from inside it as Quagg flung his cape about in mimed protest, 'I just want to get up this plaster dust before it gets tracked into the carpet!'), lit from behind – or rather from atop: Scarborough had drilled holes through the ceiling and mounted table and floor lamps up there above the sheeting. At the cavemouth, Teresa stood naked and frightened ('I feel so stupid,' she was complaining, trying to cover, not her breasts – which Gudrun was rouging – or her genitals, but the whitened rolls of fat on her tummy), while nearby Jim leaned over Ros's cadaver, laid out amid pilaf, cheese balls, and sliced salami on our dining room table, a butcher knife in his hand. He seemed shorter than usual. 'No, no, I want the video camera *inside* the cave, looking *out* at the *audience!*' Quagg shouted over the sweeper's roar, and Scarborough cried: 'Goddamn it,

Fats, get outa here! You're knockin' everything over!' 'I'm just trying to help, Scar!' 'Well, go help Gudrun!' Oddly, this was all reminiscent of something I'd seen before, as though – I was thinking about Inspector Pardew's whimsical speculations about 'the geography of time' – I'd somehow got switched onto some kind of reverse loop (had I just heard Goldy say something about this to Eileen? Now certainly she said: 'Sounds like the story of my life,' but perhaps he'd been describing his shunting operations), such that though the space had changed and the approach was from an opposite angle, this was a point on time's map I'd passed through before. I squeezed my eyes shut, shook my head.

'They said the dining room table was too high and wanted to saw the legs down,' my wife said suddenly beside me, 'but I talked them out of it.'

'*What*— ?!' I lurched back, banging my head on the doorframe.

'I didn't mean to startle you, Gerald. It's all right.' What was happening? It was as though we'd jumped over something! One moment she'd been vacuuming the carpet and Quagg, prancing about in his white unitard, had been shouting over the noise, the next she was in front of me discussing the dining room table, Louise was carting the sweeper off, Fats was on his knees, smearing Teresa's legs with clown white, and Quagg, wrapped up like a sleeping bat in his purple cape, was quietly explaining to Alison's husband ('In theater, dialogue *is* action, man!') what the play was all about. What had happened to that moment *in between?* 'I made up something off the top of my head about the proper height of altars, and luckily they accepted it.' Behind her there was a reek of pot and incense. 'No, no, *no*, Fats!' Gudrun was exclaiming. 'I said *not* in her bush – now go away, *I'll* do it!' 'In fact, I overdid it, I'm afraid, and then the table turned out to be too low, so they had to raise it up on some of your records.'

'Ah. Good.' I really didn't know what I was saying. Regina came sweeping in, drew up short when she spied Teresa, cried out: 'How come *she* got the part?!' and went storming out again in a stylized pique I was sure I'd seen before. I was totally confused. I didn't know whether the night was running forward or backward. I was afraid the doorbell would ring and it would be Ros at the door. Backing out, her cloak wrapping her, her welcoming hug dissolving into a wishful fancy – and then the doorbell *did* ring! 'Oh no!' I cried.

'Not *more* people!' my wife groaned, and took my arm. But it was: little Bunky Baird, the actress who'd played 'Honeyed Glances' in *The Lover's Lexicon*, one of Lot's daughters, and Jesus's nymphomaniac sister in *The Beatitudes*, escorted by some older guy in his fifties and a young gigolo who might have been partnering either or both. Quagg had just been explaining to Alison's husband that, 'So what we're going for here is the transmutation of stuff from deep down in the inner life, see, into something out front that we can watch, something made outa language and movement, you dig, to show forth the –' when Bunky let out a terrible shriek from the doorway: *'Stop him! he's going to kill her!'*

Teresa squealed as though Gudrun, now rouging her bottom, might have jabbed her with something, Olga yelped and dropped her drink, Jim looked up: 'Don't be silly,' he sighed ('We need a butterfly on that float at the mouth,' shouted Scarborough), shaking his loose shock of gray hair, 'I'm only trying to chip this damned plaster off.'

'It's all right, Bunky,' Quagg explained, his arm around her. 'She's already dead. It's Ros.' 'Okay, hit it – that's it, now make it hot!' 'She had a big heart, I wanta use it in this production.'

'It's getting so confusing,' my wife murmured, her hand on my leaden elbow ('Yeah, I heard a rumor you had something going on the boards, Zack – looks fab!' Bunky was saying, calming down as deftly as she'd aroused herself, and Vachel, flipping irritably through Anatole's script, complained: 'Wah, don't I getta do any *fucking?*'), 'I don't even know a lot of these people.'

'That's good, kill it!'

'Hey, what took you guys so long?' Quagg asked, as Steve the plumber and Horner came in, lugging the ping-pong table.

'Catchin' the reruns in the pit, Zack.'

'Isn't that your athletic supporter Vachel is wearing on his head?'

'Looks like it.' Also my golf shoes and Bermuda shorts, my ski goggles on his bulbous rump, and Mark's blue SUPERLOVER sweatshirt.

'This where you want it?'

'Yeah.' They set the table down, still collapsed, at the entrance to the cave: apparently it was meant to serve as a kind of stage. 'See what you think, Hillie,' Quagg said, then, shifting his penis from the left to the right side of his unitard crotch, turned to Bunky: 'What're you doing these days, kid?'

'I'm, uh, between shows, Zack.'

'I – I don't know what to say,' I said, and my wife said ('C'mon,' Quagg smiled, 'we'll spot you in'): 'I'll go put the coffee on.'

'Thanks, Zack,' said Bunky softly, touching him under the cape. She already had her coat off, her two men bumping past me into the dining room with it, on their way to the sideboard. Back there, I could still hear Vic babbling on helplessly: 'Turned to salt . . . *what—* ? . . . exactly the problem . . . ice all gone . . . who – *whoof! harff!* – wanted that . . . ? *No*, goddamn it!' Yes, I thought, feeling a little better, coffee would help.

'Now lemme see that script, kid.'

I moved out of the traffic toward Jim (he seemed suddenly very weary, his hair in his eyes and square jaw adroop, as he dug away at the plaster on Ros's breast), Hilario rapping out a vigorous staccato on the ping-pong table as I passed that sounded like machine-gun fire. Behind his fierce rat-a-tat-tat, I could hear Anatole explaining excitedly that his play was really a kind of metaphysical fairy tale, a poetic meditation on the death of beauty and on the beast of violence lurking in all love, Vachel grousing in his squeaky voice: 'Yeah, but at *least* I oughta get to squeeze some goddamn *tit*, hunh, Zack?' 'Christ, so much – *gasp!* – waste . . . over and over . . .' You could hear him all the way in here, growling and spluttering. 'Got a side for me, honey?' Bunky asked. 'Am I right . . . ? story – kaff! snort! – what? *kills!*' 'Vic's in bad shape, Jim,' I said. It was a relief to be around a familiar face. 'I think he needs you.'

Jim sighed, staring down at Ros. 'Some damn party *I'm* having,' he said. One of Ros's bagged-up hands was in the pilaf. There was a loose scatter of paper napkins, turkey bones ('Damn it, you gotta dumb it down, kid,' Quagg was remonstrating, Alison's husband hovering over his shoulder, trying to read the script, 'you're outa school now, so cut the fancy shit – this is *theater!*'), Alison's silk sash, chorizo chunks, somebody's vibrator, used silverware. Like Time's dropped breadcrumbs, I thought: no, we were not going around in circles, Ros wasn't anyway. And the sash: it was greasier than ever. There are no reverse loops, it seemed to say. The borders are absolute. Things end. Replay, instant or delayed (the TV cameraman had just moved off Jim's hands to focus on Teresa, clown white from head to toe, except for her bright red breasts and bottom, now being urged up onto the ping-pong table to dance with Hilario, Scarborough meanwhile nailing my skis to the front corners of the table, apparently creating some kind of proscenium arch, the raps of his hammer syncopating contrapuntally with Hilario's chattering tapdance and Zack Quagg's barking lecture to a deflated Anatole: 'You might as well learn right now, son: keep it simple! The mystery just gets chewed up in all this razzamatazz. If you got something to say, come straight out with it!'), was a manipulation not of time but of matter. Benedetto came in, pulling on Roger's bloodsoaked business suit (this was new): 'It's still *sopping!*' he complained (he hadn't said this before), trying to stretch it around his operatic belly. 'Gudrun, old sock, could you let this out a bit?' 'How's the shoulder, Gerry?'

'Stiff . . .'

'Just remember, kid, the most mysterious sentence in the world has only three letters in it. Everything else is nothing but a fucking footnote to it, variations on a – hey, why so glum?'

'There's only about an inch or so back here,' Gudrun said, examining the seam in the seat of Roger's pants, Benedetto peering down at her over his shoulder. 'Why don't we just make you a codpiece?'

'I'm sorry, Mr Quagg. It's my fault. I guess I really don't know much about this—'

'Whaddaya mean, you're doing great!'

'I am?'

'Hey, Scar, look what I found!' exclaimed Horner, coming in with Mark's pedalcar. Scarborough was up on a stepladder, his mouth full of pins, hanging our drapes over the ski uprights like theater curtains, so folding them as to make the splotches of blood resemble large crude hearts. 'Terriff,' he called down lugubriously, taking a tuck, 'see if he'll fit,' and Vachel squeaked: 'No, man, I'm *not* getting *in* that thing!' Gudrun was meanwhile measuring Beni for his codpiece and it reminded me, as I settled back against the table, accepting it all now, Ros, Roger, Tania, the police, the wounds and bruises, everything, or almost everything ('Sure, kid! You got *bucketsa* talent!' Quagg was booming), of the time Ros, holding the head of my exhausted member up in the air, said: 'I don't care how big it is, Gerry. I don't even care how hard it is. I just care how *here* it is . . .' Yes, I thought – I was watching Teresa's crimson cheeks bob like ripe apples as Hilario, looking pained, clapped her along – this is the one sweet thing we have: the eternal present. Our only freedom. It seemed to flatten out beneath me, all resistance crumbling at last.

'Gerry . . . ?'

'I mean, I *love* the fairy tale bit, kid, that old granny in the ice castle, little orphan Ros at the door – like, we'll put her in a basket maybe, shaking a rattle or sucking a dildo or something – flash all that in the hello frame to key some motifs, ring a few bells, then punch in this torture number to set up the death dance and Last Supper routine: shit, man, it's a fucking *classic!*'

'It is?'

'No, no, no, Teresita! You are the, how you say? the goddess off *loave*, no?'

'And this line about bats in daylight – I mean, *wow!*'

Clock time might take things – Ros, for example – further and further away, or seem to, but human time ('So awright, kid, get *on* with it!') – what had the Inspector said?

'Now, anybody here get off on a git-box?'

'Gerry, you're, uh . . .'

'You muss *leeft!* and *leeft!* So!'

Pulsations, yes. Perhaps. (He said.) But flow, no.

'Whew, I don't *believe* this!'

'How 'bout *me*, Zack? Gimme a kit, I'm magic, man!'

'Vic's daughter plays, I think.'

'Gerry . . . ? Hey . . . !'

'What?' I realized Jim had been trying to get my attention for some time. I leaned back toward him ('She's in the dining room, Zack. Her old man's got a problem . . .'), cradling my numb arm in my live one and recalling that game Ros and I used to play with our toes and noses – toeses and noses, we called it – and the delicious pucker of concentration on her lips, the tip of her tongue slithering out between them like an animal's erection . . .

'Okay, sign her on. Now – hey, sweetheart, whaddaya *doing*— ?!'

'. . . Sitting on her hand,' Jim said.

'Oh— !' I lurched away from the table, and her arm swung loose. '*No . . . !*' I'd almost forgotten she was there. Jim put her hand back. The fingers knuckled, looked more like a bag of marbles inside their plastic wrap.

'This is not a singalong, baby! We're not watching the bouncing ball! This is a dance of *death!* Doesn't that *mean* anything to you?'

'It's just . . . I – I've never *done* anything like this before,' Teresa whimpered, her hands trembling, white on white, on her tummy.

'That story about Roger and Ros and the old lady, you know, is a complete fabrication,' Jim added. 'And Zack knows it.'

I nodded, feeling too weak to stand alone, yet too appalled to lean back against the table again (I still felt her brittle fingers, knuckled into my rump like some kind of summons), or even to look at it, keeping my eyes fixed instead on stubby Teresa, now trying, coached by Hilario and Quagg, to 'fly like a beard' (as Hilario said) – 'No, no, guapa! like a *doave*, not a *tour-key!*'

'Is this what you'd call a metaphor?' asked Alison's husband from under his floppy hat. Olga, it seemed to me, had her hand in his pocket.

'Ros came to see me that day. Somebody had apparently given her a hallucinogen of some kind without her knowing what it was, and she was frightened. Not by the visions, but by the feeling it gave her, she said, of being alone.'

'Mate a – *vot?*'

'Curious . . .'

'Wait a minute! *Wait* a minute! Let's get *serious!* This is *death* we're talking about, baby, *death!* – you know, the last fucking call, the deep end, so long forever: now, come *on*, what does it make you *think* of?'

'Why don't you stick a feather up her butt, Zack, and let her try it on all fours?'

'Ros hated to be alone. She even wanted someone in the bathroom with her when she was brushing her teeth or . . .'

'I know . . .'

'I – I once imitated a person flushing herself down a toilet,' Teresa offered timidly. 'Of course it was a long time ago . . .'

'His blind daughter?' Bunky asked, studying Anatole's script. Lloyd Draper had entered the room in his hat and coat, photo albums under his arm, Iris beside him. 'Yeh heh heh!' he exclaimed, discovering me, and they came strolling over.

'At . . . at church camp . . .'

'Beautiful!' enthused Benedetto, admiring the silky patch Gudrun was holding up to his gaping fly. 'Whose *were* those?'

'Awright,' Zack barked, losing patience ('Take your pants off,' Gudrun said around the needle in her mouth, 'and I'll sew it on . . .'), 'let's *see* it!'

'Everything was just delicious!' Iris exclaimed, and Lloyd agreed: 'Yes indeed! I'll second that!' He grabbed my right arm and gave it a painful shake. Someone behind me was tuning up a guitar. 'God, she's terrible!' Zack groaned, hand clapped to his eyes, peeking out between his fingers at Teresa trying to flush herself. 'We sure been travelin' first class tonight, haven't we, Mother?'

'I didn't even know he *had* a daughter!'

'Yeah,' laughed Horner. 'It's wonderful!'

'Thank you so much for asking us!' She was wearing the pecker-sweater, I saw, pinned to her dress like a corsage or a political button. 'We looked for your wife . . .'

'How is she, Sally Ann?' Jim asked behind me.

'She's probably in the kitchen . . .'

'Well, please tell her . . .'

'Still about the same.' She plunked at a guitar, picking out a chord. 'He doesn't seem to be bleeding as bad, but his mind's getting worse.'

'Can I stop flushing now?'

'Say, Mother, doesn't that remind you of those dancers we saw in the East – you remember . . .'

'No, guapa, ees byootifool!'

'Poor Dad. I don't think he's got much longer.'

'Oh yes. The red paint, you mean. It was quite lovely, as I recall, dear, and very skillful – but I didn't like the heads on the stakes after.'

'*Now* theenk like you are toilet *all stop opp!*'

'What— ?'

'And flow! Effrywhere! *Ffflo-oo-ow!*'

Lloyd and Iris Draper, saying their goodbyes along the way, had stopped to talk with Alison's husband. He pivoted toward them, causing Olga to stumble and fall to her knees. 'Well, I love my father very much,' Sally Ann was saying (someone had just asked her why she'd left him alone in his condition, in fact I had), 'but, after all, Gerry, I do have my own career to think about.' 'Don't worry, I'll check on him,' Jim assured her, as Alison's husband shrugged and glanced over at me. 'I don't know,' he said, or probably said. Olga and the Drapers, following his glance, also peered back over their shoulders.

I turned away, just as Eileen came strolling in in her khaki raincoat, collar up, hands in pockets, staring right at – or through – me. 'You look ridiculous!' she said. 'I know,' I slumped a bit, and there was an echo just behind me: she'd been speaking, I realized, not to me but to Teresa. 'Can – can you please find Wilma?' Teresa whimpered, and Eileen ('This bearded fruitcake's driving me nuts, Priss!' Zack was hissing) said: 'She and Talbot've already gone, Teresa. And we're going, too.' She bumped past me, pulling off her raincoat. 'Put this on.'

'Why don't you and Olga take the sonuvabitch up and get him laid?'

'Who, this boiled hat, Zack?'

'I don't know if I *can*—'

'Sure you can, Teresa. All it takes is two feet. Come on, I'm fed up with all this cheap sensationalism. Let's get the hell out of here.'

'Yeah, he's loaded, Priss, I'm cultivating him – *hey*, hold up there! That's our *star!* Leave her alone, goddamn it!'

'You see?' Teresa shrank into the raincoat that Eileen wrapped around her, as Horner, Scarborough, and Quagg started crowding menacingly around. Goldy, at my elbow, spat into a cup and said: 'You know, if I was them guys, I wouldn't fuck with that broad . . .'

'That's far enough, you cold-ass bitch!' Horner snarled, blocking their exit. Eileen coolly snapped her knee up and Horner crumpled, howling pathetically, the others backing off a step. 'Like I said,' laughed Goldy, and – *poytt!* – shot another gob into the cup.

'All right,' said Eileen impassively, 'who's next?'

In reply, there was a sudden gasp from the onlookers crowded up near the hallway door, and they all fell back: standing there was a weird naked figure wrapped like a mummy in plastic cleaning bags, with a condom pulled over his head. It was Malcolm Mee. He looked like something from outer space – or inner space, rather: a kind of aborted fetus. He took two bounding steps into the room (Prissy Loo screamed, Fats fell over a coffee table, pulling down part of the cave wall), paused, crouching; in his raised hand: *the ice pick!* 'Oh no . . . !'

'Hey, man, we're not ready for this!' Scarborough protested, and Mee mutely flashed the pick at him as though to strike. He was breathing heavily, erratically, through a tiny puncture in the condom, the rubber snapping in and popping out with each breath. I wasn't sure, but he seemed to be smiling. The TV cameraman was squatting, shooting up at the flapping rubber under his nostrils. Beni said: 'What is this?! I haven't even got my codpiece yet!' – but he went quickly silent when Mee turned on him, swishing the pick through the air, making it whistle.

'Christ, I think he's serious . . . !'

'Malcolm— ?'

'You've got to *stop* him, Zack!' a woman cried out.

'Shut up!' Quagg snapped, drawing his purple cape across his body like a shield, and Prissy Loo seemed to faint. Or maybe she just tripped over her heavy galoshes. Horner, clutching his scrotum and grunting painfully, dragged himself off across the carpet, out of the way, watching Mee warily. 'Shit fire . . . !'

'Is this some sort of protest— ?'

Mee leaped lithely out of the shadows onto the spotlit stage and posed there rigidly, pick upraised. Everyone crept back except Teresa and Eileen, who were seemingly unable to move. 'Please . . . !' Teresa whimpered, the raincoat falling away from her painted breasts, bright now in the overhead lights. Eileen, clutching the coat to Teresa's shoulders, watched Mee intently; Quagg knelt; Fats stared goggle-eyed, wrapped in collapsed cave wall.

'Come on, Mee,' I said, finding my voice, or some of it anyway. 'Enough's enough, damn it!'

He appeared not to hear me, took a lurching step toward Teresa as though losing control, seemingly transfixed (his dilated eyes were clearly visible through the stretched rubber sheath, the flesh around them mashed back like shiny scar tissue) by her heaving red spots, the pick quivering in his poised fist.

Beni, in Roger's ill-fitting jacket and his own theatrical longjohns, threw his arms open and stepped forward: 'Malcolm, my old friend!'

'Don't, Beni! He knows what he's doing!' shouted Quagg.

'But she's not one of us,' Beni argued, 'she wouldn't understand!' Mee's free hand shot forward and grabbed one of Teresa's crimson breasts – she squeaked in terror, slumping backward into Eileen's arms as he drew the breast toward him. Beni tore off his false moustache. 'Malcolm, my friend, it's your old comrade Benedetto, remember?'

'Isn't this getting a bit dangerous?' Alison's husband murmured, his face pale now under the drooping brim of Beni's hat, his lips pulled back in a frightened grimace. If Beni distracts him, I thought, maybe I can somehow disarm him. Malcolm was stronger than I was, though, I'd need help. I glanced around for the police: amazingly, they were watching me, not Mee!

'This is theater, man!' Quagg was saying, his voice a fierce whisper. 'Theater is hard. It's real. Did you think we were just fucking around?'

'But I thought—'

'Do me a favor, would you, dear friend,' Beni insisted, interposing himself boldly between Mee and Teresa, 'and loan me that –' Mee struck. Beni gasped, disbelievingly, staggered back a step, clutching the handle of the pick that now seemed to grow out of his chest like a thick warty finger, pointing back at Mee. '*Oh no . . . !*' he wheezed, and sat back in amazement – *splat!* – as though someone might have pulled a chair out from under him. Blood began to spread outward from the wound.

'My god—!'

'*Now* see what you've done!' I cried. I didn't know who I was shouting at – Mee maybe, Quagg, the police, or perhaps the whole damned crowd – but I was suddenly angry, a ferocious rage was boiling up in me: '*You've gone too goddamned far!*' Someone seemed to be crying. I shoved Mee aside brusquely, knelt at Beni's side: he was bleeding badly now, and when he tried to mutter something about 'a surprise ending,' blood bubbled out the corner of his mouth and down his plump chin. '*Jim—!*' I screamed – I couldn't seem to *stop* screaming. '*Someone get Jim! Hurry, for god's sake!*' But no one moved: they seemed frozen with shock or fear. I leaped to my feet: '*Jim! Come in here! Quickly!*' I yelled, then turned on the two cops: 'Why didn't you *do* something, goddamn it? What did you just *stand* there for?' They looked utterly bewildered, as though they didn't even understand the question. The room was silent except for the suppressed whimpering, Beni's rasping groans, my own labored breathing. I swung on Mee and beat him on the chest with my good arm: '*You vicious creep!*' He took my blows without response, as though stunned by his own action. 'Never seem to make it . . .,' Beni rasped hoarsely, 'to the final curtain . . . !' '*You're a maniac, Mee!*' I screamed, shoving him off the stage. '*You ought to be locked up!*'

'It's time . . . to put a silk on it, friends . . . lower the asbestos,' Beni moaned. I turned to him. He was sprawled against one of my wife's potted plants (had someone moved it there?), his eyes rolled back, blood dribbling profusely from his mouth and stabwound. 'They're . . . yanking the show on . . . old Benedetto, boys . . . it's the last stanza . . . !' Oh no . . . I leaned closer, a new fury intruding on the old: 'Beni . . . ?' He rolled his eyes back down, focusing on me, winked, pushed a half-chewed blood capsule between his teeth like a peashooter. '*Damn* you!' I snatched the pick out of his hands: a stage weapon with a contracting point! The sniggering (I hadn't been hearing whimpering at all) changed to laughter and a loud burst of applause. I looked up and found myself staring into the lens of the video camera. Mee was peeling off his facemask, smirking toothily. Even Eileen had a grin on her face as she wrapped Teresa up again, and Fats asked: 'How'd I do, Zack?' 'You were fantastic!' Quagg laughed. 'Ah, screw you guys!' I said, hurling the pick across the room, and pushed out, drawing another burst of cheers and applause.

In the dining room doorway, Kitty and that white-haired neighbor lady in the lime pants and pink-and-lemon shirt were laughing at a photo: 'Look at that cute little thing!' 'Is that Gerry?' I snatched it away from them and ripped it in half: I was tired of this abuse. They stared at me in some astonishment. On looking closer, I saw it was not one of the photographs I'd made with Ros, as I'd supposed, but a picture of Mark being held in my arms. Behind me, Quagg was saying: 'Okay, now for the second number, whaddaya say we exhume that old gag from Ros's widow play, the one where she mistakes a pick for a prick and reaches in a guy's pants—'

'Isn't that a bit slapstick for the occasion, Zack?'

'Excuse me,' I mumbled, and shouldered on past the two women, feeling like some kind of maimed and brutish fool.

'We'll play it straight – you know, reenactment of a sacred legend, take it apart and slow it down, like we did in *Bluebeard's Secret* . . .'

'Anyway, I thought it was a pecker for a pucker . . .'

I pulled up short just inside the dining room. Entering, I'd brushed silk. She was standing in the shadows by the doorway. Perhaps she'd been waiting for me. I took no hope from this: I'd betrayed her, after all, in her eyes anyway – and in my own as well (hadn't I said at the theater that night we met that the last word was, artistically, the inevitable consequence of the first, that truth was an aesthetic principle, beauty moral?), it was a goddamn mess. I couldn't even look at her. Over by the sideboard, Vic groaned. There were several people around him, but they were talking only to each other – even Jim had turned away to fix himself a drink. Above him, Tania's 'Susanna' stepped out into oblivion. 'She's making one mistake,' Vic once said of her. 'She's looking backward, back at the establishment, the elders. She's turned the pool, the stream of life, into a bottomless pit. What she ought to do is step back, turn around, and kick the shit out of them once and for all. Then she can take her fucking bath in peace.' But what if the real cause of her terror, I thought, trembling, is that there's no one back there? That it's only she who's watching herself, or rather – *what?* She was crying! I turned at last and, tears springing to my own eyes, took her in my arms – or arm: my right one was still pretty useless. 'I – I'm sorry!' I blurted out. I felt certain, somehow, she'd forgive me.

'Me too!' she sobbed. 'Poor Vic!' Vic? It was Brenda: I let go her podgy body, naked and lumpy under the silk. 'Such a super guy, Gerry!'

'Where'd you get that dress?'

'Fats found it somewhere. Is it your wife's? I couldn't get back into that damned pants suit.'

'Gerald would never let me buy a dress like that,' my wife said, passing by with a sponge cake. 'He doesn't like silk.'

'Enough? What's ever enough?' Vic moaned. I could tell him. In the living room, someone was singing about 'the old man,' Sally Ann maybe, and I could hear Kitty and Mrs Waddilow oohing and ahing over the sponge cake. 'There are strawberries to go with it,' my wife said, and Vic broke into a new fit of coughing. 'You think it's all some kinda – *wheeze!* choke! – *joke?*'

'He's such a brave guy,' snuffled Brenda, blowing her nose in the hem of the dress. I felt utterly wasted. Emptied out. Like Brenda's nose. Steve the plumber and the character with the pipe and the leather elbow patches came in behind her, talking about Mee's act ('You know, he looked a bit like that dead girl, all bagged up like that!' 'Well, that was probably his intention . . .'), laughing when they saw me, and I felt the humiliation of it all over again. Where had all the beauty gone? 'You probably ate it,' Vic might have said. That 'aesthetics of truth' line I'd used at the theater was his too actually, I'd borrowed it for the occasion. She hadn't quarreled with it ('It felt like a lifetime,' Sally Ann, or whoever, was singing, 'our little husband-and-wife time . . .'), but she'd had a reply of course. To wit: that from another perspective (mine had been of her soft lips pursed above a cup of steaming coffee that matched her eyes and velvet suit, and to tell the truth, thoughts of ethics didn't even enter into it) it was the *first* word that was the consequence of the *last*. 'And he's still got presence,' Brenda added, taking a chewed wad of gum from behind her ear and stuffing it in her jaws. She wiped her eyes on a slashed sleeve and took my arm. 'I know he's not making a lot of – *crack! pop!* – sense, but he makes you *feel* like he is.'

'God *damn* you,' he shouted now as we drew near (there was applause in the living room), and Mr Waddilow, hooking his thumbs in his vest, said: 'Isn't that a bit sacrilegious?' Mavis was sitting up now, propped against a chair, though her eyes were still glazed over and her jaw sagged loosely. Her husband, Jim, some distance away, held his drink up to the light, just under Tania's 'Susanna,' taking her fateful step, and it was almost as though she were stepping into his glass. Steve, smiling, said something to Bunky's two friends, who stared back dully, and Charley, who'd seemed locked in some kind of elbowbender's freeze (he often went rigid before falling over at the end of a night), suddenly reared up and seized Mr Waddilow's lapels. '*Damned right!*' he bellowed. Mr Waddilow rocked back on his heels in alarm.

'By the way, Gerry, who's that cute guy in the tweed jacket?'

'His name's Gottfried, that's all I—'

'Oh, is *that* the famous Gottfried . . .'

'Where are the lights? Turn on the . . . goddamn lights!' Vic begged.

'*Hey, Big Ger!*' Charley boomed out, wheeling around heavily. 'Where ya *been?*' Jim lowered his glass as though pulling the ground out from under Susanna, though of course she didn't fall. No, that abyss awaited her forever. It wouldn't even be there without her. This thought somehow picked me up a bit, like something I'd forgotten but finally remembered. 'It's been *awful* here since you been gone!'

Howard in his bra, red tie, half-lens reading glasses, and sailing cap sniffed petulantly as Steve, shrugging, reached in past Bunky's friends for the gin bottle. I remembered the older guy now: he was the angel who had put up the money for that mock sci-fi film Ros and Bunky had starred in, *The Invasion of the Panty Snarfers*. The younger one, the gigolo type, had directed it. A terrible film. Or so it had seemed at the time. Now I wished for nothing more than to be able to go sit down somewhere and watch it. Or maybe I only wanted to (I seemed to hear someone telling me to do this: sit down) sit down.

'We *miss* ya, ole buddy! Nothin' *happens* when ya go away! Eh, Waterloo?'

'I beg your pardon?' Steve asked, his hand hesitating over the gin bottle, and Gottfried, putting pipe to mouth, said: 'No, she was with some older gentleman, I believe – the one with the goatee.'

I poured myself a brandy and stared up at the 'Susanna,' thinking: My father was right, we're the products of calamity, metamorphosed by our very will to endure, meshed alive into the unraveling fabric of the universe – that's where all creation happens. 'Before I forget it, Howard,' I said, gazing at Susanna's small foot poised tenderly over the void, 'I want to buy Tania's "Bluebeard" painting.'

'Cyril? You must be mistaken,' Brenda was saying to Gottfried, smiling up at him, her jaws working strenuously, as Steve staggered back, shoved by the younger guy. The tall cop limped up with his toolbox, muttering something about a missing dynamometer, and Howard said: 'I'm afraid you can't really afford it, Gerald.'

'What do you mean? It's not even finished, Howard—'

'There's some forceps gone, too,' Bob grumbled, and Brenda, looking puzzled (Steve also looked puzzled: 'Who you calling a shitface?' he asked), said: 'They've *what* . . . ?'

'All the more reason,' replied Howard huffily ('I think I saw those on the turkey dish,' Jim said). 'It's priceless probably. You're lucky to have the pieces you own now.'

'Oh yes?' Mr Waddilow asked, reaching in his breast pocket for a pair of spectacles. 'Is this one of them?'

'*Oh no!*' Brenda cried. '*Not Cyril and Peg!*' Steve, eyes asquint, reached for the gin bottle again, but the gigolo blocked his way. 'Is that an advertisement, sweetheart?' the older man asked with a sneer, pointing to the name stitched over Steve's pocket. 'I can't *believe* it! *Fats*?— I felt I understood now what Tania had meant when she said that truth ('That's not art, it's a piece of trash,' Bob was objecting, 'she don't even know how to draw!'), dispersed into the clashing incongruities of the world, returns as beauty: which, with memory, is all we have of substance. 'You're not *listening!*' Vic yelled, and Brenda, running off ('Hey, mister, you wanting trouble?' Steve asked): '*Fats? Oh my god, Fats—!*'

'*Fuck* your shadows! Man is – *glurgle! splut!* – something *hard!*'

What? Was Vic talking to me? Kitty came over from the doorway with

Mrs Waddilow and said: 'Hey, you guys in here are missing it all!' 'Oh yeah?' yuffhuffed Charley confusedly, and Vic, breathing with great difficulty ('How much you sell your ass for, working man?' the gigolo taunted, blowing smoke), gasped out something about 'the disappearing eye' or 'I.' No, not to me or to anyone else: Vic had fallen through that hole in the world Tania spoke of, he was far away, in another place. I felt a sudden pang of loss, of disconnection from something valuable. Something like the truth. 'Ah well, what the fuck, it's all just a – *farff! foo!* – fiction anyway,' he babbled now. I turned, sipping brandy, to watch Steve take a halfhearted swing which the gigolo parried. No ('Yeah,' Kitty was laughing, 'they've got Vachel rigged out like a kind of walking joystick, smeared all over with petroleum jelly and blowing off about murder and paradox as time's French ticklers – it's a *scream!*'), not the truth so much, but commitment, engagement, the force of life itself: this is what Vic had meant to me. The *idea* of *vocation*. The young plumber, wary now, drew himself erect, flexing his strong shoulders. The older guy ('Look at this interesting painting, dear,' Mr Waddilow said) knocked his cap off. 'Yes, it's very nice. Did you see the icon in the front room?' 'We've *got* to have revolutions,' Vic used to argue, banging his fists on the table, or bar, or lectern, wherever he was, 'hope'd *die* if we didn't!' It was beautiful (Kitty, speaking of little Bunky Baird's new makeup job, had just said more or less the same thing): 'Watch out for art,' he'd exclaim, 'it's a parlor trick for making the world disappear!' Or: 'You know what I hate, Gerry? The idea of original sin – in *any* disguise! Do it new! Don't be afraid! Change yourself, goddamn it, and you inhabit a renovated world!' I didn't believe any of it, of course. But I loved the fervor.

'No, Bunky's playing "the Lady in Red," and she's really in great form! Regina tried to upstage her by swooping in wrapped in nothing but herself, but unfortunately her birthday suit's about fifteen years outa fashion!'

'Yeah, I just saw that on the box!' laughed the man in the gray chalk-striped suit, joining us from the TV room, an empty glass in his hand. 'The poor toad!' Steve, lurching blindly to his feet – reaching down for his cap just a moment before, he'd taken a chop in the neck, a kick in the ribs, a drink thrown in his face – crashed into him. '*Whoa!*' the man whooped as his glass went flying, and Kitty, ducking (Bob, watching her, reached for his revolver), said: 'Are they showing it on TV?'

'Yeah, the best bits anyway, along with – hey! talk of your show stoppers!' he hooted, picking up his glass and pointing at me. 'You really tumbled for that old chestnut!'

'Whuzzat?' Charley grinned, swiveling his big head back and forth between us: it was the only part of him that still worked, the rest seemed totally immobilized. Bob had relaxed again, was showing Howard some of his own drawings of the crime scene.

'A stage sticker!' the guy in the chalkstripes laughed. 'The old collapsible pick trick – ha ha! he really cut a gut!'

Charley's face sagged. 'Whuzz funny 'bout that?' he wanted to know. ''Assa fuckin' *trazhedy!*'

'Well, certainly they show skill, sensibility, a consciousness of form and architecture,' Howard was expounding, peering down at arm's length through Tania's narrow spectacles at Bob's drawings. 'But they lack, what can I say, a certain density, mythic complexity, innovation . . .'

'Argh . . . ,' groaned Vic as though, were he at all rational, in mockery, 'say it . . . *kaff!* ain't so!'

'How about, uh, percipience?' Bob asked hopefully. The kitchen door swung open and Woody and Cynthia came in, holding hands. 'If by percipience you mean a discerning eye for detail, yes,' acknowledged Howard, 'but true intuitive apperception: not yet.' Bob looked a bit downcast, but Gottfried, removing his pipe from his mouth (over his shoulder, the gigolo had Steve in a hammerlock, and the other guy was kicking him in the stomach), leaned intently toward Howard and said: 'Ah! you're interested in myth, then . . . ?'

'Gerry, thanks for the party,' Woody smiled, as Bunky's older friend took the monkey wrench out of Steve's back pocket and shoved it in his mouth, 'but we've got to be going.'

'So soon?'

'You've been very kind,' Cynthia said, and gave my hand a squeeze, her own hand knobbled with rings. There was a soft flush in her cheeks and just above her cross-strapped bra, partly hidden by the vulgar fur she wore around her shoulders. 'We both appreciate it.'

'Hey, you're not goin', are ya, Woodpecker?' Charley protested. Beside him, Howard was talking to Gottfried about orchestral renderings of symbol and prophecy, and the dark roots of creation, Vic wheezing and blowing agonizingly below. 'Night's still young, goddamn it! Like you'n me!'

'I'm afraid so, Charley. I've got a big case tomorrow, and now all of Roger's damned work besides. Sorry.' Cynthia let my hand go.

'An immersion into mystery, don't you see, into pain . . .'

'So what's . . . next, Howard?' Vic gasped. 'The old – *hah! harff!*– "language of the fucking wound" – ?' He was getting testy again. His face was haggard, bleached out, his mouth gaped, blood stained his blue workshirt darkly and his pants were wet with urine. 'The artist-as-visionary shuh – *whooff!* – shit?' Howard's eyes were watering up in anger. I too felt unaccountably annoyed (he was still clutching that silly fork) and turned away to watch Bunky's friends haul Steve, kicking, still eating his monkey wrench, out of the room toward the front door. All that hard-won wisdom, that shrewd and stubborn intellect, turned to pudding in the end: a lesson I really didn't need tonight. 'You're a fuh – *fooff! shit!* – fucking whore, Howard!'

'Have you seen Noble, by the way?' Woody asked, raising his voice to be heard. Bob, staring deadpan at me, winked. As did Earl Elstob, wandering in, when Charley asked him: 'What? Back awready, Earl?'

'Ah, I think he—'

'Yup, well, huh! as one rabbit – shlup! – said t'other: This won't take long, yuh huck! *did* it?'

'Last I saw,' said the guy in the chalkstripes, 'your coz was in high gear – even his gold eye was lit up and blinkin' like a turn signal!'

'I see. Well, Noble deserves a little fun. If you see him, tell him I'll call him in the morning.'

'What I – *huff! whoo!* – hate,' Vic rattled on fiercely, 'is fucking contrivance! Triviality, obfus . . . obfuscation . . .'

'Poor old Jack the Forker,' said Scarborough morosely, coming in from the living room with Gudrun. 'Still at it, is he?' He held a bottle up to the light. 'Tenor's farewell,' remarked Gudrun. She was smeared randomly with greasepaint, though her hands were principally scarlet: as she rubbed her nose (' . . . All that – *wheeze!* – "all-is-vanity" horseshit!'), she moustachioed herself. 'Bah!' Scarborough pitched the empty bottle over his shoulder impatiently. It hit the doorframe, clattered into the TV room.

'There's more underneath—'

'I want . . . *lucidity* . . . Authen – *gasp!*—'

'Uh, huh! you seen sister?'

'What do you suppose this one could do?' Gudrun mused, looking Bob over.

'Ole Glad's relaxin', Earl! Don' worry, you juss zip up there'n 'n *joy* yourself.'

'Well, he sure as hell can't dance,' muttered Scarborough, squatting.

'Yuh, I thought I'd just leave it open so's I don't hafta – huh! – lose time!'

'Could you repeat that?' Gottfried asked, bending toward Vic. It was true, I saw it now: he did have a tape recorder.

'What I want . . . in art . . . is a knowing . . .'

'*Everything's . . . changed . . . ,*' Mavis intoned gravely. She was on her feet now, leaning against the wall, legs spread wide, eyes staring zombie-like into some remote distance. Bunky's young friend, back and breathing heavily, took a swig from the brandy bottle, handed it to the older man. '*I seem to remember . . . a statue . . .*'

'Say, yuh know what's – yuh huh! – worse'n pecker tracks on your zipper?'

'*. . . A knowing moral center!*'

'*. . . Of ice . . . with mirrors for eyes . . .*'

'Well, who doesn't?' snapped Howard, glancing contemptuously down at Vic ('*. . . And a little man where the heart should be . . .*'), Gottfried sidling in between the two men with his mike. 'But that's simply too narrow a view of art. Every act of creation, no matter how frivolous it might seem, is, in its essence, *an act of magic!*'

'Ah, that's very good,' said Gottfried, stopping up one ear against Mavis behind him. Gudrun clapped her scarlet hands, as Scarborough, rummaging around in the shelves below, came out with a bottle of Tennessee sourmash. 'But by "magic" do you mean— ?'

'*. . . Showing his behind . . .*'

'No, goddamn it, that's . . . too narrow a view . . . of action!' Vic cut in, snorting and spluttering. 'It takes a long . . . a long – shit! can't seem to . . .' As he sucked in air, it made an awesome bubbly sound, rattling through him as though ripping everything apart in there. His eyelids fluttered open, but his eyes were rolled back, unseeing, half-screened by his unruly gray hair. '. . . A long time to find out . . . that the only *magic* in the world . . . is *action!*'

'*. . . With a wart on it . . .*' Mavis pushed herself away from the wall and stood there, her feet planted far apart, rocking unsteadily.

'God, that poor devastated sonuvabitch has had it,' murmured Bunky's gigolo friend, taking the brandy bottle back. It was true. Vic looked feverish now, an unnatural flush in his craggy cheeks, his breath coming in abrupt little gasps. The gigolo, taking a deep swig and pushing the bottle away ('Is there anything left to eat?' Gudrun asked, accepting a tumbler of whiskey. 'If I toss this down the void, it'll take me with it!'), belched and said: 'He's gonna get put beddybye tonight with a fucking shovel, that one!'

'Don't count on it,' laughed the older man, picking up the bottle again. Vic tongued his swollen lips – Howard was carrying on grandly about art as 'man's transcendence of the specious present, his romance with eternity, with timelessness' ('But then what about Malcolm's tattooed prick?' Kitty interrupted) – and his eyelids fluttered again. 'Doesn't *exist!*' he bellowed. 'I beg your pardon?' said Gottfried. 'Yes, it does,' Kitty insisted. 'I've seen it.' 'I think some strawberry shortcake passed me, going into the living room.' '*Eternity!*' 'Doesn't sound like the right thing to go with bourbon.' 'What're they up to in there now?' the man in the chalkstriped suit asked Scarborough. 'Another . . . fucking *illusion!*' Vic yelled. It was pathetic to watch him. 'I once knew a guy,' this was Bunky's older friend, putting the bottle down after a long guzzle ('And the present is . . .') and carrying on, 'got shot like that and took *days* to die.'

'. . . Is *not* specious . . . goddamn it!'

'Some kid's grisly visit-to-the-underworld spasm,' Scarborough replied ('That guy's death rattle *alone* lasted eight hours!'), 'called "Rec Room Resurrection," or some such shit,' and Gudrun reminded him: 'He's still just a boy, such things are important to him right now. He'll grow out of it.'

'Did I . . . only imagine it?' Mavis asked herself, rocking gently.

'What you're trying to say, as I understand it,' Gottfried interposed, leaning toward Vic with his mike, 'is that action is a sort of rude language, emanating from the reflex centers of the—'

'*I'M NOT FINISHED YET!*' roared Vic, startling us all. 'Sorry,' whispered Gottfried, having reared back into Howard, and Mavis, still mumbling hollowly to herself, added: 'And am I . . . imagining it now . . . ?' Earl Elstob was wheeling about, doubled over, yuck-yucking noisily: someone told him to shut up. 'Huh – ?' We waited. This was it. Or might be. Vic sucked in air, let it rattle out again. There was a trickle of blood at his lips: he licked at it. 'What was I . . . ?' His eyelids fluttered open, his eyes rolled down out of their contemplation of the top of his skull, searching for me. 'Is . . . is that you, Gerry . . . ?'

I squatted in front of him and his eyes closed again. 'Yes. Take it easy, old man. It's all right . . .'

'Don't . . . shit me it's all right, goddamn it . . . I know better. Listen . . . is one of those – *oof!* damn . . . ! – one of those cops around?'

'Yes, but—'

'This is *important*, goddamn it!' Mavis had lumbered slump-shouldered away, rocking heavily from one foot to the other, still half-dazed, but the rest of us were crowding around, watching Vic. He wheezed and snorted laboriously. 'Ignore him, he's a stupid and intolerant monomaniac,' Howard declared petulantly, but in fact it was Howard who was being ignored. 'Can he . . . hear me?'

'Sure.' I glanced up: Bob watched Vic without emotion, leaning against the sideboard.

'All right. Tell him . . . tell him I did it . . . I killed them!'

'What? Killed who, Vic?'

'*All* of them, goddamn it!' He struggled to sit up, but his coordination was gone, and the effort seemed to be tearing him apart. 'Ros, Roger . . .'

'Vic, listen, you don't know what—'

'Who else?' he groaned. 'Who *else*, goddamn it – I can't *think*—!'

'You mean Tania?'

'Yeah, that's right . . . Tania, stabbed her . . . too!'

'She wasn't stabbed, Vic.'

'Strangled, I mean!'

'She was drowned.'

'Drowned, that's what I . . . what I – *choke!* – said!'

'Hey, listen, nice try, Vic, but—'

'No! I held her under, I – just look at my hands . . . ! They're the hands . . . of a murderer, they – *what* – ?!' His chin shot up, one leg straightened, a shoulder twitched. 'Where *are* they? My *hands*, Gerry! *Where are my goddamn . . . hands—* ?!'

'Here, Vic, easy . . . !'

'You see?' sniffed Howard.

'Jesus,' somebody muttered softly, 'someone oughta put the poor bastard outa his misery!'

'Oh shit,' Vic was weeping, 'I can't . . . I can't *feel* them . . . I can't feel *anything!*'

I glanced up at Jim, who shook his head sadly. Howard looked disgusted. 'You'd be doing him a favor,' the police officer said.

'What?'

'It's true, Gerry,' said Jim quietly. Indeed, it was very quiet all around, broken only by Vic's rasping breath, the ice tinkling brassily in someone's glass, Earl's chronic sucking noise. The cop took his revolver out of his holster, checked the chambers. 'It'll only get worse for him.'

'A *drink!*' he yelled, making us jump. '*For chrissake, Gerry——!*'

Jim handed me his own glass. I sniffed it. 'Is it——?' 'He won't know the difference.'

'Where *is* everybody——?'

'Right here, Vic.' I held the glass to his lips. He sucked and slobbered, most of it ending up as a kind of bloody foam that dribbled down his chin and shirtfront like baby drool. 'Easy now . . .'

'*More!*' he demanded, jerking his head about, batting the glass with his nose, thumping his head on the wall. Once, when I was very small (I was thinking of this now, watching Vic try to keep his head up, his eyes open), we found a dead tomcat in my grandmother's backyard. A few nights later, she incorporated him into her bedtime story about the climb to heaven. The cat was not well-suited for this climb and I probably fell asleep very near the bottom, but I did hear the preamble and remembered it still. Interested in a lady cat next door, the tom had come out to serenade her and had got shot by an irate neighbor who didn't want his sleep interrupted. At the entrance to the stairway, there was a kind of ticket-taker, like the ones outside carnival rides and circus tents, and the cat complained to him about the injustice of being shot for singing: 'Is that what you get for bringing a little beauty into the world?' he protested. 'It's not fair!' 'What do you mean, you were lucky!' the ticket-taker replied. 'There's no big deal in a long life – what counts is the *quality* of the *departure*. Yours was beautiful! You died quickly, more or less painlessly, and at the moment of your greatest happiness!' 'No, you don't understand,' the cat objected, 'the singing was only the *preparations*.' 'Exactly!' smiled the ticket-taker. Indeed, now that I

thought about it, I'd said something very much like this to someone
earlier tonight, only . . .

'Ah, *listen!*' Vic barked.

'*What*— ?!'

'I said, listen, damn it! I'm talking . . . about what's happening . . . here
tonight . . .'

'Ah . . .' My heart was pounding. Bob, I realized, was holding his gun
out to me, butt first. Jim took the empty glass. 'But . . . do you really
think— ?'

'You *know* . . . what kind . . . what kind of a world . . . we live in . . . !'

'You can see for yourself,' said Jim. 'The size of the wound, the blood
lost, kidney and bowel dysfunction, numbness in the extremities—'

'So why . . . are they letting you . . . ?'

'And that rattle means his lungs are filling up: he's slowly choking to
death, Gerry. Then, as he loses oxygen, the brain – well, just listen to
him . . .'

'. . . Letting you even . . . *have* parties like this?'

'The poor guy,' said Gudrun. Howard snorted scornfully. 'Yeah?
Whuzzamatter?' asked Charley blearily.

'I – I've never . . .'

'Here,' said Bob, showing me the safety catch. 'It's easy.' There was
a soft whirring noise behind me and the lights brightened: the guy with
the video camera again. 'Angle's bad,' he said. 'Hang on, I'll get a chair.'

'Damn it, Gerry! I . . . asked you— !' Vic burbled.

'What? I don't know, Vic. Maybe they don't know any better.' The
weight of the thing surprised me: I nearly dropped it. It seemed nose-
heavy or something. 'Oh, I *love* the *cowboy boots!*' Patrick was gushing
behind me in his swollen lisp. 'They're so well *tooled!*' My sudden shadow,
which had been clouding Vic's chest, now fell off him below my knees.
Certainly he was a mess, I couldn't deny that. 'Grip it a little higher up
the handle,' the cop said, and Gudrun asked: 'How are the skin tones?'

'Don't . . . underestimate them . . . !'

'Not bad – could use a touch at the back maybe,' said a voice high
above me. 'Under the hairline.'

'Whoa! Whoozat tall sumbitch?' Charley asked.

'He's not tall, Charley, he's on a—'

'No? Jesus, then maybe's *me!* Maybe I'm *shrinkin'!*'

My shoulder ached with this sudden awkward weight. Vic looked ghastly in the hot glare: it hurt to see him like this. 'I've got a lot of things to do. I don't think I like this . . .'

'You're okay, just hold it steady.'

'Grrr-rrr-*rr-rr*!' said Patrick, drawing a nervous laugh or two.

'That's it. Now all you have to do is squeeze.'

'I just want to *eat* them!'

'You get any goddamn spit on my boots, you old tart, and you'll get one of 'em down your fucking throat – now get that mike outa the way!'

Gottfried ducked down beside me, squatting into my shadow. 'Oh, what a *brute!*' exclaimed Patrick giddily. 'Isn't he simply fe-*ro*-cious!'

'Don't pull on it or jerk it, just close your fist, easy-like,' said Bob.

'In some way or other,' Vic gasped, his shaggy head lolling under the bright lights ('Hey, where you off to – is it getting too much for you?' somebody asked), 'you're . . . *useful* to them . . .'

'No, I wanta catch it live on the tube.' Someone was stroking the back of my neck ('It's live here . . .'), taking the pain away. 'I-I don't think they know I exist, Vic,' I sighed ('Yeah, but I miss the zooms!'), and Bob said: 'Listen, maybe you oughta use both hands.'

'And pivot about thirty degrees, so I can see your cannon!' the guy on the chair called down. 'Wow! Funkybuns! C'mere! Lemme see ya!' 'Whaddaya mean . . . ?' Vic growled, just as little Bunky Baird, stark naked and painted a gleaming scarlet from head to toe (stark, that is, because even her hair was shaved away, her skull a gleaming red dome, her pubis sleek as a creased plum), pranced into the light between us. '*Hey*—!' 'Isn't it just *smashing?*' she exclaimed breathlessly, one hand on hip, the other behind her ear ('They're *here*, Gerry,' came the gravelly voice between her legs, 'it's a matter of record . . . !'), switching through a sequence of fluid poses to make the paint sparkle. 'Gudrun here did it! It's a *masterpiece!*' I stepped back out of her way, gave my arm a rest. She was bound loosely with a fine metallic thread that made her flesh bulge in peculiar places, and decorated with little silver ribbons, randomly attached to the thread. She looked like someone who'd got tangled up in the tail of a kite. 'It's for Zack's *terrific* new *show!* It's called *Party Time*, and I've got this *great* part – it's so *exciting!*' She glanced up at the lights as though discovering them for the first time, flashed a bright innocent smile ('Watch out you don't shoot your foot,' Bob muttered irritably in my ear): 'Oh, hello! Am I interrupting something?'

'Yeah, stop catching flies, sweetie, and move your fat act! We got something heavy going down here!'

'What—?' She turned to gaze down at Vic, gasped audibly, her hands before her face. She held this pose rigidly a moment, then let her fingertips slide slowly down her seamed body ('Even pleasure . . .,' he was muttering on the other side, 'has its fucking consequences . . .'), coming to rest just at the crease between thighs and shiny buttocks, her shoulders bowed but back straight, bare feet straddling his body. When she turned around, two tears glistened in the corners of her uplifted eyes.

'Oh yeah!' applauded her younger friend ('Gesture, stylized gesture,' I'd remarked that night at the theater – perhaps it was her uplifted eyes that had reminded me of this, or else the heavy weapon in my hand – 'is really a disguise for uncertainty: which is why we're so attracted to it' – but perhaps I'd been wrong about this), and the older one said: 'Ha ha, come over here, baby, and see what your old man's got for you!'

Because it might just as well be said (I wish I'd thought of this at the time) that what fascinates us is not the ritualized gestures themselves – for, in a sense, no gesture is original, or can be – but rather that strange secondary phenomenon which repetition, the overt stylization of gesture, creates: namely, those mysterious spaces *in between*. 'What . . . what are you going . . . to do, Gerry . . . ?'

'Pardon?' His eyes were open. One of them anyway: it was fixed on the revolver in my hand. 'Ah. I'm sorry, Vic,' I said, waggling it about ambiguously ('God, it's *gorgeous!*' Bunky was raving behind me, and Howard, staring grimly at my hand, said: 'Would you watch where you're *pointing* that thing, Gerald?'), 'I'm only, you know . . .' I lowered it. His open eye ('Is it a sapphire?') rolled up to meet mine briefly, then closed. 'Ah well, it . . . it beats . . . senility, I guess,' he wheezed, and effected a jerky little movement with one shoulder that was perhaps meant as a shrug. 'Yeah, a little something to celebrate your new success, baby – slip it on your pinkie, there!' 'Anyway, it's – it's almost over, Vic,' and I thought—'

'*No*, goddamn it, it's *not!*' he blustered, spewing blood. 'The sooner you get it over with, the better it's gonna be for everyone,' Bob growled in my ear. 'It's so *big!*' 'More's . . . more's gonna happen, but I won't . . . be here . . . to see it . . . and that . . . that scares me . . .' I shared his dread:

that door closed forever. Not being. Eternal absence. 'Well, you're a big *star*, sweetheart!' It made me shudder just to think about it. This consciousness was what I had and, like him, I didn't want it to – 'I *don't . . . want it . . . to end!*'

'I know,' I said through the catch in my throat. 'In fact, oddly, I was just—'

'If I had a wish,' he spluttered ('Hey, don't get that red stuff all over me!' laughed the gigolo behind me, as Bunky passed out thanksgiving hugs and kisses), 'I'd wish always to have . . . one . . . more . . . *minute* . . . !' Of course, death itself caused no suffering, only this gnawing terror of it – it was, more or less, what I was saving him from. 'Is . . . is my daughter . . . ?'

'She's in the next room, Vic. She's got a part in Zack's play. Shall I – ?'

'No . . . just tell her for me . . . tell her to watch out for words like . . . like mind and . . . and soul, spirit . . .'

'You better point it a little higher,' Bob murmured, 'or you'll just cause him more useless damage.'

Jim knelt and tipped Vic's head to one side. 'The best place, Gerry, is here behind the ear . . .'

'All that junk . . . just . . . just a metaphor, tell her . . . old animistic habit . . .'

'That way, you'll penetrate the medulla at the top of the spine, which is the center for regulating all the internal functions . . .'

''Assa pretty bad *sunburn*, li'l lady,' Charley was rumbling behind me.

'. . . There's nothing in there, goddamn it . . . no me, no I . . .'

'Breathing, for example.'

'. . . The brain . . . just makes all that up . . . the first person . . .'

'Or speaking.'

'Iss even got *scabs!*'

'. . . Is a hoax, an arrogant sham . . . the first person . . .'

'That little place does it all?'

'Yes, the smallest damage to it causes death in a few minutes.'

'. . . Is no person . . . at all! Tell her . . .'

'So what's all this baloney about thinking with the whole body, old man?' I muttered hoarsely to myself as I took off the safety.

'Did I say that?' He looked up at me, cocking one yellowish eye (this startled me), and a wet sardonic grin formed at one corner of his mouth. He seemed disconcertingly alert all of a sudden. 'Well, just watch me . . . *twitch* after . . . !' he grunted.

'Vic?' But he was delirious again, rumbling on about 'militant time' and 'the living organic arena . . .' ('That often happens,' Jim was explaining softly, 'a kind of involuntary hypoglossal reflex . . .') '. . . of choice and freedom . . .' I heard someone behind me say something about 'the host,' then ask for a drink. Or perhaps offer one. 'Yeah, he's a sweet guy . . .' Vic was fondling his knee with his free hand (he clutched the fork in the other still like some kind of credo) and I supposed he was thinking about Ros again. Well, why not? For all his dogma about the oppression of the past: who was I, locked even now in reverie (that quiet talk we'd had earlier in my bedroom, now so poignant: it was ancient history!), to hold him to it? This unexpected weakness had in fact endeared him to me even more. 'One in a million,' someone murmured, and my wife called out from somewhere back there: 'Gerald, can you help with the coffee, please?'

'Yes, in a minute.' My shoulder throbbed, and something was blurring my vision. Tears maybe. I couldn't see his face at all, it was like that face in Tania's painting.

'Why don't you . . . wise up, old buddy?' he gasped. I found the place. I hoped Jim was right. 'There's not . . . much time . . . !'

'To tell the truth, Vic,' I sighed, 'I wouldn't know where to start.'

'Famous last words,' he grunted, and I squeezed the trigger.

There was less kick than I'd expected, less noise. I'd been braced for worse. And Vic was mistaken. I waited patiently (no, that's not true, it wasn't patience: I was rooted to the spot, frozen, a waxworks figure, legs spread, body and neck rigid, arm outstretched, lips pulled back over my clenched teeth – I wasn't any good at this), watching him, but nothing twitched. Except my shoulder, after the cop pried the gun out of my hand. 'That wasn't so bad, was it?' he said. Jim, kneeling by Vic with his stethoscope, looked up at me and nodded solemnly. He reached for Vic's eyes, now wide open as though startled by something he'd just seen (or remembered?), and closed them. 'Okay!' someone said, a chair scraped, the lights dimmed – then brightened again and wheeled around: '*Daddy—?*' My arm dropped and my fossilized spine unlocked and sagged as the light spun away. '*Oh no! Daddy—!*'

As Jim rose, concern pinching his tired face, to gaze over my shoulder toward the living room door, I turned the other way, weary of concern itself. 'How do you feel about nihilism, then, as a viable art form?' Gottfried was asking, the mike thrust in front of my face, but I pushed away, out past Scarborough and Patrick and the guy on the chair, across the room ('Gerry, your wife –' 'I know, I know . . .'), and on through the swinging door into the kitchen.

'Ah, just in time, Gerald,' she said, switching off the oven timer. 'The coffee's ready. Could you take that tray of cups in, please? We'll get the chocolates and the whipped cream—'

'*In a minute!*' I snapped. I'd made it as far as the butcherblock table in the middle of the room, and stood there now, leaning against it. The stains were gone, it had been scrubbed clean.

'You look exhausted, Gerald.' At least she was able to see that much. I could feel her ego, callous and swollen, billowing out of her, packing the kitchen, crushing me. Or perhaps that was my own ego, her own infuriating in its evanescence. Or maybe Vic was right, maybe it had nothing to do with egos. 'Is Vic . . . ?'

'He's dead,' I shot back.

'Well,' she sighed, 'it's probably for the best.' She brought the bowl of whipped cream over and set it on the butcherblock. I clutched my head in my hands. 'Oh, I'm sorry, Gerald, I forgot about your shoulder – don't worry about the cups. Instead, why don't you –'

'My god!' I cried. 'What's the *matter* with you? He's *dead*, I tell you, his life is *ended*, it's *all over!*'

'I know, you just—'

'But how can it be for the *best?* That's *crazy!*'

'Yes, I'm probably mistaken, Gerald, please don't shout at me.' She glanced back over her shoulder. 'Maybe what you could do is bring in the brandy. And anything else people might like with their—'

'*You* get the damned brandy! I'll – I'll—' I felt like picking up the bowl in front of me and heaving it across the room. I had to struggle to get control of myself. '*I'll bring the whipped cream!*' I yelled.

'Well, if you wish, but Alison had offered—'

'What?' All along I'd been seeing Louise over at the breakfast bench, as usual. But it was Alison. She sat there, watching sullenly, huddled up in a heavy checkered overcoat. 'Ah . . .' I wiped my eyes with my sleeve. Her hair was snarled, her makeup gone, her eye shadow smudged. As she got up, I saw she was barefooted as well, and there were welts on her ankles. 'I'm sorry, it's all right, I'll, uh, take this in, then—'

'No, I'm the novelty act here tonight, allow me,' she cut in acidly and snatched up the bowl of whipped cream. She glanced briefly at me as she padded by, her brown eyes hard and dull like hammers.

'Does she always walk that way,' my wife wondered as the door whumped shut behind her, 'or is it just the funny coat . . . ?'

'Does the Inspector know she— ?'

'Oh, is that whose it is? She came in hungry and cold, so I fixed her something to eat, while Woody went to find her a wrap. She seems to have misplaced all her own things.' She put on mitts, opened the oven door, and took out a pie, set it on the counter, reached in for another. 'I must say, Gerald, I've never known anyone to have such an uncharitable view of you.'

'Well . . . I probably deserve it.'

'Oh no. She feels slighted, but I'm sure you've done everything you could, Gerald. It's all these extra guests.' She sliced the pies, ran her fingers along the knife blade and licked them, wiped them on her apron (it was that handwoven red-green-rye-and-gold one that we'd bought at a mountainside roadstand on our way back from Delphi), sprinkled some powdered sugar on. 'Just because she didn't get enough attention, that's no reason to blame you for everything that's happened! Even poor Roger, and Cyril and Peg – really, she got quite nasty about it, said it was all your fault, you were no better than a petty thief!'

'Yes . . .' She'd mentioned thievery that night at the play. Or I had. The theatrical transaction . . .

'She might have been talking about her watch, I don't remember, but it got Louise so upset she went storming out of the kitchen!' She filled a large basket with fresh fruit from the refrigerator, brought in some boxes of chocolates from the pantry, got down a stack of dessert plates from the cabinets, stood on a chair to reach a pair of silver bowls on the top shelf. 'Honestly, I'd just fixed her a nice hot soup and some fresh spinach crêpes; you'd think no matter what had happened to make her so grouchy, she might have been a *little* more gracious.' She topped up the sugar canister, filled the cream pitcher – 'But some people are just never satisfied!' – then touched the coffeepot gingerly. 'Good, still hot. If you can bring in the coffee and the fruit, I can carry the rest.'

'Sure. Is that all?' I felt much subdued now.

'I think so. For now. Except . . . well . . .' She smiled up at me, wrinkling her nose slightly as though looking into the sun. 'I know Alison's acting rather unpleasant, Gerald, but she *is* our guest. I think you should try to make it up to her somehow.'

'I don't know really . . . what I could do . . .' I tried to recall that happier time, now so long ago, when her eyes had another look in them, but all I could think of was her husband on the back porch, blocking my way into the house. What had he said? 'It was as if the very geography of the world had shifted.' Yes, 'something anarchical and dangerous' – it was coming back to me now. 'You were stroking her thighs,' he'd said, 'she bent down to put your—' 'But I'll try,' I said.

'And please forgive me for what I said before. I'm truly sorry about Vic.'

'Vic?' I looked down at her. She was smiling still, but there were tears in the corners of her eyes. 'Oh, right . . .'

'Hey, you two lovebugs!' Fats sang out, thumping grandly in through the dining room door, the Inspector's gray fedora, its crown punched out, perched on top of his big head like a party hat, Scarborough, Gudrun, Michelle, Benedetto, Earl Elstob, and others in his wake. 'You get outa here now and go enjoy yourselves! Ole Fats is takin' over!'

'Oh dear. Fats, I've just cleaned up in here— !'

'No backtalkin', little lady! We got some citizens with a desp'rate belly-wrinkles crisis, but you has done did your duty!' He warbled out a striptease tune while untying my wife's apron, jigging around her as he peeled it off. 'La-la-la-*la*-la-la-la!' sang Beni, practicing his scales and strutting around in his silken codpiece. 'We is gettin' up a *do!*' He tied on the apron on his way to the refrigerator, tipped the fedora down over his nose as he peered inside. 'Whaddawe got? Cottage cheese? Good! Cocktail onions, grape jelly, ketchup – what's in these little tin cans?' 'Why are we here?' Michelle asked vaguely, looking around, and Beni, a halftone higher than before, responded: 'La-la-la-LA-la-la-la!'

My wife glanced at me, shrugged helplessly, picked up the tray of cups. 'What's that you're tracking in, Mr Elstob?'

'Huh? Aw – yuh! – whuppin' cream!'

'I'm afraid it's all over your hallway floor,' Dolph said, lifting a foot to show us. 'I think they're trying to ski in it or something.'

'Oh dear . . . I think that was the last of the cream . . .'

'Here, Gerry, I'll help with that, if you'll rescue Zack,' said Gudrun, picking up the bowl of pink pears and melon balls in her scarlet hands and bumping out backward through the door ahead of me. 'Come on, there's some old bawd in here queering the pitch, and Zack's going bonkers.'

'Ho-boy! Get ready to sink your pegs into the real bony fido, friends! Ole Fats is homin' in on the range!'

'La-la-la-*LA*-la-la-la!'

Out in the hall, people were laughing and cheering: 'Go get her, gangbusters!' they shouted up the stairs. 'Hair *wut?*' I glanced hopefully into the dining room where the brandy bottles were ('*Can*-busters, more like! Ha ha!'), but she wasn't there: only Sally Ann, wearing Tania's heavy peasant dress now and wistfully cradling her dead father in her arms in front of the cameraman's bright lamps and video lens; Patrick was helping with the lights, and Gottfried seemed to be interviewing Brenda, or vice versa – they were drifting, heads bent over the mike, past the abandoned sideboard toward the TV room – but all the rest were gone, and it seemed peculiarly barren and lonely in there. Some awful absence . . . 'Okay!' the cameraman barked. 'Now tip his head the other way!'

'It's nice to have those guys around, they add a little *color!*' Horner laughed, turning away from the foot of the stairs, and Mr Waddilow, standing on the landing, blushed perceptibly. Or perhaps he was trying to lift something up. Beneath him, Daffie stepped out of the toilet, holding her forearm pressed against one bare breast. 'Hey,' she said with a vague glittering smile. Malcolm Mee was still in there behind her, under the red darkroom bulb, back to the open door. 'Eet wass like night off fool moon, no?' grinned Hilario, picking up the fallen overcoat, just as Zack Quagg came fuming out of the living room, sliding through the floor's flocking of whipped cream, his dark cape flying: 'Where the hell's Hoo-Sin? *Hillie—*? Jesus! What am I *working* with here, a buncha *amateurs?* We got a fucking *show* on the boards in there, goddamn it! Where's that extra grip? *Horner—*?'

'Easy, Zack,' Horner said, 'that mudlark's been pulped.'

'*What*— ?! Holy shit, Jacko! We've lost our goddamn band, half the deck crew, our new end-man's off banging tail, that bearded dude's pulled his lens outa the show – *we're gonna die standing up in there, if we don't move our ass!*' He kicked the fallen cream bowl across the hallway in pale-faced anger.

'Awright, screw your tits on, Zack, we're doin' what we—'

'*Aha!*' Quagg cried, grabbing my arm. 'I been *looking* for you!' He dragged me toward the living room. 'There's some old scud in here *murdering* our production! She's up the fucking *flue*, man, and taking me *with* her! You gotta *do* something!'

My mother-in-law stood calmly on the collapsed ping-pong table, her arms folded. That's what it was now: a collapsed ping-pong table. Her presence had quite effortlessly disenchanted our living room. The sacred cave had become a bunch of dirty laundry, the altar a table with a dead body on it (this latter, most of the skirt now cut away, was being removed by Vachel and Gudrun to make some room, my wife, bracing one edge of the tray of cups and plates against the table, instructing), the proscenium arch merely my skis with nailholes in them. I half-expected the lamps to drop off the ceiling in sheer embarrassment. 'It's time to go home,' my mother-in-law said flatly.

'*Put it down! Put it down!*' Vachel screamed, his head slick still with petroleum jelly. '*Yeu-uck!*'

'You see what I *mean?*' moaned Zack, waving his arms around wildly. My mother-in-law only set her jaws tighter. 'Thank you, Vachel,' my wife was saying. 'I know it's not pleasant, but it can't be helped. Now could you move that bowl of fruit nearer the center, Louise?' 'You *gotta* get this dry hole *outa* here, man!'

I glanced questioningly at my wife, now spreading the cups and dessert plates out on the table: she smiled toward her mother and shook her head, sent Louise off to the kitchen for the pies, slapped at Vachel's fingers as he dipped them in the chocolate sauce. 'I'm afraid there's not much I can do, Zack,' I said. 'She's not going to budge.'

'You can't be *serious!*' He clutched at his hair ('God! I'm starved!' said Gudrun, peeling a banana) as though to tear it out. 'We've just hit the nub, man, the weenie, the *payoff!* This is everything we've been *working* for tonight! What are we going *to do*— ?!'

'Well, Zack,' my wife put in, taking the coffeepot from Michelle, who stood dazedly by, 'I suppose you'll just have to exercise your imagination. Could you please move the strawberries, Gerald, so I can set the coffee down?'

'Maybe we oughta fold it up, Zack,' grumbled Gudrun around her mouthful of half-chewed banana.

'No, wait,' he said, gazing thoughtfully at my mother-in-law ('That's funny,' said my wife, lifting up the sponge cake: 'where did the plate go?'), 'if the old bat wants to become part of the set, then, goddamn it, we'll just build the show *around her!*'

'Actually, there's an old lady *in* the next scene,' Anatole pointed out. 'It's the dream sequence in which—'

'Hey, you're right! Lemme see that script a minute!' My mother-in-law looked disconcerted, but stubbornly held her ground. 'Meanwhile, kid, go in there and get our guitarist back – even if you have to pick her ass up and *haul* it in here— !'

'Yes sir, Mr Quagg!'

'I once had a dream about an old woman,' Michelle remarked languidly. 'She was standing on a mountain, or some high place. She said she'd been there for a long time.'

'Do you suppose someone took it?' my wife asked. I gazed down at the cake, sitting there on the bare table as though after a pratfall, trying to think what it was that was bothering me.

'Her clothes were all worn away and her skin was covered with sores and scabs and a thick dust almost like sand . . .' Michelle touched her breast, her privates—

'Oh no . . . !'

'What is it, Gerald? What's the matter?'

'This woman in the dream, I mean . . .'

I turned toward the dining room: yes, it had been nagging at me since I left the kitchen – that peculiar sensation of barrenness, of erasure . . .

'"But the worst thing about getting old," she said,' Michelle was saying, '"is what happens to your navel . . ."'

'Right! The Ice Palace, the wet dream stuff, free will versus necessity, the Old Lady – this script is terrific! The kid's got talent!'

'The "Susanna" . . . !' I whispered.

'What? What are you talking about, Gerald?'

'It keeps getting deeper and deeper . . .'

'Hey, Jack! Go find the Scar! Tell him we want the panes out of all the windows in the house and as many mirrors as he can lay his hands on! We still got a *show* here!'

'It's gone.'

'Gone?'

'Yum!' enthused Bunky, stepping over Ros's body and plucking a melon ball.

'Tania's painting,' I explained, my throat constricted.

'I saw it now. The navel. In the middle of the old woman's tummy. Like a nailhole.'

'I just realized—'

'Only much bigger . . .'

'It isn't there anymore.'

'What— ?!'

'. . . Like a kind of tunnel, going nowhere . . .'

'And Gudrun! Listen, go strip all this red shit off Bunky!'

'"You can go in and look around if you want to," she said, but I was afraid.'

My wife rushed over to the doorway. Those thoughts of oblivion I'd had when entering from the kitchen, glancing toward Vic (I'd been looking for something): almost as though she had somehow, after all, completed that terrible step . . .

'I want her midnight blue now, top to bot! With a scatter of sequins if you can find some – and a silver skullcap!'

'Right, Zack,' Gudrun stuffed the end of one banana in her mouth, picked up another and pointed with it. 'Wha' you wahme do wiwode wady?'

'What?'

'But I did see lots of things crawling in and out of her navel,' Michelle said now, scratching idly, 'and at the very back there was a little spot of light, like when you turn the TV off . . .'

Such an emptiness, that wall: it wasn't even a wall in my mind's eye, but infinite space, appallingly indifferent. I felt her disappearance as if it were, in part, my own, and great relief when my wife came back ('Ah, the old lady – leave her like she is, Gud! This is gonna be the weirdest goddamn peel you ever saw in showbiz!') and took my hand: 'Do you suppose . . . it's been stolen?'

'That's where heaven is,' someone said – 'I think it was one of those things crawling in and out . . .'

'Hey, that was Prissy Loo's part!' Vachel was objecting (she released my hand as though I'd answered her – in fact, I had), and Zack said: 'She's off doing a little business for me, Vaych, she'll never know – now listen, you said you wanted a sex scene, right?'

'. . . But I didn't believe it.'

'Someone must have overheard you,' my wife suggested ('Yeah! Hey, can I have the guitarist? Hunh, Zack?'), 'when you were negotiating with Howard.'

'Yes . . .'

'No, she's the only orchestra we got, Vaych – I was figuring we'd use Bunky for the—'

'Bunky?'

'When I looked closer,' Michelle went on, 'I saw that these little things crawling in and out of her navel were tiny people . . .' I gazed at her there, clutching her thin arms, lost in her dream story ('Okay! Great! Luff-ly! Thanks, Zack! I get Bunky!' 'Well, not exactly, Vaych . . .'), thinking: she seems younger suddenly, as though she were shrinking back into her vanished image . . . 'And whenever they turned their heads and looked at me . . .'

'Actually, this is a kind of dream sequence . . .'

'. . . They curled up like waterbugs and dropped off somewhere below . . .'

'No kidding!' grinned Anatole as he came through the door with Sally Ann ('At first it *seems* like Bunky, you see – or what she stands for,' Zack was explaining, my mother-in-law looking on with increasing apprehension), her guitar slung round her neck: 'You too? Tonight?'

'But when I tried to see where the little things fell to,' Michelle murmured, 'I discovered I was standing there all by myself . . .'

'Oh *no*— ! Wait a minute, *wait a minute!*' squawked Vachel, backing off. '*Not* this moldy old *crowbait*— !'

'Yeah, well, almost,' said Sally Ann, glancing darkly up at me as she passed, and my wife, breaking out of her worried silence, exclaimed: '*Oh, Louise!*' She stood there behind us, her round face red as a beet, holding two steaming hot pies in her bare hands. 'Why don't you use the oven gloves, for goodness' sake?'

'What *is* this shit, Vachel? I thought you were a goddamn pro!'

'Well, sure, but – *cheez!*'

'. . . The wind was blowing, it had gotten dark . . .'

'Well, look at the *power* in this scene, man! the *risks!* the levels of *meaning!*' He grabbed the hem of my mother-in-law's skirt and dragged it up past her garter belt: she turned pale, staggered back a step, her jaw dropping. 'This ain't *beautiful* enough for you, goddamn it? Is *that* it?'

'The old lady was gone, I was all alone.'

My wife cleared a space on the table and helped Louise set the pies down. Louise clapped her hands in her armpits ('Actually, my original idea,' said Anatole, 'was to take a couple of old archetypes and re—' 'Right!' Quagg rolled on, slapping my mother-in-law's corseted behind. 'It's original, it's ancient, it's archetypal – I mean, are you *good* enough for this or *not*, Vaych?'), her eyes damp and bulging, and Michelle said, as though from some distant place: 'All my clothes had blown away somehow . . .' My wife glanced up at Michelle, a flicker of a smile curling her lips. '. . . And now *mine* was the navel with the hole in it . . .'

'I think this is where I came in,' my wife said. 'I'll go see if I can win the kitchen back from Fats.'

'*No* one,' said a commanding voice from the hallway door, 'goes *anywhere!*' It was Inspector Pardew, clutching his lapels, white scarf draped loosely around his neck, thick moustaches bristling. 'Oh oh,' someone said. 'Where's the, uh, toilet?' 'It's all right, m'um,' Pardew added, nodding firmly, and my mother-in-law took a deep breath, smoothed her skirt down with trembling hands. 'We have all we need now. Thank you for your assistance.'

'Wait a minute— !' objected Zack Quagg. My mother-in-law straightened her back, drew her chin in, and, glaring at Quagg, stepped down off the ping-pong table. '*Hey*— ! You can't do this! We're just *cli*maxing this spasm!' Others had started drifting in, some shepherded by the two police officers, Bob and Fred. 'I'll check upstairs,' said Fred. My wife, taking my arm, whispered: 'I'm afraid the coffee's going to get cold,' and the Inspector glanced up sharply: 'Did someone say something?'

'Yeah, *I* did, you hick dick! This is *our* pitch, man, get outa here, this space is *booked*— !' Bob lashed out with his baton: '*Whuff-ff-FF-FOOO!*' Quagg wheezed, crumpling to the floor, curled up in his purple cape. 'I hope,' said the Inspector, withdrawing his briar pipe from a jacket pocket and tapping it in the palm of his hand as he gazed around at us all (Anatole interposed himself between Zack and the cop, Sally Ann kneeling to whisper: 'You okay, Mr Quagg?'), 'there will be no further disturbances.'

He filled the pipe from his leather pouch, cupping his hand around the bowl to form a funnel, then, tugging the drawstrings of the pouch closed with his teeth (Quagg groaned and stretched out: 'Ow, something's . . . caught . . . !' he gasped), stepped aside as Fred came down the stairs behind him, herding a group of people toward us, Hilario leading the pack and showing off with a complicated set of hops and pirouettes down the steps, followed by Kitty, Dolph, Janny and Hoo-Sin in each other's clothes, Charley, Regina, the guy in the chalkstriped suit – or pants rather: down to an undershirt on top now and a towel around his neck. His jaw gleamed as though he might have been shaving. Regina, wrapped up in one of our sheets (Sally Ann, on her knees, was tugging speculatively at the seam of Zack's white crotch: 'Here, you mean, Mr Quagg?'), swept past Hilario into the room, eyes rolled up and the back of one wrist clapped to her pale forehead, crying: 'Is *nothing* sacred?' 'Caught her jerking off,' Fred explained to the Inspector behind his hand, Dolph meanwhile slipping off behind him, unnoticed, toward the kitchen. 'There's a few more upstairs'll be down in a minute, Chief. Meantime I'll go check out back.' Pardew nodded, slapped his pockets for a light. Bunky's gigolo friend took a wooden match from behind his ear, popped it ablaze with his thumb, and held it, shielded with his cupped hand, over Pardew's pipebowl. 'Ah! Thank you,' said the Inspector, Zack Quagg echoing him throatily from the floor (Sally Ann, stretching the crotch of his unitard down, was carefully easing his testicles to one side). 'Now, I've gathered you all together here in this—'

'Hey, *big Ger!*' Charley boomed out, stumbling heavily into the room through a tangle of collapsed cave wall, his arms wrapped around Janny and Hoo-Sin. Janny looked radiant in her kimono, Hoo-Sin in the wrinkled pink outfit oddly weathered and innocent at the same time. 'I've riz *up* in the *world* again, ole son! I'm standin' *firm!* Thanks to these two lovely ladies, I got a *bone* t'pick with *anyone!*'

'Easy, Charley,' I cautioned, nodding toward Bob, who was just behind him, scowling darkly, club at the ready.

Charley reared up heedlessly, swung round, his big head swiveling. 'Who, ole Bobbers here? Nah, he's one a my bess *clients*, Ger! Him'n his pardner both, I give 'em a fan*tas*tic deal! A – yaw haw! – *joint policy!*' He grinned expectantly, his head bobbing drunkenly. 'C'mon, ole scout, 'sbeen a long night, give us a smile! A *joint* policy!'

Bob had turned toward the dining room door, through which Fred was now prodding another group of guests: 'Whoa, man, you gonna make me char the hash!' Fats was protesting, the Inspector's gray fedora rocking back and forth on top of his head.

Pardew, pipe clamped in his jaws, was smoking vehemently. 'Now, as I say, I have called you all here, here to the scene of the crime, in order to –'

'All I'm sayin' is you guys got no respect for the inner man!' Fats complained, then '*Rrnkh-HH!*' grunted as Fred suddenly jabbed him fiercely in his aproned belly with the end of his nightstick, doubling him over: the hat fell off, Fred caught it, handed it to the Inspector. 'Ah . . . yes . . .'

''Swhut I love about you, ole buddy,' Charley rumbled, wrapping a fat arm around me, 'you laugh at my jokes. Goddamn it, ole son, you *lissen!*'

'What?'

'Where do you want these, Zack?' called out Scarborough, carrying in, with Benedetto helping, a stack of windowpanes, and Earl Elstob asked: 'Hey, huh! yuh hear about the gal who couldn't tell putty from Vaseline?' Charley winked at my wife, Regina flung herself on the couch in seeming despair, Dolph popped the top on a can of beer, and Kitty, helping Fats straighten up, said: 'Well, that's one way to kill an appetite!' Pardew, brushing irritably at his hat, looked up as though about to speak, but just then Charley hollered out: '*Whoa!* I smell *coffee*, girls!' and pushed away, startling Louise, who, backing off, stepped crunchingly on Fred's foot. '*Oww! SHIT!*' he yelled, and whirled on Louise, nightstick flashing – Dolph reached up, almost casually it seemed, and caught it on the upswing, stopping it dead. He handed his beer to Earl and slowly, Fred resisting, brought the club toward him, gripped the end of it with his other hand, and – *crok!* – snapped it in two. 'Thanks, Dolph,' Louise said softly, her face flushed. Fred, scratching the back of his head above the neckbrace, gaped in amazement at the shattered stub of nightstick in his hand, and Earl said: 'Yuh, well, huh! all her windows fell out!'

'Ah, fuck everything,' said Daffie vaguely, and left the room.

Pardew, biting down on his pipe, continued to fuss with his fedora, but, attempting to put the crease back in, chopped at it so fiercely in his rage that he knocked it out of his own hand. Angrily, he reached down for it, but somehow managed to step on it at the same time. 'Damnation!' he mumbled around the pipe. '*Cream 'n sugar, girls?*' Charley called out. '*SSSHH!*' Patrick hissed. 'Hunh?' Charley looked around blearily at the quiet that had descended. We were all watching the Inspector. He was trying to lift his foot off the hat, but it seemed stuck to his shoe. He studied the situation, one hand in a jacket pocket, the other holding the bowl of the pipe in his mouth. Bob approached him, but he waved him away, knelt, untied the shoe, took his foot out. Except for a light titter from some of the women at the holes in his sock, the room was hushed. Regina was sitting up now, watching; Zack, too, helped by Sally Ann and Horner. The Inspector lifted the shoe off the hat: no problem. He gazed quizzically at the sole of the shoe, shrugged, put it back on, tied it. Unfortunately, he was stepping on the hat as he did so, and when he lifted his foot, he found the hat was stuck again. He scratched at the back of his neck, under the scarf, thinking about this. He stepped on the hat with the other foot to hold it down, tried to lift the first foot off but without success. Then he discovered that the second one was stuck as well. He struggled with his problem for a moment, doing a kind of sticky shuffle, peevishly muttering something about the sense he'd had all night of having 'intruded on some accursed place, some forbidden domain, which was not what it seemed to be.' Finally he looked up at the taller cop and nodded toward his holster: Bob handed him the gun. The Inspector checked the chamber, sucking thoughtfully on the pipe: 'One thing about homicides I've learned to watch out for,' he said around the stem, his pate gleaming under the overhead lights, 'is the murderer's attempt to conceal the fact that what we've got is indeed a murder.' He took a firm grip on the revolver with his right hand, took the pipe out of his mouth with his left. 'There's been no limit to the ingenuity of murderers in masquerading their act – or even of removing all evidence of both victim *and* act. Bodies have been burned, blasted, buried, embedded in concrete, dissolved in acid, disassembled, and devoured.' Sighting down the barrel, he let his arm fall in a slow arc until pointing between his feet. 'You name it, it's been tried.' There was a terrific explosion that startled us all, even though we'd been expecting it. 'Of course, in this case, we've not only got a victim plain to see,' the Inspector went on, handing the revolver back to the policeman, taking his feet off the hat, and reaching down to pick it up, 'she's also got a hole in her' – he held it up and brushed at it lightly – 'as big as your hat!' This got a burst of applause and laughter, led by Patrick (even Zack Quagg was joining in, if reluctantly), and the Inspector, handing the hat to Bob, nodded curtly.

'Damn! I missed it!' whispered the cameraman, staring at the equipment in his hand.

'Nothing, however,' Pardew continued, beginning to move slowly about the room, gazing first at one of us, then another (Scarborough and Benedetto, grunting, set the windowpanes down against the table), 'is ever so straightforward as it seems on the face of it. We have facts, yes, a body, a place and a time, and all this associative evidence we've so painstakingly collected – but facts in the end are little more than surface scramblings of a hidden truth whose vaporous configuration escapes us even as it draws us on, insisting upon itself, absorbing our attention, compelling revelation.' He peered abruptly up at the guy in the chalk-striped pants and undershirt, who was wiping his face with the towel but now stopped. 'Yes, *compelling!*' Pardew repeated, raising one bony index finger, and the man stepped back a step. 'Deduction, I am convinced, is linked *au fond* in an intimate but mysterious relation to this quest for the invariant, the hidden but essential core truth, this compulsive search for the nut.' Dolph, who had just picked one up from the bowl, put it back. 'It is, at any rate, *my* main desire,' the Inspector went on, continuing his rounds, followed now by the TV cameraman, 'and in pursuit of it, I had to ask myself' – and now, pausing for effect, taking a contemplative puff on his pipe, he glanced up at my wife (her hand tightened on my arm, I clasped it, he watched this) – '*why?* Eh? Whatever possessed – and I choose my words with care – whatever possessed our perpetrator, or perpetrators' – he squinted briefly up at me, then turned to the others – 'to commit this foul deed, this useless insolent vanity? I ask you!' He had, moving on (my wife's hand had relaxed and dropped away: 'Were those once mine, Beni?' she whispered over her shoulder), stopped in front of Regina, who, startled, shrank back, cronelike, in her bedsheet. 'Was it fear? Jealousy? Moral outrage? Cupidity?' Regina made a little squeaky noise and shook her head. Beni was whispering something to my wife about the inexpressible gratitude of his pudenda. 'Well, I hope they were clean,' she said. Pardew cocked his head up toward the rest of us. 'Of course, all crime – even fraud, perfidy, indecent exposure, excessive indulgence' – he was staring at each of us in turn, as the cameraman panned past the gaping faces – 'all crime is at heart a form of life depreciation, a kind of psychic epilepsy, and so, in a real sense, there is always only one motive. Nevertheless . . .' He gazed off, drawing meditatively on his pipe, then pinched the back of his neck under the white scarf. He studied his fingers and, smiling faintly, pressed a thumbnail against the pad of his index finger. 'I was reminded,' he said around the pipestem, brushing his hands together ('They take an empty fist as containing something real,' Hoo-Sin was murmuring to Janny, 'and the pointing finger as the object pointed . . .' '*Really?!*'), 'of a curious case I had some years ago in which the murderer, as it turned out, was an unborn fetus. The victim was its putative father, who in a drunken rage had struck the pregnant woman several times in the stomach. The fetus used the only weapon at its command: false labor. It was a wintry night, the man was heavily inebriated, there was a terrible accident on the way to the hospital. The woman, who survived for a time, spoke of maddening pains en route, and it seems likely she grabbed the steering wheel in her delirium or lashed out with her foot against the accelerator. Was the fetus attacking its assailant or its host? This was perhaps a subtlety which, in its circumstances, escaped it. Certainly it achieved its ends, and though it could be argued that it had acted in self-defense, it seemed obvious to me that the true motive, as so often, was *revenge*.' He paused to let that sink in, striking a fresh match to his pipebowl. 'The strawberries are starting to go soft,' my wife whispered. 'In any event, we'll never know. Prosecution was impossible because the fetus – a harelip – was stillborn. But the point—'

'Wait a minute,' Dolph interrupted. 'You trying to suggest Ros was killed out of revenge?' Pardew watched Dolph without expression, holding the match over his pipebowl. 'I dunno, I just can't see that, not Ros.'

'Nor can I,' said Pardew, looking around for some place to drop the match; he chose one of the potted plants Scarborough had lined up around the cavemouth. 'No, revenge is a noble passion, an instinctive search for order, the effort to restore a certain balance in the universe. Our murder here tonight seems much more sinister than that: a search for disjunction, a corrupt desire to disturb, distort – a murder committed perhaps out of curiosity or impudence' – my wife, watched by a frowning Pardew, stifled a yawn ('Sorry,' she murmured) – 'or even love, which is well known for its destructive powers. No, what reminded me of the Case of the Vengeful Fetus was the sense that the motive here was not merely irrational, it was *pre*rational, atavistic, shared by all, you might say, and thus criminal in the deepest sense of the word. Once I recognized this, my task was eased. It was simply a matter of recalling certain ancient codes, making the obvious associations, then following the discretionary principles of professional criminalistics. Whereupon our crime was, for all practical purposes, solved.' He nodded toward his two assistants, and they fanned out, blocking the two doorways, cutting Fats off from one, Bunky's boyfriends from the other. 'Yikes,' someone said. The TV guy lowered his camera, looked around as though for an exit. Suddenly it wasn't amusing anymore. 'Who . . . ?' Howard shrank back toward the far window, Michelle seemed to offer herself up. Earl Elstob was trying to close his lips around his buckteeth as though to draw a curtain. The Inspector, spotlit from above, watched all this, hands in pockets, pipe in mouth, as though, silently, weaving the final strands of his web – then, glancing toward Fred and turning his back, he jerked his thumb toward the rest of us. '*Now!*' 'Ah, shit,' Charley groaned, slumping a bit, and Fats whimpered: 'Hey, wait a minute, anybody seen Bren?' Fred, hand on holster, pushed past him (he yipped reflexively), headed in my direction. Ours, rather: my wife tightened her grip again. 'It's all right,' I muttered huskily (others were ducking, stumbling back) – and so it was: Fred broke past us in pursuit of Vachel, who, squeaking in alarm, went scrambling behind pots and props. 'It's a *frame-up!* I been *skunked!*' he screamed, shoving the pedalcar in Fred's direction. Fred went crashing, but Bob had joined him in the chase and now tackled the dwarf cleanly (Charley in confusion cheered him, and Regina wheezed, falling back: 'God! I thought it was going to be me!') near the back wall. Vachel, greasy with petroleum jelly, slipped a foot free, brained the cop with the fireplace poker, and took off running, but by now Fred was on his feet again and had him in a bearhug: Vachel's little legs churned in midair, going nowhere. Bob, enraged, holding his bloodied head, staggered toward them. *'Let me go, you shitheads!'* Vachel shrieked, feet and fists flying. *'You can't do this to me!'* 'Pop him one on the gourd there, Bob!' Fred grunted, hanging on desperately, and Bob, leaning into it on his short leg ('Oh dear,' my wife said, wincing), brought his stick down so hard that it did indeed sound like he'd crushed a pumpkin. 'Shit,' Quagg sighed from the floor, 'there goes our show,' and Fred, now holding the unconscious Vachel under one arm like a duffelbag and picking up his hat with the other, said: 'Whew!'

'If that don't beat my grandmaw!' Fats gasped, and someone belched eloquently, Dolph probably. 'Vachel! Who'da guessed it?'

'Guessed what?'

'Eet wass how you say a brow-eye leefter, no?' exclaimed Hilario, rolling his eyes.

'Fucking little degenerate!' growled Bob, still sore, blood streaming down past one eye, and he gave the dwarf another blow which oddly made his feet bob as well as his head.

'That'll do,' said Pardew. 'Come along now,' and my wife, letting go my arm, said: 'I'll see them to the door.'

I sat back against the arm of the couch where Regina lay all akimbo in a crumpled white heap, the back of one wrist pressed melodramatically against her brow ('Goodness, Sally Ann – that dress is still wet!' my wife remarked in passing, there were people crossing now between us, I could only catch glimpses), taking great heaving bolts of air. I too felt short of breath, one half of me sinking leadenly, the other half dangerously afloat. 'Do not try to grasp it,' I could hear Hoo-Sin murmuring to Janny out there somewhere in that unfocused blur of movement before my eyes: the tension in the room had dissolved into a kind of generalized backstage flutter, as people slipped out of folds in the cave wall or crept out from behind one another, exchanging laughter and snorts of relief, ducking off for drinks or helping themselves to the dessert and coffee. 'Casual thought is for fools. It is the burying of oneself in emptiness.'

'You said it, Hoo! Juss what I been doin' for – *ruff! haw!* ('*Ffoof-hrarf!* I swallowed one of those damned – *choke!* – cookies *whole!*' rasped the guy in the chalkstriped pants) – twenny years!' laughed Charley, drawing both of them into his arms. My grandmother had had a story about this, or something like this, I remembered, something about a dead cousin. 'I *love* it!'

'*Now* what, Mr Quagg?'

Or aunt. I pushed off a canvas shoe, and scratched my foot.

'*Hroaf! ch-wheeze!*'

Beside me, the cameraman was changing cartridges, Zack Quagg was doing deep kneebends, Gudrun was tying Janny's hair up in a tight coil, powdering her face white. 'Don't worry, kids,' Quagg panted. 'We'll – *grunt!* – clean it up and recast it, mount the whole uproar again!' Janny sneezed, Scarborough swore, Regina groaned, and the guy in the chalkstripes – '*Pwwfff-FWWOOO!*' – spewed cookie as Kitty reached round from behind and squeezed his diaphragm. 'We'll call it "The Feast of Saint Valentine," use Mee as the vampire, make it a revue maybe, a kinda funerary tribute to the bourgeois theater . . .' 'That better?' 'What happened?' asked Brenda, standing dim-eyed in the traffic of the dining room doorway, Gottfried peering sheepishly over her shoulder. The green charmeuse dress hung askew on her, one plump arm sticking out of the sleeve's slash instead of the cuff. She pulled a string of gum out of her mouth, let it droop ('Write some new tunes, give it some bounce!'), then lifted her chin and nibbled it back in again. 'We were, um, watching TV.' Regina sat up and studied her nails. 'It's so unfair!' she said, and Fats, lapping up pie and chocolate sauce, spluttered: 'You'll never believe it, Bren!' 'You know, uh, I think I've lost my tape recorder,' said Gottfried, reddening. 'They've just took *Vachel!*' 'Unfair?' 'Poor old Vachel, I mean,' said Regina. 'Enh,' Horner shrugged, rolling himself a cigarette, 'he made a good exit . . .' 'Yeah, but does he *know* that?' 'Oh *no!* not – *snap!* – *Vachel!*' yawned Brenda (it was catching, my own jaws began to spread), and Michelle said: 'I think I'll put a record on.'

'That reminds me,' said the Inspector, turning around at the door. 'Our ice pick . . .'

'I got it,' said Bob, holding it up, then he tucked it back in his rear pocket.

Fred must have seen my gape of surprise (I'd been caught mid-yawn) as I rose up off the couch arm, because he winked and came over (I pressed my jaws together), wagging Vachel under his arm. 'One of the Old Man's favorite tricks,' he grinned. 'His probe, he calls it. Stick it in, see what surfaces. You know.'

'I thought somehow I – I'd— !'

'But of course we couldn't fool you! Oh, and by the way . . .' He leaned closer, switching Vachel to his other arm. It was my bloated self I saw in Vachel's goggles, dwarfed twice over by the lenses' convexity. 'I just wanted to tell you: you know that ultraviolet exam . . .' He nodded toward the hall door, where my wife stood, smiling wearily. She was waiting for the Inspector, who, stopped now by Patrick, was patting his pockets helplessly. 'Well, sir, clean as a whistle!' He gave me a knowing nudge. 'Just thought you'd like to know . . .' He sidled closer. Kitty, poking around at Vachel's head behind his back, scrunched up her nose and said: 'Ouch!' 'And listen, that wasn't blood on the knife the Chief found, it was tomata juice – we knew that, we knew it all the time.' He slapped my butt with his free hand. 'You got a great little lady, fella. Hang on to her!'

Vachel's dripping head bobbed at Fred's rear under the blue SUPERLOVER sweatshirt as the officer walked away through what was left of the proscenium arch. One of my skis, cracked at the binding, tipped forward now at a crazy angle, making it seem as if the stage were reaching out to stop him, and Scarborough, trying to right it, snapped it in two. 'Piss on it,' he grumped and planted the broken end impatiently in a fern pot.

'Forget it, Scar, we're blowing this stand,' said Zack.

'Hey, where's ole Earl?'

'We're moving the show up-country!'

'Yeah? Who's providin' the nut?'

'Cyril? Out back with Malcolm, I think, Charley.'

'Probably getting stoned, the poor bastard.'

'Don't worry, I got somebody. We're working on him now.'

'Naw, I meant—'

'Is it true Peg left him because he liked to do it with mirrors?'

'No, that was someone else.'

'I hear it was because she wanted to surprise him on their silver wedding anniversary, and it was the only thing she could think of.'

'I *love* it!' Charley yuff-huffed. ''Ass like the ole folks who went back t'their honeymoon hotel, an' . . .'

'You mean Peg and— ?'

'You know, I don't think that guy's playin' with a full deck!'

'Lissen, this'll knock your pants off! They went back t'the goddamn hotel, see . . .'

'Well, according to Cyril . . .'

'Say, did you hear about that play Ros was in where she was supposed to pick up this deck of cards and cut it?'

''N – hee hoff! – the ole fella says . . .'

'That's not the way I heard it . . .'

'Ros?'

'Yeah, and – ha ha! – the director says—'

'Well then . . .'

'No . . .'

'He says . . .'

'*He* said . . .'

I was tired of stories and moved away. Perhaps my wife needed me. I remembered her hand on my arm a few moments ago, clutching at it as though for strength, and then the paleness of her face a little later as she smiled vacantly, sorrowfully, into the room past Pardew before she led him out. As I crossed to the door, little particolored Bunky Baird came bouncing through it, shouting: 'Zack! Zack! they've done something to Vachel!' 'Yeah, I know, they popped his blister, Bunko – and ours too. The show's blown, kid. So get outa your skin, we're pulling stakes!' A proscenium arch, I thought, passing under it, is like a huge mouth, but the sensation that it is the audience that is being fed through it is just another of theater's illusions. Theater is never a stripping down (Bunky was bright blue and pimpled with sequins from the waist up, scarlet still from the thighs down, but in between a damp fleshy smear, ugly and shockingly naked), but always a putting on: theater fattened on boxed time. To be a member of the audience, then (so many thoughts, one after another, I staggered on, feeling myself consumed by my own consciousness), was a form of martyrdom . . .

Gudrun as I lumbered past gave me an understanding glance as though in sympathy with my troubled thoughts ('Okay, before we go, everyone together for the flash!' Zack shouted) and rubbed her nose with a blue finger. 'I think someone stole your wife's dressing table,' she said.

'Come on! Curtain calls!'

'What— ?'

'This is *exciting!* You know, Mr Quagg, *I really love the theater life!*'

*

I leaned up against the doorframe. Even the dressing table . . . My wife was at the front door, saying good night to Inspector Pardew and Fred. They didn't seem to want to leave. Or maybe they didn't know how. She wanted me near, I knew – I caught it in her sorrowful gaze as she glanced up at me from Vachel's lifeless and begoggled buttocks – but between us the tall cop Bob had Patrick slap up against the wall, jabbing him with his stick, cursing him out for being a nuisance and a whore, and I lacked the will, or maybe even the courage, to push on past. 'If you don't stop bugging the Inspector, you scummy little poufta, you're gonna get your goddamn place of business tweezed!' 'Well! Is that a *promise?*' Patrick simpered brazenly, twitching his puffy lips up at the black-bearded TV cameraman now looming beind the cop's shoulder. 'You goddamn pervert— !' 'You got problems, little buddy?' asked the cameraman, taking a fierce grip on Bob's neck that made the cop whistle and drop his nightstick. In the living room (to be at a crossroads, I realized, was actually to be nowhere: there was unexpected comfort in this) applause erupted as the actors took their curtain calls, Mee joining them now, sliding spookily past me out of the toilet, as though sucked in by the slapping hands. Scarborough focused the lights, Regina doffed her bedsheet (there was a lot of good-natured booing), Zack dragged Fats on stage to take a bow. Fats, feigning shyness, shuffled up doing a little hunched-shoulders soft-shoe routine, hands in his pockets and rolling his eyes. 'Spread it, sweetie!' laughed Brenda, clapping the loudest: 'Let's hear it for him, folks! the one and lonely!' 'Now if you'll just pick up my gear there, pardner, and haul it along with us,' the cameraman said beside me, making Patrick gasp and flutter his lashes ('Oh my! yes!'), then he highstepped the cop to the front door, one hand gripping his skinny nape, the other the seat of his pants, Bob's gimpy leg brushing through the scum of whipped cream on the floor like a dangling plummet. 'Hot it up, Scar!' shouted Quagg. My wife opened the door and the cameraman heaved the cop through it, then turned to wait for Patrick. 'Okay, strike it and take it away, crew, we're sloughing this dime museum!' People were starting to head out this way: I joined my wife.

'Such in the main are the degenerate dregs of humanity, whom we have never, I regret to admit, learned to curb or eliminate,' Pardew was saying, as though into some kind of closing recitation, 'characterized chiefly by their stupidity and depravity and their inability to play the game—'

'Oh yes?' said my wife vaguely.

Patrick, his hands full of camera gear, paused at the door to pucker his battered lips at me and wink, then pranced out after the cameraman, my wife still holding the door open. Her lips moved as though she might be counting. Behind us, the actors, laughing and shouting ('And their, eh, deformed personalities, you see . . .'), were flowing into the hallway. 'Well, back to selling pencils!' 'Christ, Vadge, get those things in a hammock before somebody steps on 'em!' 'No, believe me, baby, we *got* a *backer!*' 'I believe you, Zack. Call me at the beach.' 'Somebody gimme a chaser!' Fats called out, hauling on his down jacket. 'A tailpiece for ole Fats – *lemme hear it from the heart!*' The Inspector had long since fallen silent. He peered down at my wife, nibbling his moustache. 'Thank you so much for coming,' she said.

Fats chasséd past us, waggling his hands beside his face and singing, 'You're gonna miss me when I'm gone,' my wife pushing the storm door open just in time to keep him from crashing through it. *'Ta-DAAA-AA-aa-aaa . . .'* The police marched out behind him. 'Watch where you step,' I could hear the Inspector mutter peevishly, his voice echoey in the night. 'It's really too bad about Vachel,' my wife said with a sigh.

'Yes, well . . . I never did like him very much, though.'

'I know.' The actors had applauded Fats' exit and Brenda was now giving them all a hug. 'But he was always good with children.'

'Next party at our house, everybody! Promise!'

Hilario leaned toward us and said: 'Your keetchen, do you know, she ees smokeeng!'

'What – ?!' Yes, I could see it, rolling in from the back like some kind of mephitic vapors.

'It's all right, Gerald,' my wife said. 'Fats just left some things on the burner. As usual.'

'Ees what you call a bloody mass, no?'

'Shall I go see if— ?'

'No.' She took my arm. 'I already turned it off.' There was a peculiar gentle flush in her cheeks. 'Dolph and Louise are back there, making up,' she whispered.

'Ah . . .'

'Bren!' cried Fats, staggering wide-eyed back in through the front door, making us all jump. 'My *god*, Bren! It's that plumber! *Whatsisface!'*

'What—? Oh *no!* No—?!' She came rushing silkily past us, but paused to give us both a hug – 'You're a super guy, Ger,' she breathed in my ear, her gum snapping, 'you've got a great heart . . . and *wonderful* hands!' – then clambered on out behind Fats: '*God!* I can't *believe* it, Fats!'

'Hey, poison curls!' Zack Quagg exclaimed. 'Our angel descends!'

I looked up, we all did: it was Alison's husband, escorting Alison down the stairs in front of him, followed by Olga and Prissy Loo. Alison was dressed now in Brenda's red pants suit, a couple of sizes too big for her, stained at the knees, the cuffs flopping around her bare feet. The actors all applauded. Alison, her makeup smeared across her face, hair snarled, stumbled when she saw me. Her eyes searched mine. Was her lip quivering? She held the baggy-kneed red pants up with one hand. There was a patch sewn on the crotch now, probably one of Sally Ann's, which, even from here, I could see was in the shape of a road sign.

'And have *we* got a show for *you!*'

Alison's husband sniffed. 'Theater,' he said frostily, 'is dead.'

'What—?' Zack laughed, staggering back a step. 'I told you, Zack.' 'Is it time for my part?' asked Prissy Loo. She was wearing Beni's plumed hat and false moustache, my fingerless golfing gloves, and one of my mother-in-law's girdles, ornamented with what looked like rolled-up bloody socks. Olga was trying to stretch my wife's yellow nightie down below her high muscular croup. Zack spread wide his caped arms as though unfolding a curtain. 'Hey, ha ha! you gotta be *kidding,* man!'

Alison's husband shook his head. 'No, it's dead. All over. I see that now.' He prodded Alison on down the stairs.

'Aw, goddamn it, Prissy, you overdid it!'

'Well, that was a short run.'

'Don't blame me, Zack, it was Olga's idea.'

'What idea?'

'Yah, goot! In a minute!'

'DANGER: BUSY CROSSROADS,' the patch said. She stood there in front of me, echoed dismally in the hall mirror, clutching the baggy pants, looking lost. 'Did you bring a coat?' my wife asked politely. 'It's boring, it's repetitious, and it's dead-ended,' said Alison's husband. 'And it's a lie.'

'Wait a minute, what do *you* know about theater, you dumb fuck?' Quagg exploded.

'Hell, he's nothing but a goddamn preacher, Zack.'

'One goddamn night of pissing around, and you think you've seen it all? You weren't even in at the death, fer chrissake!'

'Don't *tell* me it's all *over!*' Prissy Loo wailed, her moustache listing. 'Zack, you *promised!*'

'What do you know about blocking and backing, asshole? Glue guns and gobos?' Alison's husband only smiled faintly. 'What about conventions, eh? Peripety, goddamn it? Teasers, timing—'

'Timing?' Alison's husband gazed round at us, stroking his beard. 'Peripety?' He reached forward suddenly and yanked at the top half of the red pants suit as though to whip it off: Alison clutched at it and her pants fell down. He stepped on them and, as she bent over to grab them up, he shoved his hand in under his shirt and cracked a mock fart in his armpit. She blushed, tugging frantically at the trapped pants; he reached forward and grasped the nape of his wife's neck, pressing her head down. He poked his finger up her rectum, felt around, came out with one of Ginger's kerchiefs – in fact a whole string of them, knotted together: out they came, one after another, fluttering in the air as he tossed them high, more kerchiefs than you could imagine there'd be room for in there. And at the end, knotted to the last kerchief: the Inspector's white silk scarf! The door opened behind us: it was Fred. 'Excuse me, the Chief seems to have left his – ah! thank you . . .' There was a burst of applause and whistles (Fred backed out with the scarf, hand to holster, looking non-plussed, or pretending to), even Zack had to join in. 'You know, I think that sonuvabitch was just using me!' he laughed.

'*You!*' cried Prissy Loo.

'Yah?' said Olga.

My wife was giggling beside me; I think it was the first time I'd seen her laugh all night. I smiled: just as Alison straightened up, flushed and hurt, to stare at me. I tried to erase the smile, but it seemed frozen there, as though stretched forcibly over my teeth. 'The bright moon is serenely reflected on the stream,' Hoo-Sin said, gazing into the hall mirror behind Alison: 'What is it for?' Well, I could only hope she understood. I tried to think of some way of explaining it all to her ('Gosh, I give up,' Janny yawned, 'can you give me a hint?'), or at least of deflecting some of her anger, something about theater perhaps, or time, but before I could come up with anything, she had stumbled out past me, red pants binding her ankles, had tripped at the threshold, and completed her exit on her hands and knees, chased by another round of laughter and applause.

'Whoo-*hoo!*'

'Look at them blue hereafters!'

'Just as well her parents missed that,' my wife murmured.

'That was somethin' *special!*'

Alison's husband paused at the door, all eyes on him still, his on me. Out in the front yard, someone shouted: 'Hey *hey!* What *wuzzat* just creeped past?' 'I dunno, Dugan, but it was wearin' the biggest *smile* I ever seen!' 'I believe you still have our watches,' he said.

'Oh yes, sorry! I'll get them!' But my wife stopped me: 'I'm afraid someone . . . they're not there anymore, Gerald.'

'The watches, too— ?!'

'*This* way, squad! I think we found the *source!*'

Alison's husband snorted disdainfully and touched his beard. Outside there was drunken laughter, curses, stumbling on the steps: 'Wah! Look out! This place is *alive!*'

'However, if they turn up later—' my wife began, reaching forward to take his hand, but he turned his back on her and strode stiffly out the door, a final ripple of appreciative applause trailing in his wake.

'*Whoa!*' exclaimed someone outside who, from the sound of it, had just tumbled down the porch stairs.

'*Down boy!*'

'*Yowzer!*'

'Where was *that* dude goin'?'

'Hard to say, Doog, but he was either *awful sober* – or *awful drunk!*'

'I dunno when I've had so much fun!' Charley Trainer laughed, throwing his arms around us both. Janny stood by with her hands pressed together below her chin, eyes closed, listening to Hoo-Sin, while around us, some people I'd never seen before were pounding and clattering through the door, singing, shouting greetings, brandishing bottles and bits of clothing. 'Oh dear,' my wife sighed, shrinking into Charley's arms. One guy was carrying a woman, wall-eyed with drink, on his shoulders: she failed to see the doorframe as he passed under it and smacked it with her face. 'Somebody knock?' asked the guy confusedly, swinging around, still holding the woman's ankles and so wearing her collapsed body over his shoulders like a cape. 'Ha ha! Who's there?' called another and Charley hugged us close: 'You guys're the *cream!*'

'*Leda!*'

'Leda who, Moose?'

'I *mean* it, Big G! My heart is *full!*'

I could feel my wife's heart emptying out, but she smiled and said, her voice catching: 'I – I'm so glad you could all come . . .' No one heard her but me – and Charley Trainer, who, pitching forward drunkenly, knocked his head on hers and growled: 'Me too – but lemme tell ya, *I hadda work like hell!*'

'Hey hey hey! Izzat little Bunky Baird?'

'Leda horse to water?'

'Axel!'

'Do we know these people?' I whispered.

'Naw! Guess again!'

'And I'll tell you no lies?'

'I think we may have met some of them at Wilma's house a long time ago, when she was still married to Miles . . .'

'Miles?'

'*Benedetto!*'

'A Leda goes a long way?'

'*Gwendoline! My love!*'

'*Love* the silk pocket, Beni! Très charmant!'

The new arrivals were spreading recklessly through the house, as though the place itself were hemorrhaging. 'Please,' I said, but no one was listening, they were all ('Ha ha, we give up, Moose!') hooting and laughing. 'My oh my, look what's *not* in that nightie!' 'Hey, I'm looking for Serena!' 'Is that rhubarb pie?' 'She ain't here, Ralphie!' 'Vot's hoo-bob?' asked Olga, grinning stupidly and pushing the nightie down past her navel: at the back, it climbed halfway to her shoulders. '. . . Like so many particles of dust . . .,' Hoo-Sin was murmuring in Janny's ear, and Charley ('Am I drunk, or are those lamps up onna ceiling?'), dipping his heavy head, smirked hopefully: 'Hey, Ger, heard any good jokes lately?' At the back, they were fanning the kitchen door ('*Leda me beside distilled waters*— !') to clear the smoke. I could hear the refrigerator door whumping, drawers being opened and closed like marching feet.

'. . . Floating, rising . . .'

'You're drunk, Claudine – *and* the lamps are on the ceiling!'

'. . . Disappearing like clouds . . .'

'– *Before da party's* SOBER!'

'Send your ole dad home with a l'il chuckle, whaddaya say?'

'Haw haw!'

'I'm fresh out, Charley. Nothing's funny.'

'. . . In the vast emptiness of unending space . . .'

'Moose, you're a scream!'

'Aw, c'mon, Big G, have a heart!' Charley pleaded, and Janny, her head tipping to Hoo-Sin's shoulder, sighed: 'You've got such a nice voice, Hoo-Sin . . .'

'Do you think they'll want something to eat, Gerald?'

'*No!*'

'. . . It nearly puts me to sleep . . .'

'Well, y'don' hafta be *sore* about it, buddy!'

'Sorry, Charley, I meant—'

'Whatever thoughts you have, they are not to dwell on anything,' Hoo-Sin said softly as Janny's head snuggled in under her chin and her hands dropped to her sides. 'That's easy, Hoo-Sin . . .'

'Why don't you tell him the one about giving the testicles to the girl, Gerald,' my wife suggested, looking small and vulnerable under Charley's arm.

'Testicles?' Charley grinned broadly.

'You already have,' I said.

Hoo-Sin reached down under Janny's sagging knees to pick her up. 'We return to the origin,' she whispered, as Janny wriggled closer, 'and remain where we have always been . . .'

'Flo! Where'd you find the fodder?'

'No, the one about how you find out if she's ticklish or not.'

'In the back there, Rocco, but you gotta scrape it off the pans . . .'

'How you find out – oh Jesus!' Charley doubled up, roaring with laughter.

'You find that funny?' I asked in some amazement. At the foot of the stairs, Prissy Loo shook her plumed hat ('Chet!') and stamped her foot. 'But you said you'd *wait*, Zack!'

'I guess – *whoosh! hah!* – I guess it's all,' Charley wheezed, falling back on the hall bench, holding his quaking sides ('Ha ha! Not *Chet!*'), '*in how you tell it!*'

'I knew he'd like it, Gerald,' my wife said. 'Now go ahead and tell it.'

Whereupon Charley, tears in his eyes ('You're a real heel, Zack!'), nearly fell off the bench.

'You kids off?'

'Careful, Charley, you'll hurt your back again.'

'Oh shit! – hoo ha hah— !'

'Yes, thanks a lot, Mr Quagg! As soon as we're in our new place—'

'– I awready did!'

'Better come quick, Zack! One of those drunken yobs gave Olga something heavy and she's freaking! She thinks she's a bird and keeps throwing herself at all the walls!'

'What am I, some kinda nursemaid?' Zack protested.

'Say, where'd you hide your sewing machine?' asked Prissy Loo, slapping over ('Well, keep in touch, kid— !') in her big galoshes. 'I went in there to sew these sanitary napkins on my costume and—'

'You mean it isn't there?' my wife exclaimed.

'And let me see what you write!'

'It *probably* cost me my part!'

'That's right,' someone said ('You bet!'), 'your dressing table was gone, too,' I said.

'Unh, Big G . . . ? I – *hoof!* – I can' get up . . . !'

'The dressing table! But that old thing is worthless!'

'Well, aw-*moss!*' yuff huffed Charley, struggling clumsily, 'but, Jesus, don' go *tellin'* everybody!'

Anatole gave me a hand pulling him to his feet, while Hoo-Sin stood patiently by, holding Janny, now breathing deeply, in her arms. Howard had joined us and, peering down through Tania's half-lens glasses, was trying to button his coat, while at the same time holding on to the sheaf of drawings the tall cop had made of the scene of the crime. 'Here, let me help, Uncle Howard,' Sally Ann said.

'What I don't understand, Gerald, is how they got all those things *out* of here?' In the dining room we could hear Olga crashing around, yelling: 'Tveet! Tveet!' 'Tell her she's a fucking *flower!*' Zack was shouting. 'Or a *stone!*'

'Cute,' said Prissy Loo, fingering Sally Ann's dirndl.

'You gotta catch her first, Zack!'

''At wuzza bess laugh I had all night! *Hoo!*'

'Do you think they had a truck?'

Anatole cleared his throat. 'Uh, do you want to tell them, Sally Ann . . . ?' he said, blushing.

'Well . . .' She took Anatole's arm, looked at each of us in turn.

'Tveet – *squawk!*'

'Oh oh,' said Prissy Loo, puckering up.

'We're . . . we're going to get married.'

'I knew it!' wailed Prissy Loo and burst into tears. 'I always cry at the clinches!' She planted a blubbery moustachioed kiss on Sally Ann's cheek and Anatole's ('That's wonderful,' my wife was saying, 'I'm so happy for you!'), then went clopping off into the living room in her plumed hat and decorated girdle. 'Whuzzat? Whuzzat?' asked Charley blearily, careening around, and I said: 'But how will you live?'

'Oh, Gerald!' my wife scolded, taking my arm. 'Hush now!'

'That's all right,' said Sally Ann gently. 'I knew he'd be upset.'

'I'm going to drop out of school and write for Mr Quagg,' Anatole explained. 'And Dickie's getting Sally Ann a job in one of his massage parlors.'

'You see, Gerald?'

'And we're going to live with Uncle Howard,' Sally Ann added, taking the older man's arm. 'He needs us, and we need him. Now that . . .' Her voice broke and Anatole's eyes began to water up.

'I assume you are aware, Gerald, that the "Susanna" is missing,' Howard said in his rigid pedantic way.

I nodded. 'And not only that, Howard, they even took—'

'Such carelessness, Gerald, is utterly inexcusable.'

'Come along now, Uncle Howard,' Anatole said huskily.

'Whoa there, young fella!' exclaimed Charley, holding Anatole back. ''Sa tough ole world out there, son – you can' go get married on nothin'!'

Anatole looked offended. 'It's not nothing, Mr Trainer. Mr Quagg says I have a lot of talent and—'

'No, hell, I know that, but juss hole on, goddamn it!' He fumbled in his pockets. 'Art, Gerald,' Howard harrumphed, scowling at me over the spectacles, 'is all we have. It is not a joke.' Olga came bounding through on all fours, more like a lamb or a goat now than a bird, the yellow nightie up around her ears, pursued by Gudrun, Zack, and some of the newcomers. '*Maaa-aa-aa!*' she bleated, frisking along into the living room,

her head stretched high. 'Come here, Olga! Stop that!' 'It is not a decoration, simple bric-a-brac. It is *not* a mere entertainment.' 'Maybe if she
thought she was a dog, we could get a leash on her!' *'Maaa-aa-aa!'* 'Just
so she don't start droppin' pellets!' panted Horner, limping along behind,
and the guy with him stopped and pointed: 'Hey! I know you jokers! Ha!
I seen you in the photos!' 'Art, Gerald—' 'Photos?' my wife asked. ' – *Is
the precipitate of the human spirit. . .'* Charley dumped all his change into
the pockets of Sally Ann's dress – or in that general direction: coins
splattered the floor, rolled at our feet. 'Yeah, some guy from the newspaper's floggin' 'em out in your front yard like souvenirs.' 'There! 'Sall I
got, kids,' said Charley, emptying his wallet and thrusting the bills at
Anatole, 'but, well – I mean, god-*damn* it— !'

'I don't go much for the shots of stiffs or all the blood and shit . . .'

'Oh, Uncle Charley!' cried Sally Ann, throwing her arms around him.

'. . . The repository of the only meaning we *have* in this world . . .'

'. . . But there's one of some ole girl peein' off the teeter-totter out in
the backyard that'll – Christ! – break your heart!'

'I know, Howard, but—'

'That must have been Wilma,' my wife said.

'In the end, Gerald, and I say this with all seriousness, you are a
dangerous person!'

Hoo-Sin, carrying Janny, bowed slightly and backed out the door,
Howard ('I intend therefore to sue you for the remaining pieces in your
possession,' he declared, and my wife said: 'Yes, you must come again
soon!'), Anatole, and then Charley following. Some of the people
chasing Olga had peeled off here in the hallway and it was filling up
again. Not a familiar face among them. 'Is that the only bottle you
could find, Carmody?' one of them asked. I recognized it. Alas. Central
to the art of love, I knew ('Yeah'n taze like piss, buh' this time nigh',
who givshit?'), as to the art of theater, was the essential fusion of
process and product, an acknowledgment of the inherent doubleness
– one's particularity, one's universality, one's self, one's persona – of
the actor/lover. In fact ('I'm so glad you found each other,' my wife
was saying, 'it's just about the nicest thing that happened all night!'),
I'd said something like this to her earlier tonight, and she'd agreed,
probably it was while she was fingering my nipple, we'd seemed in
perfect harmony, perfect collusion, and yet . . . 'Gerry?' I realized Sally

Ann, hanging back from the others, had taken my hand. 'Try not to be so sad, Gerry, it's for the best, believe me – but I promise I'll never forget you!' Her eyes were full of tears and they were tumbling down her cheeks. 'I – I was blind until you opened my eyes to love . . . !' She tried to say something more, but it was choked off by a stifled sob. She kissed my mouth and went running out the door.

My wife, looking on, smiled and took my arm. There was a loud spewing sound behind us, someone gagging. 'Young love . . . !' she sighed.

'Goddamn it, Carmody! This *is* piss!'

'We'll have to think of something for a wedding present . . .'

'Hey, you guys! Come in here! You don't wanna miss this!' I could hear toward the back what sounded like ('"Fya don' like it, shifface, giv't back!') wild guttural laughter, utterly insane, and the crack of whips. Or belts.

'Madre de dios! ees getteeng roff!' Hilario gasped, staggering out of the dining room just as the others (something crashed) went pushing in. He wobbled toward us with his legs exaggeratedly bowed and his eyes bugged out. 'Now Olga theenk he ees a horse and everybody ees rideeng heem! Hair.'

'Where have they all come from, Hillie?' This never used to happen. Michelle's dream of the old lady's infested navel came to mind: it's what comes from growing old. 'What am I going to *do?*'

'You wan' get reed?'

'Sure, but— ?'

'Seemple like a tart, Cherry! Don' cry!'

My wife, rummaging through the hall closet, said: 'My good fur wrap is missing, too.'

'La serpiente – what you say the dance-sneak, no?' He reached forward as though gripping a waist and did a little rumba step. The guy they were calling Carmody, hugging his pale green bottle and muttering, 'I *know* wha'm *doing*, wobbled past us (*'Yippee! Let 'er rip!'* shouted someone in the dining room) and disappeared through the front door.

'*Look out!*'

'Yow— !!' *Crash!*

'Eet *always* work!'

'That would be nice, Hillie, I'll put some music on,' my wife offered, but just then Charley came banging back through the front door and grabbed us both: 'Wait, you guys! I forgot!' 'Pairmeet me!' Hilario smiled, bowing from the waist. He shuffled gracefully off toward the living room, hands still on the imaginary waist. 'I sold my car!'

'Your car?'

'Yeah, the big station wagon. Your buddy – travel agent guy. Hey, whaddaya cryin' about, Ger? I got a fan-*tas*-tic deal!' He fished around in his jacket pockets, came up with a crumpled check. The crazy whinnying had stopped. I could hear the music now in the living room. Hilario was turning the volume up. 'See? Awmoss *twice* what I paid for it!'

'Charley, isn't this check signed "Waterloo"?'

"Ass right – hah! ole Waterloo – you 'member! That dumb shit!'

I glanced up at my wife: she sighed and shook her head. 'I showed them everything . . .'

'Whuzzamatter?' He stared in puzzlement at the check, held it up to the light.

'Listen, Charley, you take my car for now.' I handed him the keys. The music was getting louder.

'Hunh? Oh yeah, thanks, ole buddy!' He wrapped his arms heavily around me. 'Hey, I *love* ya, Ger! I *mean* it!' He hauled out his handkerchief and wiped my eyes and then his own. Over his shoulder I could see a line of people, hands on one another's hips and led by Hilario (he winked and raised his long fingers in a V), come hopping and kicking out of the living room, all singing along with the music, now turned up full volume: '*Don't LAUGH, it may be LOVE . . . !*' The woman who'd hit the door lintel with her face was still out cold, the guy who'd carried her in now dragging her along by one ankle. As they wound toward the back into the dining room ('Hey! wait for me!' people shouted, grabbing on to the tail), Dolph and Louise came squeezing out past them, holding hands, looking flustered and confused. Beside me, my wife caught her breath, and Charley, pulling away (*'It's YOU I'm thinkin' OF!'*), said: 'Great goddamn party, Big G! Bess I ever wen' to!'

'I guess we gotta second that,' Dolph grinned.

'Is it true, then?' asked my wife, and Louise blushed and nodded. They fell into a big tearful embrace and then Dolph hugged my wife and Louise hugged me: she was trembling and I thought I heard her gasp something about 'love you' or 'because of you,' it was hard to tell because things were getting pretty noisy. They both hugged Charley, who seemed to have no idea what it was all about, then hugged us again (they'd been standing in the smoke too long and smelled a bit charred), Louise now almost unable to breathe for excitement. While Dolph had his arms around me ('I *love* it!' Charley was saying. 'God-*damn* it, Louise!'), I stage-whispered in his ear: '*If you grab my buttocks, Dolph, I'll bite your ear off!*' Dolph laughed, a squeaky but joyful laugh, unlike any we'd heard in over a year, and my wife, in tears, hugged them both again. 'I'm so happy for you!' she cried, and Charley, punching Dolph in the ribs, said: ''Sbeaut-iful! I *mean* it!'

Hilario's snake dance, meanwhile, had come winding out of the living room again, led now by Olga, who seemed to think she was a frog: she was down on her haunches, hopping along, her big cheeks bouncing rhythmically off the floor, and shouting '*Borp!*' every time she leaped into the air. The line coiled to the rear of the hall, Olga going '*Borp! Borp!*' in front of them, then swung round and hopped toward us again.

'*Life is ONLY what you SEE . . . !*'

Dolph said something about influence, but the noise in the hall was deafening. 'WHAT— ?'

'I SAID YOU GUYS—'

'*Borp!*'

'Here they come!'

'*So come DANCE along with ME!*'

'Look out— !'

My wife flung the door open and we pulled apart to let them by, but Olga, as though in panic, stopped dead at the threshold. Hilario prodded her effectively – '*BORP!*' – in the behind.

'You're a genius, Hillie!' I shouted.

He laughed, kicking. '*I promeese dem all w'en we outside we EAT de FROG!*' And then he was gone, the long line hopping and whooping behind: '*Won't you TRY to under-STAND . . .*'

My wife seemed to be saying something. '*WHAT?*' I cried. Horner had his hand up the skirt of the woman in front of him: she bounced rigidly as though on coiled springs, her eyes glazed, mouth agape.

'*I said, I get the feeling half my wardrobe walked out the door tonight!*' She pointed at Beni, who, one hand cupping his silk codpiece affectionately, winked and shouted out a '*Ciao!*' '*Or hopped!*'

'*If you're the GLOVE, then I'm the HAND!*'

A guy with a runny nose and what looked like dried vomit down his shirtfront staggered out of the line and threw his arms around us.

'G'nigh'!' he shouted. *"Nkyou fr'inviding us!'* He seemed to be crying. *'C'mon, Boomer! you'll get left behind!'* ' *'S been so . . . shit! . . . so—'* 'Soup's on, Boomer!' *'So goddamn . . . I don' know howta . . . God! yareally SWELL!'* he sobbed and grabbed up my wife's hand and kissed it. Or maybe he was only wiping his nose on it. Then he stumbled back into the line, disappearing through the door.

Slowly the sound wound away from us as the dancers snaked past. A guy with an eyepatch waved a bottle at me, Bunky blew a kiss – *'Noble said to say thanks, Gerry, thanks a lot!'* – Scarborough moved lugubriously out of step. *'If I'm the HAND, then you're the GLOVE . . . !'* they sang, kicking, the music still blasting away. The woman getting dragged along at the tail seemed to be coming around at last. 'Phil . . . ?' she asked as her head bumped over the threshold. 'Where am I, Phil . . .'

'So don't LAUGH . . .'

I shoved the door shut, leaned against it, turned the latch. *'Whew!'* I gasped.

'What happened to Dolph and Louise?' my wife asked, looking around in amazement. *'And Charley—!'*

'I don't know!' I said. We were still shouting. *'They must have joined in!'* She shrugged, then said something I couldn't hear. About the kitchen maybe: she wandered off that way. *'I'll go turn the music down!'*

In the empty living room, Michelle danced alone, wan under the bright lights from the ceiling, drifting wraithlike through the wreckage, hands crossed at her breast, eyes closed. When I rejected the tone-arm, the sudden silence was shocking, almost physical in its impact, and I heard her gasp faintly, frozen in her movement. 'I guess it's that time, Michelle.' The deadly silence was eery and I was almost tempted to put another record on. I thought: it used to be more subtle than this.

'Have you been crying?' she whispered.

'Yes, well,' I said, and wiped my cheek, 'I hate goodbyes.'

'Once, when I was modeling for Tania . . .' She hesitated. '. . . This was a long time ago . . . I was young then . . .' Her head dipped slightly. '. . . Just a little bit of hair . . . "like a boy's moustache," she said . . .' She seemed lost in her own reverie. '. . . Trying to help me feel more . . . relaxed . . .'

'Michelle?'

'What? Yes . . .' She clasped her hands at the back of her neck, her elbows in front of her face. Her intricate lace blouse was unbuttoned, tails out over a wrinkled skirt. 'That day, she was apologizing for keeping me in the same pose for so long . . . and it was true . . . my whole body ached . . . it was awful . . . I wanted to fly right out of myself . . .' She lifted her head, stretching her neck against her clasped hands, then let her hands separate to slide forward and support her chin. '"But an unfinished painting frightens me," she said . . .' Yes, 'a bare patch of canvas,' she'd once remarked to me, 'is like some terrible ultimate nakedness . . .' '. . . I can still see her face as she said it . . . her eyes . . .' '. . . Reality exposing itself obscenely . . .' '"I can't sleep," she said, "I can't eat, I can't even think properly until I've completed it . . . I become cruel to myself and cruel to others . . ."' I remembered how she'd turned away and seemed almost to shudder. '. . . "And then . . . when it's suddenly done . . ."' Michelle dropped her hands limply at her sides, lowered her chin. '. . . "There's this terrible emptiness . . ."'

I watched her drift away, stepping barefoot through the butts and crumpled napkins, spilled food, the debris from Scarborough's set (near the cavemouth, Malcolm Mee's cast-off plastic wrap lay like an insect's husk, glittering and dead), and, though I wanted her to leave, I felt abandoned at the same time, left behind in a room (why were the windows so bare, the lights so harsh?) full of grave disquiet. The bloodied drapes and linens had turned dark and dirty. Sticking out from under the collapsed ping-pong table: the chalk drawing of a pair of legs. Scarborough had rigged the cords of all the lamps to a kind of switching system in a box dangling just behind the proscenium arch, but I was afraid to touch it. It had a rickety yet lethal look, as though it might go off. I needed a drink, but I didn't want to go in where Vic was, so I stepped into the makeshift cave, away from the flat lights and stripped windows, and sniffed at the half-filled glasses. I found one that smelled more or less like scotch, but just as I tipped it back, I noticed what looked like pubic hairs floating in it – I spat it out. But it was only someone's false eyelashes. I sank back into the gold couch in there, feeling suddenly very tired. We'd have to clean up tomorrow. Outside, in the hallway, I could hear my wife saying good night to Michelle, her voice thin in the hollow silence ('Goodness, Michelle, where did you – *yawn!* – get those nasty toothmarks . . . ?'), and it reminded me of the time when, spelunking in Greece, we'd come on this cavernous pit of human bones. What she'd said then – thinly, hollowly – was: 'Did you notice? None of them have heads . . . !'

Of course . . . that wasn't my wife . . .

'Somehow,' she said now, gazing around wearily (she was standing in front of me, easing her shoes off: I hadn't seen her come up), 'parties don't seem as much fun as they used to.' She sat down beside me, curling under my arm, the one I could still move, and tucked her feet up. 'It's almost as though the parties have started giving us instead of us giving the parties . . .' She loosened my shirt, lay her head sleepily against my chest. 'It gives me a . . . funny feeling . . .'

'Yes . . .'

'Still, I guess it's worth it . . .'

The woman in Greece had said something much like that about making love. She'd had an appetite for the unusual, the perverse even, and I too was pretty jaded in those days, frustrated by the commonplaces of sex, bored with all its trite conventions – the state of the art, so to speak – and so in need of ever greater novelty, ever greater risk-taking, in order to arouse myself to any kind of performance. What worked for her – and thus for us both – was to be unexpectedly violated in a more or less public place, the key to a successful orgasm being not so much the setting or the use of force, as the element of surprise. It was a kind of essential trigger for her – like having to scare someone out of her hiccups. Thus, I might walk her through public parks, churches, department stores, taunting her with exotic possibility while yet denying her, only to jump on her back in the busy hotel lobby while asking for the key. Or I might arrange a night out at some mysterious destination, coax her into dressing up elaborately, then get her out of the hotel, hail a taxi – and suddenly violate her on the sidewalk just as she was stepping into the cab. I don't know why I thought that pitful of decayed atrocity victims would work. Perhaps because it seemed so unlikely. But nothing happened. In fact it was a disaster. We got filthy, she hurt her back on the bones, got her nose bloodied, I cracked my elbow, we were both choking with dust, and when it was over – or rather, when there was no point in going on – she told me just to leave her alone and go away. I never saw her again, my last vision of her being sprawled out there in the – '*Ouch!*'

'Sorry, Gerald, is something . . . ?' She had been stroking me through the trousers and had caught the place where Jim had nicked me. She opened my trousers carefully, eased my shorts down. 'Oh, I see . . .' She licked it gently, then took the crown into her mouth, coating it with warm saliva. 'Bat's a bad bwuise, too,' she observed, touching my tummy, then let her mouth slide gradually down the shaft. I reached for the hem of her dress and she shifted her hips, turning her knees toward the back of the couch.

There was a sudden crash, the whole house shook – I lurched away, reared up – and then a scraping, another crash, a rumble, something rolling in the street. She closed her mouth around my penis again, curled her hands behind my hips, tugged at the back of my trousers.

'But . . . my god, what *was* that— ?!'

'Pwobabwy Chawwey puwwing out ubba dwibe. . .

'Ah . . .' She eased my trousers down below my hips – outside, there was another crunch, the distant squealing of tires – then pulled them away from between my thighs. She put my hand back on the hem of her dress. There was a tag there, I noticed, stamped by the city police department. 'Wewacsh, Gewawd,' she whispered. I liked the pushing of her tongue against the consonants and, surrendering to that, slid down toward her knees. 'Tell me again . . .'

'Wewacsh, Gewawd . . . ?'

'Yes . . . good . . .' It all comes down to words, as I might have argued with Vic. Or parts of them. 'Is this a new dress?'

'Yeumf,' she said, working my trousers down to my ankles: I lifted one foot out and raised it to the couch. 'Do woo wike it?'

'Right now, it's in my way . . .'

'You say the nicest things, Gerald,' she sighed, taking her mouth away. She located the fastener, unhooked it, pushed at the skirt: I pulled it away and, stretching forward, eased it past her feet. 'What are you doing with pancake makeup on the back of your neck?' she asked.

'I don't remember.'

I tugged at her panty girdle, stretching it down past her soft hips, and she took my penis in her mouth again, warming it all over, closing one hand tenderly around my testicles. She kneaded them softly, pulling them toward her as though gently pumping them, sliding her other hand around to stroke my buttocks, finger my anus. Only one arm worked for getting her clothes off her: I left the dead one between her legs for the time being and she squeezed her thighs around it. 'Just . . . a minute . . .' The panties and stockings came off in a tangle. I ran my tongue slowly up her leg from her calf, past her knee, and up the inside of her thigh: she spread her legs and, as I nosed into her vulva, lifted the top one over my head. 'Mmmmf!' She had her finger up my anus now and was sucking rhythmically, her mouth full of foamy saliva like a warm bubble bath. I had found the nub of her clitoris with the tip of my tongue and now worked against it as though trying to pry it open. I reached round from behind, dipped my fingers into her moist vagina, pushed one of them up her rectum – '*Ouch!*' she cried, letting my penis go.

'Sorry . . .' I pushed my nose deeper between her thighs to have a closer look: her anus was drawn up in a tight little pucker, inflamed and cracked, slightly discolored as though rubbed with ashes. 'How did you— ?'

'You know. The police.' She paused, holding my penis by the root. Perhaps she was studying it. Or simply reflecting.

I pressed my chin against the hood of her clitoris, gazing thoughtfully at her crinkled anus, remembering now her position on the butcherblock (as though being changed, I'd thought as they lowered her), her thighs stretching back, belly wrinkling, tiny little red lines running down her cheeks. 'What . . . what's an exploding sausage . . . ?' I asked uneasily.

'Oh, Gerald!' she laughed and wagged my penis playfully. 'Don't you know a joke when you hear one?'

'Ah . . .' I stroked her buttocks gently as my penis returned to its soothing bath, rubbing my chin rhythmically against her pubic knoll. Like veined marble, they'd seemed to me at the time, as I remembered, something like that, though now they sparkled with a kind of fresh dewy innocence (it was the kind of feeling I had between my own legs now) under the bright overhead light. She was beginning to grind vigorously against my chin, thighs cuffing my ears, so I moved my mouth back over her rosy lips, dipping my tongue into their warm mushy depths – I was aswim in warm mushy depths, we were both—

'Say, uh . . . where the hell *is* everybody?' someone asked. I peered up between my wife's convulsing thighs, my own hips bucking against the cushions: it was Knud, standing bleary-eyed over us, rubbing the back of his neck. 'Crikey!' he muttered, his voice phlegmy with sleep. 'You'll never believe the dream I just had!'

'Everybody's gone home, Knud,' I gasped, my chin sliding now in the dense juices beneath it.

'Hunh?' He frowned at his empty wrist. My wife had stopped pumping her head up and down the shaft of my penis, but she was still sucking at it rhythmically and stroking it with her tongue, marking time, as it were, her throbbing clitoris searching for my mouth. 'Even Kitty? Jeez, what time is it?'

'*Everybody's* gone, Knud. It's *late.*'

'Holy cow, I must have slept through the whole goddam party,' he rumbled, still staring at his wrist. He yawned, belched. 'Boy! What a dream, though!' My wife's hips had stopped pitching. She held my testicles and one buttock firmly, but had let my penis slide past her teeth into one cheek. 'I was like in some kind of war zone, see, only everyone was all mixed up and you didn't know who was on your side—'

'Not now, Knud,' my wife panted, letting me go and twisting round to look up at him. Her buttocks spread a bit, giving me a clearer view of Knud: he was puffy-eyed and rumpled, tie undone, shirttail out, pants damp and sticky, and he looked like he needed a shave.

'No, listen, it was a lot longer. And really weird. Since you couldn't be sure who anybody was, see, just to be safe you naturally had to kill everyone – right? Ha ha! you wouldn't *believe* the blood and gore! And all in 3-D and full color, too, I kid you not! I kept running into people and asking them: "Where *am* I?" They'd say: "What a *loony*," or something like that – and then I'd chop their heads off, right?'

'Please, Knud— ?'

He glanced down at my penis withering in my wife's hand, at her buttocks flattening out in front of my face. 'Oh, right . . . sorry . . .' He gazed around at the living room, running his hand through his snarled hair. 'Say, do you remember, was I wearing a watch when I came here tonight?'

'Well . . .' my wife began tentatively, raising herself up on one elbow, and I cut in: 'I can't remember, Knud.'

He seemed to accept that. He squinted up at the lights on the ceiling for a moment, yawning. 'Kitty been gone long?'

'No, you can probably catch her.' I was beginning to feel my wife's weight: I gave a little push and she lifted herself off my face.

'Don't get up,' Knud insisted. 'I can find my own way out.' He stumbled away, stuffing his shirttail in. My wife, sitting up, let her hand fall idly on my hip. We could hear Knud peeing noisily in the toilet bowl. It was a lonely sound, but not so lonely as the silence all around it. 'At least it's working,' my wife said. She picked up her stockings and panty girdle, toweled between her legs with them. 'Hey, thanks,' said Knud from the doorway. 'See you at the next one.'

'Flush it, please, Knud!' my wife called, but he was already out the door. 'Oh well.' I curled around her from behind, hugging her close, and she patted my hip with sleepy affection. My penis nuzzled between her cheeks. It felt good there. It was something to think about. 'Do you notice a kind of chill in here?' she murmured sleepily.

'Well, all the windowpanes are out,' I said. I ran my hand along her thigh where it met the couch. 'We could try the TV room now that Knud's vacated it . . .'

She smiled, a bit wearily, then took my good hand and pulled me to my feet. I kicked off the trousers, still tangled around one foot, and, holding hands, we stepped out from under the tented drapes and linens into the glare and wreckage of what was once our living room. She drew close to me suddenly, pressing her naked hip against mine. I was feeling it, too. As though the house had not been emptying out so much as filling up. The windows, stripped bare and paneless, seemed to crowd in on us, letting the dark night at their edges leak in like some kind of deadly miasma. Hugging each other's waists, we picked our way barefoot through the shards of broken pots and glassware, the food squashed into the carpet, the chalk outlines and bent cocktail skewers. The wall next to the dining room doorway was splattered and streaked with a mince pie someone must have thrown, and even that, innocent as it was, seemed to add to our feelings of apprehension and melancholy.

The wall above the dining room sideboard was eloquently vacant, the picture hooks sitting on it like a pair of pinned insects. Bottles lay tipped like fallen soldiers, liquor still, amazingly enough, gurgling from one of the open mouths. 'What exactly happened to Vic?' my wife whispered.

'He . . . got shot . . .'

'He makes you think of Tania's painting, doesn't he? The one with the eyes . . .'

'Well . . .'

★

I tugged her on into the TV room. We seemed safer in here somehow. Maybe because the lights were softer ('Our antique lamps are missing,' she remarked quietly as though in explanation) or because the drapes were still on the windows and the furniture more or less where it ought to be. Or just the soothing blueness of the walls. I could feel my wife's hip soften and I too seemed to walk less stiffly, my knees unlocking, my scrotum sliding back into place. Snow played on the TV screen, making a scratchy noise like a needle caught on the outer lip of a record, but I didn't want to turn it off. It was company of sorts. 'I'll put a cassette on,' I said, letting go her waist, and she sat down on the sofa to wait. 'Don't be long, Gerald,' she yawned.

I couldn't seem to find any of our old tapes, but there were plenty of new ones scattered about to choose from. 'How about "The Ancient Arse?"' I proposed, reading the labels. 'Or "Cold Show at the Ice Palace" – or here's one: "The Garden Peers."'

'I think that's *pee*-ers. I've seen that one. I don't want to see it again.' Ah. I understood now. 'Below the Stairs,' 'Butcherblock Blues,' 'Party Time,' 'Life's Mysterious Currents,' 'The Host's Hang-up,' they all fell dismally into place. 'Candid Coppers.' 'Some Dish.' 'Special Favors.' I felt defeated even before I'd begun. There were tears in my eyes and a strange airy tingling on my exposed behind, like a ghostly remembrance of cold knuckles. I shuddered. 'Put on "Hidden Treasure,"' my wife suggested, unbuttoning her blouse and jacket.

I searched through the pile of cassettes, intent on doing my best, getting through it somehow, but my appetite had faded. 'It . . . it will never be the same again,' I muttered, my throat tight.

'Tsk. You said that last time, Gerald. After Archie and Emma and . . .'

'Yes, well . . .' It was true, I'd all but forgotten. 'But Ros, Vic, Tania . . .'

'Roger, Noble . . .'

'Yes, that's right, Roger . . .'

'Fiona . . .'

'Fiona—?' I took off the cassette labeled 'The Wayward Finger,' and inserted 'Hidden Treasure,' rewound it to the beginning, punched the 'Play' button, wishing it were all so easy as that.

'Yes, that was why Cyril was so upset.' She was completely naked now, stretched out on the sofa, hands behind her head, eyes half-closed, scratching the bottom of her foot with one toe. 'How do you think Peg found out?'

'Found out what?' I took off my shirt, folded it neatly over the back of the sofa, stalling for time. On the TV, my mother-in-law was getting Mark into his pajama bottoms. 'That's better,' she was saying. Mark was holding Peedie, which now had one of Sally Ann's patches sewn on its underside. 'HOT TWOT,' it said.

'Well, she was pregnant.'

'Peg was?'

'No, Fiona.' I sat down beside her and stroked her thighs, pushing into the warm place between her legs, but my heart wasn't in it. Mark, on the television screen, was asking: 'What's a "twot," Gramma?' Behind him, his bedroom door was all smashed in. 'That's the whole point, Gerald. Didn't you notice? It was very obvious.'

'It's a . . . a faraway place,' my mother-in-law was explaining. 'A kind of secret garden . . .'

'I'm not sure I saw her all night,' I said. Maybe it was the scar, cold and bluish in the light from the flickering TV image, that was bothering me. I looked around, spied one of her aprons hanging over the edge of the games table.

'Is it always hot, Gramma?'

'But you heard Peg carrying on when she left – she was telling everybody!'

'No, it's warm. Like a bed. Now you crawl up into yours there, young man.'

'I guessed I missed that.' I brought the apron over: 'Listen, do you mind— ?'

'But then that's why everyone was feeling so sorry for Cyril after.' She raised her hips so I could tie the apron on. 'Will I ever go there someday?' Mark was asking. 'You know, to lose them both in one night . . .'

'Both— ?'

'It seems inevitable, child . . .'

'Yes – my goodness, Gerald, where *were* you?' I slid my hand up under the apron: yes, this was better. There was a faint stirring at last between my legs, which my mother-in-law appeared to be overseeing from the TV screen, her face marked by a kind of compassionate sorrow mixed with amusement. 'Tell me a story about it, Gramma,' Mark was pleading sleepily, as she led him to the bed. 'You missed just about everything!'

'About what?' she asked.

'You know, the Twot,' said Mark, as my hand reached my wife's pubis. I let my fingers scratch gently in the hair there, while my thumb slid between her thighs and curled into her vagina. 'Well, once upon a time,' she began, lifting Mark onto the bed, and I too lifted slightly, then let her down again. 'You know . . . sometimes, Gerald . . .,' she sighed, closing her hands gently over mine, '. . . it's almost as if . . .' 'There was a young prince . . .'

'. . . You were at a different party . . .'

'Was his name Mark?'

I edged closer to my wife's hips, my thumb working rhythmically against the ball of my index finger ('Oh yes . . . good . . .'), and she took my wilted organ in her hand. On the television screen, my mother-in-law was tucking Mark in. 'All right then, a young prince named Mark – but get down under the covers, or I won't tell it.'

I pushed my thumb as deep as it would go, while at the same time stretching my fingers up her belly, her pubis thrusting at me under the apron, closing around my thumb, her own hand (my mother-in-law had already launched Prince Mark out on his 'unique adventure,' but Mark wanted to know: 'Where's his mommy and daddy? Is he a orphan?') stroking me with a gentle but insistent cadence, slowly helping me forget what I'd seen sticking out from under the games table a moment ago when I'd reached for her apron: a foot, wrapped in a plastic bag, one toe poking out. Its nail painted. Cherry red. 'No, he was the little boy of Beauty and the – her husband . . . ,' my mother-in-law was saying, as the prospect of orgasm swelled in my mind like a numbing intuition. I gazed down at my wife, her hair unrolled now and loose about her pale shoulders, her thin lips parted, nostrils flared, and thought I could hear Ros whispering: *Oh yes, lets!*

Oh no . . .

'. . . But he was a big boy now and it was time to leave home and seek his own fortune . . .'

I was frightened and wanted to stop ('We are in it, Gerry, we cannot get out of it,' I seemed to hear Vic mumble right outside the door – had he moved somehow?!), but my wife was blindly pulling me toward her, spreading her legs, the apron wrinkling up between us, and my genitals, it seemed, were quite willing to carry on without the rest of me. 'We can only stand up to it or chicken out . . .'

What? Vic— ?

'Was the Beast nice now?'

'Oh yes, yes . . . !' my wife was gasping.

'Most of the time . . .'

I'd let go my thumbhold on her pubic handle and, twisting my hand around, my mouth sucking at a breast now (ah, what was it I *really* wanted? I didn't want to think about it . . .), had slid my handful of fingers down there instead, my bodily parts separating out like a houseful of drunken and unruly guests, everybody on his own. She tugged still at that most prodigious member, the host, as it were ('He paused at the edge of the Enchanted Forest: it was dreary and dangerous and . . .'), pumping it harder and harder, her other hand grasping my testicles like a doorknob: she gave them a turn, opened, and, going up on my knees as though to offer my behind to the invading emptiness ('And . . . dark?' asked Mark fearfully, hugging his Peedie under the blankets), mouth still at her breast, I crossed over between her legs.

'Yes . . . !'

'Hurry, Gerald!'

'I'm afraid, Gramma!'

There was a congestion now of fingers and organs, a kind of rubbery crowding up around the portal ('But he was not alone,' my mother-in-law was explaining in an encouraging voice), but then she slipped her hands out to snatch at my buttocks, yanking them fiercely toward her as though to keep them from floating away like hot-air balloons – perhaps I'd been worrying about this, I felt like I was coming apart and falling together at the same time – and as her legs jerked upward ('little Prince Mark was protected by his faithful companion Peedie the Brave Rabbit . . .'), I dropped in through the ooze as though casting anchor. *This*, I was thinking with some excitement, and with some bewilderment as well – what *is* this 'we' when the I's are gone? – is my *wife!* Under my tongue, her nipple ('. . . and by his Magical Blue Shirt . . . ,' her mother was saying) had sprung erect like a little mushroom stem ('. . . for forfending demons . . .'), and I moved now – I say I, certainly *something* moved – across her flushed and heaving chest to suck intrepidly at the other one.

'. . . And his good Fairy Godmother, who watched over him wherever he went . . .'

'Oh, Gerald! You're so . . . so . . . !'

I gripped her buttocks now, one taut flexing cheek in each hand ('Did she look like you, Gramma?'), feeling the first distant tremors deep in the black hole of my bowels ('A bit . . .') and remembering one night at the theater when, the stage littered with fornicating couples meant to represent the Forms of Rhetoric (the sketch was called A Meeting of Minds'), she'd leaned toward me and whispered: 'I know they want us to feel time differently here, Gerald, more like an eternal present than the usual past, present, and future, but the only moment that ever works for me is at the end when the lights go down ('No, Peedie doesn't die,' her mother was saying, 'not yet . . .') and the curtains close. And I'm' – her feet kicked up over my back, crowding her own hands away, so she reached up to clutch my neck and hair – 'not sure I like it.' '*Great!*' she moaned now, her head tipping back off the edge of the sofa, her back arching, her hips convulsing, and mine too were hammering away, completely ('Don't worry . . .') out of control – it was a kind of pelvic hilarity, a muscular hiccup (had Pardew compared this to murder?), our pubes crashing together like remote underwater collisions, as ineluctable as punchlines.

'That's what fairy godmothers are for . . .'

Only not too soon, I begged (as did my wife: 'Wait, Gerald! Not . . . *ooh! ah* . . . *!* yet . . . !'), wanting to hold on to this moment, like so many before, but her vagina seemed to have filled up like a fist and to be clinging to my penis for dear life, pumping and pumping in tight muscular spasms, and even as I was looking forward to its arrival, it was already ('*Yes— !!*' my wife cried out, her head out of sight) gone.

I lay sprawled across her breasts, my head jammed into the linty corner between the armrest and back of the sofa, trying to conceive of the idea of eternity as a single violent spasm. I couldn't even imagine it. For that matter I couldn't imagine much of anything. It was as though I carried my semen in my head and orgasm had sucked it hollow. Distantly, I could hear my mother-in-law describing for Mark the 'mysterious Walled Garden' in the middle of the Enchanted Forest, 'where fairies play and rubies hang from bushes like berries and you never get old or lose your way,' which might have been quite soothing had she not sounded like she was scolding. We were still linked in a soft aromatic congestion. I wanted to say, 'I love you,' but instead found myself saying: 'You focus . . . my attention . . .' 'Oh, Gerald,' she sighed from below, reaching up to pat my hip, 'your sweet nothings are not always sweet . . . but at least . . .'

We slipped apart, my wife's pelvis sliding away to the floor to join the rest of her. Mark's grandmother was telling him about a hidden treasure in the Walled Garden, 'guarded by a wicked and spiteful Tattooed Dragon that breathed both ice and fire.' As I fell back, I seemed to catch her televised eye: a kind of warning . . . 'And what the Prince had to do to reach the treasure,' she went on as my wife sat up and reached for the off button ('Sorry, mother . . .'), 'was chop –'

Click.

There was a sudden dreadful silence. 'Goodness,' my wife murmured, looked around, 'I almost don't know where I am . . .' Somewhere, I seemed to hear some sort of knocking sound. Like darts hitting a dartboard. 'Do you think we should . . . ?'

'No, leave it all till morning.' I was thinking about the ice pick, that improbable object. When the officer carried it away, I was glad to see it go – I thought at the time: Free at last! But now I was not so sure. I seemed to feel its presence again, as though it had got back in the house somehow.

She struggled to her feet, then turned to gaze down at me with a compassionate smile. She was still wearing the apron. It was the one with the candystripes. From Amsterdam. 'I love you, Gerald.'

'I know . . .' Or Monaco.

'You might as well stay where you are.' Her eyes were damp, I saw, the pupils dilated, and her lips were flushed and puffy. 'I'll sleep on the studio couch in the sewing room.' Perhaps I frowned at that, or looked puzzled, because she added: 'Our bed's filled up, I'm afraid. Mr and Mrs Elstob are evidently staying the night.' There seemed something wrong with that, but I couldn't remember what. 'It will be a while before we want to use *that* bed again.' She leaned over, her breasts brushing my arm, and kissed me. 'It's all right, Gerald,' she whispered, resting one hand on my tummy. I seemed to hear Vic snort at that ('Don't shit me it's all right!'), and I trembled, so she took her hand away. 'Is anything – ?'

'No . . . well . . . it's like there's an echo in here. Or . . .'

'That's probably the people out in the backyard,' she said, rising.

'The backyard? But what are they doing out there?'

'Nothing. Just telling stories, as far as I could tell. You know, the usual stragglers. But don't worry, I've locked up. Tomorrow . . .' Her voice seemed to be receding. 'No, wait— !' I called, but she was already gone. Only the faintest fragrance remained and that, too, was fading. I lay there on my back, alone and frightened, remembering all too well why it was we held these parties. And would, as though compelled, hold another. At least she had turned the TV back on. Perhaps I had asked her to do this. Prince Mark was now riding through the Enchanted Forest. Or maybe this was the Walled Garden, maybe the Tattooed Dragon was dead already, quite likely. ''Ass usin' yer ole gourd, Mark,' Peedie was saying, with a loose drunken chortle. 'I think we're awmoss there, ole son – juss keep it up'n – yuff! huff! – *don' look back!*' 'Look! There she is! I can see her now! She's *beautiful!*' Yes, this *was* the Garden, I could see her, too: she was running bouncily toward me through the lotus blossoms, radiant with joy and anticipation, her blond hair flowing behind her, eyes sparkling, arms outstretched, her soft white dress wrapping her limbs like the frailest of gauze. I felt myself awash in glowing sunshine. 'Gerry!' she cried, leaping across some impossible abyss, and threw her arms around me. Oh, what a hug! Oh! It felt great! I could hardly get my breath! Tears came to my eyes and I hugged her back with all my strength. But then suddenly she grabbed my testicles and seemed to want to rip them out by their roots! I screamed with pain and terror, fell writhing to the ground. 'No, no, Ros!' I heard someone shout. I couldn't see who it was. I couldn't even open my eyes. 'That's "Grab up the *bells* and ring them," goddamn it— !' Oh my god! Get up! I told myself. (But I couldn't even move.) Turn it off. 'Gee, I'm sorry . . .' (But I *had* to!) 'Now c'mon, let's try that again! From the beginning!' No! *Now— !*

Contemporary ... Provocative ... Outrageous ...
Prophetic ... Groundbreaking ... Funny ... Disturbing ...
Different ... Moving ... Revolutionary ... Inspiring ...
Subversive ... Life-changing ...

What makes a modern classic?

At Penguin Classics our mission has always been to make the best
books ever written available to everyone. And that also means
constantly redefining and refreshing exactly what makes a 'classic'.
That's where Modern Classics come in. Since 1961 they have been an
organic, ever-growing and ever-evolving list of books from the last
hundred (or so) years that we believe will continue to be read over and
over again.

They could be books that have inspired political dissent, such as
Animal Farm. Some, like *Lolita* or *A Clockwork Orange*, may have
caused shock and outrage. Many have led to great films, from *In Cold
Blood* to *One Flew Over the Cuckoo's Nest*. They have broken down
barriers – whether social, sexual, or, in the case of *Ulysses*, the
boundaries of language itself. And they might – like *Goldfinger* or
Scoop – just be pure classic escapism. Whatever the reason, Penguin
Modern Classics continue to inspire, entertain and enlighten millions
of readers everywhere.

'No publisher has had more influence on reading habits than Penguin'
Independent

'Penguins provided a crash course in world literature'
Guardian

The best books ever written

P E N G U I N (🐧) C L A S S I C S

SINCE 1946

Find out more at www.penguinclassics.com